House of Monsters

Lindsey Acosta

LINDSEY *Acosta*

AUTHOR

MAYHEM | MURDER | MYSTERY

To my husband
Tony Acosta
I may not be the ray of sunshine in your life but thank you for loving me as your little ray of pitch black. You healed pieces of me you never broke, and I'm a better person because of you. Thank you for loving me endlessly, unconditionally, and wholeheartedly. I love you more than you know.
If you're a bird.

ACKNOWLEDGEMENTS

Thank you to everyone who played a role in getting my story from mess to masterpiece. My life is forever changed because of your love and support! But, as always, I'd first like to thank my husband. Thank you for your unwavering support and encouragement.

Dr. Erin Hanson: this book doesn't exist without you, literally! Your expertise in DNA made this story possible. Thank you for answering all of my many questions and being so patient with me as I worked out the plot. I'm so appreciative of you!

Dr. Bryanna Fox and students: creating a sadistic serial killer was such an interesting process. I'm so thankful for your expertise and willingness to answer my questions and help me create a monster that gave readers nightmares but was also as accurate as possible.

Jon Avery: thank you for answering all of my police procedure questions. You truly helped me bring Sergeant Moretti and Detective Reid to life.

My publishing team managers | Kyrsten Burley and Kristin Turcio: From the bottom of my heart, thank you so much for all you do for me long before pub day and long after. You both are such a gift!

My beta readers and editors | Susannah Pearson, Karissa Blakeney, Leah Fowler, Lauren Schugg, and Meghan Ginelli: you see my manuscript long before it's ever polished and yet you still believe in my vision. You all are the reason I'm able to turn this dream in head into a book worth reading.

And, of course, thank you to my readers. This wouldn't be possible without you.

ARC Team:

Aaishah Emritte, Abby Florez, Alexandria Linde Andersson, Alicia Hudson, Alisha Carroll, Alkira Jabus, Alyssa heuerman, Amalia Stoica, Amanda Copeland, Amanda Crosby, Amy Fodchuk, Amy Hricko, Angela Yodice, Annie Pruitt, Ashleigh Campbell, Ashley Tucker , Astrid Pizarro,

Bethany Fawcett, Bianca Gasca, Bianca Norfleat, Brandy Aker, Brittany Armstrong, Brittany Boudreau, Brittany Whitman, Brooke Helt, Brooklynn Tobin,

Carina Powers, Cassandra (Cassie) Yagos, Cassandra porga, Celeste, Cheylynne Abreu, Christina Faris, Corri Shelton,

Danielle Folk, Denita Holman, Dominique Gould, Emily Booth, Emily Chamberlin, Emily cisar, Gargi Vyas, Gillian Butler, Hailey Wilkinson, Heather Flaherty,

Jamele Medina, Jamie Boyd, Jen Jensen, Jen Slagel, Jenna Seward-Hatfield, Jennifer Horton, Jessica Banwart, Jessica Hall, Jessica Harris, Jessica Shafer, Jessica Woren, Jessie Swisher, Jodi Fajardo, Jodi Souza, Julia Force, Julianna wagner, Julie Maleski,

Kaitlyn Skiscim, Kamil Jackson, Karly Briggs, Kate Forsman, Katelynne Hummer, Kayla Rupright, Kayla Snyder, Kayla Wagner, Kelsey JoAnn Kozderka, Kerri Grace, Kimberly Barrerr, Kimberly Searles, Kira Ross, Kizzie Roulhac, Krissy Beal, Krysta Orr, Krystle Holt, Kyla Grant, Laura Graham,

Lauren Lynch, Leilani Laurencio, Lindsey Hillyer, Lisa Kaminski, Luaren Baker, Lyndsay Di Varano,

Makenzi Hutton, Mallory Sorrells, Marie Cashel, Mary Baumgarten, Mary Kuhlmann, Maylin Gonzalez Gonzalez, Megan Dick, Meghan Barron, Melanie Thomas, Melissa Dressler, Melissa Duchaine, Melissa Hoyt, Melissa Ingram, Melissa Turk, Michaela Baker, Michelle Shamy, Micki rawling, Molly Barr, Monica Simmons, Monique Muro, Myesha Pryor,

LINDSEY ACOSTA

Nancy carroll, Naomi Jones, Nicole Hine, Nikki LeLand, Nikki Trocchio, Nina Plete, Olivia Griffin, Paige Gunn,

Rachel Scott, Reagan Hopper, Rebecca Nelson, Renee Arieno, Rhianna Khramez,

Sabrina Bailey, Samantha Burgess, Samantha Burns, Samantha Cooper, Sara carver, Sarah Morgan, Shania Caines, Shannon Demaio, Simone Machado, Stacey Stephens, Stefani Rae Lange, Stephanie Bulcamino, Stephanie Mellon, Susan Heun, Susan McAulay, Suzan Larson,

Taylor Sheppard, Teresa Brock, Teressa Oliverio, Tonya Hoselton, Tori Clancy, Tricia Powell, Yinka Boudreaux

PROLOGUE

1983

C ynthia Anderson. *Cynthia Anderson. Cynthia Anderson.*

I chant my name over and over again, terrified I'll forget who I am.

In the month I've been here, he has beaten and raped me. Ridiculed and mocked me. Tormented and tortured me.

He's the monster you read about in fairytales. But the devil didn't appear crowned with horns. No, he slithered in, adorned in charm and allure.

I was captivated the moment our eyes met, pools of warm molten amber taking my breath away. And his smile was an invitation to trust him, despite the alarms that had reverberated through my body the day he had asked for my help. Even his laughter had deceived me.

And now I'm paying the price for my naivety.

At seventeen years old, I have become captive to a man whose only intention is to bring me agony. I am but a toy to him, and he enjoys the torment I suffer at his hand. He laughs at my tears, mocks my cries, and takes pleasure in my screams of terror as I call out for someone to save me.

I hate him for what he's done to me. He has stolen my innocence in more ways than one, and my soul is broken beyond repair.

At first, I tried my hardest to oppose the devil, to battle the demons of torment that came with him. But my fight has long since left me. I've lost all sense of hope and have such little strength, both physically and mentally. My only desire is that death will come quickly.

It would be much better than the hell I'm enduring now.

But I miss my mother and father. And though my older brother may have bullied me relentlessly growing up, I even long to look into his beautiful blue eyes one last time.

The door to my personal prison creaks open ever so slowly. He always opens it slowly, intent on causing my heart to nearly beat out of my chest and my limbs to go numb as I shake in terror. But as footsteps beat on the stairs, I realize they are much too quiet to be his.

A faint smile tugs at my lips. *She* has come to visit me today; a bright light in the darkness that has become my life.

Her face appears as she turns the corner and I'm always taken aback by her beauty. She smiles slightly, but her eyes are etched with the usual pity that haunts them. I must look pathetic chained to this bed. I've withered away to nearly nothing as he all but starves me.

I was beautiful before he took me, with long luscious hair and eyes that gleamed like emeralds. Now, I'm a broken version of myself. One that's covered in bruises, gashes, blood, and dirt.

As she walks toward me, her fist is balled tightly at her side. I'm eager to know what she's brought me today. She always comes with a gift when she visits. It's her way of absolving herself from the part she's played in the terror I've endured.

The first time, she brought me a can of Slice soda, and I cried when I drank it. Then, she brought me Big Chew gum. But because of the beating I'd received the day before, I couldn't chew it without pain shooting through my jaw. Part of me hopes she's brought a Fireball candy because those are my favorite, though I know the heat from the cinnamon would surely cause me more pain than it's worth.

She sits on the floor in front of me and the sadness that fills her eyes is alarming. Though she's never cheerful when she visits me, she still radiates hope. A hope I will overcome the hell that is slowly burning me alive. A hope I may be freed. A hope that I will live.

But today, that hope seems to elude her.

My heart jolts and I whisper, "Am I dying today?"

She tilts her head, and a tear slips down her cheek. "I'm sorry I couldn't save you from all this pain, but I can't let him kill you."

I furrow my brows as hope floods back through my body. "Are you here to let me go? Am I finally free?"

She looks away from me, and I immediately know the answer, though I can't say I'm surprised. She's under his power just as much as I am. She may be free to leave this damned room, but she's every bit as chained as I am. She's merely bound to the devil while I'm shackled to his demons.

No, I'm not surprised she hasn't come to save me. I knew as soon as he took me, he would kill me. And today is that day.

Her eyes meet mine, then she glances at her closed fist that's resting in her lap. She lifts her arm and extends her clenched hand to me. I reach out and she drops her gift into mine.

A diamond ring glistens in the dim light.

My eyes dart to her face, looking for an explanation.

She softly says, "I bartered for your life. And if you accept his offer, he won't kill you."

"I...I have to get married?" My heart beats quickly and my vision begins to blur at such a thought. My body sways slightly, but I steady myself by inhaling deeply.

She simply nods. "I can't lose you. You're my best friend. Please say yes when he asks you to do this. If you don't, he *will* kill you."

I study her face then hold up the ring. How am I supposed to get married at seventeen years old? How am I supposed to marry the very monster that has raped and tormented me?

I nearly vomit at the thought.

But I don't want to die.

I glance at her and realize she's been holding her breath as she waits for my response. A tear falls from my eye and hits the dirt below as I slide the ring on my finger. This is a calculated risk where so many things could go wrong. But to refuse would be to sign my own death warrant. So, I will play the devil's game. And while he believes I'm still wrapped in his shadows, I'll be lying in wait. *Planning. Plotting.*

And before long, the devil will become the prey.

I wipe at the tears that are falling down my cheeks. "I'll say yes, but it's only to bide time."

She furrows her brows. "For what?"

"Until *we* can escape." I say it with a boldness I don't feel.

She vehemently shakes her head. "I can't leave. He'll hunt me down and kill me. And he'll do the same to you. I've seen what he's done to all the women before you...what he's done to *you*."

I take her hands in mine. "We will do this together. Promise me when the time is right, we will do whatever it takes to escape from this place."

"I can't leave. But I'll help you get away, even if I die trying." She closes her eyes and unbuttons her shirt to reveal five circular burns on her chest, just above her left breast. My heart nearly stops beating.

She's been marked. She's been claimed. She's his now. *Forever.*

She offered herself in my place.

I pull her into a hug and she doesn't pull away, despite the blood and dirt that is surely to soil her crisp clothes. I whisper, "I'm not leaving without you. We are sisters now, and that means something. I won't leave unless you leave."

"But-"

I cut her off by pulling away and putting my pinky into the air. "I promise I won't leave without you. But you have to promise to leave when we finally have the opportunity. *Together forever.*"

She considers me for a moment, then nods her head as she wraps her pinky around mine. "I promise."

Suddenly, an eerie feeling fills my chest, but I quickly push it aside as she releases me from my restraints and leads me up the stairs I've so desperately wanted to climb since being dragged into the devil's darkness.

If only I'd known how that promise would alter my life in ways I never could have imagined. I thought I had lost my innocence to the monster who violated me, but it was actually the *promise* that would eventually take my innocence in the most intricate of ways.

That promise of hope would very quickly turn into the darkness in which my own monster would hide. It would unleash a part of me I didn't know existed, a part of me I wish would have died in the basement the day *she* came to see me.

That promise made me a monster.

And that promise would ultimately kill me.

CHAPTER 1

2024

Pain raged through Bianca's naked body as she lay on the cold cement floor, shivering as the winter temperatures slowly dropped. She didn't know where she was, only that she was in some type of basement. Maybe a cellar or bunker or storm shelter?

The single window at the top of the room acted as a clock, her only connection to the outside world. She'd been there seven days, though now they bled together, much like her body. Bianca glanced out the small window, wishing she could find beauty in the dusk that painted the sky. But she couldn't. It was now a reminder she'd spent another day captive. And as she studied the hues of pink and orange, she prayed for death as her hope slowly faded with the sun.

Glancing to the far side of the room, she wanted to sit on the bed that was in the corner of the dimly lit cellar, but she couldn't bring herself to touch the disgusting fabric. After what he'd done to her, she couldn't even look at it without nearly having a panic attack. So, she positioned herself on the opposite side of the room, as far away from the mattress as possible.

How could she have been so stupid? Hadn't her mother spent years warning her not to go home with strangers? As always, she didn't listen. She never thought it could happen to *her*. Yet, here she was.

What's worse, Bianca hadn't even seen any warning signs of danger. She had bumped into Tall, Dark, and Handsome as she had come out of a coffee shop, causing him to spill his latte all over his white dress shirt. She had bought him another coffee, a lousy excuse of an apology. Then he had made her laugh with a lame joke and they had found themselves walking around downtown Lakeland, Florida. After a few minutes, they had sat down on a bench under a canopy of trees.

He had been hesitant at first, but relaxed the more they had talked. Bianca had found it easy to be with him and, even more so, flirt with him. He was sexy with a perfect smile. He had a charm that made her feel safe and noticed. Plus, she couldn't miss the gold band on his finger, which had made him all the more enticing.

She had always been attracted to married men. Even as a teenager, there was something thrilling about the thought of being with someone who had already been claimed. Eventually, she had found she quite enjoyed the challenge of convincing a man she was better than his wife, even if it was just for a night. Though, sometimes that night turned into much longer.

Abel hadn't been the first man to leave his wife in order to be with Bianca.

She had momentarily thought about the ring on her own finger but quickly pushed those thoughts aside. Since she and Abel had separated, she hadn't slept with anyone in over a month. Her marriage was nearly over, so what did it matter if she had a little fun? It wasn't as if wedding rings and marriage vows had ever stopped her anyway.

She had given Tall, Dark, and Handsome a sly smile and placed her hand on his inner thigh as she had leaned in to gently kiss him. His eyes had pierced her soul and sent a yearning shiver up her spine. It was a look she'd seen over and over again, always filled with lust and desire. That day, she had wanted to be wild and find someone to rock her world with an afternoon quickie. So, she had gone home with Tall, Dark, and Handsome.

But how wrong she'd been.

He was Tall, Dark, and Evil.

She visibly shivered as she recalled the last few days of her own personal hell. The first day, he had raped her repeatedly...and brutally. He wanted her body to instinctively fear him as soon as she heard his footsteps in the distance.

But he had waited a day or two before inflicting his next form of torment, claiming he wanted to give her body rest from his punishments. She had known better than to believe his kind eyes and soft tone. He had wanted to torture her, both physically and mentally.

Eventually, Tall, Dark, and Evil had waved a cattle brand in front of her face, wanting her to see the tool he would use to torment her next. Bianca had sobbed, despite trying her hardest not to show any weakness. Tall, Dark, and Evil had laughed at her, exhilarated by her terror. The hot metal had seared her skin with a sharp hiss, and she had screamed so loudly she thought her vocal cords would bleed.

He hadn't waited for the burn to fully heal before pulling out a whip the next day. It was the kind she had seen in those old western movies her grandfather would watch before he had passed away. And she hadn't been prepared for the leather to slice through her skin with such ease.

By that time, she had nearly become numb to the suffering she was enduring.

Now, the branded 'A' on her chest was beginning to scab, as were the cuts that covered her body from the lashes she'd received. There wasn't a single place on her body he hadn't brought pain to. And she knew the pain would continue as long as she was held captive by this monster, which she knew she'd never escape from.

When she was first taken, she had prayed someone would hear her screams and rescue her, but such thoughts had long since dissipated.

No one was coming.

She would die here.

And honestly, she welcomed the darkness of death as if it were a friend.

Bianca brought her knees to her chest, lying in the fetal position. She despised the vulnerability that pierced her heart as she quietly hummed a lullaby her mother had sang to her as a little girl. What she wouldn't give to have her mother hold her close and tell her she would be okay. That it was only a nightmare and she was safe. But she wasn't. This nightmare was real, and the monster who hurt her was worse than anything she could have dreamed up.

A tear slid down her blood-stained cheek and into the dirt as the door squeaked open, announcing the monster's arrival. She detested her body's fearful response to him; heart racing, lungs constricting. She was terrified of what he would do to her today.

He slowly descended the stairs, rolling up his sleeves as he did. "Have you learned your lesson? Marriage vows shouldn't be tainted."

Bianca quickly nodded and tried to scoot away from him as he walked toward her. Taking in her naked body, his eyes trailed every inch of her, and he smiled at her powerlessness. It was a smile she was accustomed to, one that had once brought her so much pleasure knowing she had used her body to make men fall for her. Now, she loathed it. Was disgusted by it. She had thought her body brought her power, but this man had proved it was actually her greatest weakness.

She cowered on the floor, trying to cover herself. Bianca didn't dare sit on the bed in case he tried to rape her again. Though she knew it was a pointless gesture. He would do it if he wanted, no matter what she did to try to stop him.

He towered over her, and in one swift motion, he reeled his arm back and his hand connected with her cheek. She shrieked in pain. "Please stop! I promise I learned my lesson. Please stop hurting me."

Tall, Dark, and Evil crouched down and put his nose to hers. "Whores like you never learn their lesson."

Bianca sobbed, knowing he was going to do more than rape her today. She could tell simply by the darkness in his eyes. She wanted to barter with him, to tell him she would do whatever he wanted if he didn't make her bleed again. But no matter how much she begged and pleaded, no matter if she played along or fought him off, he would continue to hurt her.

She hadn't noticed the wraps around his knuckles until his fist connected with her head once again. She yelped in pain and tried to move away, her body's natural reaction to danger. But he grabbed her foot and dragged her back to him as he brought his fists down all over her, despite her screams of terror.

Agony tore through her. Her family wouldn't even be able to identify her when they found her body.

Because she was, after all, going to die.

He would make sure of it.

After what felt like a lifetime, he finally inhaled deeply in an attempt to calm himself. Bianca found herself thankful for the moment of peace, and that thought was jarring.

He slowly stood and she prayed the beating was her only form of punishment for the day. But she heard the hiss of his zipper, and she knew he wasn't done. He claimed her with his vile body, ignoring the dirt and blood that covered her. And just as he did every time he raped her, he whispered in her ear, "You wanted a married man, didn't you? I'm giving you what you wanted. Now, admit you're a whore and I'll end your torment."

Bianca clamped her mouth shut so tightly her jaw ached, just as she had done every other time. She wouldn't say it. She refused to give him the satisfaction, nor did she want to die. She missed her mother and father. She felt guilty for fighting with her sister a few days before she was kidnapped. Would Layla know Bianca loved her?

And truth be told, she didn't want her marriage to be over. She wanted to make amends with Abel, promise to uphold their vows and finally be the loyal and faithful woman she enviously wanted to be.

Yet, as Tall, Dark, and Evil defiled her again and again, something in her spirit broke. As much as she wanted to live, she was also ready to die. She wasn't strong enough to withstand his horrific torture.

Finally, she sucked in a breath as tears flowed down her cheeks. "I'm a whore," she whispered.

He put his lips to her ear. "I can't hear you."

"I'm a whore!" she cried out, shame welling up in her chest.

A smile stretched over his lips as he kissed her and she recoiled.

Then, pain exploded in her lungs. Bianca let out a blood curdling scream as she tried to protest, but no sound crossed her lips. His grip tightened around her throat and a single tear flowed down her cheek as she thought about her family.

She hadn't meant it. She didn't want to die.

She clawed at him, flailing wildly as she made one last attempt to escape. But dark spots threatened her vision and she could feel her body floating away. "Please, stop," she mouthed.

But Tall, Dark, and Evil wouldn't stop.

Because Bianca had begged to die.

CHAPTER 2

S ergeant Jaxon Moretti tugged his leather jacket closer, trying to warm himself, but it was useless. Despite the sun shining brightly, the temps read fifty-four degrees, and Jax was instantly annoyed by the cold breeze that stung his face. Though it rarely got cold in Florida, anything below seventy was deemed a winter's day.

A loud honk and screeching tires met his ears. The city of Winter Haven was buzzing with life as people hurried to get to work in the early morning hours.

Jax stood in downtown, the city's historic district. He studied the large fountain set in the middle of the park. Surrounded by shops, restaurants, and various businesses, the structure brought a touch of tranquility to the busy area. And just like every popular spot in the city, the fountain was now decorated for the winter holidays. However, he didn't think the crime scene tape surrounding it was part of the decor.

A few officers stood near the yellow barrier to ensure no one tried to get through while the crime scene techs looked for and collected evidence. Dr. Norman Reeve, the medical examiner, knelt next to the victim as he studied the cuts and bruises that covered the woman's body.

Jax spied his partner, Detective Juliette Reid, as she parked her car and got out, making her way to the first set of officers. Her blonde hair was pulled into a ponytail, accentuating a bold red lip. When Jax had first met Jules three years ago, he had been surprised to see she wore a full face of makeup every day. And she would surely die if she was to ever get caught in sweats and a t-shirt. The woman took pride in her appearance, and she wasn't embarrassed to let everyone know it.

Juggling two to-go cups, she flashed her badge at one of the officers. The man nodded to her, and she lifted the tape and ducked underneath. Jax silently watched the cop's gaze discreetly follow her movements, and Jax didn't think it was her back the man was watching. The cop noticed Jax's stare and quickly turned back around.

Jules smiled and handed Jax one of the cups. He eyed her drink. "Hot chocolate?"

She took a sip. "You know it."

"I don't know how you drink that stuff. It's too sweet."

She shrugged. "You know I don't like coffee and it's too early for a Coke."

Jax sipped his own drink, welcoming the carbonation.

Despite the cool air, it was still a beautiful day. Sadly, it was overshadowed by the death that lay in front of them. The dark-haired woman lay naked and exposed to the elements, her once olive skin now pale and blue, covered in the early morning dew. They both crouched down next to Dr. Reeve to study the victim.

Sighing, Jules nodded to the body. "Do we know what happened?"

Jax said, "Same as the others, but she's been beaten pretty badly."

The girl was hardly recognizable with the amount of blood that caked her skin. The bruising and swelling that overwhelmed her body would make it nearly impossible for them to use any type of facial recognition as a means of identification. Jax felt a pang of sadness for the family who wouldn't be able to recognize their loved one.

Though he had seen numerous dead bodies before, Jax looked away to regain his composure. He gritted his teeth and took a deep breath, trying to calm his racing heart. He was tired of seeing the tortured bodies of women being tossed in the streets. He had two older sisters, and every time a body turned up, all he could see was Savannah and Mara gazing up at him.

What he wouldn't give to beat the shit out of the man responsible for the torture and deaths of ten women.

"Was she raped?" Jules asked.

Many cops would have rolled their eyes at the question; the victim was naked, which almost always indicated rape. But Jax knew better than to judge his partner by her seemingly ignorant questions. And while she would endure countless dumb-blonde jokes by other officers who assumed she wasn't good at her job, Jules simply wanted confirmation. She never made assumptions, and she worked hard to ensure she knew her cases inside and out. Every detail, every shred of evidence. He'd even seen her memorize victim and witness statements.

There was no doubt in his mind, Juliette was anything but dumb.

Jax looked back to the victim and ran a hand through his blonde hair. "There was a lot of bruising around her thighs to indicate she was raped repeatedly."

"And brutally," Dr. Reeve said as he peered at Juliette over his glasses. "We'll know more after I do the autopsy, but there are enough indicators for me to believe she was raped, just like the other victims."

Jules closed her eyes and slowly shook her head. "Do we know her name?"

To Jax, one of Jules' best qualities was her kind heart. Victims weren't just a case number or poor unfortunate soul to Juliette Reid. No, to her, they were people who mattered, who were missed and loved. It made her a great detective and an even better partner.

Not that Jax didn't feel the same way, he just wasn't as attached as she was. He sometimes wished he could be, but his own traumas taught him to compartmentalize and shove his feelings down as far as they would go. He grew up in a family of police officers, so it wasn't surprising he learned that tactic early on. He was a walking poster child for the poor coping mechanisms of most cops.

Jax shook his head. "Not yet. We'll run prints, but there was no ID or anything else left to identify her." He gently lifted her left leg, showing a seashell tattoo above her ankle. "Bianca Preston, the girl who went missing a week ago, has a tattoo like this one and in the same place. She has black hair like our vic, too."

Dr. Reeve nodded and said, "I will compare Bianca's dental records with the victims' to be certain, of course, but I am inclined to think it's her."

Using a gloved hand, Jules gently pushed the girl's hair behind her ear, revealing a once beautiful face now swollen and bruised beyond recognition. "Who did this to you, sweet girl?" Jules motioned toward the ring on the woman's finger. "Now we know why she was beaten so severely."

It had taken nine victims to see the initial pattern of beatings. If the woman was married, this monster would beat her so horribly she would be unrecognizable. If the victim wasn't married, she was spared the horrific beating that left four victims nearly unidentifiable.

Jax indicated to the woman's neck. "She was strangled like the others, as well. And he left his mark." He pointed to a burn on the left side of her chest, just above the victim's breast. The wound had started to scab when she'd been killed, forming a dark red letter "A."

"Shit. I was afraid of that." Jules said.

"He's back. After two years of silence, he's killing again."

She clenched her jaw as the fire in her blue eyes burned bright. "We can't let there be a twelfth victim, Jax."

He touched her hand. "I know."

The two stood and Jax took one last look at the body, looking for this killer's signature.

Dr. Reeve noticed and said, "The flower?"

Jax nodded.

The man pushed open the victim's mouth and Juliette cringed.

That was new. Normally the flowers were scattered in the victim's hair.

But the blue hue and small petals couldn't be mistaken.

The Scarlet Letter Killer was back.

And he left a forget me not flower to let everyone know he was hunting again.

CHAPTER 3

J ax had been in court most of the day, which resulted in a murderer receiving three consecutive life sentences. He had been planning to go home after but wanted to check on Jules and their current Jane Doe. There hadn't been much traction in the case since finding the woman three days ago, but he hoped Juliette had gotten lucky while he was out of the office.

Once inside the conference room, he saw Jules sitting at the table, files in hand, just as he'd seen her do for the last three years. Her emerald green top made her eyes pop, despite the sadness that filled them. This case was weighing heavily on her, and he could plainly see it was beginning to take an emotional toll on his partner. Jax was getting more worried by the day and made a mental note to mention it to Cameron Knox, Juliette's boyfriend.

Cam and Jules had met six months ago at a robbery-homicide crime scene and had hit it off instantly, dating only two weeks later. The man worked as a prosecutor with the D.A.'s office, so Jax had been surprised when the brass didn't protest the relationship. But Jax assumed it was due to Cam's connections with the mayor and other local politicians.

Jules eyed him as he shrugged off his jacket and collapsed into a chair. He said, "Have we heard back from Dr. Reeve about our Jane Doe? I want to figure out who she is ASAP."

She shook her head. "No, but maybe if you show some leg, it'll speed up the process."

Jax grinned, amused by her rare sassiness. "You're a little feisty. Did Cam piss you off?"

"Cam is about to be yesterday's news. He doesn't understand my work schedule and the fact that I don't dictate when bad guys decide to break the law; something he really *should* understand." She sighed. "He was mad I had to come in early."

Jax lifted a brow, surprised by her outburst. Jules was typically very happy and easy-going. She rarely showed any type of anger or annoyance, and it was yet another reminder of how this case was affecting her.

Regretting her outburst, Jules shook her head. "I really like him, and this is the first fight we've had since we started dating. But I hate that my schedule causes issues in every relationship."

Jax nodded. "I know it's hard. But if he really cares about you, he'll figure out how to make it work."

He inwardly cringed. *What a lame thing to say.* But truthfully, he didn't have much advice to give, though he understood the frustrations of dating someone who didn't understand their line of work. It's a common theme in the police force. The late nights, the numerous calls that interrupted even the most special moments, the depressing nature of the work... It strained relationships, and it wasn't a secret that most cops had been divorced a handful of times by the time they retired.

But it helped that Cam was a prosecutor, so he understood Juliette's schedule more than most. Plus, he was good to Jules, so Jax didn't necessarily want them to break up. He just didn't like that it made working together a little murky since Cam was co-counsel to the D.A. on the Scarlet Letter Killer case. If their relationship prevented a conviction once they caught this guy, he'd be pissed.

But Jax kept that comment to himself. Juliette was one of the most kind and gentle people he knew, and she didn't let the darkness of the job affect her desire to bring peace to so many hurting people. Jules deserved to be happy, and he wouldn't be the one to screw that up for her. Especially if their bosses didn't have a problem with it.

Jules stood and walked over to the crime board. She added Jane Doe to the list of ten victims by tacking her photo to the board.

Hannah Seymour.

Traci Vazquez.

Sierra Brown.

Felicia Taver.

Jade Scott.

Ashley Judd.

Anya Jones.

Emilia Santos.

Kiara Short.

Serenity Raver.

Now, Jane Doe.

Eleven victims. Eleven families ripped apart. Eleven women who met a horrific demise because they mistook a monster for Prince Charming.

From what they could gather, the Scarlet Letter Killer began killing in 2012 and would kill once a year. In his earlier crimes, SLK murdered his victims within forty-eight hours and didn't seem to bother as much with the torture that would notably appear in later cases.

Then, in 2015, SLK began holding the women for a week, torturing them while they waited to die. All of his victims were whipped, brutally raped, and branded- all peri-mortem. Some of these poor women were unfortunate enough to receive an awful beating. Then, he would suffocate them.

He stalked the cities of Polk County, kidnapping women who were known to cheat on their spouses or enjoyed the company of married men. And after enduring horrific acts of torture, he would kill them and dump their bodies in a significant part of the city.

Felicia Taver had been taken from a bar in Davenport and was found at Haines City's Community Theater. Jade Scott was last seen in Lake Wales but was found at Hollis Gardens in Lakeland. Kiara Short's body was laid across the steps of the Bartow Courthouse, despite being taken from a laundromat in Frostproof.

The Scarlet Letter Killer wouldn't be minimized to a single area. He wanted the entire county to fear him, for people to know this was his hunting ground and no one was safe.

Until he seemingly disappeared in 2022.

For the last two years, the Scarlet Letter Killer had been quiet, something the whole state was glad for. But with this new Jane Doe, it was apparent he was back. Which meant most of Polk County would soon be in a panic.

Jax studied each victim's photo that was tacked to the board. He couldn't imagine what these women went through in their last days. It made him sick to know someone was hunting women and deliberately torturing them.

Jules pulled him from his thoughts. "Well, now we know our theory about married women was right. He seems to brutalize them far more if they had on a wedding ring."

Jax nodded. "I'm not surprised. We know the brand on their chest is his way of telling us these women were adulterers. And the torture is a clear indicator of a deep-seated hate for them. I just don't know how that information helps us right now."

Jules tossed the files down, and they landed with a thud. "We need to call the FBI. We're not trained for this kind of shit."

"I know, but the brass is refusing. They don't want to look incompetent since it's an election year."

Jules opened her mouth to protest but was interrupted by a tap at the open door. They both turned to see Dr. Reeve. "Sergeant, maybe this will help."

It was clear the man was on his way out for the evening, donning a furry cap pulled over his ears and a thick trench coat. He carried his briefcase in one hand as Jax watched the medical examiner lay a folder on top of the table with the other hand.

Jax's heart raced. "Did we get an ID?"

"We were correct. The victim is Bianca Preston, twenty-five. The contact information for her next of kin is in the folder."

"Thanks, Norman," Jax said.

Dr. Reeve nodded. "Get this guy, Jaxon. I'm tired of seeing brutalized women come across my table."

When the man left, Jax rubbed his face. He wanted to break something. They should have been able to catch this guy long before now. Before there were eleven women who had been terrorized, tortured, and killed at the hands of some sick piece of shit. But every lead they thought they had turned cold, and this killer had been careful not to leave any DNA behind. Or at least, nothing the CSI techs could find or use for testing.

They had hoped the families could shed some light on a potential suspect, but so far, none of the victims had anything in common other than having black hair and green eyes. They didn't attend the same church or work in the same building. They didn't frequent the same restaurants, nor did they go to the same gym. They didn't even live in the same cities or have much overlap with travel.

All previous ten victims were strangers, and it made nailing this bastard even more difficult. Jax didn't think that would change with Bianca's case.

He stole a glance at the single headshot that hung under their suspect list. Philip Murray. He'd been seen visiting some of the spots the bodies had been dumped. And after they'd done more research, they'd quickly found he was a convicted rapist who liked to beat, rape, burn, and choke prostitutes.

Though, his first victim was his wife.

And despite having done this to multiple women, Murray had only served seven months. Jax knew it was because detectives could only tie him to a single case. And since it involved a prostitute, the courts didn't care about justice. Which infuriated Jax.

Then, ironically, Murray had moved to Georgia, and the Scarlet Letter killings stopped.

Curious about Murray's current whereabouts, Jax did a quick search in the database. The criminal's name popped up on the screen with a home address in Polk City, Florida. Jax clucked his tongue. "Look at that, Jules. Mr. Murray is back. Wonder if he's still choking prostitutes in between tormenting the rest of the women of Polk County?"

"That could be what he does in between kills since he's dormant for such long periods of time. Maybe he's roughing up some working ladies to hold off his urges," Jules said.

Pulling his phone out of his pocket, Jax added, "I'll text my CI and see if he can ask some local prostitutes if they know anything more recent about Murray. Maybe he's been hanging around the street corners again."

"It's definitely time to pay him a visit, see what he has to say about this little coincidence." Jules pointed at the computer screen showing Murray's new address. Then, she sighed and stood. "Come on, let's go notify Bianca's family. Murray can wait until tomorrow."

Jax nodded and followed her out the door and into the parking lot. Once outside, the two of them trotted to the car to get out of the frigid air. Jax climbed into the driver's seat and blasted the heat as Jules sat in the passenger side, rubbing her hands together quickly.

God, he hated the cold.

They made their way to Lakeland, where Bianca's parents had put down roots. Passing a shopping plaza on the south side of the city, Jax asked, "So, are you really thinking about breaking things off with Cam?"

Jules gave a soft smile. "No. He's a good man. And he's been so patient with my job and my schedule. I think the constant change of plans and canceling finally caught up with me."

Jax shook his head. "I'm telling you, being single is the best."

Jules chuckled and swatted at Jax's arm. "You're such a man-whore."

"True. But you also don't see me having relationship troubles, do you?"

She side-eyed him as he parked in the driveway. Christmas lights twinkled as dusk flooded the sky and smoke billowed from the chimney. He welcomed the aroma of winter that filtered into the car, the faint scent of wood burning with a hint of a sweet toasted smell.

The Christmas decor on the lawn reminded him of the many Christmas Eves he had spent baking cookies with his grandmother as a child. He would stay up late watching Christmas movies, hoping to catch Santa bringing him gifts while his grandmother sipped hot cocoa in her rocking chair.

Jax took in the Preston home. It wasn't particularly special, but he somehow knew it was filled with love and laughter.

And now that laughter would turn into grief.

Jax and Juliette became somber as reality set in. Neither he nor Jules made a move to get out of the vehicle. This was one of the worst parts of the job. No one wanted to deliver the news that a loved one had died. But someone had to take on the burden. So, he reluctantly bore the weight of grief and sadness that he brought to many of the families he encountered.

Inhaling deeply, Jules got out of the car, and Jax followed.

She rang the bell, and Jax instinctively knew she wanted to be the one to break the news.

A petite woman answered the door, her dark hair brushing her shoulders in a bob cut. "Can I help you?"

"Are you Maria Preston?" Jules asked.

"Yes."

"I'm Detective Reid and this is Sergeant Moretti-"

"You found Bianca?!" The woman called out for her husband. "Carlos! They found Bianca!" She took Jules' hand, and Jules let out a stifled gasp, caught off guard by the gesture. "Where is she? Is she at the hospital?" Mrs. Preston snatched her coat as her husband's footsteps rumbled through the house as he came to the door.

He met Jules' eyes and Mr. Preston's shoulders drooped, his last bit of hope shattered with Jax and Jules' appearance. He gently took his wife by the hand. "Honey, that's not why they're here."

Tears began falling down his cheeks, and she pulled away from him. "No, she's safe! She's only twenty-five. She has so much life left to live!"

Jules continued, "I'm sorry to inform you-"

"Don't say it! Don't you dare say it!" the woman shrieked.

Jules closed her eyes for a moment, then said, "I'm sorry to inform you, but your daughter, Bianca, was found deceased three days ago."

The woman wailed as she collapsed into her husband's arms, her body shaking as grief tore through her. "No! No, no, no! My baby! My Bianca!" She slowly fell to the floor as her husband knelt to the ground and pulled her close, both crying out in angst.

Jules' hand flew to cover her mouth as she choked back a sob. "I'm so sorry," Jules whispered. Unable to hold back her own tears, she quickly walked back to the car.

"I'm sorry for your loss," Jax said as he hung his head.

He didn't need to tell them they would be back with questions. They all knew. And he hated that he had to do it at all.

Leaving the couple to grieve their new reality, Jax climbed into his vehicle where Juliette cried softly and Mrs. Preston's shrills vibrated his windows.

CHAPTER 4

T his time, it was Jax's turn to bring their morning pick-me-ups. Holding the to-go cups, he nodded at the other officers who stepped into the elevator alongside him. Once the doors opened, they all dispersed, going their separate ways.

Jax walked over to Jules who sat at her desk, typing away. "Find anything good?" he asked as he set her cup on the desk and sat in his own chair.

Jules shook her head. "No, just finishing up some reports." She aggressively hit the 'enter' key and glanced up at Jax. "And now I'm done. Let's go talk to Murray."

He was thankful Jules was eager to question the worm of a man. Jax hadn't been able to sleep the night before, playing potential scenarios in his mind. Would Murray pull out a gun and Jax would need to subdue him, being dubbed a hero in the process? Would Murray try to attack Juliette, not knowing she was trained in three types of martial arts? Would they finally be able to catch the Scarlet Letter Killer?

Of course, his mind wouldn't quiet down, so Jax had decided to drink. He'd lost count of how many glasses of bourbon he'd had. It had been just enough to quiet his mind but not enough to make him pay for it in the morning.

Now, he was eager to see if they had finally found the serial killer that had been stalking their streets for the last decade. Looking back at the computer screen, he wrote down the address, and they walked out of the precinct, hurrying to the car.

Twenty minutes later, he and Jules pulled into Philip Murray's driveway. Jax had a gut feeling this guy might actually be the Scarlet Letter Killer. Steeling himself for the potential interaction with the monster they were hunting, the two of them climbed out of the car and made their way to the front door.

Jax knocked, and a man appeared in the entrance way, his dark hair only just beginning to gray and his blue eyes bright and observant.

"Can I help you?" the man asked.

Flashing his badge, Jax said, "I'm Sergeant Moretti, and this is my partner, Detective Reid. Is Philip Murray here? We're investigating a homicide and think he may have information that can help us." He and Jules had both agreed to treat Murray as a witness instead of a suspect, hoping he would be more forthcoming with them.

Murray pushed his shoulders back. "I didn't do anything, and I don't have any information on a homicide, officer. I know you're standing in my doorway because of my record, but those women were liars. I never once touched them. I gave them a lift home and the next thing I know, I'm in cuffs for something I didn't do."

Jax knew better than to fight with him. The man would never admit the truth, and Jax wasn't about to waste his time, risking Murray clamming up.

Jules intervened, knowing she could calm him. "I'm so sorry you were treated badly, but that's why we're here. We want to make sure it doesn't happen again. And if you help us, we can put in a good word and make sure people know you're actually a hero."

"Miss, I really don't have anything to say."

Jules tilted her head and subtly pushed out her chest. "Please, Mr. Murray. We could really use your help."

If it wouldn't potentially ruin the interview, Jax would have laughed at how easily Jules was able to slip into a role she'd normally avoid. But she knew men fancied her, and she used that to her advantage when she needed to.

Hell, if he were a woman he'd do the same thing.

Murray slowly leered over Juliette from head to toe, focusing on her breasts for a lot longer than Jax was comfortable with. Trying and failing to hide a smirk of his own, Murray's eyes finally flickered back to Juliette's face. He simply said. "Sure." Then, he stepped outside and closed the door behind him, putting himself close to Juliette.

Jules pulled out her phone. "Do you recognize any of these women?"

Out of eleven victims, he'd been caught at five crime scenes and had even revisited those sites long after the police were done investigating. Though it may seem like harmless behavior, Jax knew serial killers enjoyed revisiting where they dumped their victims' bodies.

Murray shook his head. "I don't know them. And I don't really need the...*comfort* of a whore. I have my own girlfriends I see when I'm on the road."

Jax glared at Murray, irritated by the man's blatant lack of respect for the victims.

Jules raised a brow. "*Girlfriends*? As in more than one?"

"Yes. I treat my girlfriends like queens. When I'm traveling, I stop in and wine and dine them. I buy them nice gifts, get what I want in return, and then come back home. I take great care of the women I'm with." Murray's eyes shifted over Juliette once more, hoping to impress her with his ability to charm women. Then, he winked at her, and Jax wanted to throttle the man.

"What do you do for work?" Jax asked.

Murray bristled, annoyed that Jax would dare interrupt his conversation with Jules. "I'm a trucker."

Jax nodded. "You ever travel out of state?"

He eyed Jax. "Why are you asking?"

Jules quickly said, "Depending on where you travel, we could use that to quickly rule you out as a suspect. We want to make sure you don't get caught up in any other investigations."

Satisfied with Jules' response, he shook his head. "No, I only take loads in Florida. I don't like to be too far from my house."

If Murray never left the state while on the road, it was likely he could be tied to the victims if he and Juliette could prove Murray had crossed paths with the victims before they were abducted and killed.

Jax held up his phone, the victims of SLK showing on the screen. "So you're sure you've never met any of these girls? Because we know you were at multiple crime scenes."

Crimson crept over Murray's face. "I didn't touch them!"

Jules gently touched his arm, immediately calming him. "Philip, we know you're innocent. But you need to be straight with us or we can't help you."

He took a breath, gathering himself. Then, he calmly pointed to Kiara Short. "I had seen her at a laundromat and asked if she needed help getting her clothes to her car, but she was checking out another guy who was there and basically ignored me."

"Do you remember what the man looked like at the laundromat?" Jules asked.

Murray thought for a moment. "He was maybe a little older than you two. Good lookin' guy. Looked like a movie star, honestly. He wore a button-down and slacks, so I knew he was a businessman, which made me wonder why he was at a laundromat."

"Do you remember anything else about what he looked like? Hair color, ethnicity, eye color?"

Murray shook his head. "I can't remember. I just know she wasn't interested in me once he walked inside."

"Why were you at her crime scene?" Jax asked.

Murray shrugged. "Curiosity mostly."

Jax narrowed his eyes. "You were curious about a woman who had been tortured and killed?"

Murray stood taller, crossing his arms. "By the amount of cops swarming the place, I figured that one killer must be back, and I wanted to see what the fuss was about."

Jax wanted to push the man for more information, but Juliette glanced in his direction and he heeded her warning. Murray was getting irritable, which meant the interview wouldn't last much longer.

Jules touched Murray's arm once again, and he smiled at her. She said, "I need to ask you about your ex-wife. It came out in your trial she had an affair. Is it possible she's behind all of these lies?"

Jax was impressed with her ability to lie so effortlessly.

Murray quickly removed his arm from her grasp and glared at her. "Don't ask me about that jezebel. Sylvia was a whore, and she ruined our family for a quick lay that ended up costing us everything. My son won't even speak to her. She may as well be dead and buried for all we care."

"I'm sorry to hear that," Jules said kindly. "But if she's behind the lies, it's important we talk to her."

This time, Murray narrowed his eyes at her. "I said we're not talking about her."

Not wanting to push him any harder, Jax said, "Can I use your restroom before we go?" He hoped to snoop while inside, knowing Jules would distract the man.

Murray put his arm up against the door jamb. "I don't think so."

Jax lifted a brow. "If you're innocent, surely you won't mind if I use your restroom."

Murray folded his arms. "Get off my property."

Jules interjected, "I'm sorry, Philip. We don't mean to be disrespectful or accuse you of anything. My partner just needs to use the restroom."

No longer persuaded by Juliette's pleas, he said, "Leave or I'll call and file a complaint against both of you." Then the man walked inside, slamming the door behind him.

CHAPTER 5

J ax parked the squad car in the only available spot, which had been the farthest from the building. Groaning, he and Jules got out and made their way
to the doors of the station. In the distance, *White Christmas* drifted through
the winter breeze as the rhythmic ring of the Salvation Army bell danced with
the melody.

He smiled to himself. He might hate the cold weather, but he loved the
Christmas season.

Picking up their pace, Jules pulled her scarf closer around her neck as she
ducked her face away from the cool breeze. Then they both jogged the last few
feet to the door and walked inside, welcoming the heat of the building.

Jules waved to the receptionist. "Hi Merisol! Hope it wasn't too crazy while
we were gone."

The woman chuckled. "No, ma'am. Everything is just fine."

"That's because you keep everyone in line," Jax said with a wink.

Merisol pointed at him. "That's right!"

They made their way back to their desks, taking off their coats and firing up
their laptops to start on their report about Murray. Detective Ramirez walked
by, nodding at the two of them as he made his way to the breakroom.

"So what did you think about Murray?" Jules asked.

Jax sat back as he waited for the device to turn on. "I think there's a good
chance he's SLK. The timing is right, plus his MO is *very* similar. My gut tells
me he's guilty, and you know my gut is never wrong."

"I agree. But we need to get a warrant to search his house for evidence. We can't arrest him on a hunch." Jules quickly typed in her password and hit enter.

"Later today, we need to talk to Cam about getting the warrant."

Jules nodded. "Let me text him and see when he'll be in the office." She felt her pocket and frowned. "Crap, I left my phone in the car." With an eye roll, she stood. "I'll be back."

Just as she disappeared around the corner, Jax's phone buzzed. He almost declined the call but thought better of it. The caller ID read Diego Reams, piquing his interest. He tapped the green button and put the phone to his ear. "I thought you were on your honeymoon."

Detective Reams chuckled. "We're about to board our flight, but Lawson screwed up, and I need you to help us out on a case. It'll be easy, I promise."

Leaning back in his chair, Jax said, "What did Lawson do?"

"He was supposed to notify the next of kin on a Jane Doe case before leaving for his vacation but never did. Can you or Jules do that? And maybe just look it over and get us started before Lawson and I come back?"

Jax wasn't surprised by the discrepancy. Though Lawson and Reams were good cops, they screwed up repeatedly when it came to time management.

"What's in it for me?" Jax asked.

"You owe *me*, remember? I bailed you out of that god-awful date you found yourself on."

Jax laughed. He had been looking for a one-night-stand, but it was clear the woman had been looking for something more... way more. She was talking about having kids together before the entrée had even made it to the table. Reams happened to be eating in the same restaurant and saw Jax's misery, so he had interrupted by "accidently" spilling his drink all over the woman."

Smiling, Jax said, "Yeah, I guess you're right. Okay, Jules and I will take a look. What case is it?"

He rattled off the case number, then said, "Twenty-six years ago, Mulberry police found a deceased Jane Doe. According to the autopsy, the girl was approximately between the ages of five and eight years old and never matched any missing persons records. It went cold pretty quickly."

Jax's heart dropped to his stomach. He absolutely hated working child-related cases. He couldn't fathom how people could be so cruel to adults, let alone children. He thought of his own nieces and felt the urge to call them and make sure they were okay.

"What was the cause of death?" Jax asked

"I'm not sure. What I told you is everything I know about the case."

Jax sat up, irritated. "You didn't look at the case at all?"

Reams hesitated for a moment. "It was kind of at the bottom of the list with all this wedding planning. Plus, we were knee deep in that triple homicide. Now that the homicide case is closed and the wedding is over, I can focus on Jane Doe."

Jax eyed Jules as she entered the room. "You mean Jules and I will do all the leg work while you sip mimosas on the beach in Cabo and get blow jobs nonstop."

Jules nearly spit out the hot chocolate she'd grabbed from the breakroom after retrieving her phone. She furrowed her brows, curious about the conversation.

Reams choked out a laugh. "Something like that. So, you'll do it?"

"Yeah, Jules and I will handle it until you get back."

"Thanks! I'll email you the DNA results, but the rest of the reports are still paper files, so you'll have to check those out."

The two said their goodbyes, and Jules lifted a brow. "Our plate is already a little full, don't you think? What case did you sign us up for?"

Jax shoved his phone back into his pocket. "A Jane Doe, approximately five to eight years old, was murdered twenty-six years ago. They finally got a familial DNA match."

Jules' face fell. "Why are people so awful? She was just a baby. She didn't even get to live."

Jax nodded. "I know. But at least we can try to bring her justice, maybe bring her family some peace?"

Jules sighed in agreement and sat at her desk. She pulled out the M.E.'s report for their latest SLK victim while Jax checked his email for the DNA results on Jane Doe. Once the email came through, he clicked on the message. He read over the report, skimming some of the scientific jargon until he came to a name: Alabama Knox.

Curious, he eyed Jules. "The name of the match is Alabama Knox. She lives in Winter Haven."

Jules paused and looked at Jax. "Cam has a cousin, but he's never mentioned her name. I know she lives in Winter Haven, though. He's not close with his family and doesn't talk about them much."

"Do you want to sit this one out?"

She shook her head and said, "No, I'll ask Cam about it later. They may not even be related."

He read over Reams' email and found the woman's home and work address. She lived close by and owned a small bookstore in downtown Winter Haven.

"Okay, then let's go meet Miss Alabama Knox," he said.

The two of them left and headed back into town. Once there, they climbed out and made their way to the library building. Before walking inside, he turned to look back at the fountain across the street, the tall structure casting a shadow over the surrounding flowerbeds.

Jax found it quite eerie that Bianca's body had been found in that very spot only a few days before. He glanced around, hoping by some stroke of luck, the killer would be standing right there. But the park was empty.

Turning back around, he and Jules made their way into the library building, which housed a few other businesses inside, including Miss Knox's. Jax wondered what would make someone want to open a bookstore, as he wasn't much of a reader, and he didn't think Jules was either. In school, the smart girls used to tease him mercilessly, all while scrunching their noses to keep their big-rimmed glasses from falling off their ugly faces. He was the jock, and they were jealous he never wanted to date any of them... or so his friends would tell him.

He'd bet his entire salary Miss Knox was a scrawny, doe-eyed woman with crazy hair and glasses too big for her face. Anyone who would deliberately own a bookstore was likely mental and couldn't be trusted.

Walking through the corridor, Jax and Juliette found the bookstore across from the library. A 'closed' sign lit up the window. Peering inside, he could make out a shadow on the far side of the room. He knocked and they waited until someone answered.

A woman appeared in the doorway and poked her head out, her copper hair falling over her shoulders. She smiled. "Hi, there. I'm so sorry, but we're closed right now. We open in an hour and would love to have you both come back then."

Jax's breath caught in his lungs. He hadn't expected her smile to be so full of life. And her eyes were the color of late autumn: deep brown with a warmth that made her impossible to ignore. The flecks of gold shimmered, like sunlight trapped in glass. Jax couldn't help but stare at her, completely speechless.

It was a good thing he hadn't made his earlier bet, because Alabama Knox was gorgeous.

Jules eyed him, waiting for him to respond. When he didn't, she said, "Are you Alabama Knox?"

The woman cringed and said, "Yes. But please, call me Ali. I hate my first name."

Jax grinned at her, and she sheepishly looked away, attempting to hide the red that painted her cheeks.

Jules gave him a weird look as she continued, "We're actually with the sheriff's department. I'm Detective Juliette Reid, and this is my partner, Sergeant Jax Moretti." She showed the woman her badge, and Jax did the same.

The woman's eyes widened. "Is my mother okay? Did something happen to my brother?"

Wanting to ease her worry, Jax said, "Oh, no, nothing like that. You submitted DNA to a genealogy site and opted in for police searches. Your DNA was linked to a case. I'm sorry to inform you, but your sister was found deceased twenty-six years ago..."

Ali furrowed her brows. "I don't understand. My sister?"

Juliette said, "Yes, ma'am. She was approximately five to eight years old when she died, but no one has been able to I.D. her. Is there any way you would be willing to come down to the station and give us more information?"

Ali shook her head. "Officers, I don't have a sister. I think there must have been a mix-up at the lab."

Jax said, "I'm sorry, we should be more direct. She's your half sister, according to the results. And I can assure you, the results are correct."

Ali crossed her arms. "Sir, I don't have a sister, so I'm not sure how to help you."

Jules asked, "Is it possible your mother had another daughter she gave up for adoption that you never knew about?"

Ali shifted slightly. "I'm really close with my mother. I don't think she would do that, let alone not tell me about it. I, uh…I don't know. I suppose it's possible, though."

Jax said, "According to our records, no one ever filed a missing person's report on her. And no one ever claimed her body when the police cycled her case through the media. If you could put us in touch with your mother, that would be helpful."

Ali nodded. "Of course. Let me write down her address for you. She's out running errands today, but I'll stop by tonight and let her know to expect you tomorrow."

She disappeared back into the shop for a few moments before emerging with a bright yellow sticky note, a smiley face pattern printed on it.

Jax took it from her. "Thank you, ma'am."

She gave a half smile and nodded as she rubbed her arms and looked to the floor. Then she said, "Hopefully my mother can shed some light on this."

Juliette nodded, and she and Jax handed the woman their cards. "Let us know if you think of anything. Even the smallest piece of information can be helpful."

Ali accepted the cards. "Of course."

"Have a great day, Miss Knox," Jax said as he and Juliette turned to leave. He glanced back at the pretty redhead, and she smiled and tucked her hair behind her ear as she quickly disappeared into the store.

Jules loudly cleared her throat. "Come on, Romeo. We've got work to do."

He shot her a look as they walked toward the car and headed back to the station.

After the officers had left her store, Ali felt guilty for not having much information to give them. And as the hours ticked by, she couldn't keep her anxiety at bay as she wondered who the little girl was. So she had quickly closed her tiny shop and drove to the police station hoping to speak with the Sergeant and Detective.

Once inside the precinct, Ali walked up to the counter. "Hi, my name is Ali Knox. I'm here to see Sergeant Moretti and Detective Reid."

The woman smiled brightly. "I'll let them know you're here."

Ali nodded and took a seat in the waiting area. While she waited, she took out her phone and scrolled through her emails, replying to the ones that were the most emergent. Hitting send on her last email, a deep voice had her glancing at the door next to the receptionist's window.

"Miss Knox, I didn't know you were stopping by." Sergeant Moretti held open the door, gesturing for her to follow.

Ali nodded and smiled. "Please, call me Ali. And I've just felt antsy since you left so I wanted to get more information about the little girl."

The two walked down a hallway and then stepped into the elevator where he hit the button for the second floor. She stood across from him, taking in his muscular build; the fabric of his collared shirt not leaving much to the imagination. She was surprised by the tattoos that covered his arms and the gold watch on his wrist. And the gold chain around his neck accentuated his tan complexion. Of course, she couldn't ignore the way his hazel eyes trailed her.

His cologne filled the small space, and Ali found herself embarrassed at the rate in which her heart was beating. She cleared her throat. "So how long have you been a cop?"

Sergeant Moretti crossed his arms as he leaned against the elevator wall. "Ten years. I joined when I was eighteen."

Just as she was about to respond, the doors slid open and he stepped out of the small space. "This way," he said as he led her to his desk.

Detective Reid was sitting at her own workspace next to Sergeant Moretti's. Ali had been surprised by the woman's beauty when she'd seen her early that morning. The blonde hair and striking cloudy-blue eyes no doubt turned heads. But more than that, there was a kindness about the woman. Something that Ali instinctively knew though they had just met.

The detective glanced up and smiled. "Hi, Miss Knox."

Ali returned the smile and took a seat across from the woman while Sergeant Moretti pulled up a spare chair and sat next to his partner. "Sorry to drop in unannounced. My nerves got the better of me. I was hoping to get more information about the little girl, maybe spark my memory or something." She sighed. "I sound crazy. I'm so sorry." Ali stood quickly, embarrassed that she had intruded on the officers' day.

Detective Reid gestured to the chair. "Please, sit. It's not stupid at all. I can't imagine what this is like for you."

Ali nodded and twirled her hair as she sat back down. "One of the girls who frequents my shop was reading about DNA and how people are able to find things about their heritage, so we did it together. We were going to read the results at a dinner party or whatever." She scrunched her eyebrows together and groaned. "Gosh, that sounds so childish now that I say it out loud." She shook her head. "Anyway, how did it end up with the police?"

Sergeant Moretti sat back. "When you submitted your DNA to GEDMatch, you were given the option to allow your DNA to be used by law enforcement. Since you opted in for that, we were able to get hits on your DNA linking you to this particular victim."

Detective Reid clasped her hands together. "Why did you upload your DNA to GEDMatch, Ali? I understand using Ancestry or 23andMe since those show your heritage and things like that. But GEDMatch is specifically used to connect you with other people. Who are you trying to find?"

Ali felt the room spin ever so slightly. She took a breath, trying to calm her racing heart. "I- uh..." Ali closed her eyes for a moment. Then, she shook her head. "No one. I was just curious to see if anyone was a match."

Ali didn't dare tell them the truth. It could ruin everything. She'd be better off keeping her secret until she absolutely had to tell the police...*if* she had to tell the police. There was no reason to think her secret had anything to do with the Jane Doe. And more importantly, by keeping her secret, she was also keeping *his*.

The sergeant and detective exchanged glances. It was clear they didn't believe her, but neither pushed for more information.

Hoping to change the conversation, she said, "Would I be allowed to see her photo? I guess I'm hoping it will help jog my memory or something. Does that sound silly?"

"It doesn't sound silly at all," Detective Reid said.

Sergeant Moretti opened up a manila folder that lay on the desk. He took a picture out and slid it across to her. Ali wasn't sure why she felt so nervous, but her heart seemed to nearly beat out of her chest. She held her breath as she slowly reached for the photo of the little girl who looked to be sleeping, her black hair cupping her face.

The girl was small, her skin grey and blue, no life within her. She almost looked like those porcelain dolls Ali's grandmother used to have.

Ali traced her face, desperately trying to conjure up who she was. Again, she felt her chest tighten, as if she should know the Jane Doe. But she couldn't bring forth a name. She stared at the photo, unsettled. The face of the little girl felt familiar in that strange, fleeting way. Like passing someone on the street, sure you've seen them before, though you can't quite place them. A vague familiarity.

Her shoulders slumped slightly. "I don't know...I feel like I've seen her before. But then again, she doesn't look familiar at all." She smiled sadly and looked at Sergeant Moretti. "I'm sorry, I'm probably not making much sense." Ali shook her head. "What happened to her?"

Sergeant Moretti said, "She was murdered, but that's all we know at the moment."

Ali's hand flew to her mouth. "Murdered?! Who would do that? She was just a child."

Guilt clutched Ali. This little girl deserved justice. To have a name, to be properly buried. But Ali didn't have the answers that would bring such clarity. And that fact nearly crippled her. According to the police, this child was her sister, and Ali didn't even know her. Her heart ached for the little girl.

"I know this is a lot to process." Sergeant Moretti looked at Ali and gently took her hand from across the desk.

Ali glanced down but didn't pull away. She found herself intrigued by the man. He was no doubt rough around the edges, but there seemed to be a silent gentleness about him. His touch was somehow comforting, and Ali didn't dare explore those thoughts.

"Is there anything more I can do to help?" Ali asked.

Detective Reid stood, as did Sergeant Moretti, and then Ali. The Detective said, "Not right now, but thank you for trying to help us, Ali. If you think of anything or find something that might help, don't hesitate to reach out. We'll try to talk to your mother tomorrow."

Sergeant Moretti nodded to the doorway. "I'll walk you out."

Detective Reid lifted a brow at her partner as he tried and failed to hide a smile. Then, she glanced at Ali. "It was nice to meet you."

"Likewise."

Before Ali turned to leave, Detective Reid said, "Oh, Ali, one last thing. Are you related to Cameron Knox by chance?"

Ali pulled her purse over her shoulder. "He's my cousin. We haven't talked in a long time though. He had a falling out with the family before I even left for college. Why do you ask?"

Detective Reid looked at her desk then back at Ali. "We're dating, actually. When I saw your last name, I wondered if there was a connection."

Ali smiled sadly. "Tell him I miss him and it wouldn't kill him to check on his kid cousin every now and then." Sadness splintered her heart. She missed him fiercely. Despite the age gap between her and Cam, he had been like an older brother to her. She had been devastated when he had cut ties with the family.

Bringing Ali back to reality, the Sergeant said, "This way." She followed him back to the elevator and as the doors closed, Ali let out a breath.

"You okay?" he asked, lifting a brow.

"I just feel so guilty that I don't know who she is."

Jax shrugged. "You can't help what you don't know."

"How do you do it? How do you deal with seeing stuff like this every day?"

"I'd like to say it gets easier over time, but it doesn't. I'm a walking cliche and have some really unhealthy coping mechanisms like a lot of cops. But at the end of the day, the job is about getting justice for the ones who were silenced."

The doors slid open and the two stepped off, making their way toward the lobby. Ali gently touched his arm and smiled softly. "Just know you're making a difference, even when it doesn't feel like it." Ali dropped her hand, and they walked in silence down the hallway.

Once at the front doors, she turned to look at him. "Will you keep me updated on what you find out?" She paused for a moment, then said, "I know she's gone, but the least I can do is check on her. No one deserves to be forgotten."

Sergeant Moretti nodded. "I'll update you with any information I can."

"Thank you." Ali said. The two stared at each other and Ali could feel the heat creep up her cheeks. Embarrassed, she ran a hand through her hair. "Well, I need to get going." She ducked out the door before Jax could respond. She felt like a schoolgirl, giddy over the popular boy all the girls had a crush on.

She chastised herself for even considering the man. First of all, he was a cop. She had no interest in dating someone in such a dangerous line of work. And no doubt women threw themselves at him, a game she didn't want to play. Plus, she had just gotten out of a bad relationship six months ago and really wasn't looking for anything.

The cold air bit at her face and she hurried to the car. Once inside, she blasted the heat before taking off toward her bookstore.

Once there, she walked down the foyer to her shop. She fished out her keys from her purse and unlocked the door. Pulling it open, she noticed a flower on the floor. She smiled to herself, knowing *he* had been there. She had wanted to get the mail slot sealed, but he used it as a way to leave flowers for her, and she couldn't bear the thought of cutting off yet another form of communication with him.

Ali picked up the flower and studied the blue hue. A forget me not.

He wanted her to know he was close by. That he was still watching over her, even if she could never see him again. Ali hoped one day those circumstances would change, that they would finally be reunited.

But for now, he would stay in the shadows. And she would keep his secret.

CHAPTER 6

Affter finishing their interview with Ali, Jules and Jax headed to Cam's office, hoping he'd grant them a search warrant for Philip Murray's home. When they walked through the door, Cam was sitting at his desk, paperwork strewn across the large wooden box.

His blue eyes brightened when glanced up and saw Juliette. "When you texted me earlier, I thought it was because you just wanted to see me." He walked around his desk and kissed her on the forehead.

She smiled to herself; happy she'd found a man who treated her so well.

Cam nodded toward her partner. "Since Jax is here, I'm going to assume this isn't a social call."

Jules shook her head and sighed. "Unfortunately, no."

Jax said, "We need a search warrant for a man named Philip Murray. When we went to talk to him today, he said he had interacted with one of the victims. He also has a history of raping, burning, and choking prostitutes."

Cam leaned against his desk and crossed his arms, his muscles pulled taut under his dress shirt. "The creep that's been documented as coming to the dump sites?"

Jules nodded. "He said he met Kiara Short at a laundromat, but she wasn't interested in him. When we questioned him about his ex-wife's affair, he got pretty angry."

Unease washed over Jules as she recalled Murray's glare. It had taken her by surprise. His initial calmness caused her to put her guard down, a mistake she wouldn't make again. Though she knew he was a monster, she hadn't been fearful of him at first. Now, she knew he was a man who shouldn't be crossed.

Cam lifted a brow. "Anything else?"

Jax shook his head. "That's it. I really think this guy is the Scarlet Letter Killer, Cam. He's a truck driver and only takes jobs in Florida. He already has a history of rape and burning victims, plus he nearly killed one of the women he assaulted. And when asked about his ex-wife, he was livid."

Cam shrugged. "He might be SLK, but you know you don't have enough for a warrant."

"Cam, this monster has been brutalizing women for a *decade* and I think we finally have him. We can't let him get away."

Cam held Jax's stare, "Then bring me more. If he's guilty, there will be evidence."

The vein at Jax's temple throbbed, and Jules cast a worried glance at her partner. When Jax got heated, there was no reasoning with him. She'd been called to one too many bar fights where she'd have to attempt to calm him down. Or put him in cuffs. Whichever worked best at the time.

The last thing she needed was for her partner to throw a punch at her boyfriend.

"Are you kidding me?" Jax took a step toward Cam who didn't flinch at the outburst. "Get me the warrant."

Cam lifted his hand. "I'm not even going to waste my time bringing this to a judge." He looked at Jules. "Am I wrong?"

She looked at Jax, then at the ground. "No. It's not enough."

Jax scoffed. "You're just like the rest of these shady-ass politicians. Your only concern is to run a great smear campaign and work your way up the political ladder while the rest of us do your dirty work so you can come out looking like a hero."

"Jax!" Juliette hissed.

Cam clenched his jaw as he crossed his arms, looking at Jax. "I want to give you a warrant, but a judge would never sign off on it. And believe me, I want this piece of shit behind bars." He shook his head. "But not like this. Not when it could potentially be the wrong guy and you're too prideful to bring me sufficient evidence."

Jax seethed at Cam's refusal, though Juliette knew Jax understood, even if he was upset by it.

"Whatever," Jax said as he stormed out the door.

Jules hung her head. "I'm sorry. This case is eating at us."

Cam tilted her head up with his finger. "I know. And I know he's not mad at me. Bring me something substantial and I'll bring it to a judge, doesn't matter the time or day. I'll call in a favor if I have to."

She smiled. "You're a good man, you know that?"

"Only sometimes." He winked.

She giggled and shook her head. "I'm hoping to stop by after my shift, but I've got a lot of paperwork to catch up on so I may be late."

He kissed her deeply. "That's okay, I'll still be here when you're done."

The two said their goodbyes and Juliette left to find her very angry partner.

Ali cradled the phone to her ear with her shoulder as she placed new books on the bookshelves in her shop. After seeing the little girl's photo, guilt tugged at her heart. So she called the one woman who could potentially shed light on Jane Doe's identity.

"Hello?" Theresa Knox whispered.

"Ma," Ali chuckled. "Why are you whispering?"

Theresa sighed. "You know today is my errand day. I'm at the grocery store. What do you need?"

Ali heard the familiar repetitive squeaking of grocery cart wheels. "You know you can talk at a normal volume, right? You're not at the library."

Theresa laughed. "Alabama, don't tease your mother." A sharp *clink* met Ali's ears as her mother set something into her cart. "What do you need?"

Ali was nervous to ask her mother about Jane Doe. Initially, she wanted to let the police do it, but Ali couldn't seem to get rid of the knot in her stomach. She wanted answers and Theresa seemed to be the only one who could give them to her. If Theresa had another daughter, she hadn't shared that with the rest of the family.

Slightly hesitating, she said, "I'm not sure how to ask this so I'll just say it...Do I have a sister? Well, a half-sister?"

Her mother took in a sharp breath just as a sudden *clash* filtered through the phone, "Dammit!" Theresa said harshly. "I'm sorry, darling. I dropped a jar, and I need to go get someone to clean it up. I'll call you later."

"But-"

Click.

Ali held her phone away from her face, staring at the screen. Frustrated, she sighed and stood up, grabbing the empty crate and placing it back in her storage closet in the far corner of the office. She still needed to catch up on some paperwork, but thankfully was almost finished since the day hadn't been very busy.

The shop had been quiet, aside from a few regulars. And to Ali's pleasant surprise, she'd gotten to chat with a woman who traveled to Winter Haven from Ohio every few months to visit family. She'd first come into the shop four years ago, and over time, she had become one of Ali's favorite customers. She'd always come in smiling, heading straight to the kid's section to find books to take back to her grandkids.

A soft *ring* drifted through the small shop, announcing another customer's arrival. Ali emerged from her office to find her brother, Levi, standing at the desk. His blond hair was styled in a neat combover, specks of gray just beginning to appear. Though Levi was forty-one years old, you'd never know it. He made it a priority to run three miles every day... after working out for an hour.

Ali wouldn't be caught dead in a gym. She'd rather eat dirt than exercise for fun.

"I didn't expect to see you today," she said as she walked around the desk to hug him.

Levi said, "I had to show a client a house on this side of town, so I thought I'd drop by."

Ali smiled at him. "I'm glad you did."

Because he'd been busy showing new property to potential buyers, they hadn't been able to have their weekly lunch meetups in over a month.

Levi leaned against the front desk. "Have you talked to Ma today? She wanted to make sure you were still on for dinner later this week."

Nodding her head, she said, "Yeah, just tell me when." She hesitated for a moment, wanting to confront her brother about Jane Doe. Being so much older than Ali, there was a chance he had heard their mother talking about her.

Sensing her nerves, he asked, "Are you okay? You seem jumpy."

Ali played with the bracelet on her wrist. "Actually, I need to talk to you about something. Can you grab lunch real quick?"

"Sure. In the mood for burgers?"

"Always," she said with a smile.

The two left the shop and Ali drove a few streets over to the burger joint as she unapologetically (and loudly) sang along to a Christmas song. Even though she hated the winter weather, the Christmas season was her favorite time of year.

Growing up, her family hadn't taken part in holiday traditions like most other families. Gramps had always claimed it was all a scheme for companies to make more money off the backs of hardworking men. But when Ali had gone away to college, her roommate had celebrated *every* holiday, no matter how miniscule. Ali had immediately been drawn to the joy it brought to their tiny dorm room, and Ali had kept the tradition alive all through college and even into adulthood.

Even now, she found the Christmas holiday quite magical.

Pulling into a parking spot, she climbed out of her car. The local burger joint was small, but the food was delicious. Since inside seating was minimal, she wanted to sit outside to ensure she and Levi had privacy. Luckily, the cold temperatures from this morning had warmed up significantly and they wouldn't be too uncomfortable sitting outside.

Ali and Levi made their way to the window and placed their orders. After a few moments, the two collected their trays and found an empty picnic table on the farthest side of the courtyard.

As Ali took her first bite, she spied a mother with three boys sitting a few tables over. She watched in silence as each boy picked up a handful of the gravel that was below their feet and chucked it at each other. Their mother hastily chastised them, sending a ripple of laughs through the boys.

Ali let out a chuckle at the scene.

Drawing her attention, Levi said, "So what do you need to talk to me about?"

Ali took a deep breath. She wasn't sure why she felt so nervous to talk to him about it. Maybe she was scared of the truth? Had her mother been assaulted and the baby was a result? She wondered if maybe her mother had a one night stand and had been ashamed of her choices, causing her to keep the baby a secret. Or maybe the child was her father's, the result of a torrid affair. After all, the man had long since disappeared from Ali's life, taking his secrets when he left.

Regardless, Ali had a half-sister, and she needed to know what had happened to her.

She put her burger down and snatched a fry as she said, "Does Ma have any other kids?"

Levi nearly spit out his drink. "I'm sorry, what?"

Ali rolled her eyes and dipped another fry in ketchup. "I know it's a weird question, but did Ma place a baby for adoption?"

Levi set down his drink, his eyes narrowing at her in concern. "Ali, are you pregnant? You don't have to give up your baby. You're perfectly capable of raising a child."

Ali laughed. "God, no! I'm on birth control." Becoming a bit more serious, she pushed him again. "I was told I have a half-sister, but I've never heard anyone talk about her."

Levi froze for a moment, then asked, "Where did you hear that? Have you been talking to Cam?"

Ali furrowed her brows. "No. Cam hasn't talked to me in almost twelve years."

A pang of sadness shot through her heart. She missed her cousin, but he had cut off the Knox family after a disagreement between him and their grandfather, Henry Knox. Ali had never been privy to the details, only that Cam had severed all ties with them and her grandfather hadn't been the same since.

Although she had been glad to see Cam at Henry's bedside when the man had passed away two years ago, Cam hadn't spoken a word to any of them. He had asked for privacy so the two of them could talk and then left after the conversation had ended. Ali had always assumed he wanted to make amends with their dying grandfather, but the brokenness of the family still remained.

"Good," Levi said. "You know better than to believe anything he says."

Ali shook her head. "What happened with Cam? It's been nearly twenty years since he and Gramps got into it. I think it's safe for you to tell me."

He took a drink of his soda, then said, "You know I won't ever tell you. You're wasting your breath."

She rolled her eyes. "Fine. Then tell me about this half sister I apparently have."

"Who told you that? Sounds like a crock of shit." Levi said as he bit into his burger.

Ali wasn't about to bend so easily. If he wanted to keep secrets, she could do the same. Plus, he'd find out tomorrow when the police went knocking on their mother's door asking their own questions.

Ali lifted a shoulder. "Look, all I'm going to say is that I have very strong evidence proving I have a half sister and I just want to know if you knew about her."

Irritated with her reluctance to reveal her source, Levi studied her face for a few moments. The faint sound of children laughing echoed through the air as a neighboring school let their elementary kids out to play on the near-by playground.

Finally, he said, "No, I don't know anything about a half sister. Are you sure the information is good?"

Ali nodded. "I'm positive."

He eyed her suspiciously, then sighed. "I don't know what's going on, but don't talk to Ma about it. It might bring up some unwanted emotions for her, and I don't think that's fair."

She gave her brother a soft smile.

Always the protector.

When Ali's father had disappeared, it had been up to Levi to be the man of the house, despite only being fifteen. And he had taken his role seriously. Ali had always admired that about him, at least when it didn't interfere too much with her life.

And he was right; she didn't need to discuss it with their mother. Ali would let Sergeant Moretti and Detective Reid do their jobs and hopefully she'd get answers.

Because even though she'd been looking for someone else when she submitted her DNA, Jane Doe was the one she was now focused on.

CHAPTER 7

A li had picked up take out for dinner but didn't have much of an appetite now that she was home. She couldn't seem to get the little girl's face out of her head. There was something familiar about her, but Ali couldn't quite put her finger on it, which both irritated and saddened her. She was Ali's sister, per the DNA results, and yet Ali had never seen her before.

Or heard of her.

She closed her eyes once again, conjuring up the dark-haired child. She tried her hardest to put a name to the face, but it was useless.

Sighing, she picked up her plate and began cleaning in an attempt to clear her mind. She wiped down the counters, put away some laundry, and made sure her clothes were laid out for tomorrow's workday. Then she hopped in the shower, threw on some comfy pajamas, and climbed into bed.

Turning on the TV, she searched for a romcom, needing a good laugh after the long day she'd had. She was surprised when her thoughts suddenly turned to Sergeant Moretti. Was he on a date? Was he at home snuggling with the beautiful girlfriend Ali assumed he had? Or was he thinking about her as much as she was thinking about him?

Rolling her eyes, she chastised herself. She had no business thinking about him, let alone wondering what he was doing at the moment. Tossing her head back, she groaned.

A soft cry from the doorway had Ali turning her attention to the black cat that strutted into the room. "I see you've come out of hiding." Ali patted the bed next to her, but the feline ignored the gesture and instead jumped up on the dresser that was next to the doorway.

"Bellatrix, get down," Ali demanded.

But the cat simply stared at her as she licked her paw. Ali got up and walked toward her pet, but Bellatrix jumped down, knocking Ali's grandmother's bible to the floor. Then, she darted to the bed and sat in the spot Ali had just been laying in.

Ali shook her head. "Real funny."

Bending down, she scooped up the bible. A sad smile tugged at Ali's lips. Her grandmother had passed away in 2012. Being the only girl, she was very close with her grandmother, and the woman's death had been particularly hard on Ali. She still found herself crying over the loss from time to time.

Smiling to herself as memories raced through her mind, she placed the book on the dresser. As she turned to sit back on the bed, she nearly stepped on a photo that had fallen to the floor.

Curious, Ali picked it up.

The candid shot must have been taken at the park near the compound, the old sycamore tree standing tall in the background. She had spent many days attempting to climb that exact tree as Levi and Cam had hidden within the branches, trying to keep from playing with her.

Ali looked to be around six years old in the photo. Her wild copper hair was pulled into pigtails and freckles lightly dusted the bridge of her nose. She was smiling brightly, revealing two missing teeth.

But what took Ali's breath away was the child who stood next to her. Ali's heartbeat quickened and she caressed the girl's face with her finger. It was the Jane Doe from the photo Sergeant Moretti had shown her earlier. The little girl had her black hair pulled into pigtails, mirroring Ali. And she smiled just as brightly; except she hadn't yet lost any teeth. The innocent twinkle in her eyes nearly caused Ali to cry.

That didn't make sense.

Who was she and why did her grandmother have the girl's photo tucked away in the family bible? Ali had no recollection of the girl the police claimed to be her sister, yet DNA said otherwise. And now her grandmother had a photo of the girl.

She flipped the photo over. In Gin's handwriting was written *Ali & Missi: 1998*

Jane Doe finally had a name.

Yet, Ali couldn't mistake the feeling of dread that filled her chest.

Ali drove twenty-five minutes to the Knox property in Polk City, Florida. The family compound was set on twenty acres, yet was only a few miles from the city. She, Levi, and Cam loved exploring the woods that surrounded their homes and would spend hours playing hide and seek around the property, despite the large age gap between them.

Of course, the boys would reluctantly drag her around the farm, sometimes leaving her stranded while they smoked cigarettes and rode four-wheelers. And even though they would pick on her and bully her, they would still look after her.

Some of her fondest memories were made right here.

Pulling up the long dirt driveway, she could make out the large farmhouse that had once been her grandparents' home. The structure was surrounded by two other houses on either side, a little cottage and a cute bungalow.

Growing up, Ali, her brother, and her mother lived in the old cottage to the left. It had been a cute little place, suited for a single mother and her two kids. Of course, Cam and his parents (Ali's Uncle Rick and Aunt Dianne) lived in the bungalow to the right.

Then, there was a barn and work shed tucked back into the woods beyond the homes. Her days had been filled with farm work or playing in the woods and getting dirty, something she had thoroughly enjoyed. But her grandparents' farmhouse had been her sanctuary.

She had spent many nights cuddled up by the fireplace where Gramps would tell her stories while Gin would bake cookies. And as her grandfather finished a story, Ali's eyes would drift closed and she'd be carried to their bed where she'd sleep soundly, tucked between them.

And when there was a thunderstorm or if she had a nightmare, she'd demand to go to Gin and Gramps. Which always resulted in Levi unenthusiastically walking her the short five minutes to the farmhouse.

Wrapped in the naivety of childhood, she was certain Gin and Gramps would keep the monsters away. But now they were gone and Ali was left to protect herself and she missed her grandparents terribly.

Sighing at the memories, Ali parked and stole a glance at the silhouette of the old cottage and bungalow that were now vacant. After her grandfather passed away, he left the farm to his kids: Rick and Theresa, which hadn't surprised Ali in the least. The siblings were close, as were Theresa and Rick's wife, Dianne. The two had been best friends for as long as Ali could remember.

Though Ali, Levi, and Cam had ventured out on their own, it wasn't a secret their parents hoped that one day the three of them would come back to live on the compound. But none of the Knox children had the heart to tell them there were no such plans being made. Ali, Levi, and Cam enjoyed their independence, as they hadn't gotten much of it growing up.

Glancing at the clock on her dash, she hadn't realized how late it was, but she knew her mother would be awake. She spied Levi's Mustang and wondered why her brother was at the house too. She climbed out of the car and made her way up the porch steps.

Stealing herself, she opened the door. "Ma!" Ali yelled.

Theresa appeared from the kitchen, holding a dish she was drying with a towel. Her copper hair was pulled into a top knot and a few gray strands peeked through, telling the world she was older than she appeared. She donned a red dress that looked as if it had come right out of a seventies housewives magazine. And though she kept her makeup simple, she was known for her bold red lip.

She smiled at Ali. "Hi, baby. What are you doing here this late?"

Ali followed her mother back into the kitchen. "I need to talk to you about something. Where is everyone else? Is Levi here?"

Theresa lifted a brow. "Your Uncle Rick was called in to do an emergency surgery and Dianne is somewhere around here. Levi is out in the shed tinkering on another one of his projects."

Nodding, Ali sat at the dining room table that was only steps away from the kitchen.

Theresa followed and did the same, eyeing her daughter. "Ali, what's wrong?"

Ali didn't answer at first. Her chest tightened and sweat beaded on her hairline as she began to work up the courage to ask her mother about the girl in the photo. Ali could be reopening old wounds and she didn't want to cause Theresa pain.

But Ali needed to know.

And Jane Doe deserved justice.

It was clear by the photo in Gin's bible the family had kept an eye on 'Missi.' Especially if they had allowed Ali to take a photo with her. Of course, that bothered Ali to her core. How could she have taken a picture with the girl and not remembered her? Surely her mother would have told Ali who she was...*right*?

For fear of losing her nerve, Ali blurted out, "Do you know who Missi is?"

Theresa started. "No. I don't."

Ali's heart dropped. She furrowed her brows and tilted her head. "Why are you lying?"

Theresa's hand flew to her chest. "Alabama, don't call me a liar."

Ali rolled her eyes at her mother's theatrics. "Ma, we played poker every time I visited from college. I know when you're lying."

Theresa tapped on the table for a moment, then stood up and walked to the kitchen counter where she grabbed Gin's cookie jar and brought it back. Ali smirked as she reached her hand inside and snatched a cookie.

Theresa did the same, setting it on the table.

"Missi was your imaginary friend growing up." Theresa said, looking down at the snack. "We had a difficult time getting you to understand she wasn't real. You would wake up from nightmares about her, and you would have the most vivid daydreams of playing with her. It wasn't normal. I think you used it to cope with your father leaving, but it got worse as time went on."

Ali vaguely remembered the nightmares. She remembered a park swing and screaming. She thought there might have been blood, but maybe that wasn't right. She hadn't thought about those nightmares in quite some time.

And now that her mother had mentioned the dreams, she could recall imagining a little girl as they played with dolls or dressed up as princesses. But if she was an imaginary friend, why did Gin have a picture of her?

"Ma, I have a picture of her. I found it in Gin's bible and-"

Theresa's face paled and before she could respond, Ali's Aunt Dianne walked into the room.

The woman eyed Ali suspiciously. "Why are you here? It's late."

Ali had always tried to stay away from Dianne growing up. The woman didn't care much for Ali, though Ali never knew why. Her earliest memories of her aunt were filled with angry stares and short answers anytime Ali spoke to her.

Theresa hesitated and then said, "Ali is asking about her imaginary friend, Missi. She thinks I'm lying and that the girl is real."

Dianne sucked in a breath as her eyes rounded. Then, she quickly ran a hand through her black hair and narrowed her eyes at Ali. "What an odd thing for your mother to lie about, Alabama."

Ali was initially stunned by the comment. "I, uh-" Ali's eyes darted to Theresa who was intently staring at her.

Ali paused for a moment and considered Theresa. She had grown up never wanting to disappoint her mother. The two were close, confiding in one another about everything. Ali found herself wondering if she was being dramatic. There had to be a simple explanation for this.

Maybe the 'Missi' from the photo just resembled Jane Doe and Ali was wrong. She'd really only looked at the photo at the police station for a brief moment. Hadn't she even heard somewhere that witness statements were frowned upon as evidence in trials because people couldn't be trusted to remember facts correctly? Had she merely mistaken the two girls?

A thud from the back door had everyone turning to see Levi, mud covering his boots and cuts on his arms and legs. He eyed the three of them. "What's going on? I haven't seen y'all this heated since Ali set the Thanksgiving turkey on fire and nearly burned down the house."

Ali scowled at her brother and crossed her arms.

Theresa looked back at Ali. "Your sister is asking about Missi. Apparently, she found a photo in Gin's bible."

Levi turned around and started washing his hands in the kitchen sink. "Ma, just tell her. Quit making it such a big deal. It's a stupid story that you don't need to perpetuate anymore. Ali's a grown adult, treat her like one."

Ali tilted her head. "Thank you," she said. Then, she looked at her mother, waiting for Theresa's explanation.

Theresa let out a deep sigh. "You saw a girl at the park one day and said it looked like Missi. You begged for a photo, so we took it and Gin made the stupid decision to print it out and act like it was real. It made it even more difficult for you to cope with your father leaving and when we told you Missi wasn't real you were nearly inconsolable."

Levi leaned against the counter as he wiped his hands with a towel. Dianne glanced from Ali to Theresa, then to Levi.

Instinctively, Ali knew they were all lying. Because at the end of the day, if that were true, Gin wouldn't have chosen *that* photo to keep in her bible. If Missi was a random stranger, her photo wouldn't have been cherished above any other photo Gin could have printed.

Irritated, Ali walked back to the table and reached into her purse and pulled out the picture and showed it to her mother. "If her name isn't Missi, then what is it? The police came to me today, asking about this little girl. They said-"

Theresa's eyes rounded as she shared a glance with Levi. "The police?"

Startling Ali, Dianne tried to grab the photo, but Ali pulled it away.

Dianne took a step closer. "Give me that photo right now."

Ali took a step back. "No. Not until you tell me who Missi is...who this girl is."

Dianne's hand connected with Ali's cheek. Pain stung her face and Ali gasped as she brought her hand to the wound.

"Dianne!" Theresea screamed.

Levi put himself between the two women, gently moving Ali away from their aunt.

"Give me that photo right now!" Dianne demanded.

Ali clutched it to her chest as tears stung her eyes. "I'll show you, but you can't take it." She couldn't risk her running off with the photo before Ali could get answers. Clearly, the girl meant something to Dianne.

"Ali," Levi said with a sigh as he shook his head, but she ignored her brother. Dianne knew who this girl was.

After a moment, her aunt nodded in agreement, but Theresa grabbed Dianne's arm. "Dianne, no..."

Dianne ripped her arm free, glaring at Theresa as she walked toward Ali.

Ali slowly turned the photo around, revealing the nameless little girl.

Tears flowed down Dianne's cheeks as she gently reached for the photo. She clutched it tightly to her chest. "Oh Missi. My sweet Missi." As if realizing what she was doing, she shoved the photo back into Ali's hands, then abruptly left the room.

Theresa rushed to Ali and took her by the arms, startling Ali. "You need to leave and put that picture back where you found it. Forget about it and forget about this conversation.'

"But the police-"

"Alabama, I'm serious. If you've ever trusted me, you will listen to me."

Ali looked at her brother who nodded and said, "Come on, I'll walk you out."

Her mother shared a glance with Levi and then dashed up the stairs where Dianne's faint sobs could be heard.

Seething, Ali let Levi walk her to the car. Once outside, she quickly turned on her heel and thrusted her finger in her brother's face. "What the hell is going on?"

He shoved his hands in his coat pocket and looked around. "Nothing you need to worry about. Do what Ma says and forget about that girl."

She threw up her arms. "I can't! She's dead, Levi. And my DNA matched hers. She's my half-sister and the police want answers."

He ran a hand through his hair. "Shit. Okay, just..."

"Who is she?" Ali demanded.

Levi hesitated. "She's going to be what gets you killed if you're not careful."

Angry, Ali crossed her arms. "Stop trying to scare me. I'm not a little kid anymore."

Levi sighed and clenched his jaw. When he didn't respond, Ali continued, "You know, I initially thought maybe Ma had a baby and she'd been put up for adoption. But after seeing Aunt Dianne's reaction, I don't think the little girl belonged to Ma at all."

Levi's lips twitched ever so slightly, confirming her new suspicions.

"Did my father have an affair with Dianne and Missi was the result? Is that why he left?" She glared at him, wanting her brother to be honest with her. But then, her expressions softened as she studied his face.

She and Levi had been close growing up. He'd always protected her, doted on her. He'd taught her to ride a bike, saddle a horse, and muck stalls. He'd taught her how to play chess and how to fight.

He'd been there with a tub of ice cream and a chick-flick when she had suffered her first breakup. He'd been on the front row when she had graduated high school and college. And she had no doubt he'd give her hand away in marriage when the time came. Though they would argue occasionally, Ali had always known she could trust and depend on Levi.

Which meant, if he was lying, she could trust he had a good reason for it.

But a little girl was murdered and Ali needed answers.

Finally, he took a deep breath and said, "I love you, Ali. And I'm sorry if this hurts you, but you need to let it go. I'm not exaggerating when I say you'll end up dead if you don't."

Ali thrusted up her chin. "Fine. You want to act stupid, go ahead. But I'm going to find the one person who can tell me all our family secrets."

Levi scoffed. "Yeah? And who would that be?"

Out of spite, Ali ignored her brother and climbed into her car. As she drove off into the night, she worried she'd just started something she couldn't finish.

CHAPTER 8

L evi watched as Ali tore down the dirt path, feeling a little guilty for hiding the truth from her. But it was for the best. Or at least it had been until now. Now, it was time for the truth to come out. The police would figure it out anyway.

He just needed to sever a few loose ends before they did.

He waited until her tail lights disappeared into the night before he went back inside. The aroma of garlic and herbs assaulted him. His stomach growled, reminding him he was starving after having worked on his project all evening.

He found his mother back in the kitchen, hands shoved into a bowl, mixing together ingredients for homemade bread. It's what she did whenever she was overly stressed. And he had no doubt she was anxious after the conversation they'd had with Ali.

Levi leaned against the counter next to Theresa, crossing his arms as he did. "We need to tell Ali the truth."

Not bothering to look at him, Theresa sternly said, "We will do no such thing."

"She needs to know. It's time."

Theresa quickly lifted her head, her eyes darkening. "The truth will get us all killed. Will get *her* killed. That's why we've kept it from her for all these years."

"You and I both knew we would eventually have to tell her. Keeping everything a secret is no longer going to keep her safe. If the cops are involved, it's only a matter of time before our demons are discovered. And I'm not just talking about Missi."

She clenched her jaw and shook her head. "The truth will break her. Once she knows, she will never speak to us again, and that's if she doesn't wind up dead first. "

"As if making her feel crazy is going to help?"

She glared at him. "That was for her own good and you know it. Just like it was twenty-six years ago."

"Just listen to me-"

Theresa shoved her finger into his chest. "If you bring this up again, I'll tell *him* about what you've been doing."

Levi tensed. How did she know? He had worked hard to keep his secret. Too much hung in the balance for him to be discovered.

She smirked. "That's what I thought." She turned back to her mixing bowl. "Now be a dear and get me the salt."

Levi clenched his jaw. He hated that she had the upper hand, that she could control him at the snap of a finger. But he did as he was told then walked to the front door. He stopped before turning the knob and said, "She's going to figure it out. And when she does, all hell will break loose for this family."

Theresa ignored him and sang the children's song she had been singing the day Missi had died, sending a shiver down his spine.

Jax blinked quickly to clear his mind. But no matter how hard he tried, he couldn't focus. The Vodka had started as a welcomed burn as it heated his throat, but eventually, he hadn't even noticed the slight pain. By that time, he wasn't sure how many drinks he'd had.

After work, he had needed to turn off his brain. He was tired of feeling so helpless. They weren't any closer to catching SLK, and Jax hated the guilt brought on by that burden. Not to mention the booze was feeding the anger that burned through his veins. Despite Cam doing his job, Jax was still livid with his friend. The man could help them arrest the guy responsible for torturing eleven women, but he was stonewalling their investigation.

No. Cam was right. They didn't have enough for a warrant and that had pissed Jax off even more. So, he'd ordered another drink, brooding and sulking.

Eventually, he'd hit it off with a girl- Becca? Betsy? No, maybe it was Blakely... he couldn't remember now. She hadn't wasted any time taking a seat next to him. Their conversation had started off with general questions, and while she was hot as hell, Jax had slowly lost interest.

And the more he drank, the more his thoughts wandered to the copper-haired, un-nerdy, surprisingly beautiful, bookstore owner. Alabama Knox's face clouded his thoughts with every sip. So, he kept on drinking.

And drinking and drinking and drinking...

Now, he was stumbling around downtown Winter Haven with the rest of the drunken patrons that were falling into Ubers or throwing up in the street. Jax tried to focus again. *Left foot. Right foot. Left foot, right...*

He paused when he saw an empty bench outside another bar. He staggered toward it until it was at arm's length, then he sloppily threw himself onto it, worried it would grow legs and walk away. Jax quickly pulled out his phone and searched for his friend's number.

He let the device ring and chuckled cynically when it went to voicemail. Through slurred words, he said, "Cam! You piece of shit. You're letting SLK get away because you're too much of a coward to call up a judge and tell them we need a warrant. How many more women need to die, huh? Do you want more blood on your hands? Because I have enough on mine."

Jax paused for a moment, his breathing labored as he collected his thoughts. Guilt rippled through his chest. Cam was his friend, and he was working just as hard as Jax and Jules were. Jax wiped at the tears that had sprung in his eyes. "I'm sorry, buddy. I didn't mean it. I just...I hate feeling so hopeless. I want this guy caught. I love ya man. And Jules loves you and she's like my little sister..."

He shook his head, losing his train of thought. He sat up and shoved the phone back into his pocket and made his way down the street. He had no idea where he was going, only that he needed to keep moving.

Once to the four-way stop, he stepped out into traffic. A loud honk vibrated his body and he turned to slap the hood of the car that had nearly hit him, despite it being his own fault. Unable to make his body obey his mind's commands, he simply stood there.

"Sergeant Moretti, are you alright?" a woman said.

Jax's head shot up as he realized the driver had emerged from her vehicle. He would know that copper hair anywhere. He smiled. "Miss Knox, how are you this evening?"

She lifted a brow and mumbled, "Better than you."

"Sorry to keep you waiting. I'm just going... Well, I don't know. I probably need to call Juliette." Jax wanted to smack himself for sounding so stupid. But no matter how hard he tried to focus, he couldn't get his head to stop feeling so fuzzy. He ran a frustrated hand through his hair as he tried to walk away from her.

"Sergeant!" she called out. "Why don't I take you home?"

"No, no. I can't ask you to do that," he slurred.

A car behind her honked wildly and she gracefully ignored the angry resident. She quickly approached him and gently laced her arm through his and led him to the back door of her vehicle.

Without much protest, he slid inside and laid down on the seat, hiking up one knee as he stared at the ceiling. Her door clicked and the buildings began to blur as they picked up speed.

Jax's eyes drifted closed as he heard her ask, "What's your address?"

He rattled it off and let the alcohol lull him to sleep for what felt like a minute before a small hand shook his leg. "Sergeant Moretti, we're here."

Jax's head swam.

Who is that?

Whose car is this?

It wasn't Jules, she wouldn't be so gentle with him. She'd have dragged him out of the car and tossed him into the grass. And it wasn't either of his sisters because they would be doting all over him.

Groggy, he slowly sat up but had to stop for fear he'd vomit all over the car.

Shaking his head, he slowly looked up to see bright brown eyes staring at him. Crimson painted his cheeks. "Oh, it's you."

Ali giggled. "I saved you from getting into trouble. Now let's get you inside."

He climbed out of the car but lost his balance and collided with Ali and they both crashed into the grass. Ali laughed hysterically before Jax could even process what had happened. Then, he too, started laughing.

After a moment, Ali slowly stood and guided him to his front door where he fished out his keys from his pocket. He shoved open the wooden barrier, and she followed him inside, stopping in the doorway.

He placed his arm above her head and put his face close to hers and whispered, "Why don't you stay with me?"

Ali tucked her hair behind her ear and smiled as she shook her head. "I think you've had enough fun for one night, Sergeant."

"I like when you call me that," he said, his eyes moving to her lips. He sounded like a tool, but he was having a hard time controlling anything that was coming out of his mouth.

He also couldn't miss the subtle throbbing at the base of her throat as her pulse quickened. Or the soft shade of pink that rosied her cheeks. Her only response was a sly smile that tugged at her lips ever so slightly.

"A man can try," he said with a shrug. Sighing at his loss, Jax dropped his arm and nearly fell backward.

Ali reached out and grabbed his arm to steady him. "Come on, let's get you to bed."

She guided him to the back of the house where he collapsed onto the heaps of laundry that had been tossed on top of his comforter. As one last ditch effort, he patted the mattress. "You sure you don't want to stay with me? You know, in case I need more help?"

Ali shook her head and laughed. "Goodnight, *Sergeant*."

Quickly drifting asleep, Jax never heard her leave the house. Then, Ali Knox consumed his dreams.

CHAPTER 9

L acey Pits slammed her drink down on the bar top. "Hit me, Reggie."

The bulky bartender lifted a brow but complied.

She couldn't believe her misfortune. Her boss had come into the office today, pissed off because she had misquoted something to a client. He had fired her on the spot. Then, her car had broken down, and her sister had called to complain about Lacey's incessant need to leave her clothes strewn all over the house.

Who cared? Tasha was always with her boyfriend, anyway. And Lacey wondered why she didn't just move in with him. Lord knows Lacey was ready to have her place to herself again.

She wanted to be able to bring home bar flies without getting disapproving looks from her sister. It had been months since she'd been able to let loose in her own house, and she was over it. God, she missed crazy sex with some rando she could shoo out the next morning and not have to commit to. But no. Tasha berated her anytime she brought home a guy, saying it was trashy to give it up on the first night.

Lacey threw her shot of tequila back and cringed as it heated her throat. To hell with Tasha and her judgements. She could move out if she didn't want to hear Lacey's cries of desire and moans of pleasure.

Freaking prude.

Tonight, though, Lacey sat at her favorite bar, the one she frequented weekly. She waved Reggie back over and ordered a margarita. Mixing her drink, he said, "I'm gonna have to cut you off soon, Lace. You've got about three more drinks before I call you an Uber."

She threw her arm up. "I'll be fine! Hopefully you won't have to if I can convince someone else to take me home." She winked at him and he smiled. Reggie knew she loved being the life of the party. Having fun was her M.O. He was no stranger to her mischief. Or her bed. But that wasn't something she wanted to think about.

Lacey checked her watch and saw it was only midnight. Damn, the night was young, and she was getting bored. And even though she was feeling down, she'd be damned if she didn't make a night of it. She didn't have any responsibilities now anyway.

She looked around, trying to find a man who might want some company. It was a Friday night in Lakeland, and the place was full of men huddled together, shouting as they watched the latest hockey game. A chorus of boos and cheers filled the room when a team scored, and Lacey shook her head at how easily men were entertained.

She eyed a man across the bar, sitting alone. He was tall, dark, and handsome with striking features and a perfect smile. Lacey thought he'd fit perfectly with the celebrities that had graced the cover of People Magazine's "Sexiest Men Alive" edition.

He noticed her gaze and looked her up and down. She brought her mouth down to her drink and seductively lapped up the straw. He lifted a brow and smiled but then sheepishly looked away.

Lacey could take a hint. She got up and sauntered over to him, taking a seat next to the gorgeous man.

He yelled over the crowd, "Can I help you?"

"Maybe. Let me buy you a drink first."

He hesitated for a moment, then lifted his hand to show a wedding ring. "I don't think my wife would like that."

Lacey put her mouth close to his ear. "She doesn't have to know."

He chuckled and nodded. Men were predictable. And weak. Their satisfaction level was a measly zero. Most of them couldn't commit to just one woman for life, despite the vows they claimed at the altar.

Which was just as well for Lacey.

She didn't make a habit of sleeping with married men, but she most definitely wasn't opposed. Most of them had spent years having to clamp down on their sex drive and they needed release, which almost always ended in great sex for her.

She held up a finger to Reggie, and he rolled his eyes at her and laughed, knowing he wouldn't need to call her an Uber after all.

Tall, Dark, and Handsome said, "So what's a girl like you doing in a bar like this?"

"That's the best pickup line you've got?" she chuckled.

Smirking, he said, "No, but the other ones are too dirty for a first conversion."

"I like dirty." She brought a finger to the "v" of her top and caressed it.

Lacey glanced at his wedding band again and he followed her gaze.

"That bother you?" he asked.

She bit her straw coyly and tilted her head. "Quite the opposite. It turns me on." She slowly drug her heeled foot up his pant leg and then dropped it. His eyes trailed her and Lacey nearly shivered with anticipation.

Her phone chirped and she saw her sister's text. Tasha was already home, wondering where Lacey had wandered off to. Annoyed, she turned off the device and shoved it into her purse, not wanting any interruptions with the smoking hot man in front of her. Soon to be on top of her if she was lucky. Or maybe she'd be on top of him.

Compliments of the three shots and margarita she'd had, Lacey stood and walked toward the back door, casting a glance back at him. She smiled and gestured for him to follow. Of course, he did as he was told, like all men.

Once outside, she didn't wait before kissing him deeply. His hands rushed to fondle her body and her hair. He walked toward his car, still embracing her as he did. She wouldn't be the one to break their kiss as his tongue collided over hers, heat creeping through her body.

He forcefully pressed her against his vehicle, and she let out a seductive grunt. Lacey quickly undid his belt and unbuttoned his pants as his hands found their way up her dress. Not caring about the stares from other patrons, Tall, Dark, and Handsome claimed her body.

Euphoric from climaxing, Lacey giggled as he whispered in her ear, "My wife is out of town. Wanna go back to my place?" He kissed her neck. "There's a lot more where that came from. And a lot better too."

She licked her lips. "Only if you promise to show me a good time."

"Oh, don't worry. I will."

Lacey lifted a brow and smirked, then climbed into his car.

CHAPTER 10

Ali hadn't been able to sleep much as she replayed her interaction with the sergeant all throughout the night. Initially, she'd been taken aback by his drunkenness, but had quickly revoked her judgments knowing she didn't see such terrible things on a daily basis.

And when she'd almost hit him with her car, she was glad he had agreed to let her take him home. Which, of course, landed her in the middle of his yard laughing hysterically. And she couldn't forget the way her heartbeat had quickened and her breath had caught in her lungs when he'd placed his arm above her head and leaned toward her.

God, she read way too many romance novels.

The Sergeant was in no way interested in a boring bookworm like her.

So, she'd gotten up before the sun had finished rising and headed to work. The drive was relatively short as the morning traffic hadn't quite picked up. Once she parked, she walked to the adjoining coffee shop and placed her usual order. She chatted with the barista for a few minutes before grabbing her coffee and making her way to her shop next door.

After an hour, Ali had finished setting up her store for the day but realized she'd forgotten a stack of books in the trunk of her car. Irritated, she made her way through the large hallway and out the back door toward the parking lot behind the library. She clung to her jacket as the wind whipped her hair around, causing her to shiver and quicken her pace.

Once to her car, she went to unlock the vehicle when she noticed Levi's Mustang parked a few spots over. Normally if he was on this side of town, he'd stop by to see her. But after last night, she didn't think he'd be doing that any time soon.

A pang of hurt splintered her heart as she recalled his refusal to tell her the truth. He clearly knew more than he was saying about Missi, and she was angry at his silence.

Of course, she didn't dare tell him about her plan to start searching for her father. Levi likely would tell her not to bother since he'd left them without so much as a goodbye twenty-six years ago. Though Ali's heart had been ripped from her chest the night her father left, Levi's had been too.

Jared Schultz hadn't been Levi's biological father, but he'd raised Levi as his own. He had loved Levi just as much as he'd loved Ali and had been a prominent role model in Levi's life. But, when Jared left, Levi had been devastated and refused to talk about him.

If she told her brother she was searching for Jared, it would break him.

And what he didn't know, wouldn't hurt him.

Since no one else in her family would tell her the truth, she hoped her father would be willing to level with her. She couldn't imagine he'd want to keep their secrets after staying hidden for the last two and half decades. The man was all but a ghost to the Knox family. And where there's ghosts, there's secrets tucked beneath the floorboards.

She slowly scanned the parking lot. Confident no one was around, she made her way over to his car, cupping her eyes over the glass. Levi kept a spare house key in the middle console, and there was no way he'd give it to her if she asked for it. So, she'd just have to *borrow* it and put it right back.

Since her brother was a realtor, he had access to background search engines that she didn't. But she would need to use his computer...which he kept at home. So, she'd sneak into his house, see what she could find about her father, then leave. And Levi would never have to know.

Steeling herself, she glanced around one more time, then yanked on the handle.

Ali immediately brought her hands over her ears as a deafening shriek reverberated through the air. She began panicking, trying to silence the car alarm. "Shit! Oh gosh. Shhh! Shhh!" She put her hands out in front of her in a panic, hoping the movement would somehow make the ringing subside. "Damn it!" she exclaimed.

"Hey! What are you doing to my car!" a man called out.

Ali quickly spun around, her cheeks bright red and eyes wide. She glanced into the window once more and realized there was no FSU lanyard hanging from the rearview mirror.

This wasn't even Levi's car.

Maneuvering his sports bike into a parking space across from the library, Jax's heart pounded in his chest. He hadn't been able to stop dreaming about Ali all night or thinking about her all morning, despite his best efforts to lead his thoughts elsewhere.

He'd woken up with a nasty hangover and the sting of embarrassment. He couldn't remember everything from the night before, only that Ali had been in the street, he'd fallen over her in the yard, and he had tried to convince her to sleep with him.

He kept trying to forget about last night, but he couldn't get the memories to stop playing like a damn reel in his head. Taking off his helmet and setting it on the seat, he rubbed his face, hoping the gesture would somehow make him feel less mortified.

He had been such a creep and he owed Ali big time for still taking care of him. If there was ever a sign he should leave her alone, last night was it. A man like Jax didn't deserve a woman like Ali. Plus, she was potentially involved in a case, and that was not only messy but against police policy. And more importantly, he wasn't much of a man of commitment. He didn't want to be tied down or have a responsibility to a single person.

Yet, her face seemed to consume his thoughts.

And even though he knew he'd kick himself for it later, he was now walking toward the library building hoping to see her. And as he got closer, a flash of copper caught his eye a few yards ahead. A smile pulled at his lips and his stomach flipped.

God, he was going to lose his man-card if he didn't pull himself together.

Picking up his speed, he watched her peek into a car, pull on the handle, and was met with a blaring wail. She quickly covered her ears and began yelling at the vehicle, her eyes wide, as she attempted to diffuse the situation. He laughed out loud as he heard her try to quiet the alarm, but the laughter was replaced with concern when a large man emerged from the building, demanding to know what Ali was doing.

Shit.

Jax waved a hand at them both and flashed his badge. He said to the man, "Excuse me! Can you turn this off please?"

The man hit a button on his key fob and the alarm quieted. Ali's face darkened three more shades of red when her eyes met Jax's. *Damn, even when she was flustered she was attractive.*

"Officer," the man said, "this woman was trying to break into my car."

Jax raised a brow at Ali who quickly looked to the ground. "Is that so?"

"Yes. I watched her do it."

Ali's head snapped up. "I didn't try to break into your car, sir. I mistook your car for mine, and I'm so sorry."

"Would you like to press charges?" Jax calmly asked the man.

Ali's mouth gaped open and the man eyed her, then sighed. "No, I've done that before myself." He stuck his hand out to Ali. "Sorry for the confusion."

She shook his hand and the man walked off, got into his car, and drove away.

When he did, Ali bent over and let out a breath. Then she stood up and swatted at Jax's arm. "Sergeant, your jokes weren't funny. What if he had wanted to press charges?"

Jax chuckled. "After last night, I think you've earned the right to call me Jax. And I would have handcuffed you myself, but we wouldn't have gone to the police station." He winked at her and she smiled, looking away in an attempt to hide the pink that dusted her cheeks.

So, the bookworm had a fun side to her.

He continued, "So what were you really doing? You drive a Camry. And while I'd love to make a sexist women-being-confused-about-cars joke, I don't think that would be flattering of me."

She shook her head as she crossed her arms. "You're right, it wouldn't be flattering." She paused for a moment, then said, "If I tell you, you can't arrest me."

Jax lifted a brow, then took a step toward her and stared down at her. "Only if you let me take you to dinner."

"What if I'm already seeing someone?"

"I'd say drop that zero and get with a hero." He raised his arm and flexed his muscles. "I *am* a hero, by the way. I've been shot twice while saving damsels in distress."

Ali tossed her head back and laughed. Then, she eyed him for a moment before saying, "Okay, I'll agree to dinner. And I thought it was my brother's car. He keeps a spare house key inside the console."

"Why didn't you just ask him for his key?"

She shifted slightly. "I'm throwing him a surprise party."

This time, Jax laughed. "No, you aren't. Spill it."

Ali played with the bracelet on her wrist. "I asked my family about Jane Doe last night. I found a photo of her in my grandmother's bible."

Jax furrowed his brows. "Do you know who she is?"

"I think her name is Missi. My mother refused to acknowledge her, though. She said she was some random girl I wanted to take a picture with. But my Aunt Dianne sobbed when she saw it and said the girl was 'her' Missi. My brother, Levi, told me to leave it alone. I thought he might have access to records or something at his house since he's a realtor."

Jax was intrigued. Ali's family definitely knew more than they let on. Maybe a visit from him and Jules would get them talking. First, he needed to confirm it was the same girl. "Do you have the photo?"

"I left it at home, but I can bring it in on my lunch break."

"If you're willing to do that, I'd like to take a look," he said.

"I can be there around one, if that's okay."

Jax nodded. "I'll let the receptionist know to expect you." Jax's phone buzzed and he saw he had a text from Jules. "I hate to take off, but Juliette...er Detective Reid is already at the office so I probably need to head to the station."

"Yeah, of course," she said as she turned on her heel to walk inside. Then, she quickly turned back around. "Actually, what were you doing here anyway? Did you have more information on Jane Doe?"

He rubbed the back of his neck. "I came to apologize for last night and see if you'd let me take you on a date. You know, to make up for being an ass. Which you already agreed to."

Ali giggled. "Well, you got what you wanted. And it's not that big of a deal." She shrugged. "I've had my fair share of drunken nights that I'd love to forget."

"So, the bookworm isn't boring at all?" he teased.

"Hey, just because I like to read doesn't mean I don't like to have fun. I just don't have much time for it, is all."

"Then I'll make our date extra fun. And I won't even bring out the hand-cuffs." Jax winked.

Ali swatted at his arm again. "I appreciate that." She chuckled. "Well, let me walk you to your car. It's the least I can do since you didn't arrest me."

"It's across the street and you've been out in the cold long enough. Don't worry about it."

Though her embarrassment had subsided, the winter breeze had continued to make her cheeks and nose bright red.

"Oh, no. I'm walking you to your car, *Jax*," she said, shaking her head.

He smiled and nodded and the two began walking toward the street, weaving in and out of a few cars as they did. Avoiding a fallen tree limb on the sidewalk, Jax sidestepped. "So how long have you owned the bookstore?"

They looked for oncoming traffic before crossing the street. Ali said, "A few years. I spent a lot of time reading as a kid, so this was a dream come true. I worked at the library as a teenager, too. I actually thought about being a teacher, but this is better."

Jax smiled. "You have kind eyes. I bet you would have made a great teacher."

She looked away and grinned. Then, Jax stopped walking, taking her by surprise. She looked at him, then at the motorcycle he was standing next to. She lifted a brow. "A bike? That's brave."

He chuckled as he grabbed the helmet off the seat. "I'm a bit of a daredevil. I like to play it close to the edge."

"I'm not surprised by that, seeing as how you're a hero and all," she mocked.

He nodded. "If you ever feel daring, call me and I'll take you for a ride."

She smirked. "So, where are we going tonight?"

"Why don't we keep it simple and have dinner and go to a movie around six?"

"It's a date," she winked. Ali eyed the bike. "Just don't make me ride that thing. It's too cold."

"We'll save the bike for warmer weather."

She tilted her head. "We'll see how tonight goes first." Then, Ali turned and left, hurrying back across the street.

Jax reluctantly tore his gaze away from the pretty redhead as he watched her walk away, mesmerized by her movements. She casted a glance back at him and smiled, and he nearly melted into a puddle.

What was this? High school?

You'd have thought he'd never met a pretty girl before.

Rubbing his face, he shoved his helmet over his head and took off toward the precinct. Ten minutes later, Jax strolled into the conference room, a huge grin plastered on his face.

Jules lifted a brow. "Cupid in town?"

"What?" he said with a laugh. "Why would you say that?"

"That's the look you have when you meet a pretty girl. Did you meet someone while you were out drinking and leaving mean voicemails for my boyfriend?"

Shit. He forgot about the voicemail.

He immediately picked up on her irritation, and he shook his head. "I'm sorry, Jules. I'll call Cam and apologize. I'll even give him tickets to the FSU game, and I'll have him take you instead of me."

Jules eyed him. "That's a start. So, what has you all giddy this morning?"

Jax settled into his desk chair and put his helmet on the floor next to it. "While I was out in my drunken state, Ali happened to be driving and saw me, so she took me home. I acted like an ass, so I went to apologize to her this morning."

"Ali Knox?" Jules lifted a brow.

"Yes. I wanted to make sure I didn't offend her, nothing more."

Jules rolled her eyes. "Nothing more my ass. You wouldn't be smiling like a schoolgirl if there wasn't more involved."

He put his hands up. "Okay, we have a date."

"Jax!" she chastised. "She's potentially linked to a case. You know that's against policy."

Jax frowned. "You're one to talk. Plus, I figured you'd be happy someone else was taking me off your hands."

Jules clucked her tongue. "Respectfully, she's too nice for you. We both know you're going to break her heart."

It wasn't a secret he'd had his fair share of one-night-stands, which he preferred since he didn't want any type of commitment; something his mother hated. His job was taxing and called for him to give too much of himself, which meant there was nothing left for a relationship.

But that didn't mean he couldn't have a nice dinner with a pretty girl every now and then, though. Jax shook his head. "Oh, come on, Jules. You know I'm not a bad guy."

Jules lifted a shoulder. "You're not exactly Mr. Housewife, either. Your nickname is Hugh Hefner. You think Ali is a one-night-stand kind of girl? No. She's the type to settle down and have a family. Something you're set on *not* doing." She tilted her head. "See? Heart break."

Jax scowled. "Butt-out." He ran a hand through his hair, irritated, even though she was right. Juliette was like a kid sister. He both adored and got annoyed with her. And right now, he was annoyed.

Wanting to change the subject, he glanced at the files laid out on the table. "Do we have any updates on Bianca?"

Jules nodded. "Patrol talked to some of her co-workers. She was well-liked for the most part. She was last seen at a coffee shop on her way to work, but no one saw her talking to anyone. We're running down cameras in the area, but there's a lot of ground to cover."

"Any enemies?"

"Not really. But her friends confirmed she was into married men. That's actually how she met her current husband."

"Classy," Jax said dryly.

Jules shook her head. "She's still a person, Jax. It's not our job to judge her morality. This monster degraded, terrorized, and tortured her. No one deserves that, not even adulterers."

Jax sighed. "You're right. I'm sorry. I just don't get why people cheat, you know?"

"Trust me, I get it." Jules said.

Jax knew that was true. Juliette's last boyfriend, Orette, had cheated on her with her now ex-best friend, Katrina. And despite the fact she was happily with Cam now, Jax wasn't sure she had completely moved past the heartache and betrayal that had been a result of it.

Jules lifted a bag out of the evidence box and set it on the table. A forget me not. These flowers were used to remember those who had died, and the special moments had with them. This monster wanted everyone to know he wouldn't forget his victims. That his face was the last face they saw. It made Jax want to vomit.

He walked over to the board and eyed the large "A" burned into each victim. "I just don't get this guy's logic. He brands them with the "scarlet letter," insinuating they're cheaters, but wants to remember them for eternity? How does that make sense?"

Jules tossed the flower back into the box. "I was talking to Cam about it. I guess he knows a lady who owns a flower shop, and she said they don't just symbolize remembrance."

Jax was intrigued. "What else do they symbolize?"

"There's a myth of a love story about a knight who was walking by the river with his lady, and forget me not flowers had been thrown into the river. She loved the flowers, so the knight jumped in to get them for her but was carried downstream. They say he yelled, 'forget me not' as the current took him away." Juliette shrugged. "She wore those flowers every day until she died."

"Doesn't sound like much of a love story."

Jules sat back in her chair. "Yeah, well, us romantics swoon over stuff like that. It's like Titanic or The Notebook." She began twirling her chair, smiling as she did. "I want a love like that one day. A love where you know that person is your soulmate. And you're so devoted and in love with one another that no one else matters."

Jax lifted a brow. "Sounds like you have someone in mind."

Juliette chuckled and looked at the floor. "Maybe. It's starting to feel that way, at least."

"So what else did your soulmate say about it?"

She laughed and made a face at him. "The flowers symbolize eternal love and devotion beyond the grave. If you give someone a forget me not, it's like saying you won't ever forget them and you have them in your heart forever. 'Til death do us part. Makes sense seeing as how the knight and lady were so devoted to each other. Makes it bizarre that this guy would use them as part of his signature."

Jax sat on the edge of the table, still looking at the board. "He's definitely a creep. He calls them adulterers but is devoting himself to them? Is he promising to love them forever and never forget them?" A chill ran up his spine. "The amount of torture tells me he hates them. But the flower makes me think he also loves them."

Jax stood up and pulled the flower back out of the box, studying it and the photos of the victims. The Scarlet Letter Killer kidnapped, raped, and tortured these women. He branded them, their wounds forever reminding the world of their immorality.

Jax thought over the story of Hester Prynne. She wore the letter "A" as a form of punishment. Despite it being a work of fiction, Jax wondered if the woman had felt shameful, or even degraded by the mark the townspeople had placed on her.

Jax froze. The red "A" in the story was used to degrade and punish Hester. He closed his eyes and tilted his head back. "He's degrading them."

Jules leaned forward, placing her elbows on the table. "Well, yeah. Look at what he does to them."

"No, I mean, that's what he's using the flower for. These women did not respect the loyalty and devotion that comes with wedding vows." He held up the evidence bag. "You said when you give someone this flower, it's like saying 'til death do us part,' right?"

She nodded and scrunched her brows, not following his train of thought.

"He's mocking their memory. What's more degrading than having the man who tortured, raped, and killed you, mark you for all eternity. Then he leaves a flower that symbolizes love and devotion, knowing you did not uphold those virtues?"

This SOB was more deranged than Jax had initially thought.

Jules gestured toward the board. "This guy is sick, Jax. Like, really disturbed, and I hate him for hurting these women."

Jax clutched her hand for a moment. "I know. Me too."

This case was weighing heavily on him. How could they not have any solid evidence after a decade of this guy's reign of terror? How many women would have to die before they figured out who this prick was?

He thought about Philip Murray. He definitely fit their profile. But again, there was a lack of evidence. And while Jax thought Murray was the Scarlet Letter Killer, the man would keep slaughtering women until Jax could prove it in the court of law.

"Maybe we need to ask friends and family if there was anyone in their lives that overreacted to these women cheating?" Jules suggested. "A lot of the men these women cheated *on* had alibis, but it could have been a friend or relative that wanted revenge."

Jax nodded. "If that's the case, we need to look over Hannah Seymour's file since she was the first victim." In cases involving a serial killer, there was typically a strong connection between the killer and their first victim. If they looked at Hannah's case through a magnifying glass, they may have a chance to catch this guy. "And let's see if any of the friends and families had ever seen Murray around."

Juliette rubbed her face and stood. "I'm gonna grab a hot chocolate first. Do you want something?"

Shaking his head, he said, "No. I'll be fine."

Jules nodded and walked out of the room.

He grabbed Hannah's file and sat silently for a minute before opening the file. Part of him wanted to quit on the spot, hand this case over to some other poor unfortunate soul. But he wouldn't be able to live with himself if he did that. These women deserved justice, and he would try like hell to bring it to them.

Still, he was getting burnt out and needed a damn vacation. He thought of white, sandy beaches and the warm sun on his face, a Corona in his hand...Ali in a bikini. Jax let his mind wander for a moment, wondering what it would be like to kiss her, to feel her body against his.

Closing his eyes, he shook the thoughts from his mind. There might be time for that tonight if he was lucky.

Focus, Jax.

He opened the file and began reading but quickly stopped when he realized the file wasn't Hannah Seymour's. It was the file for Jane Doe. One of the officers must have absentmindedly put it in the pile of SLK files.

He moved to place the folder on the far side of the table but stopped himself. It wouldn't hurt to take a glance at the file while he waited for Juliette to come back.

Sitting back down, he began reading over the case.

The girl had been found in a dense part of the woods somewhere in Mulberry, Florida. Two teenagers had gone to have some alone time when they had stumbled upon her. She had been naked, aside from a bracelet she wore on her tiny wrist.

Local police didn't think she had been out there all that long, maybe two or three days. Surprisingly, her body had been in decent condition considering she had been found in the woods. Photos had been placed in the local newspaper in an attempt to locate her family, which had yielded no results. The detectives combed through numerous reports of missing girls and runaways but never found any matching Jane Doe's description. The case went cold pretty quickly when they couldn't identify her.

No one had ever claimed this little girl.

Jax's heart broke for her. She was a child. She must have been terrified in her last moments.

He then looked over the list of suspects. Two lonely names. One was a known pedophile in the area, but there was no evidence he had any contact with the girl. The other was the boy who had found her. The police had claimed he seemed jumpy, but that was all they could come up with to support their suspicions.

Jax moved to the ME's report, something he was dreading. It was bad enough seeing what could happen to adults, let alone to innocent children. He held his breath as he looked over the sexual assault exam and sighed heavily when he saw the results were negative.

Then, his heartbeat quickened as he scanned the evidence report. A wave of nausea hit him.

No, that couldn't be right.

Jax stood and quickly walked to his desk, opening Jane Doe's small evidence box that sat on top. He frantically sifted through the items. He found what he was looking for and held it up, clenching his jaw.

A single forget me not flower had dwindled away in the evidence bag.

CHAPTER 11

A li bobbed her head to the Christmas music that played over a speaker into the street as she walked toward the front of the police station. The festive music, twinkling lights, decorated shops, and ribbon-wrapped lampposts brought the Christmas spirit to life, despite the lack of snow on the ground.

She pulled on the glass door and walked into the waiting area of the precinct just as she'd done the day before. She let the receptionist know she was back to see Jax and Detective Reid.

As she waited, Ali studied the framed photos that decorated the lobby walls. To Ali, all the photos told stories of the men and women who protected and served. Some photos revealed generous hearts as officers brought Christmas presents to families in need. Some were snapshots of an intense game of basketball with neighborhood kids. Others celebrated graduation and award ceremonies.

Ali grinned when she spied a younger Jax playing football in the rain with some teenagers, all covered in mud.

Finally, she took a seat to wait. Twirling her hair, she thought of the photo hidden inside her purse and the conversation she'd had with her family, especially with her brother. He'd all but threatened her life, and that was a side of Levi she'd never seen before. Though he'd been known for his bouts of anger when he was a teenager, he'd never aimed it at Ali.

"Hi, Ali," Detective Reid said, pulling Ali from her thoughts.

Ali smiled and stood from the chair. "Hi, Detective. Sorry to be coming in at lunchtime. I'm sure y'all are hungry."

"It's no worry at all, we have snacks," she chuckled. The Detective held open the door. "Jax said you had something to show us?"

"I found a photo in my grandmother's bible, and it looks like Jane Doe."

Detective Reid led her back through the hallway and the two stepped onto the elevator. There were two other officers who followed them inside, and Ali briefly smiled at them while Detective Reid greeted them.

After a moment, the elevator doors slid open, and Ali followed the cop back to her desk. Jax was already there, talking on the phone. He noticed her from across the room and grinned.

Ali's stomach did a flip, and she wanted to scream at herself for being so childish.

He hurried off the phone, and Ali took a seat across from him, Detective Reid sitting on the edge of Jax's desk.

"Long time no see," he said with a wink.

"I just wish this wasn't the reason for it." Ali reached into her purse and pulled out the photo, handing it to Jax. He laid the photo on his desk and retrieved the folder reserved for Jane Doe. He carefully took out the snapshot of the little girl and laid the two next to each other.

Both he and Detective Reid studied the girls.

The Detective pointed to the girl's chin in both photos. "Look, those are identical scars. I really think that's her."

Jax nodded. "I agree. We need a positive identification, though." He flipped the photo over. "Missi." He looked back up at Ali. "Is that name familiar to you?"

She shook her head. "No. I'd never heard of her before last night."

"Would anyone in your family be willing to come look at the photo and give a positive ID?"

Ali sighed and shrugged. "Cam might. But I don't know if anyone else will. They don't really like the police. And from my mother's reaction, I don't think the rest of my family will be forthcoming. They acted as if this girl wasn't real. That I saw her in a park and had some type of unhealthy attachment to her, I guess... I don't know what to believe."

She anxiously played with the bracelet on her wrist. She was still upset about her family's reaction the night before. Her mother hadn't called her and seemed to have no desire to make amends. And she wasn't even sure she wanted to see Levi. Of course, Ali's cheek still slightly stung from Dianne's outburst.

Jax stilled. "Can I see the bracelet you're wearing?"

Curious, Ali extended her arm. "My mother gave it to me when I was a kid."

Jax studied it and then stood, leaving them for a moment. Ali looked at Jules who simply shrugged. He came back carrying an evidence bag then carefully put on gloves and retrieved the item. He said, "This was the only thing left on Jane Doe when she was found."

Ali's breath caught in her lungs, and she let out a soft cry. She didn't look at him. She only looked at the jewelry in front of her as she raised her own arm, showing an identical gold bracelet with a butterfly charm, a sapphire stone set in the middle of the creature.

It was then that memories came flooding back to her. She and Missi exploring the woods together, playing hide and seek, laughing and running through their grandparents' house. She remembered picnics and playing dress up and card games. She remembered harassing her brother and Cam, games of chase and tag.

She even remembered the day Missi got the scar the detectives had pointed out in the photos. She had climbed onto the kitchen counter to get a cup and slipped and fell, splitting her chin in the process. Surprisingly, there had been a lot of blood, and the two had screamed in terror until Gin had run in and taken care of Missi.

And Ali remembered sitting next to her under the twinkling lights of the Christmas tree, where they both had quickly opened their gifts. Inside a tiny black box were best friend bracelets, because they swore to be inseparable. No matter what.

She slowly took the photo of the girl, her voice just above a whisper. "That's Missi." She reached up to wipe the tears that were streaming down her face. Ali brought the photo to her chest and put her head down. She said through sobs, "I'm sorry, Missi. I'm so sorry I forgot about you."

How was this possible? How could Missi be dead? How had so much time passed, and Ali hadn't even realized she was missing? Why had her family kept this from her?

Why hadn't she remembered?

Suddenly, Ali's lungs constricted as she desperately tried to suck in air. She clawed at her throat as her head spun and she swayed, gripping the arm of the chair to steady herself.

Detective Jules said to Jax, "She's having a panic attack." She walked around to Ali and took her hand. "Put your head between your knees and breathe with me."

Ali focused on the detective's breathing rhythms, mirroring the woman. After a few moments, Ali calmly wiped at her tears as the panic slowly left her body.

Detective Jules softly said, "You remembered her, didn't you?"

Ali closed her eyes and gave a sad smile. "Mississippi Elenore Knox, born September 14th, 1992. We're one day apart. Our mothers named us Alabama and Mississippi because the two states touch. They said it was a tribute to the closeness of their friendship." She opened her eyes and looked at the photo. "Her favorite color was purple, and she wanted to be a doctor. We used to play hide and seek on our grandparents' farm. We tried to play with Levi and Cam, but they didn't want anything to do with us. It was us against the world."

Jax reached out and held her hand. His touch made her jump, but she didn't pull away. She held tightly to him, desperately needing the comfort. She clutched his hand as tears welled in her eyes. "This isn't real. Please say it isn't real. She was my best friend. She was-" Ali froze as her eyes darted from Jax to Juliette.

Jax furrowed his brow. "What's wrong?"

Feeling as if her heart would beat out of her chest, Ali quickly stood and turned to leave. She couldn't sit in this chair anymore. She couldn't look at Missi's photo. She couldn't think about what had happened to her best friend. "I'm sorry, I need to go."

Jax stood. "Ali, wait."

But Ali couldn't stay. She needed to find out what her family was hiding. And she knew the black sheep of the family would have the answers.

CHAPTER 12

A li waited in Cam's office, looking at the photos and accolades that lined the walls. She hadn't realized how prominent and well-respected he was. He had made a name for himself in the law enforcement and political community, and pride swelled in her chest.

She was also hurt he hadn't shared this part of his life with her, that he had chosen to shut her out. Growing up, she'd been close to him. Maybe not as close to him as she had been to Levi, but Cam had still been an influential figure in her life.

After he had left, she had tried to ask why he had cut off the family, but he had refused to return her phone calls or see her. She was actually surprised he had agreed to meet with her today.

A sharp click met her ears, and Ali turned to see his rugged face emerge from the waiting area as he opened the door. A big smile was plastered on his face as he gathered her in his arms in a bear hug. "Ali! It's so good to see you!"

She held him tightly, savoring the only affection she'd had from him in over a decade. They both released each other as she said, "You know, you could see me more often if you'd return my calls or let me come see you."

He ran a hand through his dark hair. "I know, I'm sorry. I just... Well, there's no excuse. I needed to separate myself from the family, and you were collateral damage."

Ali furrowed her brows. "I wish you would have said something. What happened that was so bad for you to cut us all off? Especially Gin and Gramps." She looked at the floor. "Especially me."

She recalled the bursts of anger and shouting between Cam and Gramps the day he had left the compound. She'd been thirteen at the time and had come home, drenched in sweat after having walked nearly a mile home from the bus stop.

She'd set her bag down near the front door of the farmhouse, beelining for the kitchen in search of a snack. She could have gone home, but she enjoyed telling her grandparents about her day, so she always made it a point to see them first.

Ali had heard faint shouts upstairs, followed by Cam nearly running down the stairs, fuming. Gramps had followed behind him, his footsteps echoing through the home. *"And you better not step foot on this property until you can control yourself!"*

Cam had slammed the door, and she hadn't seen or heard from him until Gramps passed away two years ago. Well, that wasn't entirely true. When she went off to college, she'd waited outside his work to see him and he'd humored her. But after that, he refused to see her.

Until now.

He crossed his arms. "I really am sorry. Don't take it personally. Just know I love you."

She gave him a soft smile, nodded, and made her way to the leather seat that was placed in front of his desk. He followed her lead and got comfortable in his own chair behind the wooden block as he rolled up his sleeves.

He said, "So what's up? You seemed a little frantic when I heard your message."

Ali quietly said, "The police found Missi."

Cam stilled. "What?" he choked out.

Tears sprang in the corners of her eyes. "The police matched my DNA to a Jane Doe case. They came to my shop yesterday, but I didn't have any information for them." She nearly panicked again as she forced out, "I didn't even remember her until an hour ago."

Ali let her tears flow, and Cam didn't offer any encouragement. Instead, he buried his face in his hands and sat silently. After a moment, he lifted his head and wiped at his face.

"I'm sorry, I just never thought we'd find her." He sighed. "Gosh, I haven't talked about her since the day she disappeared, but I've never stopped thinking about her. Which officers are overseeing her case?"

Ali took in a breath, "Sergeant Moretti and Detective Reid. She said you two are dating?"

Cam smiled. "Yeah, we've been seeing each other for about six months now. And they're both some of the best cops, so they will be thorough and they'll do everything in their power to find out what happened."

Ali nodded. "Detective Reid is really nice. And Jax, er, Sergeant Moretti seems like he won't stop until he finds answers."

Cam lifted a brow and tilted his head. "*Jax*? Interesting you're on a first-name basis with him. Have you met him before?"

Pink crept over her cheeks, mortified her face was giving her away. Growing up, Cam had teased her mercilessly about the boys she liked. He always knew when she had a crush and it never took him long to figure out the boys' names, constantly singing the *K-I-S-S-I-N-G* song. Levi would join in, harmonizing terribly as she would clench her fists and her face would turn bright red.

She looked to the ground and smiled. "We kind of hit it off, and we're going on a date tonight." Ali lifted her head. "Please don't say anything to his boss. I know it's probably against policy."

"Relax, I'm not going to rat you out, Ali." Cam chuckled. Then, turning the conversation back to Missi, his face became somber. "What happened to her?"

Ali twirled her hair, not wanting to say the words out loud. Somehow, admitting the truth made it far more real, and she wasn't sure she was ready for that. But Cam deserved the truth. "Missi was murdered. That's all I know."

He sucked in a breath. "Okay, I'll talk to Juliette later today and see what I can find out."

Ali opened her mouth to say something, then closed it quickly, not sure she wanted to press for answers.

Cam eyed her. "What is it?"

She bit the inside of her cheek, contemplating if she wanted to know the truth about her family. She knew secrets could tear a family apart, but she feared the truth could be just as damaging.

But Missi deserved the truth.

"Why did everyone lie about her? Why did they make me feel like I was crazy and had only imagined her?" Her heartbeat quickened and she raised her voice slightly. "They went so far as to take down all of her pictures. They wiped her from my memory. For the last twenty-six years, I had forgotten about my best friend. And from what Jax has said, they never reported her missing."

Cam reached across his desk, holding out his hand. She placed her hand in his and he gently squeezed. "They were trying to do what was best the only way they knew how. It doesn't make it right, but they were trying to protect you. And I think they secretly hoped if they pretended she never existed, then they wouldn't have to admit she was gone. People do crazy things when they're grieving." He pulled his hand away and ran it through his brown hair. "And they never reported her missing because they don't like cops and were worried Levi and I would get blamed."

Ali furrowed her brows. "Why would they blame you two?"

"What do you remember from the day she disappeared?"

She shrugged. "Not much. Just that we were at the park playing on the swings. Then everyone at home was screaming at each other. I remember being scared and confused. But that's it."

Memories of that day filtered through her mind, but they were muddled and vague. She tried her hardest to grasp anything more, but nothing came to her. As a six-year-old, she didn't quite understand what was happening. And when the adults wouldn't stop screaming, she ran upstairs and hid under her grandparents' quilt on their bed, tightly closing her eyes until she drifted off into a deep sleep.

Cam sighed. "Levi and I had taken you and Missi to the park, and instead of watching you, we were smoking pot behind the building. Next thing we know, Missi is gone, and then all hell breaks loose. Our parents were worried we'd get blamed."

Before she could respond, the phone on his desk rang. "D.A.'s office. Cameron Knox speaking."

A pause.

"Yes, sir. I can be there in ten minutes," Cam responded.

He hung up the phone and looked back at Ali, his eyes sympathetic. "I'm sorry, I need to go meet with another lawyer to discuss trial strategy. But I'll talk to Juliette today and see what I can find out."

He stood up and she did the same. He walked back around his desk and wrapped her in another hug. "I won't wait so long to see you again, okay? I didn't know it upset you this much."

Ali nodded into his chest. "You're like a brother to me, of course it upsets me." She pulled away from him and said, "But if you promise to keep in touch, I won't tell Juliette about all the ways you used to bully and mock me growing up. Or any other embarrassing stories I might have."

He chuckled. "You're a brat, you know that?"

She smiled brightly. "Only to you and Levi."

She gave him one last hug and walked out the door, hoping he didn't just lie to her face like the rest of her family had.

CHAPTER 13

J ules glanced up from her desk and smiled wildly. "What are you doing here?"

Cam walked toward her holding a bouquet of roses, his brown hair styled in a neat comb over. He leaned in and gave her a soft kiss. He said, "I wanted to see you. I saw these at a little flower cart when I stopped for coffee this morning and thought they'd brighten your day."

Jules took the vase from him and set the flowers on her desk. She would no doubt get mocked by some of the other officers, but they could kiss her ass. She was a romantic, and she loved that Cam happily obliged her expectations.

She stood and wrapped her arms around his neck and kissed him again. "I'm sorry my work schedule has been crazy. Now that we have another SLK victim, I don't think I'm going to get much free time." She sighed. "Thanks for sticking with me."

He traced her jaw with his thumb. "Well, you're worth it."

She smiled again, and he sat in the chair across from her desk, hanging his coat on the back of the chair. He looked around the room. "Where's Jax?"

Juliette sat back down at her desk. "He went to grab us lunch. Did he apologize for the voicemail yet?"

"You're only concerned because you want to go to the game," Cam teased.

Jules dramatically placed the back of her hand on her forehead. "How could you think such a thing?"

Cam let out a laugh. "Yes, he apologized. And yes, you and I are going to the game in a few weeks." He paused for a moment, his face becoming sullen.

She tilted her head. "What's wrong?"

"Ali came to see me." He shook his head. "Surely you connected the dots that I'm related to your Jane Doe."

Jules looked away from him. "You don't like to talk about your family, so I didn't want to bring it up until I had something concrete. And initially, Ali didn't remember her. Plus, the DNA didn't show whether their connection was maternal or paternal. I found out Missi was your sister a few hours ago, when Ali remembered." She paused for a moment. "Why didn't *you* tell me about her?"

She was hurt Cam hadn't confided in her. But she understood people grieve in their own way and it wasn't her place to tell him her opinion. She had no idea the amount of anguish he was in, and she had wondered if talking about the girl was simply too painful for Cam.

"There's a lot to explain," he sighed. "But can I see a photo of her first? Of Missi? I just need to see it for myself...that she's really gone." His voice cracked. "I've spent the last twenty-six years wondering if she'd ever come home. I need this closure."

Jules was surprised by the request but quickly stood. "Yes, of course."

She hurried to the conference room and brought back the photo and the bracelet, still encased in the evidence bag. She held them both to her chest. "Are you sure you want to see this?"

"I appreciate the concern, but I need to know it's her." He looked to the floor, then back at Jules. "Please?"

Juliette held her breath to keep from crying. She'd never seen Cam so vulnerable. She couldn't imagine how he felt, finding out his sister was dead after being missing for over two decades. She hated how much it was clearly hurting him.

She nodded her head and laid the photo on her desk in front of him.

Taking the image, he blinked rapidly and cleared his throat, trying to hide his tears. "That's her. That's Missi." He put the photo back down and looked at the bracelet through the plastic. He smiled sadly as he glanced back at Jules. "Ali has the other one." He paused for a moment. "That's been the hardest part, you know. Watching Ali grow up, not knowing if Missi ever got the chance."

Jules' heart broke for him. She'd never seen him cry, despite knowing he was a soft-hearted man. She appreciated the strength it took for him to be vulnerable with her, something she greatly admired.

Jules looked down at the photo. "What happened, Cam?"

He closed his eyes for a moment, then let out a breath. "She was kidnapped. Theresa was supposed to be watching Ali and Missi, but she got into a fight with Ali's dad, Jared, so she sent me and Levi to the park with the girls. We were smoking pot behind the bathrooms." He rubbed his face. "We saw a man dragging her into a grey truck. We tried to run after him, but we weren't fast enough. We were only fourteen and fifteen at the time. Ali was inconsolable."

Juliette's heartbeat quickened as the scene played through her mind. They were all children at the time; they must have been terrified.

When she didn't continue with her questions, Cam pushed her. "It's okay, Juliette. I know you have to ask me some hard questions."

Jules sighed and tilted her head, feeling guilty. She hated that it would seem as if she was pointing fingers, but they needed the facts in order to figure out who killed Missi. "Why didn't your mother call the police?" she asked.

Cam shrugged. "She didn't want us to get in trouble. My family doesn't trust the police, and they were afraid we would get blamed or even get jammed up for the pot. We figured there would be a ransom call, but we never got one. And by then, it was too late to involve the police. If we did, there would have been a lot of questions and maybe even jail time. They had lost one child and didn't want to lose another, I think."

Jules recalled her own fair share of bad choices as a teenager. They had both grown up when it was much easier to sneak off and get into trouble without getting caught. Back then, there weren't cameras posted at every corner or home.

And she couldn't pretend to understand why the family initially hesitated to call the police. Since she didn't have kids of her own, she had no business judging his parents' actions. Nothing makes sense when your kid goes missing. She'd seen that almost daily when she delivered death notices to families.

"And what about Ali?" Jules said. "She claims everyone manipulated her into believing Missi wasn't real. She said there were never any photos of her, and if she tried to talk about her, your family would deny it. You all convinced her she was crazy."

Cam rolled his eyes and shook his head. "I hated that everyone wanted Missi to be a ghost. But Ali was absolutely hysterical. She wouldn't eat or sleep.

She was catatonic by the end of the week. We all made a decision to act like Missi never existed so she could move on. She was six at the time and couldn't understand what had happened. And then, on top of that, her father took off, so the whole family was in shambles."

"That seems like a pretty extreme response."

Cam nodded. "Even at fourteen I thought as much. But we were kids, so we did what we were told." He shrugged. "I think we hoped if we just listened to the adults, it would somehow get better, like she would randomly appear." He looked down at his hands and softly said, "So much time has passed. It's strange talking about her."

Jules sighed. "I can't imagine how hard this is."

He searched her eyes and reached out for her. She took his hand across the desk, and he simply said, "Thank you." Then, he furrowed his brows. "How did you even find her? How did you figure out she's related to Ali?"

"Ali submitted her DNA, and we got a hit." She paused for a moment. "Cam, there's something you need to know."

"Okay..." he said, holding his breath.

"According to the DNA results, Missi is *Ali's* half-sister."

Juliette wasn't expecting his deep chuckle, and she nervously smiled in response.

He said, "I knew she was my half sister long before the rest of the family found out about it. My mother and Ali's father, Jared, had an affair, and Missi was the result of that affair."

Jules couldn't mistake the anger that flashed in his eyes. He continued, "It all came out when Missi was kidnapped. Nearly broke up my parents' marriage, ruined my mother's and Theresa's friendship. My grandparents had enough to worry about with Missi gone and then had to deal with that whole debacle."

Jules' mouth turned down. "You're still angry about it..."

Cam shook his head. "It sounds so childish. I'm forty years old and still get angry thinking about it. Don't get me wrong, I'm glad Missi came out of the affair, but Jared put our family through hell. Especially when he left. It wasn't right. Theresa and the kids deserved better."

Jules nodded. "What about Levi? How did he feel about his father leaving?"

"Jared isn't Levi's father. I mean not biologically, anyway."

Jules tilted her head. "He and Ali are half-siblings?"

"Yeah. Theresa had Levi when she was seventeen."

Her eyebrows shot up in surprise. "That's young. Were they high school sweethearts?"

"No. It was my grandfather's brother. I guess he had been abusing her since she was a little girl, but once she had Levi, he was long gone. He had lived on the compound, but once my grandfather found out, the man all but vanished. At least that's what my father says."

"And your father is..."

Cam laughed. "I know, my family tree is confusing. My father, Rick, is Theresa's older brother. He met my mother, Dianne, and they had me. Theresa had Levi, then met Jared and had Ali. At some point, my mother and Jared had an affair and had Missi, but no one knew the truth about her paternity until she went missing. We all assumed Missi was also my father's."

Jules was speechless. The Knoxes seemed to harbor one too many secrets. And that was a little unnerving. She was curious about the man who seemingly disappeared when turmoil seeped into the family.

"Have you heard from Jared since he left?"

"Not since he took off, and not that I care."

Juliette nodded slowly and leaned back in her chair. "Does Levi know Jared isn't his father? What was his reaction to the affair and to Jared leaving?"

Cam leaned his elbows against his knees and looked at the ground for a moment. Then he looked back at her. "He knew who his real father was at an early age, but I don't know how he dealt with that truth. We didn't talk about it. Although, he was pretty distraught when Jared left. Jared was his hero." He sighed and shook his head. "Levi was angry at my mother when we found out about the affair, and I was angry at Jared. There was a lot of animosity, and we fought for months afterward. But we were grieving and didn't know how to deal with it. Neither did the rest of the family. We were looking for someone to blame, and we got into a lot of trouble."

Juliette had a hard time picturing Cam getting into trouble. He was strait-laced and thrived on law and order. She had never been shocked by his career choice as a prosecutor, except to say he may have made a great cop.

"Does your family have any idea who might have taken Missi? I'm sure they've had theories over the years."

"I truly don't think they've ever spoken about her again. My parents were completely traumatized. Theresa was, too, I think. And of course, Levi and I have always felt guilty as sin, but we were kids, so we couldn't have done anything anyway."

A frown tugged at his lips as he fought back tears. Twenty-six years later and he was still clearly haunted by his sister's disappearance. The weight of the guilt he's carried for the last two decades was undoubtedly soul-crushing.

She pushed him a little more, though she hated to do it. She felt as if she was invading his privacy. "Is that why you don't talk to them anymore?"

He shrugged. "Essentially. I know Ali didn't deserve any animosity, but it was hard seeing her grow up while Missi faded from our memories. Plus, my family became very unhealthy after that."

Juliette got up and sat next to him, gently cupping his face and making him look at her. "I'm sorry about Missi."

He kissed her forehead and smiled sadly. "Me too. She was a good kid. Spoiled, but good."

"I'm going to find out what happened to her, I promise."

He caressed her cheek. "I know you will." Then, he kissed her gently on the lips. "I'll see you later. I've got another meeting to get to."

Nodding, Juliette watched him leave and then went back to her desk, where she began working to find Missi's killer.

CHAPTER 14

J ax walked over to his desk carrying two Publix subs. The grocery store had been a madhouse and his lunch run had taken twice as long as he'd anticipated. He eyed the flowers on Jules' desk. "I see your knight in shining armor stopped by."

Jules giggled. "You're just jealous." She paused and then said, "He actually came by to tell me about Missi."

Jax raised his brow. "What did he say?" He handed Juliette her buffalo chicken wrap and sat down, opening his own ultimate sub.

Then, Juliette reiterated everything Cam had told her. When she finished, Jax whistled. "Sounds like there's potentially a lot of family secrets. I think it's time we talk to them."

Nodding her head, she said, "Let's do it after we eat. I'm starving."

Jax agreed, and they scarfed down their food. Then, they grabbed their coats and headed to the patrol car. The drive to the Knox home was only twenty minutes, and the two obnoxiously sang along to the Christmas tunes that blared from the speakers.

Finally, they drove up a dirt path and parked in front of the main house on the property. Climbing out of the car, they looked around and saw what looked to be two empty houses in the distance. Walking up to the farmhouse, Jax rang the doorbell.

After a moment, a burly man opened the door. He was tall and stocky with dark features that had a subtle softness to them. His button-down was crisp, though unbuttoned at the collar, and Jax wondered if he'd just gotten home and removed his tie.

"Can I help you?" he asked politely.

Jax flashed his badge. "I'm sorry, sir, we don't mean to intrude. I'm Sergeant Moretti, and this is my partner, Detective Reid. Are you Richard Knox?"

The man shifted slightly. "Yes."

"Who is that, Rick?" A woman appeared in the doorway behind him. Had it not been for the bright copper hair, Jax might have assumed her to be Dianne. But there was no doubt the woman was Theresa Knox, Ali's mother.

"It's the police, Theresa." Rick didn't look at the woman. Instead, he kept his eyes focused on Jax and Jules. She tried to shove past him, but he didn't let her, asserting his dominance.

"What do you want?" she demanded.

Jules looked at Theresa and gave a gentle smile, then looked back at Rick. "I think the conversation would be best to have inside. May we come in?"

The man didn't respond immediately, but Jax couldn't miss the subtle intake of Theresa's breath as the woman waited for her brother's response. Finally, he simply gave a nod and stood to the side, all but pushing his sister out of the way.

Jax and Jules followed Rick into the living room, where a dark-haired woman was sitting on the sofa. Jax recognized the popular print instantly: brown and burnt orange florals. It was identical to the couch his grandmother had kept since the seventies. The memory pulled a quiet smile from him.

Theresa made herself comfortable on a loveseat to the right while Juliette took a seat on the opposite couch, Jax following her lead. Rick sat next to the mousy woman who slightly shifted away from him. He gestured toward her. "This is my wife, Dianne."

They waited for Dianne to acknowledge them, but she sat motionless, staring at the floor. Her quietness made Jax feel uneasy. She reminded him of a psych patient, catatonic and unresponsive.

After a moment, Jax cleared his throat and said, "We're sorry to inform you, your daughter's remains have been found. Your son made a positive ID earlier today."

Dianne's head snapped up, and she quickly stood, pointing her finger at the two officers. "No! That's not true!"

Startled by his wife's outburst, Rick gently took her by the arm and guided her back to her seat. Then, his eyes seared into Jax, his jaw set. "I want proof. Don't bring your lies here."

Jax nodded and took out the photo of Missi. Rick studied it, then closed his eyes. After a moment, he took Dianne's hand, then gave a curt nod.

Dianne's wails of grief tore through the air as she dropped to her knees.

Theresa quickly went to her sister-in-law and wrapped her in a hug, but the woman shoved Theresa to the ground. "This is your fault, Theresa! I hate you!"

Jax was taken aback by Dianne's response to Theresa. Though he initially found her to be a meek and mousy woman, her outburst proved otherwise. There was a fire burning, hidden under the surface.

Rick glared at his sister. "Go away, Theresa."

She furrowed her brows. "Rick, she-"

"Leave!" he commanded.

Irritated, she huffed away, and a loud thud echoed from the front of the house as Theresa slammed the door behind her.

Rick knelt beside his wife and held her close as her body shook and her screams eventually turned into quiet sobs.

Jax moved to stand, but Rick stopped him. "Please, just get this over with so we can move on. I know you have questions, and I'd rather you didn't ever come back here again."

Jax turned to Juliette. They both knew she was typically better at talking with family members. She was sympathetic, kind, and patient. Grieving families seemed to gravitate toward her, and she offered comfort just by the way she carried herself.

She nodded and joined the couple on the floor, wanting to meet their grief where it was. "Answering these questions may be difficult, and we can stop at any time if it's too much for you. We just need you to be honest." Jules looked from Rick to Dianne. "Can you tell me what happened the day she disappeared? We searched the databases and didn't find any missing person's report filed for her."

Rick said, "Theresa was watching the girls, but at some point, she and Jared got into an argument. She sent all the kids to the park so they could have some privacy. Back then, you could let your kid walk around town unsupervised and nothing would happen. Until it *did* happen."

Guilt flashed behind the man's eyes. It was an unbearable weight that plagued many parents who blamed themselves for the disappearance or kidnapping of their children. Rick Knox blamed himself for letting his daughter go to the park, for allowing her to simply be a child.

"I got home right in the middle of the argument, and it was heated. My mother and father had gotten involved, and Dianne was crying. Maybe thirty minutes later Jared takes off. Then the boys and Ali come running back home hysterical. They said Missi was kidnapped by a man in a grey pickup truck. We all went out looking for the truck but couldn't find it." Rick rubbed his face. "We never saw her again."

Dianne's shoulders sagged, and Jax couldn't imagine the hell this woman had been through.

Jules said, "I'm sure that was hard on you all. I'm so sorry this has happened to you." She reached out to gently touch Dianne's hand and the woman visibly jumped so Jules quickly put her hand back down. Moving on, she asked, "Did Jared ever come back?"

Dianne shook her head as her eyes met Rick's. "We never saw him again." Then, she looked away from her husband. Jax knew a brokenhearted woman when he saw one, and it was clear Dianne was still in love with Jared, though Jax couldn't tell if Rick knew that or not.

Jax asked Rick, "Why did he leave so abruptly?"

"He was a shitty father and husband, though Theresa would have sworn he hung the damn moon."

"You didn't like him?" Jules asked.

Rick shook his head. "No. Everyone else thought he was charming, but I saw through that facade the day Theresa brought him home."

Jax was curious to know what Rick might have seen that the rest of the Knox family hadn't. Was it merely a sixth sense, or had he seen a darker side to the man who was now a ghost?

Jax pressed them. "Is there any reason to believe he took Missi? Maybe paid a friend to do it?"

Dianne's head shot up, and she vehemently shook her head. "He would never do that. He wouldn't have taken Missi from me."

Jax simply nodded. He didn't know if that was true, but Dianne definitely believed it to be.

"What makes you think he would have taken her?" Rick asked.

Jax said, "We know Missi was Jared's daughter, Mr. Knox."

Jules looked at Dianne, who wouldn't meet her eyes. "That's what the fight was about, wasn't it? Somehow Theresa found out and confronted Jared...maybe even you?"

Rick stood quickly, startling Juliette. Jax's reflexes were quick, and he stood, placing a hand on his taser.

Rick said, "This conversation is over."

Juliette climbed to her feet and looked at Rick. "I know this is very difficult to talk about, but we need to know what happened in order to help bring Missi justice."

Rick crossed his arms. "She's dead, Detective. Justice doesn't matter. Now, leave."

Jules sighed and looked at Jax, who nodded. Jax said, "I'm sorry for your loss."

As they walked toward the front door, Jax stole a glance back at Dianne, who was staring right at him, her eyes a dark void. An eerie feeling swept over him as he realized Missi was the spitting image of her mother, and Jax felt as if he was looking into the eyes of the dead girl.

Chills raced down his spine as he followed Jules outside, where they spotted Theresa walking back up the long dirt drive.

"Think she'll talk to us?" Jules asked as she shoved her hands in her coat pocket.

Jax shrugged, doing the same as the winter breeze whipped at his face. "Who knows? She was clearly trying to hide something."

Theresa continued to walk toward them, unaware of their presence until she was nearly inches from them. When she looked up, she froze. Then, she squared her shoulders and gave them a dirty look, pulling her scarf tighter. "Can I help you?"

Jules nodded. "Ma'am, we'd like to ask you some questions."

"I have nothing to say," she said as she shifted.

"All we want to do is find out what happened to Missi. Don't you want that too?" Jules said.

Theresa tensed. "Of course I do. But that doesn't change the fact she's gone, and you can't bring her back."

"You're right," Jules said softly. "But doesn't she deserve to have her killer brought to justice?"

Theresa's jaw tightened, and Jax couldn't mistake the fear that flashed behind the woman's eyes. Pulling out a notepad, Jax said. "What do you recall from the day she went missing?"

Theresa sighed and looked at the ground. "Jared and I were fighting. I told the boys to take Ali and Missi to the park; they didn't need to hear about our problems. Next thing I know, Missi is gone and my whole family fell apart."

Jules nodded. "You found out Missi was your husband's daughter."

Theresa clenched her jaw. "You've talked to Cameron, I see. And for the record, Jared was *not* my husband."

Jules furrowed her brows. "I'm sorry. We just assumed he was."

Theresa let out a deep sigh. "We never got married; it wasn't really his thing." She nodded toward one of the structures near the farmhouse. "We just lived together in the cottage. And when the bastard cheated and left, I changed Ali's name back to Knox so she wouldn't have any ties to him."

"How did you find out about the affair?" Jax asked. "Did he let it slip? Did you find evidence to suggest an affair?"

Theresa crossed her arms. "Does it matter? I realized he was in love with Dianne. From there, it all just spiraled."

Jules tilted her head. "It does matter, Miss Knox."

She shook her head. "He used to give me and Ali gifts. Then I realized he was giving the same gifts to Missi." She looked at the ground. "A woman just knows, so I started snooping and found those same gifts in Dianne's drawer. *Bastard.*"

Jax nodded. "He left when Missi was taken, right?"

She nodded.

"Where did he go?"

Rolling her eyes, Theresa said, "I don't know."

Jules said, "Your family says Missi was taken by a man in a gray truck. Is it possible it was Jared?"

Theresa's head snapped up. "He never would have hurt her."

Jax nodded. "Even if it meant to save his relationship with you?"

"No. He loved Missi just as much as he loved Ali."

"That must have made you angry. Maybe something happened? Maybe it was an accident?" Jax suggested.

The woman gave him a venomous stare. "I didn't murder Missi, if that's what you're getting at."

Jax lifted a brow. "We didn't say she was murdered, Miss. Knox."

She jutted up her chin at them. "Am I under arrest?"

"No ma'am," Jules replied, shaking her head.

"Talk to my lawyer," Theresa said as she walked away and disappeared back into the house.

Once the door slammed shut, Jax rolled his eyes. "That went well."

Jules couldn't help but giggle as they climbed into their cruiser, glad to be out of the cold. Jax maneuvered the vehicle down the path and onto the main road, where the quiet melodies of Christmas music filled the silence as the two retreated to their thoughts.

After a few minutes, Jax sighed. "I want to talk to Ali's brother. He and Cam were the last ones to see Missi and, according to everyone else, they saw the truck that took her."

Jules nodded. "We may need to see if Ali remembers anything else, too."

Jax ran a search for Levi and found he was a local realtor. When they couldn't get a hold of him via phone, his secretary told them he could be found at one of the homes he'd listed.

The two parked in the driveway next to Levi's Mustang and walked up to the front door to knock. But before they could, Levi threw it open and hurried outside, nearly colliding with Juliette.

Startled, he said, "Oh, I'm sorry. Can I help you?"

The two pulled out their badges and introduced themselves. "We didn't mean to startle you, Mr. Knox." Jules said.

He waved a hand. "No worries. I just finished a showing, so I wasn't expecting anyone." He nodded toward Jax. "I'm assuming you're here about Missi. Ali mentioned the police had talked to her. My mother sent me a text about it earlier, saying you had been by her house."

"Yes," Jules said. "Can you tell us about what happened the day she went missing?"

Levi shifted slightly and then began walking toward his car. The two followed and he stopped in front of it, leaning on the door with his legs crossed at his ankles. "My mother found out Jared was having an affair with Dianne. They got into a huge fight, so she sent all of us kids to the park. Cam and I decided to smoke and then we heard the girls screaming. That's when we saw a guy in a grey truck snatch her up and drive off."

"Did you get a good look at the guy?" Jax asked.

"It happened fast, and it's been a long time." Levi rubbed his chin. "Maybe brown hair? Average height? I don't know."

Jax was a bit disappointed. That description fit millions of men. "Was it someone you might have seen before?"

Levi opened the driver's side door and placed his briefcase on the passenger seat. "Like I said, it all happened really fast, and we were also worried about keeping Ali safe."

Jules asked, "Do you remember anything else that may help?"

Levi shook his head. "Not really. I was young, and it was kind of traumatizing."

Nodding, Jax handed him a card. "Call us if you think of anything else."

The man nodded and climbed into his car and drove off, leaving Jax to wonder what skeletons the entire Knox family was trying to keep hidden.

CHAPTER 15

This time, the car ride wasn't filled with its usual joyous sound of Christmas music. Instead, Jax and Juliette focused their attention on the Knox family in silence. Jax turned down a side street and said, "They're hiding something. There's no way they're not."

"I agree," Jules said, nodding her head. "Tell me what feels off to you."

"Everything seemed rehearsed, and their recounts of that day are all nearly identical. No one added in little details or got off track when explaining what happened."

Juliette turned the vent toward herself, welcoming the heat as it warmed her icy skin. "Yeah, I didn't like that either. It was too on the nose. And I don't like that Jared up and disappeared after Missi was taken."

Jax slammed on his brakes as a stray dog ran in front of the cruiser, and Juliette cursed. Irritated by the animal, he shook his head, then continued, "The whole thing is weird. If he didn't take her, why would he completely disappear?" He sighed. "It's sketchy as hell."

After a moment, he smiled slyly and said, "But you kind of have an in with Cam."

Juliette lifted a brow. "You want me to talk to him about it again?"

"He's going to be the most forthcoming. He's removed from the family, and he came directly to you to talk about it. Plus," Jax shrugged. "He loves you, so he'll be straight with you."

Jules smiled widely. "I like how you threw that last part in there."

"Just trying my best to convince you," he chuckled.

Jules shook her head. "Okay, I'll talk to him, but you're not off the hook, *Mr. Hefner.*"

He gave her a look. "I'll talk to Ali *after* our date." He mumbled, "I need to get her to like me before I start interrogating her."

"Deal," Jules said.

Jax pulled into a parking spot at a gas station. "I'm grabbing a drink. You want anything?" he asked.

Jules thought for a moment, tilting her head. "I don't know what I want, so I'll go in with you."

Jax turned off the car, and the two reluctantly stepped out into the winter weather. Jax nodded to the Salvation Army volunteer who stood outside, then pulled open the door for a mother and her toddler as Jules followed behind the patrons. Browsing the aisles together, Jax said, "I think we also need to consider the fact that Missi is potentially tied to SLK and see where that leads us."

Jules shook her head as she grabbed a bag of gummy bears. "I'm not completely convinced they're related. Sure, a flower had been left with her body, but there's no burn, and she doesn't fit his victimology at all. Plus, SLK didn't start killing until 2012. If he had started in 1998 when Missi died, we would have seen more victims."

Jax said, "Unless we're right about Murray being SLK. He has a clear history of harming prostitutes and abusing his wife dating all the way back to 1995." He shrugged. "What if Missi was his first kill? Or even an accident?"

Jules paused and looked at him. "I don't know, Jax. There's no evidence to support any of those connections."

Jax snagged an energy drink and made his way to the boiled peanuts, Jules following close behind. He said, "I trust my gut. And my gut tells me Murray is SLK."

"Then the evidence will prove that," Jules said as she filled a to-go cup with hot chocolate. Then, she ventured over to another aisle where she picked up a sunflower keychain to add to her already growing sunflower item collection.

Feeling agitated that Juliette didn't agree with him, Jax got a place in line behind the mother and toddler who'd come in before them, Juliette following on his heels.

The two paid and walked back outside, where the rhythmic jingle greeted them again. He stopped to pull out a bill from his wallet and placed it in the red bucket. "Merry Christmas," he said to the woman.

She smiled brightly. "Thank you! Have a merry Christmas!"

Jax turned around and saw that Jules had already climbed into the car, ready to be out of the breeze that stung Jax's ears. He did the same, readily cracking open his energy drink and taking a long sip.

Continuing the conversation, he said, "Listen, regardless of who we think SLK is or isn't, I think we should look at similar crimes, especially ones involving prostitutes. I don't think a man who's this sadistic just randomly became confident in his skills. He would have practiced, and I doubt his victim pool would have included low-risk women like a mother or nurse. He'd want to make sure his victims wouldn't be missed, or even if they were, the police would be less likely to care."

Jules dumped a handful of gummy bears into her hand, eating the red ones first. "I agree. He would definitely target prostitutes or drug addicts until he felt confident he could successfully carry out his M.O."

"Let me call Haze and see if he can help us," Jax said. Pulling out his phone, he found his C.I.'s contact information and hit the call button.

Sean Rosario, known as Haze to Jax, was a name that carried weight in any criminal circle looking for a drug connection. Jax met the man a few years back when Jax had helped with a drug bust looking into none other than Sean.

Jax had kicked in the dealer's door as the man had calmly sat at the table, counting nearly one hundred grand. He had glanced at Jax, unfazed by the five officers training their guns on him, and blew a few smoke rings as he exhaled the marijuana that had filled his lungs. Thus, Jax had given him the nickname Haze.

Then, Haze had gently set down the blunt, slowly stood up with his hands on his head, and let the officers take him without protest.

Once in the interrogation room, Jax had somehow convinced the vermin to rat on his supplier in exchange for Jax finding Haze's little sister a good foster home. Jax held up his end of the bargain and had actually kept up with Sasha Rosario over the years.

Haze had been Jax's C.I. ever since, often working with other cops as well.

After waiting through four rings, Haze answered, "I'm working."

"Can you set up a meeting with a reliable prostitute who runs in your circle? Preferably one that's been around for a long time and knows everyone's business."

Haze chuckled. "Is Jules going to be there? You know the girls won't talk to you without her."

Jax wasn't offended. Jules had a way of getting people to trust her. And their trust wasn't misplaced, either. She truly cared for those women just as much as she did the missing mother of four or the millionaire who seemed to have every connection in the state.

"Yes, she'll do the questioning."

"Let me see what I can do." Haze hung up, ending the conversation whether Jax was finished or not.

As he merged into the other lane, Jax pressed on the brakes as the light turned red. He watched carefully as a young man walked through the crosswalk, his earphones popped into his ears, not paying attention to the surrounding traffic.

The light turned green, and Jax continued their drive.

He felt good about the prostitute angle. Plus, there were too many coincidences with Murray for him not to be involved. He made another call, this time to his boss.

"Sheriff James."

"It's Jax. I want to run discreet surveillance on a suspect for the day. It will be low-key, just me and Detective Reid."

"For the Scarlet Letter Killer case?" James said.

Jax sighed. "Yeah, I have a gut feeling about this guy and no evidence. The prosecutor won't go to a judge for a warrant."

The man paused for a moment. "Okay, go ahead. But do it by the book so we can nail this bastard."

When Jax hung up the phone, Jules lifted a brow. "You're very sneaky, Jaxon Royale Moretti."

"And you're a goody-little-two-shoes, Juliette Lorane Reid."

She swatted his arm. "You're the worst! You know I hate my middle name."

"That's why I said it," Jax said with a smirk.

The two drove back to Polk City, where Jax parked a short distance from Murray's house.

Jules studied the home. "Doesn't look like anyone is home."

Climbing out of the car, Jax shrugged his shoulders. "We should probably double-check."

She rolled her eyes and followed him to the door, where he knocked loudly.

They waited for a few moments, and when no one answered, Jules turned to Jax and said, "Come on, let's go back to the car and start our surveillance."

Jax paused and tilted his head. "You know what? I think I hear something coming from the back yard."

Juliette's eyes widened. "Jax, stop."

But he didn't listen. If Jax thought he was right, nothing but hard proof could convince him he was wrong, another unflattering trait he'd gotten from his father.

He quickly walked through the back gate, not caring much about proper protocol, and Jules reluctantly followed behind. A tabby cat darted out from the bushes, and Jules let out a gasp.

The two looked around the yard, but nothing seemed out of place or as if a serial killer was living there. Jax walked the perimeter close to the home and noticed the back door was left ajar. He glanced over his shoulder at Jules. "Looks like probable cause, don't you think? Could be a burglary in progress."

Jules grabbed his upper arm. "I'm not trying to lose my job because you want to be a damn cowboy. You and I both know you can't go in there without a warrant."

He ripped his arm from her grasp and turned to look at her. "So, we just let this guy get away with killing eleven women over the last decade?"

"We'll get a warrant. We just need more evidence." She hung her head. "Do it the right way, Jax."

"Yeah, and more women are going to die while we sit here twiddling our thumbs." He gestured toward the door. "All we have to do is say we thought we heard something and take a look inside."

Juliette's face reddened. "Do you hear yourself?! You want to lie? If that comes out in court, he will definitely walk. And then what?"

Jax squared his shoulders and glared at her, but she didn't falter. He wasn't surprised, though. She'd grown up with five older brothers. Of course she wasn't intimidated by his stare. Not to mention, the woman wasn't going to be persuaded to do anything she didn't want to.

Another reason she was the better cop.

Not getting his way, he said, "Fine. Stay out here. That way you won't get in trouble."

He turned and made his way into the home as Jules cried out, "Jax, stop!"

Just as his hands touched the door, faint screams echoed inside. They both froze and shared a glance.

"Did you hear that?" Jax asked.

Juliette nodded, her brows pulled tight.

They pulled out their weapons and quietly made their way inside. Once through the door, they carefully walked toward the sound, their guns held out in front of them. Jax didn't think Murray was home, but if he was, Jax didn't want to be taken by surprise. The last thing he needed was to get shot again. Or worse, for Juliette to get shot.

He and Jules came to a bedroom at the back of the house. He slowly turned the knob as Jules stood behind him, ready to shoot if the situation became life-threatening. Pushing open the wooden barrier, Jax's eyes widened and Jules let out a gasp.

A young woman was tied to a bed, naked and crying. Her face was swollen and her bloody body was covered in bruises. Startled by their presence, she began screaming loudly until she realized they were the police. Then, her eyes widened, and she began crying hysterically as shock washed over her.

"Fuck," Jax said. Despite the relief that washed over him knowing they saved this woman, he also wanted to throw up.

At the top of her breastbone was the letter "A" carved into her chest.

CHAPTER 16

A s EMS arrived, the shriek of sirens echoed through the street and neighbors slowly made their way out of their homes just as deputies roped off the crime scene.

Jules wrapped her coat around the woman and helped her walk down the driveway. Jax made sure to give the woman space, not wanting to scare her. He'd seen many rape victims become terrified of men, and he didn't want to add to her trauma.

Jules softly said, "You're okay. We've got you. Can you tell us your name?"

Through sobs, the girls said, "L...La...Layla."

Jules rubbed Layla's shoulders as she directed her toward the ambulance. "Can you tell us what happened?"

The woman quickly shook her head and froze. "No! Please don't make me remember!" Despite Juliette trying to calm her, Layla became inconsolable, screaming and clawing at Jules as they both fell to the ground. Jax stepped to remove the woman, but Jules shook her head at him and tightly held on to the girl.

Finally, she calmed down, her sobs turning into hiccups as Jules rocked her. Just above a whisper, Jules said, "Layla, I promise no one is going to hurt you anymore. I need you to tell me what happened."

Jax thought the girl was ignoring Jules as she stared at a spot on the sidewalk, unresponsive. Then, she finally said, "A man drove up next to me and dragged me into his car." She began crying again as Jules patiently waited for her to calm down, stroking her hair.

A paramedic slowly approached, and Jax put his hand up, indicating for the paramedic to wait.

Through broken sobs, Layla continued, "He raped me and hit me. And then he carved up my chest." A guttural shriek vibrated through the air as Layla's body went into shock, and Jax nearly cried watching her. She didn't seem all that old, maybe twenty-two? She had hardly lived life. She would now have scars he wasn't sure would be able to heal, and he didn't mean the physical ones. Those would just be a daily reminder of the horror she'd endured.

Jules attempted to console her again, but Layla wouldn't stop screaming and crying. Jax nodded to the paramedic who squatted down next to the two women. She gently said, "Layla, I'm a paramedic. You're going to feel a prick, and then you're going to fall asleep. We're going to take you to the hospital, and your parents will meet us there."

Completely hysterical, Layla ignored the woman. The paramedic stuck the needle into her arm as Jules clung to her and stroked her hair as Layla drifted off to sleep. Then, an EMT helped put her on a stretcher. The first responders loaded her into the ambulance just as Jax saw Cam walking toward them.

His eyes immediately darted to the blood on Juliette's clothes. Frantic, he quickened his pace just as she stood. Going right to her, he held her at arm's length, assessing her body. "What the hell happened? Are you hurt?" He quickly took off his jacket and wrapped it around her shoulders.

"Oh." Jules glanced down and furrowed her brows. "It's not my blood. We heard crying and the door was ajar, so we went in."

Jax shifted subtly, glad she'd left out the part about him almost screwing up the entire investigation.

Cam glared at Jax, knowing Juliette was lying for him but didn't say anything.

Wanting to take the attention off himself, Jax said, "I'm surprised you're here. You don't ever come to a crime scene. You usually just read the reports."

"We've never found a Scarlet Letter Killer victim alive. I needed to see the crime scene myself." He looked around. "What do we know so far?"

"Not much." Jax shook his head. "She said she was dragged into his car. Was raped, assaulted, and he carved a letter 'A' into her chest. But that's it right now. We're about to go back inside and see what we can find."

A crime scene tech walked between them to get to the house and apologized for the intrusion. Jax glanced around as more officers came on scene and began crowd control.

Cam gave a sharp nod to Jax. "Murray is already getting charged for kidnapping and a slew of other charges for the girl you found today. But as soon as you have something concrete tying Murray to the Scarlet Letter Killer murders, let me know. I have a judge on standby."

Just as Juliette opened her mouth to speak, yelling caught their attention. They all turned to see a reporter calling out to them. "Detectives! Is it true you found the Scarlet Letter Killer?"

Jax and Juliette ignored the man as Cam pointed toward the reporters who had all congregated as close to the crime scene as the officers would allow them. "Don't tell the media anything. We don't breathe a *word* of this until charges have been brought and we have sufficient evidence."

The two nodded. The last thing they wanted was for the media to get involved. It would only cause the public to look at all their choices through a magnifying glass.

Jules said to Cam, "I'll be tied up here for a while, but I should be done in time for our date."

Cam said, "Yeah, just call me." He kissed Jules goodbye and went to talk with Sheriff James, who stood with the D.A. on the opposite side of the property.

Jax pulled out his phone to cancel his date with Ali. He didn't know how long it would take for them to gather evidence and arrest Murray. He sent her a quick message, but, to his surprise, she told him she was fine to go to a late movie and was looking forward to it. He smiled inwardly, then focused on the task at hand.

He followed Jules back into the house, sidestepping other officers and CSI techs. They made their way into the bedroom, where they found photos and reports tacked to the walls. In their haste to get Layla medical attention, they hadn't noticed any of it before.

A shiver found its way up Jax's spine. Murray was a creep, making a shrine out of his murders and torture.

"Where do you want to start?" Jules asked.

Jax eyed the room. "I'll take the closet; you start with the desk."

Jules started looking through the desk. "We've got a box of zip ties and condoms. Makes me want to fucking puke."

Jax understood her unease. Though out of context, these two items were harmless. But he and Jules saw the darkest parts of humanity, and they knew exactly why the items had been used. Murray didn't want to leave any DNA behind as he raped his victims and held them against their will.

Jax clenched his jaw as he continued to look through the closet. It was mostly full of women's clothes, which Jax assumed to be those of previous victims. Murray was more twisted than Jax had initially thought.

Sifting through a box on the floor, he picked up a stack of Polaroids. "Jules, look."

She walked over to him, and he slowly flipped through the photos. They were snapshots of women tied to a bed, a bright red "A" carved into their chest.

"Think this is sufficient enough evidence?" Jax asked.

CHAPTER 17

A rresting Murray at his job had been one of the highlights of Jax's week. The man didn't fight him off. Instead, he had smiled as coworkers filmed the arrest.

Jax stood on the other side of the glass and studied the man. He didn't look like a monster at all. He looked like a man you'd hope to have around in case your wife or kids needed help. He looked like the type of man to be a deacon in a church, who helped feed the homeless, or served at a local shelter.

Jules opened the door to the observation room, and Cam followed behind her. "Has he said anything?" he asked.

Jax shook his head. "No. He won't say anything to anyone. Hasn't even asked for a lawyer. He just looks at us through the mirror and smiles every so often."

Cam nodded. "CSI finished at the house, and the victim should be awake in the next few hours." He folded his arms across his chest and looked at Murray. "I'm going to be honest: this guy is definitely a monster, but I don't think he's the Scarlet Letter Killer."

Jax whipped his head around to look at Cam. "Are you fucking losing it? Did you not just see what he did to that woman? She was branded with a letter 'A' right on her chest. She was beaten and raped repeatedly. This is his exact M.O."

Cam gestured toward Murray. "Yeah, except she wasn't branded like the other victims. He *carved* that letter 'A' into her chest with a knife. Same with the girls in the photos you found. And we haven't found a single flower in his home, his office, or his car. There's not even evidence pointing to him having forget me not flowers at all. SLK's signature is the forget me not flower, Jax. And the *branded* 'A' is part of his M.O."

Jax aggressively pointed at Murray, too. "He probably didn't have time to get the flowers." He pointed at Cam. "You're assuming he keeps them on hand, but he's methodical. He probably buys them closer to when he kills his victims." He ran a hand through his hair. "And maybe something happened with the brand, and he had to resort to using a knife."

"Jax," Jules said softly.

"No, this is our guy. I know it. My gut is telling me he's SLK. We just need to break him."

Cam sighed. "Right now, we can only charge him for this one vic. That's all we have enough for. Once we figure out who the other victims are in the photos, we can probably charge him with more if they confirm a crime occurred, assuming they're even alive. But any charges relating to the Scarlet Letter killings won't be on the docket right now."

Jax shook his head. "Cam-"

Cam put his hands up. "Prove he's SLK and I'll bring the charges. That's all I'm saying. And let's not leak this to the press. I don't want them getting ahead of the game. The last thing we need is for people to think we caught SLK if we didn't."

Cam left before Jax had a chance to argue, leaving Jax's blood boiling.

Jules leaned against the wall. "He's on our side, Jax. But he also has a job to do. I know you're stressed, and we want SLK caught, but don't take it out on Cam. This is weighing on him, too."

Jax scowled at Juliette. He was irritated she was taking Cam's side. But he studied her face and the kindness he had come to love radiated from her. She always had a knack for calming him down and putting things into perspective when he got too heated. Plus, Jax knew Cam wanted this guy put behind bars just as much as Jax did, if not more.

He looked at the floor and sighed. "I'm sorry, I'm not trying to be a prick. I just hate that we can't catch a break."

"I know." She gently touched his arm. "Why don't you call Trinity? I think we could really use her insight on this."

He nodded and left the room, trying to cool down. He fished out his phone from his pants pocket and called his long-time friend.

She answered on the third ring, her voice low with a slight rasp that most men found sexy. "Ready to be a FED or are you still a puss?" she quipped.

Trinity Harbor was Jax's longest friend and was most known for her sass and quick wit. Growing up, the two had often found themselves in a multitude of reckless antics, from trespassing to stealing gum from the local gas station. Her mouth always got them into trouble, and her father, the Chief of Police of Auburndale, was the one to bail them out.

Despite being a couple of juvenile delinquents, they had created some great memories.

He laughed. "I'm good, Trin. I actually need help on a case."

"Figures. I was hoping you weren't calling to talk shop, but I guess I suspected as much. I've been following your case on the news. You've got one sick SOB."

"Thanks for stating the obvious," Jax chuckled.

"Glad I could help. So, what's up?"

"I think we caught the guy, but our prosecutor isn't convinced."

He heard her rustling around some paperwork and wondered if she was pulling out a notebook. She said, "Why doesn't he agree?"

Jax filled her in on the day's recent events. "Cam says there's not enough evidence. Which, he's not necessarily wrong. I'm just worried this guy will get a slap on the wrist or won't even get charged for the serial killings." Another officer walked past him, and Jax nodded and smiled.

Trinity said, "What makes you think he's your guy?"

Jax leaned against the wall. "We found a shrine dedicated to SLK, and I know you've said serial killers will sometimes do that. Plus, the vic we found fits the M.O. almost to a T."

"Almost?"

"She was beaten and raped repeatedly, plus she was branded. The only difference is that the letter 'A' on her chest was carved into her skin instead of burned. And we didn't find a forget me not flower. But she was alive when we found her, so I think he didn't have time to get one."

She didn't respond for a minute, and Jax could almost hear the wheels turning in her head. "How long has this guy been killing, again?"

"A little more than a decade. Well, we just got a new case that has us thinking his first kill could have been nearly thirty years ago, but our first known SLK victim was killed in 2012."

Trinity let out a sigh. "I hate to say it, but serial killers don't usually deviate from their M.O. this late in the game. And they almost never change their signature unless they absolutely have to."

Jax groaned. "You don't think he's our guy?"

"Without seeing everything you have, I can't give you a definitive answer. Do your due diligence and look into this guy, but don't get so focused on him that you rule out other suspects because you want *him* to be the killer."

Jax hung his head back and squeezed his eyes shut. When he didn't respond, Trinity said, "What else can you tell me about the case? More specifically, the other case that may be linked."

He opened his eyes again and began pacing a bit. "We have an outlier. Her name is Missi Knox. She was six years old when she was kidnapped and killed. Her cause of death was blunt force trauma, and there was a forget me not left with the body. The family said she was kidnapped while playing at the park, but it's pretty obvious they're hiding something."

Her voice went up a slight octave. "That's interesting. From what I've seen on the news, he's never killed anyone that young nor anyone who wasn't known to be a cheater, correct? And the cause of death is different. Was she raped?"

"No, thankfully. We're thinking her death may have been an accident, and it's what set him off."

He could hear her shuffling again, followed by taps on a keyboard. "Her death likely was an accident, but I'm not sure she's connected to your guy. As much as we don't like them, coincidences do exist. And the flower is probably just a coincidence."

"What about the family being shady?"

She sighed, "You've been on the force long enough to know that anywhere from sixty to eighty percent of child homicide victims are killed by someone they know."

"Fuck me," he groaned.

"Absolutely not, perv." She mocked. She then became somber again, taking in a deep breath. "Really, though, why does that upset you?

He rubbed his face with his hand. "Because now I have to tell Ali her family might have killed her half-sister."

The clicking on the other side of the phone stopped abruptly. "Who the hell is Ali?"

"She's the woman I'm seeing," Jax replied.

"You're seeing a potential witness? Jax, are you stupid? I'm going to act like you didn't just tell me you're sleeping with someone involved in the case."

"Thanks, because I have no intention of not seeing her. And for the record, we haven't slept together yet."

Trinity snorted. "That's a fucking shock. You'll sleep with anything that moves." She sighed. "We'll talk about this later. As for the case, if you think the two are connected, see if there's a connection between him and the six-year-old. And if the six-year-old is his first vic, he's been killing for a *long* time, so there's definitely more bodies than what you know about. You first need to prove or rule out the guy you have in custody. And, actually, an easy way to see if this guy is SLK is to set him up."

Jax furrowed his brows. "What do you mean?"

Trinity sighed. "See, this is why you have to call in the big guns: because y'all don't even know how to get your suspects to incriminate themselves."

He laughed. "Screw you, Trinity. At least people like to see me coming. You *look* like a FED, and people immediately don't like you."

"People don't like you," she mimicked. "Blah, blah, blah. Cry me a river. My conviction rate beats yours right now, so kiss my ass."

"Only by 1%"

"It still counts."

"Whatever." He laughed. "So how do we get this guy to incriminate himself?"

Trinity asked, "What's something about the case that isn't public knowledge?"

Jax looked back at the door through which he came, knowing there was a monster sitting behind a thin piece of glass. "We didn't release any details about the flower.

"Ask him why he puts a daisy at the crime scene."

"It's a forget me not..." He shook his head, understanding her line of thought. "Okay, I'll see what this guy says."

"Let me know." She paused for a moment to talk to someone. When she was finished, she said, "You want me to drive over? I just finished a case in Tallahassee, and we'll be heading back that way in a day or two."

"Can you do it in an unofficial capacity?" Jax asked.

"The Brass doesn't want the FBI saving the day?"

He clicked his tongue. "It's an election year."

She sighed. "Yeah, I'll drive out in a few days. And by the way, if your suspect isn't SLK and Missi *is* connected, Ali might be in danger too."

Trinity hung up, and Jax found himself slightly frozen, phone in hand. He had already suspected Ali might be in danger, but to have it confirmed nearly paralyzed him. Which was beyond him, seeing as how they hadn't even been on a date yet.

Gripping his phone, he returned to the observation room and poked his head inside. He nodded toward the hall at Juliette. "Come on."

She furrowed her brows but followed him into the hot interrogation room. Typically, the dreary box was kept at freezing temperatures, but Jax had insisted on turning up the heat in an attempt to make Murray miserable and more likely to confess. Not that it was working. Now the two of them would be miserable along with the piece of shit who sat in the metal chair.

Jax stood in front of Murray, opening a file for a moment before closing it. "So you're the Scarlet Letter Killer? The guy who's been stalking this county for more than a decade?"

"One in the same," Murray said coolly.

Jules smiled and sat across from the man, pushing up her breasts slightly as she leaned forward. "Thank you for being honest with us. We just have a few questions." She took the folder from Jax and opened it up. Then, she laid out the photos they'd found in his office.

He studied each photo, reaching out to trace the girls' faces. The smile that tugged on the man's lips made Jax want to choke him.

Murray was proud of his work.

"What are their names?" Jules asked softly.

He pointed to the first photo. "This is Mira. She was the easiest to break. Cried for her mother right before I suffocated her. I grabbed her while she was walking her dog." He motioned to the photo of a brunette. "This is Lori. She bit a chunk out of my arm. Stupid bitch." He pushed up a sleeve to show a jagged scar. "She almost wasn't worth it but hearing her beg to die was the most beautiful sound. And this-" He pointed at the last photo. "This is Emmalyn. She didn't want to break; she didn't want to give in to her body's need for death. But eventually..." He shrugged.

Jax took out a photo of Missi and laid it on top of the other photos so it was front and center. "What about her? You like kids, Murray?"

Murray's face turned down, and he began pulling at his restraints, the first visible shift in an otherwise calm composure. "I ain't no pedo! I ain't fucking nasty."

Jules gently touched the man's hand, attempting to calm him. "This girl was killed twenty-six years ago, and we believe she may be linked to you."

Murray leaned forward, his eyes darkening. "I'm not a perv. I don't kill kids."

"Of course not," Jules said calmly. "But since we think she's connected to you, do you understand why we have to ask you about her?"

"I swear I've never seen her before."

Despite Murray being a despicable human being, Jax believed him. He didn't have anything to do with Missi's death, which both relieved and scared him. He was glad Missi hadn't been one of SLK's victims, but that also meant her killer was still out there.

Jax shared a glance with Jules, who then laid out photos of three known Scarlet Letter Killer victims. "And these? Who are they?"

Bringing one of the photos close to his face, Murray's eyes lit up. "I can't remember, but she's beautiful."

To Jax's surprise, it wasn't pride that glowed behind Murray's crystal blue eyes. Instead, it was admiration, as if he'd never seen the woman's face before.

Jules asked, "Where did you meet these women?"

Murray smiled, still looking at the photos. "I don't remember."

Jax stood next to Jules and placed his hands on the table, leaning close to the man's face. "Don't bullshit me, Philip. You remember every last detail."

He shook his head. "Sorry, don't remember." He leaned back in his chair. "But I bet they were some of my best work."

Then, in one swift motion, Jax shoved the photos off the table, sending them flying through the air and scattering all over the floor. Murray quickly stood, glaring at Jax. "Those are mine!" He yelled as he stepped to pick them up. But his restraints kept him from moving forward. His eyes darkening, Jax saw a peek of the monster that had been hiding under the charming facade.

Jax forced Murray back into his seat, and the man clenched his jaw as he tried to calm down.

Jules asked, "Why do you leave a daisy by their bodies?"

The man glared at Jax for nearly a minute. Then, he turned back to Juliette. "The daisy is the flower of death. They deserved to die."

Jax chuckled. "You're not the Scarlet Letter Killer. You're just a sick wanna-be."

Anger pooled in his eyes. "I killed those women! I showed those whores how disposable they really are. I proved that women are inferior to men, and they should show us some respect by not flaunting their bodies everywhere, causing us to sin and lust after them."

The irony nearly made Jax throttle the man as Murray continued to stare at Juliette's chest.

Taking Murray by surprise, she stood and began collecting all the photos that had fallen to the floor while Jax crossed his arms and studied Murray. "You may have killed *some* of those women," Jax said, nodding toward the photos. "But you're not the Scarlet Letter Killer. You're just some scumbag rapist who's too stupid to keep the cops from poking around."

Murray slammed a fist on the table and stood up, attempting to step toward Jax. "That's *my* work! I'm the Scarlet Letter Killer! I'm one of the greatest serial killers of this decade. My name will be remembered, just like Ted Bundy or Jeffery Dahmer." The man's chest rose and fell quickly as he worked to regain control.

Jules stood slowly and gently placed the pictures back into the folder. "You're not the Scarlet Letter Killer. Would you like me to tell you how I know that?"

He didn't answer. He simply stared at her with hatred lingering in his eyes, and Jax couldn't help but wonder if that's what those women saw right before Murray killed them.

Jules tucked the folder under her arm as she slowly walked to Murray. She stopped only inches from him, wanting him to know what it was like to not have a woman fear him. "It wasn't a daisy, Philip."

Murray yelled obscenities at them as they both walked out the door. Two officers went into the room to escort Murray to his prison cell. And as they dragged the man away, Jax's heart dropped to his stomach.

Murray wasn't the Scarlet Letter Killer. And that meant Ali was still in danger.

CHAPTER 18

J ules finished applying her lipstick, then studied her reflection in the mirror. Her makeup was perfect and she had somehow managed to make her curls listen to her after being pulled into a top knot all day. She donned heeled knee-high boots and a pink sweater dress that hugged her curves in all the right places. Happy with her appearance, she walked out the door and drove to meet Cam for dinner.

She had been surprised when he had told her where they were eating, as the restaurant was reservation-only and had to be booked months in advance. But, knowing Cam, he likely had a connection.

Parking at the upscale restaurant in downtown Winter Haven, Juliette slid out of her car and quickly walked inside. She eyed him at a table in the corner and made her way to him. Her heartbeat quickened with each step and the familiar excitement rippled through her body.

When she approached him, he stood and she kissed him gently.

"Wow, you look beautiful," he said, sitting back down.

Jules took her seat across from him. "You know I'll never deny an excuse to dress up and wear heels."

"I'm not complaining." He winked.

A young man greeted them and took their drink order, recommending the house wine, which Jules happily agreed to. After the waiter left, Juliette said, "How are you holding up? I know you've had a lot of information dumped on you."

Cam looked down at the table and Juliette immediately regretted her question.

But, after a moment, he looked up at her, his eyes soft. "Deep down, I've always known she was gone, though I'd hoped she'd be found alive. Like, maybe someone sold her to be adopted and she lived this wonderful life." He shrugged. "I know that doesn't really happen, but I was hopeful."

Juliette took his hand from across the table. "Sometimes hope is what keeps us going."

The waiter returned, setting their wine glasses in front of them, then proceeded to take their order. It had taken Juliette a minute to decide, as everything looked delicious. But, eventually, she'd decided on the roasted duck.

When the young man left, Cam sighed. "Sorry, I didn't mean to bring down the mood."

"Don't be sorry. This is your life, and I'm glad you're sharing it with me." She paused, then said, "Do you want to talk about her?"

"Maybe after dinner." He smiled. "What about you? Don't you have siblings?"

Despite having been dating six months, they hadn't ventured much into conversations about their families. Cam didn't talk to his family, and she often felt guilty talking about her large and close-knit brood, so she rarely mentioned them. Though the Reids were close, they didn't see each other often, so there weren't many get-togethers for her to bring Cam to anyway.

Jules chuckled. "I have nine siblings."

Cam's mouth hung open. "That's a big family."

"We're actually all adopted. I'm the baby." She smiled brightly. "Four older sisters and five older brothers."

He whistled as he feigned standing up. "Maybe I should just leave now."

She laughed, and he sat back down, a big grin on his face. She said, "They're pretty harmless...or so I tell people."

Growing up in the Reid household had been loud, chaotic, and cramped. The ten of them were always scheming with or against each other. Fights happened every other hour, but at the end of the day, there was no love lost. She grew up knowing her siblings had her back and she had theirs.

"Are they in law enforcement like you?"

She shook her head. "My oldest brother, Derek, is actually part of a classified unit. Gabriel is a SWAT officer with Lakeland PD. My sister, Charity, is a child psychologist. Harmony is her twin and is a social worker. Then Chase is an ER nurse. Nick was in the Marines but works in private security now. Bridgette is a teacher, and Paxton works as a PI. Connor, she's a CSI tech. And then there's me."

He raised a brow and chuckled. "So, you're well protected."

"Yeah, but they're always surprised at how quickly I can restrain them when they want to mess around, especially my brothers. Growing up they were overbearing, and liked to pick on me, but they were equally as protective." She shrugged. "Now they know I can hold my own, so they don't worry as much."

"That's how I felt about Ali. She wasn't my sister, but I looked out for her like she was. Levi did too, obviously, but he liked picking on her more." He grinned. "She would always tell me her secrets before she would tell him."

Jules laughed. "Brothers are awful. Mine didn't like me being a cop at first, so they tried every threat in the book to convince me to change my mind. But now I think they respect me more because of it."

"I get that." Cam nodded. "My grandfather and my father were not happy when I told them I wanted to be a lawyer."

A young woman approached with their waiter, food in hand. Once their plates were in front of them, Jules took a sip of wine. "So he didn't want you to be a lawyer? Most parents would love that for their kids."

"My grandfather was a pediatric surgeon, and my father is a trauma surgeon. He takes a lot of pride in his career and is actually very arrogant in terms of thinking he's God's gift to the population." He rolled his eyes and shook his head. "Truthfully, I just like the thought of putting bad guys away. My father stitches up victims while I put away the guys who cause the pain."

Jules nodded. "My father was unimpressed with my career choice, too, but he's come around. I think he gets scared for me. My mother is proud, but she makes me call her every night."

He smiled. "You probably hate it, but she just wants to know you're okay."

"Which is why I do it." She winked.

Cam smiled at her then looked down at his plate. "So, uh, do you know your biological parents?"

Juliette pushed her food around with her fork. "No, I haven't tried to find them." She looked at him. "Sometimes I get curious, but then I remember I have an amazing family already."

He nodded and took a sip of wine as the conversation shifted to other things. They talked for nearly an hour longer, and Juliette had been surprised at how open Cam had been. He'd shared many stories of his childhood and growing up on the compound. Her stomach hurt from laughing so hard. She knew him to be gentle and a straight arrow but hearing some of his stories showed he had a rebellious side that had seemed to subside once he was in college.

They hadn't talked much about their families or their pasts, but now she felt she knew an entirely different side of him. One that made her fall even more in love. Something else that surprised her.

When they had initially started seeing each other, she was hesitant to make their relationship serious. She had just gone through an ugly breakup and wasn't sure she wanted to trust someone else. But Cam had been patient with her. He had never questioned her, had never belittled her, and had never asked her to give more of herself than she could.

And now she found herself picturing a life with him. Getting married, having kids, growing old together. Even as they stood by her car to leave, her thoughts drifted to what happily-ever-after would be like with Cameron Knox.

As if sensing her thoughts, he wrapped his arms around her. "Come home with me."

Juliette grinned and laid her head on his chest. "I would, but I need some sleep. And I know if I go home with you, we won't sleep."

She stole a glance at him, and he smiled brightly. "Would that be so bad?"

"It would be for me." She giggled.

He shook his head and groaned. "Fine. I'll see you tomorrow?"

"I think we can work something out. I can come by the office."

"Good. Just don't bring Jax." He winked.

She let out a throaty laugh, and his eyes flickered to her lips. She didn't hesitate to move toward him, her lips covering his. His kiss was deep and passionate, but he pulled away, leaving her wanting more. His lips hovered over hers as he whispered, "I love you, Juliette."

She stilled as her heart skipped a beat. The words hung unspoken between them; tender, fragile. Neither wanting to rush their relationship, they both had wanted this moment to be special. They wanted the timing to be right.

He tilted her chin with his finger, his gaze holding hers like a vow. "I know you wanted this moment to be magical, and I had a whole thing planned, but I just couldn't wait to say it. It felt right."

Tears filled her eyes. "I love you, too."

He kissed her cheek. "Go home and get some rest. I'll see you tomorrow." Cam opened her car door, and she slipped behind the wheel, eager to start their life together.

Ali walked alongside Jax, scooping her ice cream as she did. Dinner had been a disaster as their reservations had been accidentally canceled, their food had come out cold, and Jax had to defuse an altercation between a drunk patron and a server.

"All in a day's work," he said.

"I'm sure you've seen much worse."

He shrugged. "Someone has to do it."

She took another bite of her ice cream, simultaneously enjoying the flavor and regretting the icy shock as a breeze swept through the night, sending a shiver down her spine. It was a clear night, the moon high in the sky as a few stars glistened.

"What made you want to become a cop?" she asked.

Briefly, his lips turned downward, and she noticed a slight sadness in his eyes. Then he chuckled. "It's kind of the family career path. My grandfather and my father were both cops. So was my uncle before becoming a CSI tech. My uncle's best friend, who is basically just another uncle to me, is actually the Chief of Police in Auburndale. And my best friend growing up works for the FBI."

Ali nodded and said, "Something tells me there's a more serious reason."

After the words left her mouth, she regretted making such an assumption. It was rude of her to ask him to share something he may want to keep private. She inwardly cringed. It was their first date, and she was already screwing up.

To her surprise, Jax answered. "When I was fifteen, my oldest sister was kidnapped and raped. She got away, but they never caught the guy. Before that, I wanted to play baseball. I actually had a few scouts interested. But after what had happened, nothing else mattered except for putting criminals behind bars."

Her eyes widened. "I'm so sorry. I wouldn't have brought it up if I'd known."

Jax shrugged. "It's just part of who I am now, I guess."

She stopped walking, wanting him to look at her. She gently touched his arm. "Still, I'm sorry."

He smiled softly. "It's okay. It's part of my past."

The two began walking again, and Jax took Ali's hand. She said, "No FBI for you?"

He laughed. "Hell no. I couldn't imagine being a FED. I'm too much of a cowboy for that. I hardly get through a shift without pissing off my boss. I can't imagine what it would be like working for the FBI." He furrowed his brows. "I'm actually surprised Trinity works for the FEDs; she's a bit of a hot-head, too."

Ali's heart dropped to her stomach and her smile fell. They weren't dating, nor did she have claims to him, but jealousy still roared in her head as he talked about another woman with admiration in his voice.

Jax gently nudged her with his shoulder and chuckled. "Are you jealous?"

Heat crept through her body, and she blushed. "No. Why would I be jealous when we've just met? We're not exactly an item."

"We could be."

She lifted a brow and grinned. "I think you may change your mind once you get to know me."

"I know you're kind. I saw you give that bum outside the restaurant a twenty-dollar bill. Most people wouldn't have even looked in his direction." Jax sidestepped a toddler who was running between his parents. "I know you're caring by the way you calmed our waitress when she was in a panic over having forgotten your ranch. I know you're a good person because, despite the lady at the ticket counter being rude to you, you still treated her respectfully. And even though we were running late, you let a mother and her teenage daughter cut you in line for popcorn because the girl was so excited to see the movie." He stopped again and gazed into her eyes, not letting go of her hand. "And you're funny, and beautiful...what else is there to know?"

Pink flooded Ali's cheeks, and she looked at the ground as she tucked her hair behind her ear. She shouldn't be surprised he had been so observant, given he was a cop. Yet she was. It made her feel special in a way that caught her off guard.

After a moment, she smiled. "Okay. But I have rules."

Jax rolled his eyes, smiling as he did. "I can't wait to hear this."

Ali's eyes gleamed. "You have to kill any bugs that creep into my house, no matter the time of day. And you can *never* invite me to play Monopoly; it will definitely end in a breakup."

He laughed loudly and then squeezed her hand. "Deal. No bugs, and no Monopoly." He led her to the middle of the shopping center, where people had gathered to listen to a local band play. Ali and Jax walked to the grassy area just as the band finished playing *Rockin' Around the Christmas Tree*.

The crowd cheered and children ran around, playing games of tag and freeze dance. The band settled down and softly strummed *Have Yourself a Merry Little Christmas*.

"This is my favorite Christmas song," Ali said.

Jax pulled her close, keeping her warm, and she leaned closer to him as the woman sang the first verse. Then, when the chorus played, Ali looked at Jax. "Dance with me?"

He looked around at the crowd, everyone huddled in groups talking to one another as kids ran through the grass, their laughs carrying through the winter breeze. He smiled and took her hand, leading her to the middle of the yard where all eyes were on them. He wrapped his arms around her waist and she melted into him as they swayed to the song.

CHAPTER 19

Lacey stared out the window at the stars that shined brightly, wishing there was a way out of this cellar. She wondered if anyone was even looking for her. Did they know she was being held captive by a fucking lunatic?

Tasha had likely thought she'd run off again with some stranger. And since Lacey no longer had a job, they wouldn't be checking on her. She had friends, of course, but they minded their business and wouldn't ask questions, likely waiting until she was already dead to report her missing.

A sinking feeling filled her stomach. *She was going to die here.*

She wasn't ready to die. She had so much to live for.

Lacey rubbed her arms, hoping to warm her naked body.

How could she have been this stupid? Granted, she'd gone home with plenty of strangers, and none of them had turned out to be the devil himself. This man had been so charming and handsome, and Lacey had thought he would show her a good time. Which was exactly what she had been looking for.

Hooking up outside of the bar had been thrilling, and she had been eager to go home with him. Tall, Dark, and Evil had driven her to a secluded road where he had pulled over. She had thought he just wanted a quickie in the car, but she had been wrong. Well, sort of. They did have sex. Good sex. But then he had quickly subdued her with zip ties and proceeded to throw her in his trunk.

In that moment, she had been terrified of what he would do to her, something she had been vastly unprepared for.

He had left her clothes in his trunk, dragging her into this basement as her body tried to keep warm against the decreasing temperatures. He had then tossed her onto a bed in the corner of the room. If she hadn't been so terrified, she would have been disgusted by the blood and other unknown bodily fluids that stained the fabric.

Throughout her first night and first day of imprisonment, he had raped her repeatedly. He had come to her every few hours to humiliate her, kissing her tears as she begged him to stop hurting her.

Now, though, she didn't cry. She had no tears left.

He hadn't been to see her since the day before last, her heart nearly beating out of her chest in terrorizing anticipation at every sound she heard. Now, Lacey laid on the ground, hoping to get some rest, praying the monster had forgotten about her.

She must have drifted off to sleep, because the creak of the door had her body involuntarily tensing, and she suddenly woke up. She quickly scooted to the wall as if there was an invisible barrier keeping him away from her.

He slowly descended the stairs. "Hello, Lacey. Are you ready to spend some time together?"

"Please, let me go," she begged. "I promise I won't tell anyone. We can keep this between me and you." She hesitated, then said, "I can be *your* secret. I'll give you my address, and we can keep seeing each other. No one has to know. We can have all the sex you want if you just let me go."

If only she could convince him to release her...

He laughed. "I don't need your permission. Your body is mine now, like the good wife you are. That's what you wanted, right? A married man? Well, married men have wives, and wives are their husbands' property."

Lacey inwardly gagged. *Wife? What kind of sick joke was this?*

He slowly walked to her, and she trembled, despite her best efforts to appear unfazed by him. But he knew. He could see it in her eyes, could feel it, could smell her fear.

Suddenly, he yanked her by the hair, her screams echoing in the small concrete room. He threw her on the bed and claimed her body as his. She tried to keep the tears from coming; she didn't want to show any weakness. But they came anyway. And then he kissed them.

Once he was finished with her, he towered over her as she huddled on the corner of the bed, pulling her legs up to her chest in an attempt to shield her body.

He glared at her. "You've gotten what you want, now. How do you like it?"

Lacey didn't respond. She simply stared at the wall, hoping he'd disappear if she ignored him long enough.

He scoffed. "You're a whore, Lacey. And soon the rest of the world will know."

She clenched her mouth shut. She didn't want to even acknowledge this monster.

Tall, Dark, and Evil shrugged. "You don't want to talk? That's fine. You'll be screaming soon."

An evil smile crept over his face, and her heart rate accelerated. She somehow knew whatever he had planned was worse than what she'd been enduring since she'd been kidnapped. And that thought paralyzed her.

"Lay down," he demanded.

Lacey continued to stare at the wall. She had no desire to listen to him. He would just have to kill her. Which was better than the hell he was putting her through anyway.

"Lay down!" he yelled, his eyes bulging.

She let out a sob and scurried to do what she was told, her knees nearly giving out as she did.

Once more, his dark eyes swept over her body. The first few times he had stared, she had thought he was getting off on her, just as she'd allowed numerous men to do before. But now, she knew he did it to mock her.

Lacey desperately wanted to cover herself but knew there was no point. He had already humiliated her and would continue his torment as long as she was in his possession.

"Put your arms above your head."

"Please no," she squeaked.

He forcefully grabbed her cheeks, and she whimpered. He said, "I won't ask nicely again."

A fire burned within her. A rush of adrenaline flooded her body, and she had the innate desire to fight against this man. She turned her head from him. "No."

Without a moment's hesitation, his fist connected with her cheek. Lacey quickly brought her hand to her face. She cried out in pain as he grabbed her by the hair and brought her face close to his. "If you defy me again, you will pay the consequences. And believe me, you will pray for death more than you already do."

Lacey didn't say anything more. She simply closed her eyes and nodded in surrender, wanting her torment to be over quickly. Tall, Dark, and Evil dropped her back onto the bed, and she bitterly brought her arms above her head. He retrieved zip ties from his pants pocket and restrained her arms.

Panic rushed over her. He had never restrained her before. Her lungs constricted, and she had to command her lungs to draw a breath. But, to her surprise, Tall, Dark, and Evil turned and walked up the stairs and out the door.

A sliver of hope washed over her. But then, a wave of nausea caused her head to spin. This wasn't his normal routine. She was about to suffer greatly.

As quickly as he'd gone, he came right back to her, her eyes darting to the stick he held in his hand. The orange glow sent her into near hysterics. It was a cattle brand. He was going to brand her as his property.

She started screaming again, fighting against the ties. Blood flowed down her wrists as the plastic tightened and dug into her flesh with every movement. "Why are you doing this?" she cried out.

He stood over her. "Because everyone needs to know what you are."

"I haven't done anything! Can't we just talk? I can give you money; my parents will pay a ransom. I swear I won't tell the police about you! Please!" She cried, but he was unmoved by her pleas.

He clucked his tongue. "Oh, Lacey, don't you get it? I'm here to show the world you're an adulteress. I want everyone to know you're tainted. And believe me, they'll *thank* me for ridding the world of you."

Her skin melted under the fury of the heat before her brain even processed the pain.

It was then that she screamed so loudly her ears rang.

And then she passed out.

CHAPTER 20

1998

I clench my jaw and let out a soft cry as I slowly peel back the gauze that's been protecting my wound. I want to scream as pain shoots through my body, but I don't let myself. I don't want him to hear me. I don't want to give him the satisfaction of knowing he is bringing me pain, nor do I want him to see me as weak.

Even though I am.

I've been stuck in this hell for fifteen years. The echo of that promise all those years ago haunts me. When I spoke those words in that dark, damp basement, I thought I was quickly on my way to freedom. How wrong I'd been. There was never an escape, only the illusion of light beyond the darkness.

And now, I will live the rest of my life in hell.

I've made peace with it. Accepted my fate. A part of me wants to fight against this reality, but the girl I once was died in the basement the day I walked up those stairs.

I reach under the bathroom sink and pull out new patches of gauze and some ointment. At first, he wasn't going to let me clean my wounds. I know he wanted to see if it would get infected and cause more pain. But, as always, *she* convinced him otherwise.

She's always been there to save me, to talk me out of the horrid thoughts that creep into my mind in the dark of night. She reminds me to keep pushing forward, that one day, we will be free. Though we both know our hope is useless.

Holding my breath, I pour the ointment on top of the broken and bleeding skin. A tear falls down my cheek, and I grip the corner of the sink and pray I don't pass out as dizziness invades my head.

This is the first time he's ever caused such a wound. Not that he's gentle. He's horrific, the monster I didn't realize was hiding in plain sight. But I've never seen him inflict this type of pain.

But then, I'm different, aren't I? My life means something different to him than the others' do. And I've now caused *him* pain. So, he punishes me.

Maybe I deserve it.

I slowly let out the air that's been burning my lungs, the sting of the ointment fading.

He wasn't always like this. But over time, he slowly grew more and more vicious. I never dreamed he'd become the monster he is now.

And, like I did fifteen years ago, I'm paying the price for my naivety.

Yet, despite this, I still love him with every cell of my being. Some may call me crazy, and maybe I am, but he holds a piece of my heart no one else can. His name is engraved on my soul, and we are tied together for eternity, even if I secretly pray for it to be severed.

Even if I hate him just as much as I love him.

I hear the front door open, and I know he's returned. He hasn't been gone long enough for another girl to have been brought here. Not that there's much for me to do about it, anyway. They're always dragged to the cellar, crying and screaming. But, eventually, the screams are silenced for eternity.

I used to think I was the lucky one because I made it out alive. But I can assure you, I'd rather be rotting away in an unmarked grave like the rest of them. At least then my soul could rest in peace. But I'm here suffering, and I hate myself for the promise I made in the basement.

I have slowly become a monster, turning a blind eye when I hear their screams and cries of terror. At first, I hated myself for being weak and fearful, never helping them. But now I'm numb to it. Now, it's simply as much a part of my days as eating and sleeping.

It's like drowning out the sound of the TV or a whining toddler. Eventually, the cries turn into white noise, and I find myself drifting to sleep to the lullaby of pain and horror. It's disgusting, I know. But it's who I am now.

I snatch the packet of gauze and rip it open with my teeth, as I'm unable to lift my left arm now. Sighing, I take a long look in the mirror. I try not to do that anymore. I despise the face that stares back at me. I hardly recognize myself. I'm but a ghost, forgotten by those who used to love me. Yet my eyes are what haunt me. They're the eyes of a heartless monster. And I hate her.

But she's what has kept me alive.

And so, the monster will continue to dwell within me until I finally find freedom in death.

I lay the gauze across the wound, covering the large "A" that will forever be branded on my chest.

Yes, I love the monster who did this to me.

And I *will* kill him.

CHAPTER 21

J ules came out of the elevator and made her way to her desk, smiling ear to ear. Despite not going home with Cam, she still didn't get much sleep. She had spent the late hours thinking about their potential future and how her stomach flipped every time she recalled the words he'd whispered to her. It wasn't how she'd pictured the moment, but it was somehow just as perfect.

She locked her purse in her desk drawer and went to find Jax in the conference room. As she got closer, she could hear him whistling, something she wasn't sure she'd ever heard him do. The longer she listened, the more she realized it was the song *Have Yourself A Merry Little Christmas*.

She leaned against the door jam, grinning.

Finally, he looked up and jumped. "Shit. You scared me, Jules. Say something next time."

She giggled. "I think you're just embarrassed."

He made a face at her, and she said, "I'm guessing things with Ali are going well?"

Jax looked at the table then back at Jules. "I really like her. I know we just met, and it sounds stupid, but I see so much darkness every day, and she is this...light."

Juliette lifted her brows. "Gosh, every woman would absolutely die to have a man say that about them." She sat down in the chair across from him and shrugged off her jacket.

He said, "Well, what's up with Cam? Didn't y'all get dinner too?"

She nodded, thinking back over the night. She picked at a loose thread on her sweater. "I think he's the one, Jax."

His eyes widened. "Really?"

Juliette sighed and slowly spun in her chair, smiling. "Yes. He's kind, he understands me, he knows when I need space and is okay with the boundaries I've set." She shrugged. "I love him, and I've never felt this way about anyone before."

"Me either; marriage will suffocate the life right out of you." Jax winked at her.

She laughed and swatted at his arm. "Whatever, man-whore. I heard you whistling, so Ali must be something special."

"No comment," he said with a grin.

Sheriff James walked into the room, his brown eyes sunken in as he sipped on his coffee. The man seemed to command every room he entered, dominating the doorway with his height and stocky build. He was in his early fifties, yet his dark skin hardly showed signs of age. Though, the crow's feet and smile lines on his face showed a happy life, despite the darkness he saw daily. "Sergeant," he said.

"Sheriff, to what do we owe the pleasure?" Jax replied.

"I have a woman who says she has information about the Scarlet Letter Killer. She's on her way in; my wife is bringing her."

"Your wife?" Jules said, furrowing her brows.

The man signed, rubbing his face. "Yes. You know Luna has a bleeding heart, and now that Darrion is off at college, she's been volunteering at a homeless shelter." He took a seat at the head of the table. "I love that woman more than life itself, but damn, she tires me out sometimes. She's always got a project she's working on. And by project, I mean person. Anyway, she says this woman seems to have good intel."

"Okay," Jax said. "When will she be here?"

Sheriff James pulled his phone out of his pocket when it buzzed. "Right now. Luna is downstairs and will bring her up." He glanced at the victim board behind Jax and Juliette. "Let's move to a different room, okay?"

"Yes, sir," Juliette said.

The man turned to walk out of the room when Jax said, "Sir, I have a request."

Sheriff James hung his head back. "This better be good, Moretti. I can't take any more stress between Luna's projects and your cowboy-ass shit."

Jax chuckled. "My contact with the FBI said she'll be in town visiting family in a few days. Can we have her consult with us on this case?"

"I don't care, Jaxon. Just catch the monster before another woman dies," he yelled down the hall as he made his way back to his office.

As Jax walked to the neighboring conference room with Juliette, she watched him send Trinity a text.

A moment later, Luna James walked in, her dark hair in stunning box braids that drew every eye in the room. "Jaxon, Juliette!" she said with a smile, her bright pink lipstick highlighting perfectly white teeth. She reached out to hug Jax, who welcomed the woman's affection, laying his cheek on her head as he held her tightly for a moment.

"Luna, it's so good to see you!" he said.

Though normally five-foot-three, her heels made her much taller in comparison to his six-foot-three stature, which meant she'd tower over Jules today.

The woman moved to embrace Juliette, who returned the gesture. Jules said, "We need another girls' day. It's been far too long."

"We do for sure! Maybe we can do some last-minute Christmas shopping," she winked. Then she turned to the woman behind her. "This is my friend, Elizabeth Norman."

The woman waved, then quickly looked at the floor, terror evident in her green eyes. She was a larger woman, close to five-foot-seven, if Jules had to guess. And her greasy black hair was pulled into a ponytail that showed off her bony face, wrinkles beginning to show.

"Please." Jules gestured to the table. "Sit."

After everyone was comfortable, Jax pulled out a recorder. "Do you mind if we record our conversation today, Elizabeth?"

"Yes, that's fine," she said softly.

The woman bounced her leg rhythmically, and Luna gently took Elizabeth's hand, calming her. "It's okay, you're safe here. And these are some of the best officers I know."

Jax smiled, then turned on the device and gave the required introduction. He looked at Elizabeth. "Whenever you're ready."

Her eyes rounded as she glanced at Luna, who clutched her hand tighter. It was clear she'd been traumatized. And while she may have put on a brave face for Luna, it was quickly deteriorating.

Jules gently said, "There's no rush. We can take breaks if you need to. You're safe here, Elizabeth."

She studied Jules for a moment before inhaling deeply, signaling she was ready to tell them what she knew. "About forty years ago, a man kidnapped me. I was working the streets then, had dropped out of school to support my dad's drug habit. He approached me, saying he would pay me to clean his house instead of sleeping with him, so I said yes and climbed in his car.

"When we got there, he sent me to his basement to get the cleaning supplies. But when I walked down the stairs, there was nothing but a bed and a flickering light hanging from the ceiling."

She paused for a moment, staring at a spot on the table for what felt like an eternity to Juliette. As much as she wanted to prompt the woman to continue, Jules knew she had retreated to her memories and needed to do this in her own time.

After nearly five minutes, Elizabeth lifted her head and said, "Next thing I know, I'm chained to the bed, and that was when my nightmare began. He would rape me nearly every day, often more than once. He would beat me if I tried to escape or fight back. He really liked to choke me while he raped me. And looking back now, I think he wanted to kill me, but for whatever reason, he didn't. He also whipped me with his belt, telling me I needed to be punished for being a whore."

She clenched her jaw, trying to steady her breathing. "I was seventeen at the time, a child. And this man thought I needed to be beaten for being raped by men who were my father's age." She closed her eyes for a moment. "Then, he would clean and stitch up my wounds, although I didn't get any anesthetic so that hurt like a bitch. I think he didn't want them getting infected because he planned to torture me for as long as possible." Elizabeth shook her head. "I endured that hell for nearly five years before he let me go."

Jules frowned, shocked by the revelation. "He let you go?"

Elizabeth nodded her head. "I thought I would die in that basement. But one day, he raped me as he always did, and then a few hours later, he loaded me into his truck. Everything was fuzzy after the rape, though. I only remember bits and pieces, and I've never trusted my memories anyway. I was hallucinating too. Saw my brother in the woods on the way to the truck, the trees contorted...I think he drugged me so I wouldn't remember anything.

"He dropped me off somewhere, and I slept right in that spot until morning. When I woke up, I was terrified and confused. I had no idea what was happening and could hardly remember anything. I tried to go to the police, but no one had even reported me missing, and I was still documented as being a prostitute and a runaway, so they didn't care. They figured I'd been doing drugs and made it up."

Jules' stomach turned. She was disgusted by officers who swore to protect and serve but only upheld the oath when they saw fit. This poor woman needed help, and they had failed her.

Elizabeth sighed. "I went back to working the streets shortly after and started doing drugs because I didn't know what else to do. I couldn't get the memories to stop replaying over and over again. Of course, it didn't take long before my story spread, and the other girls couldn't believe it. Some even added their own dramatization, and it became some type of myth or legend. Two years ago, I decided I didn't want to live like that anymore. So, I got connected with a shelter where I met Luna. I finally got clean and got my life right."

Jules gave a soft smile. "I'm glad you were able to get clean; that's something to be proud of. And Luna really is the best." She looked at her notes, then back at Elizabeth. "Can you tell us the year you were kidnapped?"

"1983," she said.

Jax nodded. "Why do you believe your captor is the Scarlet Letter Killer? I do agree some of ways he tortured you is similar to SLK's methods of torture, but there are key details that don't match."

Elizabeth sat up straight. "I'm not lying, sir."

Jax smiled gently, trying to ease her anxiety. "I believe you, Elizabeth. I know you're not used to hearing police officers say that to you, but I *do* believe you. I'm just wondering if this guy is a completely different perpetrator."

Elizabeth stood up, taking Jules by surprise. She began unbuttoning the first few buttons on her blouse, causing Jax's cheeks to redden as he glanced at Jules, then at Luna. After only unbuttoning the first four buttons, she pulled the left side of her top off her shoulder, revealing marks that had long since healed. There were five altogether, each one a perfect circle.

Cigarette burns.

Jules had seen those a multitude of times in her seven years in the field.

But these burns formed a strange pattern across Elizabeth's skin: three in a vertical straight line, a single burn horizontal from the top circle, and the last one was horizontal from the bottom circle.

Jules had never seen the pattern before but knew this was a signature. Grabbing a pen, she copied the pattern so they could use it for reference:

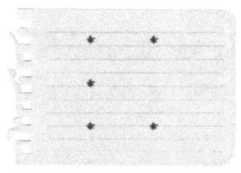

The fact that Elizabeth was reminded of her torment daily made Jules nauseous. "I'm so sorry, Elizabeth, for all of it. Do you mind if I take a photo of it and put it in our database? It may help us locate any other victims he could have had. We're going to open a case and try our hardest to find the man who did this to you."

She nodded her head, and Jax excused himself to get the county-assigned camera. A moment later, he came back in and handed Jules the device, and Jules proceeded to document the burns.

Once they finished, Elizabeth buttoned her shirt, and Luna stood. She hugged the detectives again. "Thank you both for listening to her. Let me know if you need anything else."

"We'll be in touch, especially if we get any hits when we run our search," Jules said.

Luna walked out the door and Elizabeth followed. But before she walked across the threshold, she paused and turned around. "I know you don't think the Scarlet Letter Killer is the man who kidnapped me, but it's him. I know it." She closed her eyes for a moment then opened them. "I've seen his victims; it's like looking in the mirror."

Elizabeth turned on her heel and disappeared down the hall.

CHAPTER 22

Ali was surprised to see Jax walk through the doors of her shop as she scanned an item for a customer. He smiled at her and browsed the aisles, waiting for her to finish. A stream of light filtered through the back windows, casting shadows over the carpet.

Once the customer walked out the door, Ali came around the desk and hugged Jax, smiling ear to ear. "What are you doing here?"

He wrapped his arms around her waist. "I needed a break, so I decided to come see you for a few minutes."

"I'm glad you did."

He grinned from ear to ear, not saying anything.

Ali let out a giggle. "What?"

He shook his head and tucked a strand of hair behind her ear that had fallen into her face. "The way the light hits your face, it's like this radiant glow..."

Ali raised a brow. "Do you say that to every girl you date?"

He laughed and let his arms drop. "Actually, I've never said that to anyone." He walked into her office and sat in the spare chair in the corner of the room as Ali sat at her office desk. Jax rubbed the back of his neck and looked away from her. "I need to be honest. I really don't date much. I mean, my nickname at the precinct is Hugh Hefner, and unfortunately, it's not because of all the money I make as a sergeant." His eyes met hers. "I'm not proud of it, but I felt like you should know before things get serious."

Ali's heart dropped, and her mouth turned down at the corners. She didn't like the thought of Jax with numerous women. But she considered him for a moment. She had enjoyed their date and how attentive he'd been. Even now, his honesty was somehow refreshing, despite it making her uncomfortable.

"Say something...please," he said quietly.

Ali sighed. "Is that what I am? A fling? Because if that's all I'll be to you, I don't want to pursue this any further."

He lifted a brow, startled by her straightforwardness. Truthfully, she was, too. It was rare for her to be that blunt. But seeing how easily women gravitated toward him, she wasn't sure she wanted to risk the potential heartbreak.

Jax leaned toward her, shaking his head. "Not in the slightest." He searched her eyes, contemplating his words. Finally, he said, "I've never really pursued anyone past a date or two. Most of the time, I'm just trying to cope with whatever issue I have that day-"

"You're not really helping..." she interrupted.

He held up a hand. "But you're different." Then, he chuckled. "You're this radiant glow in a world I know to be dark. And that's all I see in my job. I see sadness and pain every day, from parents grieving over the death of their child to monsters destroying innocent lives." He sat back in his seat and shrugged. "Truthfully, I don't know how things will turn out between us, but it won't be for a lack of trying. I like you a lot, Ali. I just hope that's enough for you to take a chance on me."

She studied his face. If he were truly only trying to get laid, he wouldn't be putting in as much effort as he was. If he were such a sleazeball, he likely wouldn't have been this honest with her. And despite being anxious about the potential heartbreak this man could bring, there was something in his eyes that told her he was being vulnerable. And by all accounts, she didn't think that was something Jax Moretti did.

And she couldn't deny her own feelings for him, no matter how hard she tried. He may be rough around the edges, but at his core, she knew Jax was a good man. He wouldn't have told her the truth if he weren't.

Finally, Ali got up and sat on his lap, wrapping her arms around his neck. As he brought his hands around her waist, she said, "It would be weird for me to say you're a radiant glow in my life, but I like you too." She chuckled. "And I want to see where things go."

Jax let out a laugh. "I'll have you know, I shine bright, Miss Knox."

A soft ring had Ali tossing her head in frustration for whatever patron was interrupting their moment. Smiling, she went out to greet a small family who was looking for books for their children. After about ten minutes, the family was ready to check out, and Jax came out to the main room.

As the father put his card back into his wallet, he said to Ali, "Stay safe out there, darlin'. That creep is back, and young women like yourself shouldn't be goin' places alone."

She smiled at the man. "Of course. Thank you, sir."

The family left, and Ali watched as the youngest daughter skipped out the door behind her brothers. She reminded Ali of Missi, despite sharing no physical resemblance to her.

She then turned to Jax. "I saw on the news the Scarlet Letter Killer was finally caught. I'm sure you're all relieved."

Jax rubbed his face. "Shit. That wasn't supposed to be released to the public. Plus, it's not even our guy."

"What do you mean?" she asked as she filled the candy jar that sat on the far corner of the checkout desk.

"We thought he was the Scarlet Letter Killer, but he's not. That's really all I can say."

She slowly nodded, disappointed by the news. She had been in college when she had heard about the first victim. She and her roommates never went anywhere alone, and they were weary of anyone who seemed out of place or dangerous. After a while, though, they'd forgotten about the terror that still lurked in the shadows. But then the illusion of safety was shattered when another body was found, and the cycle would continue.

She frowned. "I'm sorry. I wish I could do something to help."

He gently caressed her hand with his thumb. "Actually, would you be open to talking about what you remember from the day Missi was taken?"

Ali nodded. "I can try."

"Do you remember seeing the man who took her?"

Inhaling deeply, she squeezed her eyes shut, trying to conjure up the memories. "I..." Ali thought back to that day, the last time she'd ever seen Missi. Her heartbeat quickened as she recalled the smell of freshly cut grass and the weed the boys had been smoking. She and Missi had hurried to the swings, wanting to see who would reach the sky first. Ali had pumped her feet as hard as she could, wanting to be the winner of their little game. She tried to focus on what happened next, but all she could remember was hiding in her grandparents' room.

She let out a sigh and looked at Jax. "I'm sorry. I only remember swinging, going home to everyone screaming, and then hiding."

She felt so helpless. She likely saw the man who took Missi, and she couldn't even give him a face. Guilt ate at her as she tried her hardest to drag her memories to the surface.

Jax squeezed her hand. "Hey, it's okay. Memory loss is normal when something traumatic happens. You were a kid; there was nothing you could have done anyway."

Ali nodded and asked, "Do you have any updates?"

He shook his head. "Not really. We've talked to your family, but they're giving us the cold shoulder, so we'll have to get creative in finding more information."

She rolled her bracelet up and down her arm. "Do you think we'll ever find out what happened?"

Jax sighed. "I'd love to promise we will, but the truth is that most cold cases are never solved. But we've potentially connected it to another case, so we may get more leads."

It wasn't exactly what she wanted to hear, but she trusted Jax and Detective Reid would do everything in their power to find out what had happened to Missi. And even though it hurt her heart, she was glad Jax hadn't given her a false promise just to pacify her.

Jax's phone buzzed and he pulled it out of his pocket, checking the text that had just come through. "Jules needs me back at the office."

"I'm glad you stopped to see me."

"Me, too," he said with a smile. Then his gaze drifted to her lips, and it took all of her willpower not to press her lips against his. Tempting as it was, she couldn't let herself fall. Not without knowing he'd catch her.

"I need to go or I'm going to kiss you," he whispered.

Yet, she stepped closer, fear be damned. "Would that be so bad?"

Then, he brought his lips just above hers. "If I kiss you now, all I'll be able to think about is you, and I have a case to solve."

Ali lifted a brow. "Don't you already think of me all the time?"

"Yeah, too much." His lips lingered near hers, the space between them aching with anticipation.

"Good." Ali grabbed onto his shirt and stood on her tiptoes as she brought her lips to his. Then, she quickly pulled away and disappeared into her office, closing the door.

She leaned against the barrier, smiling from ear to ear. The thrill that welled in her chest made her feel childish, but she didn't care. Jax Moretti made her feel alive.

When Ali heard the bell ring indicating he'd left, she walked back out to the main room.

Her friend leaned against the counter, arms crossed. "I saw that," Vanessa said, narrowing her eyes at Ali.

Ali smirked. "And what did you see, V?"

"That smoking hot cop kissing you like one of the romance novels we read. Did he pull your hair a little?" she asked with a wink.

Ali rolled her eyes. "No, we haven't made it to that chapter yet."

Vanessa threw her head back and laughed, her brown hair falling over her shoulders.

"I thought you were supposed to be here an hour ago," Ali said as she grabbed her purse from the office.

"I was. I overslept and had to grab a coffee so I'm not a grouch."

Nodding, Ali said, "It should be an easy day. And thanks for letting me skip out. I need the break."

Vanessa snapped her gum. "I'm here to serve."

The two said their goodbyes and Ali headed out. As she drove aimlessly, having no plan for the day, her thoughts wandered. At first, Jax was heavy on her mind. Then, of course, she thought of Missi.

Ali felt betrayed by the lie her family had perpetuated for nearly her entire life. And it didn't seem they had been forthcoming with Jax and Detective Reid. Which made Ali question why. Why didn't her family want to find out what had happened?

Again, Ali thought back to that day. But rather than linger on her memories of the park, her mind drifted to the earlier hours of that day.

She and Missi had stayed the night with Gin and Gramps, both begging for French toast and bacon when they had woken from their deep sleep after having told ghost stories into the early hours of the morning. Of course, Gin had happily obliged. After scarfing down their breakfast, they had played in the woods for a few hours, getting lost in their make-believe games.

That's when they'd gone to Missi's house in search of a snack. As always, they had ended up in Missi's room, sprawled out on the floor as they laughed so hard tears ran down their cheeks. She'd gotten up to get a juice box and noticed the vase of forget me not flowers on Missi's nightstand...

Sucking in a breath as a car horn brought her back to reality, Ali realized *he* knew what had happened. She just needed to find him. But she would have to get creative in order to hunt him down. He had made hiding an art form, and Ali wasn't sure where to start.

She considered hiring a PI but wasn't comfortable bringing in an outsider. *He* had been clear he didn't want to be found, and revealing him to a PI might force him underground. And that's the last thing she wanted to happen.

She could ask Jax or Detective Reid for help, but that seemed worse than hiring a PI. She trusted them, but they were still cops and bound by the law. She didn't dare put him in that situation unless it were dire.

Running her hand through her hair, she let out an irritated grunt. He only made his presence known when he left her a forget me not. Always on his terms. But there was no pattern as to when he would leave one, except on her birthday; she had always received a flower on her birthday. But it wasn't until September, and she didn't want to wait that long just to *hope* she caught him.

She considered the flower and what it meant. If he communicated with her via flowers, maybe she could do the same. After all, he must be watching her from the shadows.

Ali turned down a side street and made her way to the local flower shop tucked on a back street of downtown Winter Haven. It was a cute shop with natural moody tones that accentuated the floral arrangements.

However, Lily, the owner, wouldn't be happy to see her. She and Levi had ended their engagement on bad terms when Lily admitted to getting pregnant by another man. Of course, Ali had let the woman know exactly how she felt in many colorful ways, which was quite out of character for Ali.

Regardless of their past transgressions, she knew Lily would be able to help her. And with any luck, *he* would come out of hiding, she would get answers, and Missi's killer would finally be brought to justice.

Ali just hoped it wasn't her family being led away in handcuffs.

CHAPTER 23

L evi was on edge. He hadn't realized how dire the situation had become. He had hoped his responses to the police would keep them from poking around any further, but he knew they would make the connection to the serial killings soon, if they hadn't already. And then everything would unravel.

Pulling up to the Knox property, Levi's heart dropped. Theresa was supposed to be at her weekly sewing class, but her old red Dodge Neon sat in the driveway.

He cursed under his breath. Her being home complicated things.

He had planned for Dianne to be home; the old bat never left the house. Which wasn't a surprise. She was a damn loon. Though, after everything she'd been through, he supposed he couldn't blame her.

But Levi hated her, and that hate overtook any feeling of sympathy he might possibly have.

She also irked his nerves with her incessant jumping and nervousness. She knew what she was walking into when she had chosen to be a Knox, so he had never felt bad for her. Plus, she had been awful to Ali when they were growing up, though Levi knew it stemmed from jealousy. Resentment that Jared had given Ali the same love he had given Missi and refused to leave Ali behind when Dianne had asked him to. And when Missi had died and Ali had lived, that jealousy turned into hatred.

How demented was she? As if she hadn't brought it all upon herself by being an adulterous bitch.

Taking a deep breath to calm himself, Levi maneuvered his Mustang off the dirt driveway and parked near one of the trail entrances on the far side of the property so no one would see his car. Pulling his coat close, he walked back toward the house, hiding in the shadows of the trees. When he approached the house, he carefully peered inside the windows to see where his mother was. Like he'd done numerous times as a teenager, he climbed up the lattice and peeked into the bedroom, where he saw her sleeping.

Good. She wouldn't get in his way.

He was there for a purpose and didn't want her involved. If she found out what he'd been doing, it would ruin everything. Carefully, he climbed back down, let himself into the back door, and made his way to the basement.

He hit the switch on the wall, and the dim light glowed above. Boxes sat on the far side of the room, and a few old pieces of furniture were pushed into a corner. A rat scurried across the floor, and Levi clenched his jaw.

The room had always been dark, damp, and creepy. As kids, he and Cam used to scare the shit out of Ali. The two of them had told her stories about the ghosts that lived in the basement. The stories were made up, but he had no doubt there were ghosts that haunted the space. And if he listened hard enough, he could still hear the screams that used to torment him as a teenager.

Even now, the hair on his arms stood at attention. He shivered as he recalled the blood that stained the concrete, though they had always told Ali it was paint.

Shaking his head, he walked to the far side of the room.

He probably shouldn't have waited until the police started poking around to look for such incriminating evidence. But if he hadn't, it would have raised suspicions, and there was too much at stake for that to happen.

So here he was, rushing to figure out where the damn video was.

When he was thirteen, Levi had followed Jared as he crept down the steps, curious by the way the man slipped through the house as if he were paranoid. At an early age, Levi had learned how to read people. And Jared had definitely been hiding something that day.

He had watched as Jared hid something in one of the suitcases. And not wanting to be seen by his stepfather, Levi had quietly taken each stair back to the main floor of the house.

Later that night, Levi had come back and found Jared's little stash of names and a videotape. Initially, the names had appeared to be random. But the more he had stared at them, the more he had realized they were familiar. It was a list of women who had gone missing.

He had confronted Jared, who explained the situation away, always disarming and charismatic. The man had told him who the girls were, and Levi knew he was telling the truth because he had seen their dead bodies firsthand. He had watched as the dirt filled their noses and mouths as their graves swallowed their bodies.

So, he promised to help Jared as long as Jared would help him, too. But then Missi had died and Jared was gone and it had all gone up in smoke.

Levi thought back to that dreadful night twenty-six years ago, rage boiling through his veins. Jared had left him to clean up *his* fucking mess. And now, Levi needed to figure out where he had stashed the video or he'd be screwed. He'd be tossed in a damn cell before he was able to commit his final act. To show the world the truth.

Honestly, he didn't think this day would come, though he should have. All things have to come to an end. He just wasn't ready for it. And now that the police were involved, it was finally time to finish what Jared had started all those years ago in the basement.

Levi's heart thumped wildly as he pulled down the suitcase. He heard the soft puttering of feet above him and froze. If his mother found him, he wouldn't be able to finesse his way out of this. Though he had led her to believe she knew the whole truth, he hadn't told her everything. Because as much as he loved her, she couldn't be trusted.

A moment later, the bathroom door slammed, and the pipes began to creak as water flowed to the shower. He let out a breath and set the suitcase on the floor. He eagerly snapped the clasps and lifted the lid. But his heart dropped when he saw the suitcase was empty. The only item left was an old receipt.

Clenching his jaw, he snatched the paper and crumpled it in his fist before throwing it to the floor. Levi fought the urge to hurl the luggage across the room, knowing it would only draw the attention of his mother or Dianne.

Damn it.

He should have known it wouldn't be that easy. Jared didn't have the balls to do what needed to be done back then. And even though the man had been gone for twenty-six years, he was still fucking things up.

Not wanting it to be discovered, he snatched the paper off the ground and shoved it into his pocket. Then he slid the suitcase back on the shelf and quietly made his way up the stairs. Before exiting the basement, he paused to listen and heard his mother on the far side of the house. Good, she was back in her room.

He let himself out the back door and walked the five minutes to the barn, nearly stomping the entire way. Mud clung to his clothes with every step, irritating him even more since he had a showing later today. Not that this little mess mattered after what he was about to do. He would definitely have to go home and change when he was finished.

He tried to calm the fire raging inside, taking deep breaths with every step.

Once to the barn, he slid the doors open, a loud creak echoing through the surrounding trees. No one would hear it, though. The barn was too far away from the main house.

Once inside, he went to his grandfather's old workbench and found the shovel. He eyed the bales of hay in the corner of the structure and thought about moving them. Hidden beneath the bundles was a secret room. A room that was its own hell for those unfortunate enough to be trapped inside.

Instead, he headed for the woods. And as he walked away, he could hear the girl's faint cries. Not the cries of ghosts from victims past, but cries from the girl under the barn floor. The girl no one else knew was there.

He gritted his teeth at the shrills that came from beneath his feet. She'd eventually stop crying. They always did. They always realized help wasn't coming and they would die in that little room.

Irritated by the sound, he quickly shut the barn door. In the distance, he heard tires leaving the driveway, and he knew his mother had finally left the house. He let out a sigh of relief and made his way into the woods that enclosed the property. The walk was long, and he wasn't in the right shoes to be trekking through the trees, but what he was doing was a necessary evil. His life depended on it.

Which meant Ali's life depended on it. She was tied to him, whether she realized it or not.

Once he got close to the clearing, he saw the bunches of forget me not flowers that had already withered away with the winter temperatures, another reminder that things were unraveling. Stopping in the middle of the field, he drove the shovel into the dirt. After ten exhausting minutes, a clinking noise reached his ears as the metal tool hit a barrier. He tossed the shovel aside and jumped into the hole, digging with his bare hands, though now they were numb to the cold that bit at them.

He recoiled when his fingers grazed the bony hand that had been buried in dirt. He thought they would have long since deteriorated.

But here she was, encased in time.

He dug a little deeper, and the sting of the cold metal box had him grinning. He yanked as hard as he could, and it gave way with a snap. The woman's brittle fingers fell into the dirt with a thud.

He hadn't expected it to be difficult to remove the metal from the corpse's grasp. But, he supposed, being buried for nearly twenty years will do that to a body.

Not caring about the remains, Levi quickly opened the box to retrieve its contents.

His heart fell. It was empty.

Fuck Jared for leaving him to do this all on his own!

Rage consumed him, and he yelled into the trees as he threw the box to the ground, landing next to the woman who surely haunted the Knox family.

CHAPTER 24

Lily hadn't been pleased to see Ali but had quickly helped her find the flower she needed, if only to make her leave faster. The woman had chosen a bellflower bouquet tied with a yellow ribbon. Because of the bell shape, the flower often represented a cry for help. And of course, the yellow ribbon was a quiet sign of hope while waiting for someone to return home safely.

Ali was both nervous and excited to see if *he* would come out of the shadows. In all the years he'd been leaving her flowers, she'd never actually heard from him aside from his very first letter when the flowers began. And then a second one had appeared when she was in college, both explaining how imperative it was she never go looking for him or tell anyone about the forget me nots.

And she had desperately clung to his secret, the only thing left of him.

But now she needed answers. And she hoped he'd finally give them to her.

Now, she walked through the local thrift store, trying to calm her nerves. Ali picked up a small black cat pottery piece and smiled as she thought about Bellatrix. The cat would no doubt knock it over, but Ali still placed it in the basket.

She ventured around the store, collecting trinkets, a few books, and a house figurine she knew Levi would appreciate. She'd almost grabbed an antique set of plates that reminded her of Gin, but she put them back. She knew they'd sit in her cabinets untouched like all the others since Ali wasn't much of a cook.

Walking to the checkout counter, she stood behind a lady toting a four-year-old. The little girl had her thumb shoved into her mouth, clinging to a blanket. She smiled at Ali. "Are you Ariel?"

Ali giggled as the mother turned around to smile. Ali said, "I wish I was that cool! Ariel is my favorite princess, though."

The little girl chuckled and then clung to her mother's neck, ignoring Ali.

Ali glanced at the fifty-cent bin at the end of the conveyor belt. Curious, she rummaged through the items, hopeful to find something interesting. She pulled out a Beanie Baby and nearly laughed. She'd forgotten all about these. She and Missi had collected them, and the stuffed animals had covered their beds. Ali had one that had been so well loved, it looked more like a ragged lump of fluff than the elephant that it was.

A memory flickered through her mind. It had been the beginning of summer, and she and Missi had been out in the pasture laying in the grass, looking at the clouds. They'd talked about being kids forever and never wanting to grow up. Missi had heard a story that if you bury toys, you'd never grow up.

Ali nearly laughed at the absurdity of it now.

But they'd both run home and collected their favorite items. They'd stolen a shoe box out of Cam's closet and set off into the woods to find the perfect burial spot. Not wanting to go too far into the shadows, they chose a spot where the sun still filtered through the trees.

Though they'd never admit it, they were scared of the monsters that surely lived deep within the emerald curtain. Their cries of terror had made the girls' blood turn to ice, so they tried to stay away from the trees that housed the monsters.

"Ma'am?" the cashier said, raising a brow.

Startled, Ali blushed. "Oh, I'm so sorry."

She laid her items down and waited for the woman to scan them. Once she paid, Ali thanked the woman and headed to the compound to look for the time capsule she and Missi had buried.

Once there, Ali parked at the front of the farmhouse. She would have to walk back to the barn to get a shovel, but first, she wanted to do her own bit of snooping. She wasn't exactly sure what she was looking for, but she found herself drawn to the home now that it was empty. Maybe it was her own slight against her family. Well, mostly her mother, whom she'd felt the most betrayed by.

Though Ali understood why her family chose to lie to her, she still wasn't ready to forgive them just yet.

Not bothering to knock, she quietly let herself in through the front door. Then she paused for a moment, listening for any indication of where her aunt might be. When she heard the sound of the TV in the living room, Ali tiptoed up the stairs, opened the door to her mother's room, and crept inside.

She took in the beige color scheme of the room and the dark brown sheets and curtains. Ali wasn't sure where to begin her search. She could try the drawers. Maybe under the mattress? Or her mother's vanity? She eyed the closet and walked to the door, pulling it open. She yanked on the string hanging from the ceiling and light illuminated the small alcove. There wasn't much to see aside from Theresa's clothes and a few shoe boxes on the top shelf.

Ali pulled the first one down and, because of the weight, wasn't surprised to find a pair of shoes inside. Placing it back on the shelf, she retrieved another one and found receipts. Then, another two boxes showed her mother's poor taste in shoes.

She reluctantly pulled down the last box. Pushing the lid open, she was taken aback to find old Polaroid photos. Smiling, she began looking through them.

She'd rarely seen photos of her mother as a teenager and was impressed with how beautiful she'd been. There were some of Theresa and Dianne sitting in the kitchen or standing out by the tree at the front of the compound. There was another one of Rick and Dianne on their wedding day, Theresa smiling brightly beside them.

Of course, there were photos of Ali and Levi when they were kids. But the one she was shocked to see was a photo of Ali, Theresa, Levi, and Jared. Ali studied the man's face as time had faded her memory. His sharp green eyes were accentuated by his dark brown hair and thick beard. Jared no doubt turned heads with his kind eyes and rugged features.

She'd forgotten about the large scar that sliced through his left brow. He'd told her many stories of how he'd gotten it, though they changed every time she asked, and the two would laugh at the foolishness.

She didn't find any other photos of her father, so she tucked this one into her pocket. Ali turned the light off and shut the closet door when she heard an engine coming up the drive. She quickly walked to the window and saw Theresa's car come to a stop in front of the house.

"Shit," she said aloud. She wasn't ready to speak to her mother or give her an explanation as to why she'd been inside her room.

The front door creaked open, and her mother's voice filtered through the house. "Alabama, are you here?"

Thinking quickly, Ali shoved the window open and climbed down the trellis as she'd done as a kid when Levi and Cam would disappear and she'd sneak out to try to follow them.

Once she was close enough to the ground, she let go and landed on her ass with a thud. Grunting, she pulled herself to her feet and took off in a trot around the backside of the house and headed toward the back of the property.

When she was a safe distance away, she squatted down to catch her breath. *God, she needed to work out.*

Once her heart rate slowed, she walked along the edge of the woods until she came to the old, decrepit structure. Over time, the Florida sun had faded the bright blue paint and had caused the wood to swell and splinter. As a kid, it had looked haunted, and Missi had always claimed to hear ghosts crying, so they had stayed far away from the invisible beings.

Even now, Ali found it to be rather chilling.

Pushing aside her anxiety, she shoved open the door and a loud screech echoed through the air. She closed her eyes and clenched her jaw, hoping she hadn't alerted anyone to her presence.

Her grandfather's workbench was on the far side, numerous tools and equipment hanging above. Hay bales were stacked on the opposite side, and the mower was parked closest to her.

Ali carefully closed the door behind her, leaving just enough room for the light to filter through. She slowly walked to the bench and eyed the instruments. The cattle brand was shoved into a bucket amongst other livestock tools. There were gardening spades Theresa and Dianne worked with and other implements Rick used to fix the houses. But no shovel.

Damn.

Freezing, she rubbed her arms. That's when she heard a faint cry. She wondered if a stray cat had hidden her babies somewhere inside the structure.

Turning around, she walked toward the golden bundles when the barn door creaked open.

She whirled around and let out a scream.

"Ali? What the hell are you doing here?"

She threw her hand over her heart and let out a nervous laugh. "Levi, you scared me."

He eyed her suspiciously. "You shouldn't be in here. You know Uncle Rick will be pissed."

Their uncle had been notorious for keeping her out of the barn growing up. He'd claimed there were too many hazards, and after she'd been harshly reprimanded when she was eight years old, she'd never so much as looked at it. Not that Ali ever had any reason for venturing to the place.

She dryly said, "You're here."

He shook his head and slowly walked over to her. "I'm allowed to be, and you're not. You know that."

Ali wanted to laugh at how silly he sounded. Surely Rick wouldn't still be upset. "I mean, I didn't think it still applied now that I'm an adult."

He got close to her face, and she took a slight step back. "You shouldn't be in here, Ali. Leave."

"Levi-"

He forcefully grabbed her arm and nearly dragged her outside.

"Ow! Levi, stop. You're hurting me!" she cried out. Her heart thudded wildly in her chest. Her blood ran cold, and she slowly counted her breaths, hoping the fear would subside.

Once out in the winter temperatures, he said, "Get out of here. If you come back, I'll call the cops and have you trespassed."

She attempted to rip her arm from his grasp, but his fingers tightened. She looked at his hand, then back at him, her eyes wide. "What's your problem?"

"*You're* my problem," he seethed.

"God, Levi! Ever since I told you about Missi, you've been acting so weird!" Ali studied her brother. She was admittedly scared of him in this moment, never having seen him be so aggressive with her. She looked around, realizing they were too far away for anyone to hear her if she needed help.

But this was Levi. Her brother. Her protector. He would never hurt her.

Would he?

She let out a breath to calm herself. No. Levi wouldn't hurt her.

He clenched his jaw. "What are you doing here, Alabama?"

Despite wanting to lie, she couldn't. Secrecy got them into this mess in the first place. If she wanted answers, she was going to have to be honest. "Missi and I had buried a time capsule the summer before she was taken. I wanted to find it, and I was hoping it would help me remember what happened that day."

Levi glared at her. But as quickly as the anger had flooded over him, it was dissipating. He inhaled and finally released her arm, shaking his head. "There are things you don't remember from when you were a kid, and that's for the best. So stop prying before you get yourself into something you can't get out of."

She crossed her arms and jutted her chin at him. "Are you threatening me?"

Levi tilted his head. "If it keeps you from digging around, then yes."

"You know, eventually I'll remember. So, you might as well tell me whatever secret you're trying to hide."

He took a step toward her, his eyes darkening. Her breath caught in her lungs as she instinctively took a step back.

He said, "Some things are better forgotten."

"Screw you," she bit out. She shoved past him, aiming for the barn door, when his hands gripped her upper arm again. But instead of shoving her away, he brought her close to his face. "I said, 'leave.' I'm not asking, Alabama."

Panic surged through her like a silent alarm. She was no longer looking at her brother. The man standing in front of her had transformed into someone she didn't know.

Nervous, she quickly walked away without saying another word. But as she stole a glance back at him, his eyes bore into her as they trailed her.

When she made it back inside her car, she let out a breath as tears streamed down her face.

Levi was hiding something, and she wanted to know what it was.

And she wanted to start with why he had been holding a shovel covered in mud.

CHAPTER 25

J ax watched as Ali's body moved eloquently with the music. He had been surprised when she'd requested they go dancing. He'd assumed she'd be more reserved and laid back, but the woman was full of life and energy. She confidently swayed along with the other patrons who filled the dance floor, effortlessly line dancing to an old country song. And everyone gravitated toward her. A woman smiled and laughed with Ali, eager to dance alongside her while the men ogled her.

Thankfully, the sadness that had clouded her eyes earlier had now lifted. When she'd initially told him what had happened between her and Levi, Jax had stormed to his bike, ready to brawl with the man who dared to put his hands on Ali. But, she'd begged him not to do anything, to let it be. And because he cared about her, Levi had managed to evade Jax's wrath.

Wanting to take her mind off the recent spat, she'd suggested they go dancing, and he had happily obliged. Now, Jax carefully watched Ali, smiling to himself as she did a quick twirl and her dress wrapped around her legs.

When the music ended, the DJ played another upbeat song, and Ali hurried over to where he was standing and took his hand. "Come dance with me!" Her smile was bright, and he found himself terrified that he'd never be able to tell the woman no.

Smiling back at her, he set his beer down on the table and led her to the middle of the dancefloor. Ali twirled herself into his embrace, tossing her head back and laughing as she did. Her body gracefully moved up and down as Jax held her close.

Then, he twirled her away from him, quickly pulled her close, and proceeded to dip her backward. Ali's laughter drifted through the air, and Jax found himself enthralled by her.

She wrapped her arms around his neck just as the song ended and a slower one played. Jax held her close, and she laid her head on his chest as they moved to the beat of the melody.

"So, you clearly like to dance," Jax said.

"I love it! I just don't get to do it as often as I'd like to."

Jax sidestepped a couple who were making out more than they were dancing. "I'm a little surprised by that. I didn't take you as someone who would dance."

"Because I'm nerdy?" she said with a chuckle.

"Yeah, I thought anyone who would own a bookstore would be an ugly old hag who hated the world."

Ali smacked at his chest playfully and laughed. "So, I'm an ugly old hag?"

"You're definitely not an ugly old hag." Jax kissed her deeply, her hand caressing his cheek.

She laid her head back down on his chest for the remainder of the song. Jax wasn't sure what to do about his feelings for Ali. He'd never so much as considered settling down with anyone, and yet, this copper-haired, book-loving, dancing ray of sunshine had him reevaluating his whole life.

And while he wasn't necessarily ready to go look at wedding rings, he wasn't against the idea either. And that had him feeling both excited and terrified.

The song ended, and Ali pulled away, rendering him from his thoughts. "You ready to take me home? My feet are killing me."

He caressed her cheek. "Your wish is my command."

"Don't tell me that. It'll get us into trouble," she said with a wink.

The two made their way to the car and started the thirty-minute ride to Ali's house. After a few minutes of silence, he glanced at her. Asleep, a soft rhythmic snore came from her body. He smiled to himself and shook his head.

He thought again about what their future could look like. He pictured waking up next to her every morning, vacations, late-night talks, quick kisses as they headed to work.

There was something pure about her. Something authentic that he'd never really seen in another woman before. But the hard truth? He wasn't the kind of man women like Ali fell in love with. If he had a hard day at work, he was grouchy and drank himself into a stupor. He saw the dark sides of humanity and often brought that burden home with him. Not to mention the odd hours and dangers of his job.

Was that fair to her?

Was it fair for him to bring darkness to someone who was so bright?

He didn't think so. She deserved better than he could offer her. But, despite how briefly they'd known each other, he found it hard to picture life without her. And even worse, picturing her with another man made him sick to his stomach.

He decided he would be selfish, at least for a time. But if he ever saw the light draining from her, he would let her go. She deserved that.

Before he knew it, he was pulling into her driveway. He cleared his throat. "Ali, you're home."

Yawning, she rubbed her eyes and chuckled. "Sorry, I didn't mean to do that."

He smiled. "I don't mind." Walking her to her door, he noticed a small vase of bellflowers embraced in a yellow bow. "Looks like someone left you a gift."

She shook her head. "No, I put them there."

He lifted a brow. "That's an odd place to put a bouquet."

She quickly began searching her purse for her keys. "Yeah, sometimes I just like a little bit of decoration out here."

Once she found her keys, she unlocked the door and looked back at him. "Do you want to come in?"

He hesitated for a moment but then said, "If you want me to."

She grinned. "I do."

Ali pushed open the door, and a black cat immediately wound its way between Ali's legs. She crouched down and scratched the cat's head. "This is Bellatrix."

Jax said, "You know, I'm not surprised you have a cat named Bellatrix. But I would have thought you'd name her Hermione or something less...villainy."

She giggled. "I would have. But believe me, Bellatrix fits her."

Ali walked into the kitchen, and he followed, studying the photos she had on the walls. Most were of her with friends, but he saw a few of her with her mother and brother. She kicked off her shoes and padded to the fridge, where she got a water bottle. She leaned against the counter. "Thank you for tonight, I needed it."

He slowly walked toward her, placing his hands on either side of her. "I figured. I hope you had a good time."

"I did," she said, gazing up at him.

He looked down at her, his stare burning with desire. She stood on her tiptoes and placed her lips on his, and he feverishly took her in his arms. Then, he lifted her onto the counter, and his tongue parted her lips.

She welcomed his hands all over her body as she clung to his neck. She lifted her head and smiled, scooting down to the floor. He kept his mouth over hers, hungry to take her in, as she clutched his shirt and led him up the stairs.

He paused outside her bedroom; his hands braced above her head as she leaned against the wall. "Are you sure you want this? You've had a lot going on-"

Ali kissed him again and brought her hands to the button on his pants and hurriedly popped the button. "I know what I want."

He lifted her up then, and she wrapped her legs around his waist as he carried her over the threshold.

CHAPTER 26

L acey could hardly move. Her body ached, and the burn on her chest throbbed. She knew it was infected, the swelling and pus worsening. And even after he had branded her, Tall, Dark, and Evil hadn't stopped raping her.

Every few days, he'd give her food and water, but it was merely enough to keep her alive. She hadn't wanted to eat, though. She had wanted to die. But her body had ignored her pleas and had taken in the nourishment, her body betraying her.

She closed her eyes, hoping for sleep, but they shot open when she heard his footsteps above her. Lacey let out a soft squeak, and her body instinctively flinched as her heart raced. She wished he'd just leave her here to die. She'd prefer that to the torture he so thoroughly enjoyed.

The sound of his footsteps as he descended into her personal hell had her heart beating wildly, her lungs constricting, and her head pounding. Walking over to her, Tall, Dark, and Evil studied her body like he always did.

She didn't entirely know why, but he never did anything without observing her first. She always wondered what horror would be in store for her once he was done. Sometimes he would rape her, other times he would slap her around, but the worst had been the burn. It still hurt like hell.

"Why are you doing this?" she asked softly, her voice hoarse from screaming in agony. "Please let me go. I won't tell anyone what you've done."

He stomped over to her and grabbed her by the hair, pulling her to her feet. "What *I've* done?!"

She cried out and then nearly collapsed, too weak to hold her own weight. But he wouldn't let her. He sneered. "You whore! You wanted this. You wanted to be with a married man, and this is your punishment. You mock the authority of men and have forgotten your place. Now you will pay the price."

She let out a cry. "I'm sorry! I promise I can change! I didn't mean to ruin your marriage."

He laughed. "That's what they all say."

He threw her to the ground, and she landed with a thud. Lacey whimpered. She hadn't meant to make him angry; he was so much more violent when he was angry. But she had hoped she could convince him to let her go.

"It's time for your penance."

"No! Please don't hurt me anymore!" she shrieked.

She hadn't even seen him grab the whip before he had struck her with it. She screamed as the leather tore open her skin, the lashings burning with every blow.

Ignoring her cries, he continued his tirade. "You're a jezebel, Lacey! Tempting men with your body, showing no respect for the hierarchy. Men have authority over women; *we* are your masters!" Another crack, followed by a hiss and a shriek from Lacey.

He mocked her. "Look at you, spreading your legs and tainting our power. And for what? One night of pleasure?" Tall, Dark, and Evil brought his face to hers, his breath hot as it fell over her cheeks. A wicked grin stretched over his lips. "You're weak and filthy. No man will ever love you, so you steal someone else's. And you're finally being punished for it."

This man was demented.

But he struck a chord in her. She *was* weak. She enjoyed the company of married men because they wouldn't commit. And there was something about being able to obtain something that isn't yours, a high knowing you're so beautiful you're able to steal from another woman.

Maybe she did deserve his torment. Maybe the world was better off without her.

The hiss of the whip drew her from her thoughts. But by the last lashing, her body was too numb for her to make any noise at all. And as she lay on the floor, blood flowing from her wounds, Lacey hoped he would simply kill her.

When he finished putting the whip away, he didn't even bother throwing her on the bed as he normally did. He claimed her body right on the floor in the dirt and rat droppings. Before enduring his wrath, she might have been repulsed by the filth, but now her soul was crushed, and she no longer cared.

As he violated her, he grabbed her face and made her look at him. He whispered, "Admit you're a whore and I'll stop. It'll all be over."

She knew what he meant. He wanted her to beg to die. But she wouldn't do it. "No."

"Say it!" he yelled.

"No! I won't say it!" A fire surged within her. But she was so weak. She couldn't fight back, and she crumbled under his weight, crying as he took her last spark of hope. Then, with every ounce of fire she had left, she spit on him. Wanting to end her life, she said, "You're the fucking whore."

His eyes turned into a sea of darkness, and his face contorted with rage. He forcefully wrapped his hands around her throat and squeezed.

And then Lacey's world went black.

CHAPTER 27

J ax woke with a jerk. It took him a moment to realize where he was, fragments from the night before flickering through his mind. He glanced over and saw Ali asleep, her copper hair covering the pillow. He could make out her silhouette under the sheet, and he thought about what lay just beneath the thin surface.

As the morning light filtered through the blinds and cast a radiant glow over her face, he leaned over to kiss her cheek. She was too beautiful to wake, so instead, he slipped out of the bed and padded down the stairs to make coffee.

It took him ten minutes to find the coffee machine, which had been shoved into a cabinet. Just as the last few drops fell into the pot, Ali walked into the kitchen wearing his button-up, her hair tousled from last night's passion.

"I was worried you left in the middle of the night," she said, yawning.

Jax wrapped his arms around her, and she clung to his neck as he kissed her. "I'd never do that to you."

Ali smiled and rubbed her eyes, not quite awake yet. "You found my coffee pot, I see."

"Took me long enough. Why isn't it on the counter like a normal human being?"

She chuckled, pulling away to retrieve the creamer out of the fridge. "I hate clutter on my counters. It's something I inherited from my grandmother."

Bellatrix wound her way around Ali's legs and then Jax's as he poured coffee into the mugs he had dug out of the cabinet.

A thud on the porch had Ali walking toward the front door. "That must be one of the book deliveries I've been waiting on."

Jax raised a brow and glanced at her bare legs. "Ali."

She looked down and laughed. "I'll go put pants on."

Jax grabbed her around the waist as she started to walk away. "Don't do that. Just sit and enjoy your coffee. I'll get the package." She giggled as he released her, and he made his way to the front door.

He peered out and saw the box on the edge of the step. But it was a red envelope on the welcome mat that caught his attention. Curious, he grabbed it and handed it to her as she leaned against the kitchen counter.

Her name was scrawled in messy handwriting, definitely a man's. Jax eyed the envelope. "Secret admirer?"

She laughed. "Doubtful."

Jax found it interesting that she denied the possibility of having a secret admirer. She clearly didn't realize how wonderful she was.

Ali pulled out a single piece of paper that had been folded up. Opening it, petals fell from inside the fold and she froze, her face draining of color.

Jax immediately took it from her. The paper read: "*Let the dead rest, Ali, before you find yourself resting with them.*"

His eyes darted to the petals. Forget Me Nots.

The Scarlet Letter Killer was threatening Ali. How long had she been in danger and he hadn't even been aware of it?

Jax's heart pounded, and the primal instinct to protect her roared through him. His fist connected with the table and Ali jumped. A crimson haze clouded his mind as he swore to bring this monster to his knees.

Not wasting any more time, Jax ran up the stairs as Ali followed close behind. Her eyes rounded as he retrieved his gun.

"Jax, what's wrong? Why do you have your gun?"

His jaw was set as he shoved the magazine into place. "Lock the door. Call 911 and tell them to dispatch Jules. Do not open this door until I come back or unless it's Jules. No matter what. Do you understand me?"

Ali froze, terror in her eyes.

Jax slightly raised his voice as fear grazed his heart. "Ali, do you understand?"

She quickly nodded, and he pulled back on the slide, letting it snap forward with a click. "No matter what you hear, don't unlock that door for anyone. And if someone tries to get in, climb out the window and run."

She hesitated for a moment, then he kissed her. "Promise me," he demanded. "Yes. Okay," she said, her face paling.

Nodding to her, Jax ran back down to the first floor, aiming his gun as he walked through the front door. He did a sweep of the premises, and by the time he was finished, Jules and two other patrol cars pulled into the driveway, sirens blaring.

Jules bolted out of the car, worry etched on her face. "Are you okay?"

Shivering, he realized he'd run out into the frigid air without a shirt on. Wanting to get out of the cold, he placed his gun at his side and nodded toward the house. "Come on. Bring an evidence kit, too."

Jules instructed the patrol officers to tape off the house and the surrounding yard and then followed Jax. Once inside, Juliette eyed Jax's naked chest and lifted a brow, but didn't say anything. Which was probably due to the fact that her hair was tousled and she was clearly wearing the same blouse from the day before.

Jax said, "Wait here, let me get Ali."

He took the stairs two at a time and knocked on the bedroom door. "It's me."

She slowly opened the door, now wearing sweats, but she still donned his button up. His eyes darted to her face and his heart dropped. It was clear she'd been crying, and he hated how much he'd scared her.

But he had needed to keep her safe.

Putting his gun on the end table near the door, he pulled her into an embrace, and she clung to him. Then, the tears came again.

She choked out, "What's going on? Why did you have your gun?"

Stroking her hair, he said, "Jules is downstairs. Let me put on a shirt and then we'll talk." He reluctantly let her go and snatched his undershirt off the floor and pulled it over his head.

Following his lead, Ali removed his shirt and handed it to him.

Turning to get her bra, he studied her bare back, trying not to let his thoughts wander. If she wasn't in potential danger, he might have dragged her to bed despite Jules being downstairs.

Quickly, she threw on a t-shirt that had been tossed onto her dresser. Then the two headed down the stairs, Juliette standing at the bottom tapping on the handrail as she waited.

Glancing up at them, she scrunched her brows. "Ali, are you okay?"

Ali nodded. "I think so."

"Good." Then, his partner's piercing gaze bore into him as she threw her arm in the air. "What the hell is going on, Jax?!"

He didn't answer immediately. Instead, he led them back into the kitchen, Juliette hot on his heels. His partner was undoubtedly pissed. But he couldn't blame her; she probably thought he was dead since Ali had asked 911 to dispatch her.

Once they rounded the corner, he pointed to the note and petals scattered across the counter. "Someone left this for Ali."

Jules' eyes widened as she read the paper that lay open. Her gaze darted to Ali. "Do you know who left it?"

Ali looked at the ground and shifted her body as she played with the bracelet on her wrist.

Jax instinctively knew she was hiding something. She'd done the same thing when they'd confronted her about the GEDmatch results. She'd lied that day, but he hadn't pressed her. But now that her life may be in danger, there couldn't be any more secrets.

He gently tipped her chin with his finger. "If you know who left it, I need you to tell me."

Ali pulled her head away and looked at the floor. "I can't tell you. I made a promise."

Jax cupped her face. "Ali, please. I can't keep you safe if I don't know who the threat is."

He didn't want to beg, but he would. He would gladly get down on his knees and grovel if it meant saving her. And as he studied her red-rimmed eyes, he knew he'd also kill to make sure not even a hair on her head was touched.

Searching his face, she scrunched her brows. "What aren't *you* telling me?"

Jax sighed and tilted his head. "I can't discuss an ongoing investigation."

She fiercely pulled herself away from him and shoved her finger into his chest. "Don't give me that shit. You just pulled out your gun, and I'm supposed to act like nothing happened?"

Jax looked at Jules, and he silently pleaded with his partner. The brass would have his badge if he told Ali the truth, but she deserved to know about the monster threatening her.

Juliette looked at Ali, who was now crossing her arms, then nodded to him.

He took in a breath. "*Hypothetically,* there could be a serial killer whose signature is that flower."

Ali's face paled and she steadied herself against the counter. She put a hand to her forehead. "*Oh god.*"

She slowly slid down the side of the counter to the floor, shaking her head. Her voice cracked as tears welled in her eyes. "No. He wouldn't do that. He would never hurt me or those women."

Jax sat next to her and pulled her close to his chest as sobs racked her body. She said, "It's my fault. I started looking for him." She clutched his shirt in her fists. "Are those girls dead because I didn't keep his secret?"

Jax held her tight, wishing he could take the heartache from her. It was clear she knew more than she had ever let on, and the secret she'd harbored had slowly poisoned her over time. He just hoped he could keep it from killing her.

After a moment, Ali sucked in a breath then slowly let it out. She'd released his shirt but still leaned into his embrace. Finally, she lifted her head and wiped at her eyes, mascara streaking her rosied cheeks.

Satisfied Ali had calmed down, Juliette gently touched her hand. "Ali, who is he? Who left the note?"

Closing her eyes, she whispered, "My father."

CHAPTER 28

A li felt guilty betraying her father's secret. She remembered the man to be kind and loving, always attentive to her needs. For years, she'd been convinced she was doing the right thing by helping him hide in the shadows. But good men didn't leave a trail of bodies in their wake. And as much as she'd like to deny it, monsters don't always hide under the bed. Sometimes they sit at the head of the table.

And because of that, she'd spent nearly an hour going over everything she knew about Jared Schultz, which wasn't much. Only that he didn't have family and, by all accounts, had been a drifter.

When he'd walked out on Ali twenty-six years ago, she hadn't seen or heard from him until he left the first flower for her when she was eleven. There had been no pattern to his silent returns. The forget me nots would simply appear.

She finally admitted to Jax and Detective Reid that he was the person she had been looking for when she had submitted her DNA. She had hoped to find him and either have a relationship with him or get closure if he had no desire to be in her life.

And because Jax and Detective Reid suspected Jared had killed Missi, the morning had been full of tears as Ali tried to recall anything more about the day Missi had been taken. But Ali's memories still evaded her.

Yet, despite their claims, she wasn't fully convinced her father could be so cruel. He had loved Missi just as much as he loved Ali.

None of it made sense.

Is this what her family had been protecting her from? Had he shown signs of being a monster long before he had started slaughtering women? Had they watched as he murdered his own flesh and blood, and they feared he'd do the same to her?

Finally finished with the interview, she let out a sigh as the last officer disappeared out her door. CSI had combed through her house and the property, bagging and tagging anything they thought may be evidence, which didn't seem to be much. She had helplessly watched as they dusted for prints and swabbed for DNA, grief swelling in her chest.

Ali curled up on her couch, picking at an old stain on the blanket that lay across her lap. She was emotionally exhausted and desperately needed a nap. Part of her hoped if she fell asleep, she'd wake up and this would all be a dream. But the nightmares sure to haunt her kept her from closing her eyes.

Hanging up his phone, Jax walked into the room and sat down next to her while Detective Reid stood in the doorway of the living room. He said, "Why don't you pack a bag for a few days? You're staying with me until we find your father."

Ali shook her head. "I don't know, Jax..." She didn't think her father would actually hurt her, nor did she want to put anyone in danger in case she was wrong.

Detective Reid sat on the arm of the couch. "I really think you should take this seriously."

Ali caressed Bellatrix's head as she curled up in Ali's lap. "I don't want to burden any of you or put you in any danger."

The detective chuckled. "Danger is in our job description. We're built for this."

Ali considered her for a moment before nodding her head. "But what about Bellatrix?"

"She can come too," Jax said as he attempted to pet the cat, but she pawed his hand away.

Detective Reid lifted a brow. "You don't even like animals."

He gasped dramatically and said to the cat, "Don't listen to her. She bullies me. I love you, B."

Ali laughed, but tension quickly filled the room once again. Her heart was slowly shattering as she wrestled with the possibility that her father was a murderer and not the man she thought she knew. She felt as if she was losing him all over again and that left a deep ache in her chest.

Pulling her from her thoughts, Detective Reid said to Jax, "When will Trinity be here?"

"Today, I think."

"Is that your friend with the FBI?" Ali asked.

Jax nodded, and the detective smiled. She said, "Trinity is really feisty and rough around the edges, but you'll like her. Plus, she's great at her job. " She pulled her keys from her pocket. "I'm gonna head to the station and start trying to find Jared." She looked at Ali. "Stay safe. And listen to your gut."

Ali nodded. "Thank you, Detective."

"After today, we're well past formalities. It's Jules."

Saying their goodbyes, she left and silence filled the house. After a moment, Jax stood and helped himself to a water out of the fridge as Ali walked to her hall closet to retrieve her suitcase.

"I'm going to shower before we leave, if that's okay," Ali said from the hall.

Jax stuck his head around the corner. "Can I join?"

Ali smirked. "Normally, I'd be thrilled. But I need a second to decompress."

He walked over to her and kissed her crown. "Holler if you need me."

Once in the shower, she stood motionless, letting the hot water rain down over her body.

She had been surprised by the forget me nots Jared had left her this morning. She didn't think she could summon her father from the shadows. Yet, she had.

And now she wondered: did he hide in the shadows because he was a monster? Couldn't the flowers left with the dead women be a coincidence? She wanted to believe her father would never do something so heinous. She desperately wanted to believe he was a good man, a kind man.

Sure, he'd made mistakes, but he loved her. And she couldn't live with herself if she doubted him unless there was irrefutable proof.

Sighing, she turned off the water and dried her hair with a towel, quickly throwing her hair into a clip. She didn't bother with makeup as she pulled on a sweat suit and walked to her closet to start gathering clothes to take to Jax's.

A knock at the front door piqued her curiosity, but she was too exhausted to entertain company. So, she turned to her dresser and grabbed a few pairs of underwear and socks, knowing Jax would play interference for her.

"Ali, you have a visitor," Jax yelled to her.

Furrowing her brows, she walked to the banister and saw Dianne standing just outside the door Jax held open, a cold breeze dancing through the house. Ali immediately panicked. Her aunt wouldn't have shown up at Ali's doorstep unless something had happened to Thresa or Levi.

Rushing down the steps, Ali asked, "Is everything okay, Dianne?"

"Oh, yes. Everything is fine." The woman clutched a book to her chest. "I uhm...I needed to show you something important."

Anxiety rushed over Ali. Dianne had never talked to her while Ali was growing up, let alone ever shared an important or heartfelt conversation with her. She worried the woman came bearing bad news, despite her protests against the assumption.

Nervous, Ali said, "Oh, well, come in." Jax eyed her, but she ignored his stare. She understood he didn't approve of her family, something she didn't hold against him. But that didn't mean she wouldn't be kind to them. Smiling, she said, "Let me get you some coffee."

Stepping inside, her aunt shook her head. "That's not necessary. I can't stay long."

Ali nodded, and the three of them stood in awkward silence until Ali finally said, "Let's sit in the living room."

She led Dianne to the couch while Jax waited in the kitchen, giving them privacy. Dianne sat on the far end of the sofa and looked around awkwardly as Ali moved her bracelet up and down her arm.

"Your home is really nice, Ali."

Ali tucked her hair behind her ear. "Oh, thank you."

Bellatrix came out of hiding and meowed at Dianne's feet. Dianne's eyes rounded and she smiled brightly. "You have a cat?" She reached down and patted the feline's head. "I love cats. I had a tabby before...Well, before I met Rick."

Ali nodded but didn't know what to say.

Dianne shifted uncomfortably. "I know I've not treated you kindly, but you've always been a reminder that my daughter is gone. At first, I thought the anger and grief would go away, but it never did. And after years had passed, I knew I couldn't fix our relationship, so I let it be."

"I wish you all would have told me the truth instead of erasing her from my memory." She looked to the ground, feeling like she was walking on eggshells.

Dianne sighed. "There's so much you don't understand. And I suppose it doesn't matter now. I paid the price for my sins, and it cost Missi her life."

Ali scrunched her brows. She didn't believe that's how the universe worked. Sometimes things just happened.

"Anyway, I brought you this." Dianne revealed the book she'd been holding since she got to Ali's house.

"A photobook?"

Dianne nodded. "When Missi disappeared, Rick and Gramps destroyed all of her photos. But I needed something to keep her memory alive, so I've kept these hidden all this time. They're all I have left of her." She clutched the book to her chest. "I honestly haven't looked at them since we lost her. Her face is starting to fade from my memory, and part of me wonders if I should let it. If that should be my punishment for not being a better mother."

A single tear slid down her cheek and stained her jeans as she handed Ali the book.

"Would you like to look at them with me?"

Dianne shook her head and wiped her face. "No, I need to leave before anyone notices I'm gone. Just... Please don't tell anyone I gave this to you. No one can know."

Ali nodded and walked Dianne to the door.

Before leaving, her aunt said, "You can't forget her again, Alabama. We've spent nearly thirty years trying to erase her, and I can't go to my grave knowing her memory would be buried alongside me. I need to make sure you'll always remember her."

Ali tilted her head and took her aunt's hand. "Of course I will."

Dianne smiled, and Jax emerged from the kitchen. "Mrs. Knox, before you go I need to ask you a few follow-up questions. We have some new information regarding your daughter's case."

Ali put her hand on his arm and quietly said, "Jax, not right now. Please." She was emotionally spent, and now wasn't the time for her aunt to be interrogated about her affair. Though Ali wanted Jax to get answers, she feared she would completely break if she found out the truth right now.

Jax put his hand over Ali's and looked at Dianne. "We can do it another day."

Her aunt nodded and disappeared out the door.

Jax sighed. "I'm sorry, I didn't mean to overstep. It's the cop in me."

Bellatrix slinked in and out of Ali's legs, and she scooped up her pet, stroking her fur as the feline purred. "It's okay, I know you mean well. I just can't handle that right now."

Going back to the living room, Ali sat back down. She studied the book that lay on top of the fabric, unsure if she wanted to open it. She didn't want to admit it, but she was terrified of the memories that might come flooding back.

Then she looked at the bracelet that hugged her wrist. She remembered opening it on Christmas morning the year before Missi had disappeared. They were both so excited to have matching bracelets. Her mother and Dianne had a set too, though Ali now assumed those had disappeared when the affair came to light.

Jax eyed the album in her lap. "Want me to give you some privacy?"

"No, I need you. I don't think I can do this alone." Taking a deep breath, Ali opened the book.

The first few pages were photos of Missi as a baby and a toddler. Others were of her and Cam. And of course, many were of Missi and Ali together.

There were photos of birthdays, of them playing hopscotch, and of them dancing in the rain. Missi's blue eyes twinkled with innocence in every one, not knowing in a few short years her smile would fade from the earth.

Ali traced the young girl's face. She couldn't fathom how Missi was stuck as that six-year-old girl and Ali had somehow made it to thirty-two. They had made so many plans together, their entire lives ahead of them. They were supposed to gossip about school friends and boys, sneak out to parties, and be there for each other's first breakups. They had promised to be each other's maids of honor, raise their children together, and grow old and wrinkly in a nursing home together.

They had made plans, and those plans had vanished in an instant.

She wiped at the tears that streamed down her cheeks. Life was heartbreaking. How could this little girl, so full of life, be taken away? What kind of a monster would do that? Who would take a six-year-old from her family who loved her?

Nearing the end of the book, there was one photo that caused her heart to race, though she didn't know why. But as she studied the memory, her lungs tightened as panic filled her.

Missi and Ali were sitting around the coffee table in Gin and Gramp's living room. The two of them smiled brightly as they held up their sandwiches to the camera, peanut butter and jelly smeared across their faces.

Come to think of it, the coffee table was gone. She couldn't even recall the last time she'd seen it in the living room.

Coming to the last page, Ali carefully took in each photo, not wanting it to end. Part of her feared that if she stopped, the photos would disappear like Missi had, no trace left.

Then her eyes gazed over the last photo. She and Missi had climbed into the old sycamore tree at the park, a grey truck parked in the background. And all of a sudden, her memories from that day hit her like a ton of bricks.

She remembered going to the park and playing with Missi. She remembered Cam and Levi picking on them and then disappearing behind the bathroom. She thought the smell was gross, like a skunk.

She even remembered fighting with Missi about...Something... *Gosh, why couldn't she remember*? It felt important. But they had only been six years old. What could they have possibly been fighting about that would be so important?

She remembered pumping her feet, trying to reach the clouds. And that's when she had noticed the grey truck idling by as a man stepped out, putting Missi in the back seat.

Except, Missi wasn't kicking and screaming and trying to get away. She had been excited to go with the man. She had even called for Ali to go, but Ali wanted to stay and swing.

The man had gotten out of his truck and called for her, "Ali! Let's go!"

But Ali had refused.

Clutching Jax's hand, she closed her eyes. That's when Ali realized the man in the grey truck was her father.

CHAPTER 29

Trinity Harbor spotted Jules sitting next to a beautiful redhead. She suspected it was the notorious Ali whom Jax couldn't stop talking about. Jules waved when she spotted Trinity and quickly stood to embrace her. "How was the drive over?"

"Awful. Thiago snored the whole time." She eyed her partner who stood next to her. He towered over Trinity, but she was used to his muscular frame and larger-than-life presence constantly looming over her.

She and Thiago had been partners for nearly two years, and she trusted him with her life. He was a good partner and balanced her well, despite getting on her last nerve ninety-percent of the time. The man was loud and opinionated, something he claimed was due to his Hispanic upbringing. Trinity, however, just thought it was an excuse to be an ass sometimes.

"Maybe if you napped more, you wouldn't be so cranky," he quipped.

She glared at him as he smirked, a dimple appearing on his left cheek.

Jules extended her hand to the agent. "Detective Juliette Reid. Everyone calls me Jules, though."

"Nice to meet you. Thiago Silva, her babysitter." He pointed at Trinity, and she made a face at him as he rubbed his goatee in an attempt to disarm her.

"Please. If anything, *I'm* the one making sure *you* don't eat crayons at your desk."

Jax's voice boomed as he yelled to Trinity from across the room, making his way to the group. "Well, if you weren't such a brat, you wouldn't need someone to keep tabs on you all the time."

She rolled her eyes as he pulled her in for a hug, her long black hair falling into her face. She clung to him longer than she normally would have, but she admittedly missed him. Though she'd never say it out loud.

The two had been close growing up, but when she had left for the FBI, they hadn't kept in touch as much as she wanted; despite living only five hours away in Miami.

Jax released her and gestured toward the red-head. "This is Ali. Ali, this is Trinity."

Trinity said, "So you're the one who finally has this guy in a death grip. Gotta say, I wasn't sure I'd ever see that happen."

Ali laughed. "Something like that, I suppose."

Trinity smiled, but the laughter was quickly replaced with the lingering tension from their new reality. She looked at Jax. "I hear you had a situation this morning?"

He nodded. "Ali was threatened, and there were forget me not flowers left in the envelope. We're pretty sure it was her father who left them."

Trinity arched a brow. Initially, she hadn't suspected a connection between Missi and the Scarlet Letter Killer. Now, she wasn't so sure. It was one thing to have a twenty-six-year-old Jane Doe with a forget me not at her dump site. It was another to have that same flower reappear during the monster's reign of terror and given to Jane Doe's half-sister.

Although, she was a bit curious as to why he would threaten Ali and not simply kill her, especially if he felt Ali might expose him. But then, she was working with very few details about the cases. Trinity was anxious to read the files Jax and Jules had on each victim and the little information they had on SLK.

Trinity winked at Ali. "Well, the good news is I'm very good at my job." Then, she looked at Jax. "How does it feel to have me clean up your messes every time?"

"Gosh, you do need to nap more," Jax said as he rubbed his face.

"I told you," Thiago said.

Though Trinity was known for her sass and quick wit, often offending those who didn't know her well, it was simply her way of dealing with the stress and concern that came with her job. She'd never admit it, but she was worried for her friend. It was clear this case was weighing heavily on him, and this killer had done enough damage.

Sighing, Jax nodded toward the hallway. "Let's talk in the conference room."

Trinity saw him look apologetically at Ali who smiled and said, "I'm going to make a cup of coffee and read in the break room."

Jax wrapped his arms around Ali's waist, and pulled her close as she gently laid a hand on his chest. He said, "Make yourself at home. I'll find you when we're done. Just don't leave, please."

He kissed her forehead and she disappeared down the hallway. Then, he led the group to the conference room. Jules and Thiago took a seat at the table while Jax hung back and gently grabbed Trinity by the upper arm.

Trinity stopped and looked at him, lifting a brow. "What?"

"Thanks for coming. I don't know how I'm going to keep her safe. Her father is like a damn ghost."

She shook her head. "Quit thinking with your damn manhood and start thinking like a cop, Jax."

"That's a low blow," he said and hung his head.

"It's true and you know it." She got closer to his face, softening her tone just slightly. "You're going to get her killed if you don't figure this shit out. You know I love you, but I'm also not going to let you act like a cowboy and get people hurt because your focus is on *her* and not the facts of the case."

He opened his mouth to respond, but she didn't let him. "You're scared; I get it. This case is weighing on you, and I can see it's even weighing on Juliette. But, T and I are here to help. Now, let's go catch this son of a bitch."

Trinity turned and walked into the conference room. She immediately eyed the board full of death staring back at them, something she'd grown accustomed to since working in law enforcement. There were boxes piled in a corner marked from a decade ago, and folders from current cases were scattered on the table.

They each sat down, Jax taking a seat at the head.

He looked at Trinity. "Have you seen your parents yet?"

"We stayed there last night."

Thiago's eyes widened. "Chief Harbor nearly shot me."

Trinity shrugged. "I've never brought home a man, so I think it freaked him out a little. And I didn't tell them we were coming, either."

Jax laughed, and Jules said, "What did your mother say?"

Trinity chuckled. "She tried to bake us a pie at one in the morning but burnt it. She keeps saying I don't visit enough and dad tells her to stop pestering me."

"She's right, you don't," Jax said.

She shot him a look. "I don't have much of a reason to, Jax. Miami is fine. And I'm gone on cases all the time anyway."

Jules said, "How's your Aunt Sara? The Rise Again Project seems to be going well. I heard she opened her third transitional home in north Florida."

After being released from prison and working to prove her innocence in her own mother's murder, Trinity's aunt had focused on helping other women who had been released and wanted to change their lives around. She helped them get jobs, go back to school, reconnect with their children. She'd give them any resources they needed to be successful. Sara was determined to show these women they could have a good life, that they didn't have to keep repeating the cycle.

Trinity nodded. "The homes are thriving, which is a relief. I think the project gives her a sense of purpose." She smiled at Jules. "Gavin says your brother is doing a great job running the firm, by the way."

Gavin was the head of a private security firm, but since Sara's RA Project was growing, he had recently taken a step back to help her. The two had been together for nearly fourteen years, but they hadn't tied the knot yet. Sara was hesitant to get married, despite wanting to spend the rest of her life with Gavin. But Trinity knew it was merely fear of commitment and abandonment that kept her aunt from saying 'I do.'

Trinity sighed. "Enough about my family, I want to see what you've got on this guy. I read up on the case last night, but I need to see more before I can start a profile."

Jax took a deep breath and gave her a brief summary of what they'd pieced together about SLK and his kills. They brought Trinity and Thiago up to speed on the affair, the day Missi had been taken, and how Jared had disappeared afterward. "At first, we weren't sure if Missi was connected to SLK, but now she obviously is. And with Jared threatening Ali, it makes that hunch even stronger. Plus, I think the victims might be a surrogate for Dianne. I mean, his whole life fell apart after the affair came to light."

Thiago thought for a moment. "I can get behind that theory. Do they look like Dianne?"

Jules nodded. "Yes, they all look like her. And actually, we had a lady come in claiming SLK kidnapped her forty years ago, but it didn't match his signature at all. And the timeline doesn't make sense, either. But she looks just like Dianne, too."

Thiago rubbed his goatee. "I think we should look at Missi's case again. We might be able to connect evidence to Jared now that we know what we're looking for."

"Did you record the interview with the victim that came forward?" Trinity asked. "I'm curious about what she had to say and why she thought there was a connection to SLK."

Jax walked to the case boxes and grabbed Missi's file for Thiago, then brought over the recorder for Trinity. Just as she took it from him, his phone rang. He pulled it out of his pocket and furrowed his brows, then looked at Trinity. "It's your dad." He put the phone to his ear. "Sergeant Moretti."

A pause as her father talked to him. Then Jax rubbed his face and sat back in his chair. "Okay, we'll be there soon."

She could hear her father's tone on the other line but couldn't make out his words. Then Jax looked at her. "Yes, she's coming with me."

Another pause.

"Yes, sir. See you soon."

He pushed the phone back into his pocket. "We've got another body. She was left in front of the clock tower in Auburndale."

Jules shook her head. "Another one? Are they sure it's an SLK vic? He's never killed more than once a year."

"Chief Harbor thinks so, and that's good enough for me."

Jules tilted her head. "But why would he kill again?" She looked at Trinity and Thiago. "Serial killers don't deviate from their MO, right?"

"Not usually," Trinity said. "But he's not changing his MO. He's likely escalating."

Thiago nodded. "Which means we're close to catching him and he knows it."

Jules closed her eyes. "If he's escalating, more women are going to lose their lives."

"Maybe," Thiago said. "But it also means he's more likely to slip up and get caught."

"Then let's make his worst nightmare come true," Jax said.

They all stood and headed out, but not before Jax beelined for the break room and found Ali curled up on one of the couches, lost in a book. Trinity was intrigued to see he had stopped to tell the woman he was leaving. She didn't think he'd ever be so noble.

He leaned against the door jamb and cleared his throat, but Ali didn't take her eyes off the pages, immersed in whatever world she was reading about. He chuckled. "Ali."

Startled, she looked up. "What? Oh, sorry." She giggled, red painting her cheeks.

He couldn't help but smile at her. "Don't apologize. If reading books helps you escape reality right now, I'll gladly buy you hundreds more."

Trinity nearly gagged but kept quiet.

Jax walked over to Ali. "We have to go look at a crime scene. I'm not sure how long I'll be, so stay here until I get back. If you need to leave, call me before you do so I can make arrangements."

Her smile faded. "Another woman?"

Jax sighed and nodded. "Unfortunately."

Trinity knew Ali was scared, despite her best attempts to hide the fear. But honestly, if she were Ali, she'd be afraid, too. This man was sick and twisted, not something to take lightly or underestimate. And the fact that Ali shared the same bloodline with him... Well, Trinity didn't even want to think about how she'd feel if she were in Ali's shoes.

Ali set the book on the couch and stood up, kissing Jax. "Please be careful."

He put his forehead on hers. "I will, I promise. We're just going to a crime scene, so it should be pretty routine; nothing to worry about."

Jax walked out the door and Trinity turned to follow when Ali said, "Agent Harbor."

Trinity turned back around.

"Be careful. I know you mean a lot to him. And please, make sure Jax comes home in one piece."

Home.

That single word was quiet, instinctive. But it echoed louder than Ali had realized and Trinity understood the weight of it. She nodded. "I will."

She was glad someone cared about Jax so much. He didn't let people get that close to him. And while he and Ali may not be in love yet, they weren't far from falling right into it.

Quickening her pace, she caught up with the rest of the team, and they drove the twenty minutes to downtown Auburndale.

Climbing out of the car, she glanced around the quaint area. Not much had changed since she was a teenager, except there seemed to be a few new businesses open. On a normal day, the park across the street would be bustling with families, but with the stench of death in the air, Trinity knew mothers and fathers had hidden their kids away in the safety of their homes, afraid they would be another victim.

As they walked to the clock tower, yellow tape billowed in the chilled breeze as techs moved effortlessly and collected evidence.

Trinity hugged her father who stood outside the crime scene. "Hi, Dad."

"Hey kid," he said.

Chief Trey Harbor extended his hand to Jax. "The grapevine said you caught the guy."

Jax shook Trey's hand. "No, sir. The man we arrested is definitely a piece of shit, but he's not the Scarlet Letter Killer."

Trey nodded and then looked at Trinity. "Your mother wants you home for dinner tonight."

"Of course she does," Trinity said, rolling her eyes.

"She just misses you. You really don't keep in touch. *I* get it, but she doesn't. It's hard for her."

Trinity loved her mother; she just hated coming back to Auburndale. Growing up, she and Hailey Harbor had been close. And though Trinity still felt that way, she wanted her freedom and sometimes her mother didn't understand that.

Ever since Trinity had almost died when she was thirteen, her mother made it her life's mission to make sure her daughter was never in any danger. So, when Trinity announced she'd be joining the FBI, Hailey had nearly passed out.

Thankfully, Trinity's father and Aunt Sara had talked her down. She didn't understand why Trinity would want to run directly into danger. But, given their history together, Trinity felt her mother should.

Trinity needed to put bad guys away and make the world safe. She needed to prove she could withstand the monsters of the world. And she had. Trinity could take care of herself, and she wore the emotional scars to prove it (and some physical ones too).

Jules nodded toward the body that lay a few feet away from them. "What did they find?"

Trey sighed. "We think she's a missing woman by the name of Lacey Pits. Same M.O. as SLK. Flower was found in her mouth, and the 'A' on her chest was in the early stages of scabbing when she died. She looks to be pretty badly beaten, too."

"Was she married?" Jules asked.

Trey looked at her quizzically. "No. She had just broken up with her boyfriend a few months ago. She's only been missing for four days."

Jax shook his head. "He's never killed more than one woman in a year, and he usually keeps them for a week to torture them." He indicated to the bruising that darkened most of the victim's body. "And he's only *this* brutal with married women."

Trinity said, "This proves he's escalating. Something set him off."

Thiago added, "The news report of someone being apprehended probably made him angry. If our profile is correct, he won't want anyone taking credit for his crimes." He crossed his arms. "He's becoming less controlled and way more dangerous."

"Fuck." Jax said. Sighing, he looked at Trey, "Chief, will you have your people send us updates once they know anything?"

"You'll have it ASAP." Trey turned his attention to Trinity. "And Trinity Rae."

She glanced at him and raised a brow, knowing what he was about to say. "Yes, Dad?" she said, her voice soaked in sarcasm.

He pointed to her. "You and your friends are coming for dinner. And I'm not asking."

"Fine," she said as she threw her head back. He chuckled. "I see your attitude is still intact."

"I got it from my momma."

"That you do," he said as he kissed her forehead.

CHAPTER 30

Ali clutched her stomach and wiped at tears, laughter filling the dining room as Hailey and Trey finished telling an embarrassing story about Trinity. It had been a wonderful evening getting to know more about Jax and the people closest to him. And she was glad Cam had tagged along with Juliette. They hadn't spent time together in decades. And as she looked around the room, she couldn't help but feel happy.

"So, Ali," Hailey said. "Did Jax tell you he was the ring bearer in mine and Trey's wedding?"

Ali smiled. "No, he didn't."

"Lucky for you, I have pictures."

Jax groaned and rubbed a hand over his face. "Awe, Mrs. H, don't do that."

Trinity pointed at him. "If I have to be humiliated, so do you."

Hailey excused herself from the table and retrieved a black photo album. She flipped through the pages and stopped, handing the book to Ali. Ali studied the picture of Jax standing in between Trinity and a teenage girl Ali didn't recognize. He donned a suit, but his sneakers were what caught Ali's eye. They were bright pink, and Ali let a giggle escape her lips. "I love the shoes."

He grinned as he looked at the photo. "It was a phase."

"Yeah, a long phase," Trey teased. "You and Cecilia bought matching shoes after this and wore them with everything."

Hailey let out a laugh. "Oh, I forgot about the matching shoes!"

Jax eyed Trinity. "We tried to convince you to do it, but you said you'd rather play in traffic."

Ali lifted the photo to show Jules and Cam who sat to her left.

Jules said, "I can't believe you let him wear those, Mrs. H."

"Well, I lost a bet, so I didn't have much say in the matter."

Cam said, "Oh, I'd love to hear that story."

"I bet Jax couldn't out-shoot Trey in a basketball game." Hailey eyed her husband. "I was helplessly in love and thought Trey could do absolutely anything."

Trey wrapped his arms around Hailey's waist. "*Was* hopelessly in love? *Thought* I could do absolutely anything?"

She wrapped her arms around his neck and kissed him. "I was telling a story. Obviously, I *still* think those things about you."

Juliette clasped her hands and sunk into her chair with a sigh. "Ugh. I just love how much you two still love each other." Cam chuckled and pulled Juliette close to him, kissing her hair.

Trinity on the other hand, shoved her finger in her mouth and made a gagging noise. "Get a room!"

Thiago laughed. "I don't think you should tell them that. They definitely will."

She swatted at his arm. "You're fucking nasty."

"Trinity Rae!" Hailey said sharply.

Ali chuckled and pointed to the other girl in the photo. "Is that Cecilia?"

Trinity said, "Yeah, my mom and I had to come to town for Jax's aunt's wedding-"

Hailey cut her off. "His Aunt Angie is my best friend."

Trinity rolled her eyes. "Mom, don't interrupt me." Hailey simply kissed Trinity on the forehead and sat on Trey's lap across the table.

Trinity continued, "*Anyway*, we were here for the wedding but ended up staying a lot longer- that's a story for another day- but I made fast friends with Cecilia and met Jax shortly after."

Jax grinned. "The three musketeers."

"Well, maybe you can take her back then." Thiago said as he thumbed at Trinity. "She's a pain-in-the-ass."

"Ain't that right!" Trey said. Hailey playfully smacked Trey in the stomach and he let out a huff. Laughing, he said, "But we still love her."

Trinity simply shook her head and shot everyone a look.

Ali was captivated by the Harbor family. It was clear they were close, despite everyone claiming Trinity didn't visit enough. And though Trinity wanted everyone to believe she didn't care about her parents' opinion on the matter, Ali saw through that facade rather quickly. It wasn't difficult to see the adoration in Trinity's eyes when she looked at Hailey and Trey.

A knock at the door had everyone turning toward the front of the house.

Hailey furrowed her brows and said to Trey, "Are you expecting company?"

"No," he replied, shaking his head.

Hailey shrugged. "It's probably Sara. You know she doesn't always call before she stops by."

"I'll get it," Trinity said. She walked to the front of the house and opened the door, revealing a young man with a clipboard. He couldn't have been older than nineteen years old, acne still covering his face in places.

"We don't want anything," Trinity said sternly.

She almost slammed the door, but he stopped her. "I have a delivery. I just need a signature."

Sighing, she signed the document, and he leaned down to pick up a bouquet of flowers that he'd placed by the front door. "This is for an..." He glanced at the name on the order. "Alabama Knox."

Ali's stomach knotted. Even from where she was sitting, she couldn't mistake the blue hue of the flowers.

He held out the bouquet of daisies, white tulips, baby's breath, and forget me not flowers. But instead of taking the vase from him, Trinity lifted her gun from the holster. "Put the flowers down and slowly put your hands up."

Instinctively, Trey, Jax, Thiago. and Juliette mirrored Trinity, each pulling out their firearm and acknowledging the potential threat. Shaking, the kid looked like he might pee his pants, but he did as he was told.

Ali could hardly breathe, tension suffocating the room.

"What's your name?" Trinity demanded.

His voice cracked. "Peter Cole."

"Who gave you those flowers?"

He pointed to his badge. "I work at a flower shop. It was an expedited order."

"It said to deliver here?"

"Yes ma'am," he said, quickly nodding his head.

Ali held her breath as Hailey crossed her arms, worry etched on her face. Cam must have noticed how tense Ali was, because he gently took her hand, slowing her heartbeat.

Realizing he wasn't a threat, Trinity put her gun away, as did everyone else. Then, in a chaotic blur, they all sprang into action. Trinity ushered the kid inside, commanding him to sit on the couch and not move a muscle. Trey questioned him while Jax and Thiago each called their bosses to update them. Cam offered to help Hailey make some cookies in the kitchen in hopes to calm everyone's nerves while Juliette kept watch over the flowers that were now sitting on the coffee table in the middle of the living room.

Ali stood in the corner, silently watching everyone as she twirled her bracelet around her wrist. Everyone seemed to be moving a mile a minute, the rhythmic sounds of their steps and voices muffled. She couldn't focus. She could only worry that she'd just put everyone's lives in danger.

"Y'all need to get in here," Juliette yelled, worry laced in her words.

Everyone came back into the living room, curious about what she'd found.

"There's a note attached to the vase," she said, pointing to the bouquet.

"How did we miss that?" Thiago asked.

Trey shook his head. "We were more concerned about the kid."

Juliette read the note, *"Even death can't keep me away from you."*

Cam's face paled. "Oh my god..."

He casted a worried glance at Ali, and she burst into tears. "I'm so sorry. I put you all in danger. I- I didn't think he would..."

Startled by her reaction, Jax shoved his phone into his pocket and wrapped her in a hug. "Ali, this isn't your fault."

She pulled away and rushed to one of the bedrooms and locked herself inside. Her lungs were on fire and she desperately tried to gasp for air as tears streamed down her face. She never should have put the bellflowers out for him. She never should have tried to contact him.

She should have left him in the shadows, where he'd been the last twenty-six years of her life.

But she hadn't. And now he was threatening the people she cared about.

Jax gently knocked. "Ali, can you open the door?"

Ignoring him, she dropped to the carpet and silently cried into her hands.

Grief tore through her as reality set in. Her father was a monster, and she'd kept him hidden. She had aided in his torture and murderous acts. Those women were dead because of her.

She let herself shatter like fragile glass, the shards of her heartache piercing her soul. Ali hoped she'd be able to put them back together after this was all over.

That is, if her father didn't kill her before she got the chance.

After a few minutes, she sucked in a breath and wiped at her face. For now, she had cried as much as her soul would let her. So, she walked to the door and opened it, Jax waiting patiently on the other side.

He walked through the doorway as she turned back around and sat on the bed. He stopped in front of her, tilting her chin with his index finger. He searched her eyes. "I'm sorry your whole world is crashing down around you, that everything you've known to be true is a lie. And I'm sorry about your father."

Wiping at the mascara now staining her cheeks, she said, "He's threatening me because I started poking around trying to find him. What if he tries to hurt one of you because of me?" She stood, her voice rose an octave and tears stung her eyes again. "*What if he kills you, Jax?*"

Trinity leaned against the door jamb. "You didn't start this. This is *not* your fault. He started this by killing all those women."

Ali shook her head. "But-"

"But nothing." Jax said. He put his forehead to hers. "And I can take care of myself. I'm a hero, remember?"

Ali let out a breath and sat back down on the bed. "I just hate that he's been using a forget me not as his signature. When I was little, he'd give it to me as a reminder that he would always love me. And now he uses them to degrade the women he tortures and kills. It's disgusting."

"When you were little?" Jules asked, pushing her way into the room.

Ali nodded. "Before my father left, he used to bring me and my mother flowers every week."

"He brought them to Missi and my mother, too." Ali looked up to see Cam standing behind Trinity.

She furrowed her brows. "What are you talking about?"

Cam sighed and walked into the room, standing over Ali as she looked up at him. "That's what caused their fight. You saw the flowers in Missi's room, and you told your mother. Theresa got suspicious so she started snooping and found a stash in *my* mother's drawer." He shook his head. "Why didn't you tell me you were getting the flowers after Jared left?"

She glared at him, betrayal flaming through her veins. "You shut me out, remember? You didn't want anything to do with me or our family, so I had no reason to come to you about it. Plus, *he* told me not to tell anyone."

Cam hung his head, but before he could respond, Trinity pointed at him. "So, you knew there was a connection between the flower and your family, and you didn't think to bring that information to Jax and Juliette? You're the damn prosecutor on the case, aren't you!?"

He put his hands up. "Until Missi's case was reopened, why would I have even thought there was a connection to my family? You act like no one else could have access to or a connection with that damn forget me not flower." He lifted his arm. "And even after Missi's case was reopened, there was nothing tying Missi to SLK other than the flower. And we *all* know that could have easily been a coincidence."

Jax nodded to Trinity. "He's right. You said so yourself when I called you."

Trinity sighed and looked at Cam. "If there are anymore secrets, now is a great time come clean so we can figure out what the fuck is going on with these two cases." Jax shot her a look, and she rolled her eyes. Then, she crossed her arms and sarcastically said, "Please."

Juliette took Cam's hand. "Baby, please. If you know something, you need to tell us."

But instead of Cam, it was Ali who spoke quietly. "He killed Missi."

Jax furrowed his brows. "What?"

"If you know something about what happened, please tell us," Trinity said. Ali was surprised the woman was so calm with her. But she suspected Trinity was far more kind than she let on. And Ali was thankful for it.

Ali sucked in a deep breath. "When I was looking at the scrapbook this morning, I saw a photo that triggered some memories." She shook her head. "My father was the man in the grey truck. He had called for me to come with them, but I didn't want to stop swinging. So he left with Missi."

Jax closed his eyes and shook his head. "Ali, why did you keep this to yourself? You should have told me."

She threw her arm up, startling him. "I'm scared, Jax! My father has been out there slaughtering women. He probably killed Missi, and he's been leaving me his signature flowers since I was a little girl." She looked to the floor. "What if he kills me because I told his secret? I was never supposed to tell anyone about the flowers or try to find him. And now look at what's happened." She pointed in the direction of the front door. "He's clearly leaving me a message."

Cam stood and crossed his arms. "He's not going to try to kill you. And Jared isn't the Scarlet Letter Killer."

Jax said, "What makes you so sure? The evidence is beginning to point directly to Jared."

Cam clenched his jaw and let out a breath. "Because he's dead. I watched Levi kill him."

CHAPTER 31

Ali took a step back, shaking her head vehemently. "No, that's not true. Levi would never do that. And my father loves me. He's been leaving me flowers..." Tears welled in her eyes. How could Cam be so cruel? First, he lied about Missi and now about her father and Levi?

"Ali," he said softly, "the day Missi died, all hell broke loose. Jared was trying to run away with both of you and my mother. He went back to the house to wait for you. When we got back from the park, my father was fighting with Jared." Cam shook his head. "Jared said Missi wouldn't even be here if it wasn't for him and my mother having an affair and Rick should be grateful. They shared blows back and forth, everyone was yelling. None of us realized how angry Levi was about the whole thing."

He paused for a moment, taking in a breath as he recounted what had happened that day. "I mean, he was only fifteen at the time. I remember watching him hold Theresa while she sobbed, and then," he gestured to Ali, "you were screaming bloody murder because you were terrified and he just snapped. He got a knife from the kitchen and stabbed Jared. There was blood everywhere. You were hysterical, clawing at him, and the whole house was in an uproar. At some point, you ran upstairs and hid." Ali remembered the blood. It had covered her hands. But the memory was vague and disappeared before she could grasp it.

He looked at everyone. "We didn't call the police because we didn't want Levi to go to jail."

"Why didn't you say anything when we reopened Missi's case?" Juliette said.

"And ruin my life for what Levi did? For the last twenty-six years, I've kept his secret. I'm not going to jail for accessory after the fact and any other charges that would have possibly been thrown my way. Especially not over someone like Jared! He didn't even have a family. He was a loner."

"What about me?! He had me!" Ali yelled as sobs shook her body once again. Jax brought her close to his chest as he stroked her hair.

As much as she hated her father for what he'd done to her mother, she was still that little girl he had left behind. She didn't want to think of him as dying in such a brutal way or that it was at the hands of her brother. She just wanted her daddy back. And she wasn't sure how to make sense of her conflicting emotions that were battling for center stage in her heart.

Trinity asked, "What about Missi? If Levi killed Jared, how did her body end up in Mulberry? And if Jared is dead, he isn't the one leaving Ali flowers. So, who is? And how does it all connect with SLK?"

Jax furrowed his brows and tilted his head. "Oh my god, it's Levi." He glared at his friend. "You've known this whole time he's the Scarlet Letter Killer."

Juliette clenched her jaw and crossed her arms, seething at the revelation.

Cam looked at the floor, ashamed of his secrecy. After a moment, he nodded. "I didn't get suspicious until Missi's case was reopened. When I heard she had the flower..." He shook his head and rubbed the back of his neck. "With all the commotion, we hadn't realized she'd disappeared. And when we had found her, we realized Levi had killed her, too." He brought his hands to his face as tears streamed down his cheeks. "We had all lost enough that night, so our parents decided to cover it up. They dumped Jared's body, then took Missi to the woods. Levi must have gone back and left a flower with her body."

Ali lunged at Cam, but Jax held her back. She yelled, "You're lying! That's my brother! He would never do that!" She hated Cam for claiming her brother was a monster. Levi had loved her. He'd protected her. He'd doted on her and taught her all the things her father never had.

But deep down she knew.

At the barn, she'd seen a side to him he had never shown her before. A side he had reserved for the women he tortured and killed. He was the monster hiding in plain sight. The devil with blue eyes who charmed his way into stealing the last breath of twelve women.

Cam drew her into a hug, but she pushed him away. "Get away from me! You've been lying to me my entire life. I hate you!"

Jax held her again as she continued to cry. She hated how much she was crying, but she could no longer control it. Just when she thought everything couldn't get any worse, another secret was revealed, and it broke her even more.

"I'm sorry, Ali." Cam said, desperation filling his voice. "We wanted to protect you. That lie is the reason I stopped talking to the family. I couldn't deal with any of it anymore, so I left."

No one said anything for a moment, the air painfully thin. Finally, Jules quietly said, "You knew Levi was the Scarlet Letter Killer and didn't say anything."

He put his hands up. "Juliette, you have to understand. I wanted to be sure before I said anything. I haven't spoken to Levi in almost twenty years. I don't know him anymore; he may be a completely different person than when we were kids."

Juliette wiped at her own tears. He went to her, and she put up her hand. "No. I can't do this right now. You've been lying to me, and you knew how much that would hurt me."

"Jules, I-"

"I'm sorry. I need to leave." Juliette ran out of the room, the thud of the front door echoing through the house.

"Where is Levi now?" Trinity demanded.

Cam shook his head. "I don't know. We haven't talked since the day I left the compound."

Ali quietly spoke up, "He's supposed to eat dinner with my mother tonight."

"I'm sorry, Ali. We need to bring him in. " Trinity said to Ali.

Her eyes widened. "Please, don't. Please..."

Jax stroked her hair, in an attempt to calm her. "Sunshine, you know we have to."

After a moment, she nodded into his chest as Cam said, "Ali, please try to understand-"

Jax glared at him. "Leave, Cam. You've done enough damage."

Cam clenched his jaw, and Ali felt Jax tense. She worried Cam may throw a punch, and if he did, she had no doubt Jax would lay him out on the floor.

But, he simply walked out of the house, silence filling the space. Trinity turned and went back to the living room, giving Ali and Jax some privacy.

She looked up at Jax. "Can we go home?" Her voice broke. "Please?"

He nodded to her. "Anything for you."

The two walked out to find Trinity, Thiago, and Trey sitting on the couch. "How much of that did you hear?" Jax asked Trey.

"Enough." Trey said. "Looks like this case is getting really messy."

Hailey brought out a plate of cookies and set them on the coffee table. Ali was glad for Hailey's desire to bring them comfort, even if it was through a small snack. Ali sat down next to Trinity, taking a cookie and eating it.

Ali watched Jax exchange a look with Hailey, silently thanking her. The woman nodded subtly and smiled.

Jax looked back at Ali and said, "I need to make a phone call to the D.A. and update them so we can get a warrant. I'll be right back. " He disappeared into the kitchen for a few minutes before reappearing. Shoving his phone into his pocket, he looked at Trinity. "I'm going to call in backup, but can you and Thiago go with my guys and arrest Levi?"

Thiago raised a brow. "You don't want to do the honors?"

He shook his head and glanced at Ali. "I'm not leaving her alone. She needs me."

"Jax, I'll be okay." Ali said. She didn't want to be the woman who was so broken he had to keep an eye on her.

Jax shook his head. "You're more important than making an arrest. My team is more than capable of doing it."

Trinity nodded to Thiago. "We've got it." Then, she looked at her parents. "I guess this means I'm going back to work."

Fear flashed behind Hailey's eyes. But she walked over to Trinity, kissing her crown. "You've got this."

Trinity smiled at her mother. "I'll be careful, I promise."

Thiago stood and shook Trey's hand. "Don't worry, sir. I've got her back."

Trey's grip tightened. "Good. If you don't, I'll kill you."

Though he said it with a smile, Ali knew he wasn't joking. Chief Harbor would definitely hunt down Agent Silva if anything happened to his daughter.

Trey hugged Trinity. "I know I'm just your old man but call if you need backup. I'm not *that* old."

"Dad, you're gonna retire soon." Trinity chuckled, shaking her head.

He flexed his muscles and kissed his biceps. "Hey, I've still got these guns, and they work just fine."

He sent a laugh through the room, something Ali desperately needed. She watched as Trinity kissed her parents' cheeks and disappeared out the door with Thiago. Then, Ali turned toward the couple. "Thank you for opening up your home. I had a wonderful time. I'm just sorry I put you both in danger."

Hailey cupped Ali's face. "None of this is your fault. And believe me, my family knows a thing or two about danger." She winked. "Please call if you need anything, even if it's just to look at embarrassing photos of Jax."

Ali smiled and hugged the woman, thankful for the hospitality. Hailey had Ali missing her own mother. And now that Ali knew the truth, she wasn't sure what that relationship would look like moving forward. Another sting of sorrow reached her heart, knowing her life would never be the same.

Trey stood by the door and shook Jax's hand. "Protect her, Jax."

"With my life, sir."

Ali hugged the man. "Thank you, Chief Harbor."

"Like Hailey said, you're welcome anytime." He thumbed at Jax. "And keep him in line, would ya? Hell, that's exactly what I needed at his age and Hailey made sure of it."

Hailey smiled and melted into Trey's arms as Ali ducked into the night, hoping tomorrow would bring the closure she so desperately needed.

CHAPTER 32

L evi had been surprised to see only his mother at the table. He knew Rick was working the night shift, but Dianne was never late to dinner. So when she came tiptoeing through the door, he was intrigued.

"What were you doing? You're never late." Theresa asked.

Dianne looked at the floor. "I was taking a nap." She sat down and began eating the soup in front of her.

He was suspicious of her actions, never trusting anything that came flowing from the lips of a liar.

The day Missi had died, it had taken all his will power not to toss her in a hole like the others. The only reason he'd played nice with this bitch all these years was because his mother had asked him to. Which was beyond him. How could Theresa still be friends with the woman who slept with the love of her life? Dianne tore their family apart and they were all still picking up the pieces nearly thirty years later.

Damn, he hated her.

Theresa tilted her head and furrowed her brows. "Why would you nap this late in the day?"

"I don't answer to you." Dianne gritted her teeth.

Levi lifted a brow. He had never seen Dianne angry. She was meek and timid. *Weak.*

Theresa sneered as she narrowed her eyes at his aunt. "Now, we both know that's not true." She put her spoon down and kept her voice low. "Now stop lying. We will never make it out alive if we keep secrets from each other." She lifted a brow. "Just like before."

"Fuck you, Theresa." Dianne's words were low, threatening.

Levi nearly laughed.

Theresa gasped. "What is your problem?!"

"You!" Dianne yelled. "Don't act like you have any idea what this family needs. You knew *everything* from the beginning and turned a blind eye. You're just as much of a monster as the rest of us."

Levi was nervous by Dianne's reaction to Theresa. And if she was a loose cannon, that could ruin everything.

He gently said, "Aunt Dianne, you know we have to stick together or everything we've worked for will go up in smoke. And then Missi's death will have been in vain."

She pointed her finger at Levi, and it took all of his control not to break it. She said, "Shut up! Don't say her name! Neither of you ever get to speak her name! We could have gotten out of here, but no." She pointed at Theresa. "You wouldn't leave. Missi is dead because of you, you stupid bitch!"

Theresa stood and pulled at her blouse, the buttons giving way, revealing the perfectly round burns on her chest. She glared at Dianne. "I saved your life, remember? You lived because *I* begged for your life. Because *I* bartered. It was *my* life for yours. So no, I couldn't leave." Theresa sat down, not bothering to cover herself back up.

Dianne started crying, covering her face in her hands.

Levi hated when the woman cried, which she often did. It was a mousy cry that irked him to his core. And hate welled within him at the way she had spoken to his mother.

Theresa had given everything for Dianne, and what did Dianne do? She slept with Jared and blamed the death of her own child on Theresa. If she hadn't been whoring around, none of them would be in this predicament.

But he had to hold his tongue because his mother wouldn't approve of the words he would surely use to tear this woman to shreds.

A line of cars coming up the driveway tore him from his thoughts.

Theresa followed his gaze, her eyes rounding at the realization. She looked back at Dianne. "You called the police?"

The woman put her hands out in front of her. "You know I wouldn't do that!"

Fuck.

They were here for him. That meant Cam had opened his mouth. *Bastard.*

He stood. "They're here for me. I'm going out the back and into the woods. Stall them for as long as you can."

His mother's eyes filled with worry. "Levi?"

He kissed her cheek. "Don't worry. It'll all work out. Just stick to the plan, okay? I know you aren't ready for this, but we knew this day was coming." He eyed Dianne. "We all knew our secrets wouldn't stay buried."

Theresa and Dianne went to the front door while Levi took off in a sprint and disappeared into the cold night.

The pounding on her door pulled Juliette from her movie. With an ice cream carton balanced on her lap, she'd put on a comedy, hoping the laughter might drown out her thoughts of Cam. But his face still seemed to haunt her no matter what she did.

She hadn't been able to stop crying since she'd gotten home from the Harbor's. She felt betrayed by the man who claimed to love her. Because even after knowing how much her past relationship had broken her, Cam had still chosen to deceive her. And, truthfully, Jules was terrified she'd never be able to trust him again. That their relationship was over.

The pounding continued and she quickened her pace. Peering out the peephole, she rolled her eyes and groaned. She set the ice cream down on the entryway table and wiped at her eyes before opening the door.

As the wooden barrier opened, Cam turned to her. "Please, don't shut me out."

She drew in a sharp breath, surprised by his red-rimmed eyes. She hadn't expected to see such rawness from him, causing her heart to break even more. And now she was torn between forgiveness and distance.

Jules hung her head. "Please, leave. I need space to think." She looked at him, a frown tugging at her lips. "You've been lying to me, and you knew how much that would hurt me."

He closed the distance between them. "I know. And I'll spend the rest of my life making it up to you." Cam pulled her close, his lips hovering just above hers.

Jules closed her eyes as he brushed a soft kiss across her skin, and she welcomed his touch. She knew he was telling the truth, and that deepened her ache even more. And she desperately wanted to forgive him, to forget any of it had happened. She loved him so much it hurt, and she wanted their relationship to go back to how it had been before she'd found out he'd been lying.

But they would never be the same again.

Jules gently pulled away, feeling her soul fracture even more. "Please, I need time. And I can't think when you're here because all I want to do is act like it didn't happen. I want you to stay with me; hold me and kiss me and put me back together. But you can't. Because you're the one who broke me this time."

A flicker of anguish crossed his eyes as Cam took a step back. "Juliette, I'm still the same man I was. I would *never* lie to you about anything else. I swear on everything." His voice cracked. "I'll never hurt you again. Please, believe me."

Her voice sharpened, every word tinged with anger at his deceit. "You did the *one* thing you knew would hurt me the most, Cameron. For weeks, you lied to me. And maybe it wasn't about us and our relationship, but it's still a lie."

"I would have told you if..." He let out a sigh and rubbed the back of his neck.

"If what?!" Jules yelled.

Anger burned inside her, and she resented how easily it had taken hold. She'd always guarded herself. Had kept grief and heartache from sinking too deep so she could be a spark of light for everyone else.

And Cam had been her spark. The one who made *her* shadows feel smaller.

Now he was the cause of those shadows.

He finally looked at her. "If Levi knew I told you, he would have killed me and Ali. And probably Theresa and my mother. Maybe even you."

"I don't-"

He calmly put his hand up. "Listen, I don't expect you to believe me right now or to forgive me. I fucked up, and I will spend my life proving you can trust me." He caressed her face, and she leaned into his touch. "I love you, Juliette, more than anything else in the world. And I will do whatever it takes to show you that's true."

Before she could respond, Cam slid into his car and drove off.

Tears blurred her vision, but she didn't look away until his taillights vanished into the night. Because, despite the lies, she still loved him. And as darkness settled around her, a quiet spark of hope refused to fade.

CHAPTER 33

A li woke with a headache, anxiety pumping through her. She hadn't slept much as nightmares plagued the night. And every time she'd wake up from the sleep-born horror, her thoughts would spiral as she tried to make sense of everything.

Thankfully, Jax had held her every time she cried out in her sleep, or when her body would jerk her awake, or when the tears wouldn't stop coming. Each time, he rolled over and pulled her close until she'd fall back asleep. She felt bad for the man, as he would still have to go to work after having gotten very little sleep.

But she was eternally grateful for him.

Sighing, she pushed herself out of bed and followed the rich aroma of coffee and bacon. Jax hummed a Christmas song as he flipped the pieces of meat over. Her mouth watered at the stack of pancakes next to him.

She wrapped her arms around him, kissing his bare back. "Thank you for staying up with me throughout the night. I know it wasn't all that fun."

He turned around and hugged her. "I hate that I can't make it better, so the least I can do is comfort you."

She kissed him gently, then looked at the food. "I'm starving."

"It's a good thing I made a whole meal."

Making their plates, she and Jax sat at his kitchen table. He must have cleared it off early this morning because she could have sworn it was completely covered with an assortment of items when she'd walked in last night.

It didn't take long for them to devour their food, talking about miscellaneous things like hobbies they loved or their favorite TV shows. And as she sipped her coffee, she slowly built up her nerve to ask about her brother. "Any news on Levi?"

Jax shook his head. "No. They tried to get a search team into the woods, but he had a pretty good head start and he knows those woods much better than we do. Plus, the rest of your family isn't talking."

Ali simply nodded. She couldn't make sense of the many emotions that flowed through her. She felt as if her heart would shatter into a million pieces as she mourned the brother she thought she knew. Anger surged through her as she thought about all the women he'd ripped away from the world, how he'd killed Missi and Jared, taking them from her. Guilt welled in her chest, not knowing how she had missed the signs. Because there had to have been signs...*right*?

Not bothering to stop them, tears fell from her eyes once again, followed by the usual sobs that tore through her chest.

Not missing a beat, Jax pulled her onto his lap, rocking her as she cried into his bare chest. "I've got you. Let it out."

"How did this happen? How did I not know? How could he do something so heinous?" Ali said through hiccups. "And how could my family keep it from me? They didn't even tell the police!" Finally, in a near scream, she cried out, "And my daddy is dead!"

Jax silently stroked her hair until the tears stopped, and it was only her shuddered breaths that filled the silence. And even when she'd calmed down, she didn't move. This was the only place she felt safe and she couldn't bear the thought of being anywhere else in that moment.

He held her for nearly ten minutes, not saying anything.

Finally, she lifted her head and put her forehead on his. She closed her eyes. "Thank you."

He gently kissed her, and she got up from his lap, taking her plate to the sink. "I'm sorry I'm such a mess right now."

"Don't apologize. You're allowed to be whatever way you want." Following her, he placed his plate with the rest of the dirty dishes. He pointed out the window that sat above the sink. "Look at that bird. I've never seen one like that before."

Spotting the gray and yellow creature, her eyes brightened and she smiled. "Oh, Jax! That's a yellow rumped warbler." She giggled. "I did a book report on them in school, and I've always wanted to see one in person."

Jax smiled and winked. "Apparently, I'm the bird whisperer." He gestured to the window. "You're welcome, my little nerd."

Ali swatted at him and he moved to stand behind her, placing his arms on either side of her. They both watched the creature in silence as it perched itself on the tree, chirping into the winter morning.

Sighing, he brought his face to her neck and softly kissed her. "This feels right."

Ali turned her face to him. "What does?"

"This. Us. I know we haven't known each other long, and it's been nothing but bad news since you met me, but being with you feels natural. I've never felt that way about anyone."

Ali smiled and looked back out the window, leaning her head against his shoulder. She'd thought the same thing when she'd woken up. Sleeping next to him, falling in unison as they went through their morning routine. Even watching the bird felt easy and effortless.

Happiness welled in her chest. Jax Moretti felt like home.

She wouldn't say they were in love, but she was closer than she cared to admit. Being with him was easy, much to her surprise. When he'd admitted to not being a man of commitment, that statement had nearly sent her running. But the honesty and vulnerability he'd shown that day was what convinced her he was a good man.

And she was glad she'd given him a chance.

Finally, the bird flew away, and Ali sighed as reality washed over her again.

Her life was in shambles, and she felt as if she'd fallen into a dark abyss. All because she'd wanted to find her father.

She thought back to the day she'd sent in her DNA. She'd been so excited, so hopeful. She'd pictured finding him, surprising him with a visit where he would first be shocked to see her. Then the shock would turn into tears, him pulling her into a hug as he realized she was standing in his doorway.

In her mind, they would get ice cream, catching up on the last twenty-six years he'd missed. And she would ask why he'd disappeared from her life, to which he would admit he thought he did what was best for her, regretting his decision ever since.

And now she'd never have that chance.

Because her father was dead. And her brother had killed him.

Along with her sister and twelve other women.

Ali desperately wished the roaring in her ears would cease and there would be silence. Even just for a moment. She couldn't think about the remnants of her life anymore. And while she may not be able to change reality, she could disappear from it for a few moments.

So, she turned around and wrapped her arms around Jax's neck, kissing him deeply. Wanting more, Ali tugged at his shorts, but his hand gently clamped around her wrist.

"I care about you too much to let you do this," he whispered in her ear.

Startled by his resistance, she dropped her hands and lifted her head to look at him. Anger flared through her as betrayal stung her heart. Tears sprung into her eyes. "Why don't you want me?"

Jax pulled her closer and she tried to push him away, but he held her tight. "You don't understand just how badly I want you right now. How badly I want you every moment of every day. And I'm not talking about sex, Ali." He paused for a moment. "I want you so much I can't breathe sometimes. I'm not going to take you to bed right now because you're only doing it to shut out the noise. And once the noise quiets, when you've had time to think and reflect, you will regret it. And I won't let you do that to yourself. Even if it makes you angry with me."

Without hesitation, Ali burst into tears yet again, sobs rocking her body.

For as much as Jaxon Moretti claimed to be a bad man, he sure was good to her. It would have been easy for him to take advantage of her, to be selfish. But he hadn't. And now, she was that much closer to falling in love with him.

Calming down, she said, "Why are you so good to me? I'm an emotional mess! And my family is crazy and-"

Jax kissed her then, taking her breath away. "Because you chose me when I gave you a reason to run. The day in your bookstore, when I told you I'm not a man of commitment and I make the worst decisions when I'm stressed or angry, you still chose me. And you deserve the world from me. And I'll try my damnedest to give it to you."

Ali's heart soared as she wiped at her face.

She was most definitely falling in love with Jax Moretti.

Then, Jax's phone rang, reminding them the day had started, and it was time to get back to the ugly reality that had become her life.

At least now she had something beautiful to cling to.

CHAPTER 34

J ax hated to leave Ali alone at the station, but he knew she was safer there than anywhere else. And the only way to get her out of harm's way was to catch Levi. So, he, Juliette, Trinity, and Thiago took the morning to run down the only lead potentially tying Levi to the Scarlet Letter Killings.

The Bloom Room Flower Shop was quiet, with only the soft hum of classical Christmas music drifting through the small space. This was usually his favorite time of year, but now it only reminded him that joy was a cruel contrast to grief.

How could the world be celebrating while Ali's life was being torn apart? Jax understood that life moved forward, despite the grief that pulsed through so many families, but he'd never felt the sting of it until now. And when *Jingle Bell Rock* danced out of the speakers overhead, Jax clenched his jaw, irritated by the song's forced cheer.

Leading the team, the four of them made their way to the back counter. They pushed through numerous bouquets and ferns that had been placed together to create beautiful arrangements, though Jax found most of them quite ugly.

Jules rang the bell on the counter, announcing their presence.

A petite woman emerged from a side room in the back; her blond hair pulled into a knot at the base of her head. She furrowed her brows for a moment, taken aback by the group, as it was evident they hadn't come to the shop to purchase arrangements. However, she quickly smiled, trying to hide her curiosity. "Hi, I'm Lily. Can I help you?"

They pulled out their badges as Jax introduced them. "I'm Sergeant Moretti and these are my partners: Detective Reid and Agents Harbor and Silva with the FBI."

She frowned, worry etched on her face. "FBI? What's going on?"

Jules smiled, trying to calm the woman's nerves. "Lily, we're here to ask you a few questions about a man who recently purchased a bouquet with forget me nots. His name is Levi Knox."

Lily's face paled. "Levi? What do you want with Levi?"

Jax tilted his head. "You know Mr. Knox?"

She quickly nodded her head. "Yes, sir. We were engaged." She looked at the ground. "But we called off the wedding."

"Why did you call off the engagement?" Trinity asked.

Lily opened her mouth, then closed it just as a teenage girl came huffing out of the room, clutching an iPad. "The iPad froze," she said, not bothering to hide her distaste or her attitude from the strangers she eyed suspiciously.

Lily calmly said, "Catherine, go do your homework. I'll help you in a minute."

Rolling her eyes at the inconvenience, she stomped back to the room, her dark hair bobbing as she did.

Lily looked back at the room the girl had disappeared to then focused on the group again. Playing with a piece of paper on the counter, she said, "I found out I was pregnant, and I wasn't sure the baby was Levi's."

Juliette lifted a brow. "What happened when Levi found out?"

"He was livid; yelling and throwing dishes at the cabinets." Lily shook her head. "I shouldn't have cheated on him, but he was changing and I didn't know how to break it off. I met a man who was kind and charming, who swept me off my feet while Levi all but dwindled away in his own grief. He'd just lost his grandmother, and he shut me out. He became a completely different person after that."

She sighed. "I truly believed Levi wasn't Catherine's father, and I saw it as my ticket out of the relationship. I hoped I'd finally get my happy-ever-after. Of course, I'd been wrong about that. The other man never returned my calls so I could tell him about the pregnancy." She shrugged. "A few months after Levi left, I asked his sister if she'd submit her DNA for a paternity test."

"Does Miss Knox know she has a niece?" Jax asked. He knew Ali wasn't the type to abandon her family or cut ties with them; especially a child. She was far too kind for him to believe she'd cut ties with this woman if she knew the truth about the girl's paternity.

Lily shook her head. "No. I lied to Ali once I got the results back. When Levi freaked out, I didn't want anything to do with him or his family. So lying about the results helped me do that. And oddly enough, when Catherine was about three, I bumped into the other man I had been seeing. He did the math and wondered if she was his, so I told him the truth and never saw him again."

Trinity lifted a brow. "So, you cheated on your fiancé, thought you were knocked up and came clean about it hoping to end the engagement, got what you wanted, but still proceeded to lie about the paternity results?"

Lily stiffened and Jax gave Trinity a sharp look. The woman said, "I don't need your judgment, Agent. I was only twenty-three, a damn kid. I thought life would be better with someone else." She thrusted a thumb at her chest. "I was wrong. I loved Levi and I destroyed him; I've had to live with that for the last thirteen years."

Thiago stepped in, trying to calm the woman. "I'm sorry, you'll have to forgive my partner." He narrowed his eyes at Trinity, and she glared back at him. "She's not always very eloquent with her questions."

Lily drifted her gaze over Thiago and immediately softened. "It's okay. This is just very hard for me to talk about."

Thiago smiled. "Of course, we understand." He looked at his notes then back at Lily. "I'm sorry, what year did all this happen?"

"In 2012, when his grandmother died."

When the Scarlet Letter Killer began his killing spree.

Jax closed his eyes. This truth might destroy Ali completely.

Realizing the connection, Juliette asked, "Did he ever give you forget me not flowers?"

Lily shook her head. "No, never." Then, she furrowed her brows. "Actually, the night I kicked him out of our apartment, someone had left a handful of them on my doorstep. I thought it was Levi, but he denied it. I tried to ask the man I had an affair with, but again, he wouldn't return my calls." She shrugged. "I still think it was Levi, he just didn't want to admit it."

"When was the last time you spoke to or saw Levi?" Juliette asked.

She thought for a moment, closing her eyes. "The day he left was the last time we spoke. I think I saw him in town one day, but I hid until he was out of the department store. I had Catherine with me and didn't want him to see her."

The four of them shared a glance and Thiago said, "So he hasn't come in asking to purchase forget me nots? He didn't come in last night requesting an expedited order?"

Lily said, "No. But I do remember that order because it reminded me of the breakup and it had been right at closing time. It was an older man."

Trinity nodded toward the camera mounted on the wall. "Do you still have access to the footage?"

Lily pursed her lips, still irritated with Trinity. Sighing, she walked to the laptop positioned to the left of the register. She typed in a password, then moved the mouse a few times before turning the screen around to show them the man who had purchased the arrangement.

He was tall with dark hair and appeared to be in his sixties. But it was the scar that ran down his left eyebrow and the intensity in his stare that caught Jax's eye. The man radiated danger.

Now Jax had confirmation. Levi wasn't leaving Ali flowers.

And that knowledge was somehow far more debilitating. The man in the footage was a completely unknown suspect which made protecting Ali from him far more difficult. Jax's heart dropped to his stomach. If he didn't find this guy soon, Ali would continue to be in danger. And he couldn't bear the thought of burying her if this man got to her.

Now they had to figure out if Levi was the Scarlet Letter Killer or if this stranger was the monster who had been slaughtering women for the last decade. Or were they both working together, one the devil stalking the streets and the other just a messenger threatening Ali?

They were missing something. Jax was sure of it.

Snapping a photo of the stilled frame to show Cam and Ali later, Jax said, "Thank you for your help, we'll be in touch if we need anything else."

He put his card on the counter and the team walked back to the car and drove to the precinct.

"That guy on the footage look familiar to y'all?" Trinity asked Jax and Juliette.

Jax merged into on-coming traffic. "No, he hasn't come up in the investigation at all. But I want to show Ali and see if she recognizes him."

Jules shook her head. "This case doesn't make sense. If Levi is SLK, why is this other guy leaving Ali flowers? Are they even connected?"

Silence filled the space as everyone retreated to their thoughts.

Finally, Trinity said, "What if Levi had help?"

"What do you mean?" Thiago asked.

She sat up straighter, lifting her hand. "Think about it: where is he holding the girls for a week without anyone getting suspicious? He doesn't have any type of property listed in his name that would allow him to do that. And sure, he could access abandoned buildings, but that's a little ballsy for someone so methodical. He could be discovered fairly easily if someone happened to trespass."

Jax shook his head. "But would a killer like Levi work with someone else? And how does Ali fit into this? If your theory is true, why would Levi's partner be leaving her flowers?"

Trinity shook her head. "I don't know but having this other guy buy flowers and threaten Ali doesn't make sense."

"Unless the cases aren't related," Thiago said. "Levi could be the Scarlet Letter Killer and this other guy is just a stalker."

Jax stopped at a red light, then turned right.

"But why?" Juliette asked. "That doesn't make sense either because of the familial connection to the flowers."

Trinity shook her head. "We have to stop trying to use logic when it comes to monsters." She lifted her shoulder. "That's one of the first things my mentor taught me. What these men and women do doesn't make sense. Think about all the killers we put away. Even when you know *why* they committed their crimes, it still doesn't compute. That's because it never made sense from the start, at least not to us."

Trinity was right. They had to stop using logic and start thinking like a killer. Start thinking like Levi or the dangerous stranger leaving flowers for the woman he cared about.

Pulling into the station, Jax parked the car, and they all got out. Steeling himself for what he had to tell Ali about the dark-haired teenager at the flower shop, he took in a breath to steady his wildly beating heart.

Once inside, the team followed Jax into the breakroom where Ali was curled up with a book. But this time, she stared out the window mindlessly, lost in thought.

He studied her profile as dust specs danced around her, captured by the rays of the winter sun that filtered through the windows. He would give anything to make her whole again, to see her smile and laugh like she used to. But he would have to settle for the next best thing for now and keep her out of harm's way until he got to the bottom of these two cases. And then maybe she could begin healing.

"Ali," he said softly.

She turned toward him, eyes red and lips puffy. She smiled, trying to hide her sadness from him. "How did it go?" Her gaze drifted to the rest of the group and her face fell. "You found something, didn't you?"

Jax nodded and sat on the couch next to her while everyone else took a seat at the table in the middle of the room. He took her hand. "The arrangement was from The Bloom Room."

Ali sucked in a breath. "Oh my god. I hadn't even made the connection last night." Her eyes rounded. "How did I miss that, Jax?"

"There was a lot happening," Juliette said. "And tension was high. It's not surprising you hadn't noticed."

Jax asked, "We know the owner was engaged to Levi years ago. Did you know Lily has a twelve-year-old daughter?"

Jax chose his questions carefully, not wanting to be accused of causing a bias in her answers.

Her shoulders slumped and she nodded. "I knew she had a baby, but I never knew the gender. She asked me to submit DNA for a paternity test. That's how I found out she'd cheated on him." Ali shook her head, crimson shading her cheeks. "I was livid, but I did it because I wanted to know. If the baby was my niece or nephew, I wasn't going to abandon them because he or she has a lousy mother." Ali shrugged. "Turns out the baby wasn't Levi's, so I cut ties with

Lily and haven't talked to her since. Until I went to the shop to get a bouquet myself."

Jax desperately wanted to shield her from the truth he was about to reveal. She was slowly losing her spark, and he feared any other news may cause her light to go out completely. But he couldn't lie to her. After everything she'd been through, she deserved the truth. Even if it crushed her.

Because he knew she'd never get her light back if secrets still lurked in the darkness.

Jax shared a glance with Jules and the rest of the team, each of them on pins and needles. Trinity nodded to him, encouraging him to tell Ali the truth. He let out a sigh. "She lied, Ali. The baby *was* Levi's. She just didn't want anyone to know."

Ali stood up, startling Jax. She threw her arm into the air. "Why would she lie about that?!" She slowly closed her eyes and covered her face with her hands as she sunk back into the couch. "My life is falling apart and everyone I love has been lying to me."

Juliette came and knelt in front of her, placing her hands on Ali's knees. "Your family's lies don't change who you are and who you've become. It may not feel like it right now, but you're going to get through this and we're going to be here to help you."

Ali nodded and wiped at a tear as she put her hand on Juliette's. "Thanks, Jules."

Jax was thankful for his partner and her kindness. If anyone was going to be able to help Ali, it was Jules. Because right now, he was at a loss for words. He didn't know how to help Ali and that pierced his soul.

Juliette nodded to her. "Can you handle more questions, or do you want to take a break?"

Ali shook her head and took in a breath. "I'm okay." She glanced at Jax. "Go ahead."

"We asked her if Levi had made the order for the arrangement, but she said she hasn't seen him since they broke up."

Ali tilted her head. "Then who sent the flowers?"

Jax pulled out his phone, showing her the picture of the stranger. "Does this man look familiar?"

Ali's face paled. "That's my father."

Then, she rushed to the wastebasket on the far side of the room and vomited.

CHAPTER 35

Trinity found herself feeling a bit defeated. It had been three days since Levi had gone into hiding and they still hadn't found any leads on Jared, both causing tension to rise with each passing day. And, truthfully, she was becoming more and more worried about her friends.

Ali wasn't sleeping. Jax was restless and couldn't keep his temper under control. Cam had been placed on leave from the case. And because Jules was such an empath, she cried every time Ali cried, though Trinity knew her friend was also crying over her splintered relationship.

It was a damn circus.

But she knew the only way to help them was by doing what she did best: catching monsters. So, she sat on the floor in the corner of the conference room, her shoes off, files laid out in front of her. She balanced her laptop on her legs, sipping her sweet tea.

Thiago sat at the table, quietly reading over his own stack of files. Both of them scoured for any lead as to where Jared or Levi might be hiding while Jules went to get lunch.

After checking on Ali, Jax walked into the room and eyed Trinity. "What are you doing?"

Trinity raised a brow. "What the hell does it look like I'm doing?"

He rolled his eyes. "You know what I fucking mean, Trinity."

Tired of his attitude and constant irritation, she flipped him the bird. "Lose the attitude. I might be like a sister to you, but that doesn't mean I won't whoop your ass for talking to me like that."

Sighing, he closed his eyes. "I'm sorry. I shouldn't take my frustration out on you."

Trinity tilted her head, a silent acceptance of his apology. "I like to sit this way because it's more comfortable and I focus better when I can relax."

His anger lifting, Jax sat next to her on the floor, and she scooted away from him. "Get your own spot."

He smiled and slid closer, nearly touching her and she glared at him. "Jax, quit. I don't want to be near you right now." She may have forgiven him, but that didn't mean she wasn't still aggravated by his behavior.

"That's why I'm not moving." He pulled her close to him and hugged her. "You're a brat, you know that? So, I'm dishing it back to you."

She made a face at him as she pulled herself out of his grasp and then they both laughed. As much as they fought like siblings, they really did love each other.

Jax shook his head. "Is there any way we're wrong about Levi being SLK?"

"I mean, anything is possible," Thiago said. "But it's not likely. I believe in coincidences, but there's a little too many for me to not at least investigate Levi and even Jared." He gestured toward the files. "We follow the evidence, not the theory. And right now, the evidence is pointing to Levi."

Trinity felt bad for Jax. He had to hunt down a killer all while trying to save his relationship with the woman whose family may have been harboring a sadistic serial killer for the last ten years.

Thiago tossed Jax a file and Jax settled against the wall, opening up the folder.

Trinity arched her back to stretch when her computer jingled. She opened her email to find the results of the background check she'd run when she had first gotten to town. No one else knew she'd done it. Jax and Jules would have caused a scene if they had known. But she'd be damned if she didn't have all the facts.

The Knox family was clearly full of secrets, and she didn't need any more skeletons falling out of the closet every time she opened a damn door. She saw firsthand what skeletons and secrets could do to a family; it had nearly killed her, and she'd only been thirteen at the time. Gritting her teeth at the memory, she shook her head and clicked the link to read the results she'd found for Cameron Richard Knox and Levi James Knox.

When she'd done a standard background check on the family, only Cam and Levi had a record. Cam was mostly clean, only petty theft in his early teens. But Levi had seemed to take a more violent approach to life, already receiving his first assault charge at the mere age of twelve. Over time, a handful of other charges were added to the rap sheet. Which fit the profile she had been building. Most psychopaths have some sort of criminal record when they're young since they lack impulse control. It seemed Levi had lived up to the notion.

But what piqued her interest the most was the sealed record local law enforcement wouldn't have access to. So, she'd run his name through the FED's database, and the results were finally in. Trinity clucked her tongue. Ali's brother was just as bad as they suspected, but she was surprised by Cam.

Mr. Knox wasn't as squeaky clean as he'd have everyone believe.

After reading over the charges, it seemed the two were arrested for assault and battery when they were sixteen and fifteen, not long after Missi had died. A fellow classmate had been beaten and raped. According to the reports, she'd cheated on Levi with another schoolboy. When he found out about it, he had followed her into the woods where he proceeded to beat and rape her.

Cam had been a witness, it appeared.

The detective investigating stated that Cam had given them very little fight upon his arrest, though he needed to be calmed down a bit, distraught over what he'd witnessed. Levi, however, had to be tased. And because Cam helped the police build a case against Levi, he was given no time in juvie and did most of his sentence on house arrest. Levi, though, had only been incarcerated for a year.

Trinity was surprised by the light sentences the two had received. They should have done prison time, and Levi most definitely should have done longer than a year in juvie.

Wanting more information, she found the lead detective's number. Trinity excused herself from the room and punched in the number.

The man answered on the fifth ring. "Yeah."

"Hi, this is Agent Trinity Harbor with the FBI. I'm looking for Detective Wilson."

"This is him. But I'm retired now, Sweets."

She nearly gagged at the pet name. She couldn't stand the arrogance of men who believe women would simply swoon over such empty flattery. She pushed through her annoyance. "I have a question about a case that happened quite a long time ago concerning two teens by the last name Knox. Levi and Cameron. They were arrested for the assault of a girl, a classmate of theirs. She was said to have been cheating on one of the boys. Levi raped and beat her and Cameron helped him cover it up."

"Ah yes, I was fresh meat then. Felt bad for the younger boy, he was absolutely terrified of the older boy. Wouldn't stop shaking."

Leaning against the wall, she said, "Can you tell me what happened?"

"The girl was found unconscious by some teens smoking reefer in the woods after the assault. She'd been beaten nearly beyond recognition. The ambulance took her to the hospital, and we were called in. She told us she'd been attacked and raped by Levi, the older boy. The other kid, Cameron, got there as it was ending and tried to help Levi cover it up. I think they thought she was dead."

"Is she still alive?"

"Unfortunately, she killed herself shortly after. I think the scars really did a number on her."

"Scars?"

"That boy carved a huge 'A' across her chest, Agent."

CHAPTER 36

After filling in the team on what she'd just found, Trinity made her way to Cam's office with Thiago. Now that Cam had been relieved from the SLK case, it wouldn't be wise to let Jax or Jules interview him since it was a conflict of interest, something Trinity was surprised had been allowed to go on this whole time.

Trinity flashed her badge to the receptionist and walked toward the door. Not bothering to knock, she opened it. Startled, Cam glanced up from the papers on his desk. Trinity was surprised to see his dark hair so disheveled. His eyes were sunken in and his sleeves were rolled up, adding to his chaotic appearance, which was a stark comparison to the man he'd been just days earlier.

There was a glass of whiskey sitting in the corner of the wooden block. And from the looks of him, it wasn't the first drink he'd had today. Admittedly, she felt bad for him, though he had brought these consequences on himself. Over the last few days, Trinity had grown to like Cam, but she wished he'd been honest from the start.

Blinking quickly, he sat up straight and ran his hands through his hair. "Oh, I didn't realize you two would be stopping by. Is there any news on Levi?"

Trinity didn't mince words. "I read the sealed file."

Cam froze as tension rippled through the room, so sharp Trinity thought she may have felt it graze across her skin.

Finally, he asked, "How? It's a sealed juvie record."

She sat in the chair across from him while Thiago stood by the door. "We're the FBI. We can see things no one else can."

"What happened?" Thiago asked.

Sighing, Cam picked up the glass and threw back the last swig of liquor. "I was walking home from school. We had to pass a dense wooded area to get to the elementary school and I heard muffled screaming." He shook his head. "I think I had PTSD from Missi because my brain kept telling me it might be Ali. So, I rushed to figure out what was happening and that's when I saw Levi strangling this girl from the school."

He walked over to the window, getting lost in a trance as he retreated to his memories. He took a deep breath. "Her pants were down, and her body went limp before I had time to process what had happened. Then, Levi pulled out a knife and carved the letter 'A' into her chest. When he was finished, he stood up and I think it finally dawned on him that she was dead. That's when he started freaking out, saying he just wanted to teach her a lesson."

Trinity didn't squirm easily, but any crime involving a child made her skin crawl and her blood boil. Levi was a psychopath, and his family had spent his entire life protecting him, allowing the monster to grow. And now, that monster had been released.

He turned back to them, leaning against the pane as he looked at the floor. "It was bad. She was covered in blood, he was covered in blood. I tried to leave and get help, but he attacked me. He said if I went to the cops, he'd blame it on me." Cam shook his head. "I was a kid. I was terrified of what he'd do to me. He'd already killed Missi and Jared. Plus, I was terrified I'd get locked up for a crime I didn't commit. So, I told him to cover up the body and hope animals ate it."

"How did you get such a light sentence?" Thiago asked.

Cam looked at Thiago and walked back to his desk. He sat down, leaning back. "White and rich privilege. My father and grandfather paid off a judge. Plus, my father had saved the judge's wife's life in surgery, so I think that may have been the driving factor." He shook his head. "Ever since then, I tried to stay as far away from Levi as possible."

Trinity crossed her arms, irritated by the irresponsibility of nearly everyone involved in the case. "Why didn't you tell Jax when you saw the burns on the SLK vics? Cam, they could have built a case against Levi from the very beginning."

Cam leaned forward and thrusted an arm into the air. "Because he has evidence against me! I didn't know he'd set up a damn camcorder to film the whole thing. So, when I moved her body to help cover it up, I was covered in blood. And we'd gotten into a fist fight, so I looked like I had defensive wounds on me." He clenched his jaw. "Levi said he would doctor the tape to only show the end, making it look like I was the one who killed her."

Trinity stood, placing her hands on the desk as she leaned forward. "What about after you found out she had *lived*? I saw the report. You weren't arrested until nearly two weeks later because she had to be put into a medically induced coma."

He stood, matching Trinity's energy, but she didn't cower. If he had done the right thing, even at the mere age of fifteen, they wouldn't be in the damn mess.

"We didn't know if she was going to make it." He narrowed his eyes at her. "And when she woke up, Levi went to the hospital and threatened her before I could even do anything. He wanted her to convince the cops it was me who had hurt her. And after what he'd done, I wouldn't have blamed her. But he didn't know there was a nurse in the bathroom who had heard the whole thing and called the police." He threw his arm up. "I've spent my whole life regretting my choices and living in constant shame and guilt. Not a day goes by that I don't wish I would have done more."

He slid back into his chair and buried his face into his hands.

Thiago stepped forward. "You have potentially made it impossible to get a conviction. Do you realize that? This has been a conflict of interest from the beginning. What were you thinking?"

Not caring anymore, Cam poured the amber liquid into the glass. He took a sip and then swirled it around as he looked at a spot on his desk. "When the SLK files first came across my desk, I chalked it up to coincidence. I kept my mouth shut because I wanted to see what evidence would come out. And I wanted time to find the tape before I told you about Levi."

Trinity slammed her hand on the wooden box, causing him to jump. "You have royally fucked us! It will be a damn miracle if we get a conviction. And I have half a mind to arrest you for obstruction of justice at the very least!"

Cameron Knox wouldn't be able to get a damn job by the time she was through with him. He was lucky Juliette loved him, or Trinity would have raked him through the mud.

Cam hung his head. "What now?"

Sighing, Thiago said, "Now we try to find Levi and hope SLK doesn't get to walk on a technicality. And then we find Jared."

Cam furrowed his brow. "What do you mean?"

Thiago looked at Trinity then at Cam. "Jules didn't tell you?"

He downed the whiskey. "She isn't exactly talking to me right now."

Trinity stood tall, towering over him. "Jared is alive. He's the one who sent the bouquet to Ali."

Cam's eyes rounded and he slowly stood to his feet. "That's impossible. I watched Levi kill him. He stabbed him right in front of me."

Trinity said, "Look, I don't know what happened, but he's alive. Ali confirmed it's him." Reaching into her pocket, she pulled out her phone and showed Cam the photo.

Cam's face paled. "*How*?"

Thiago opened his mouth to say something when Trinity's phone vibrated. Jax's name flashed across the screen. "What's up?"

"Theresa and Dianne are in the hospital. We think Levi went back and beat the shit out of Dianne. Theresa seems to be okay, but she may have a concussion."

Trinity froze. "How did that happen? We had a surveillance team on the house?"

"There are way too many areas we can't watch. We knew that going in. And of course, neither women are talking to us."

"Fucking great. That's just what we need." She eyed Cam. "Two more tight-lipped people."

She shoved the phone into her pocket and pinned the man with her gaze. "Your mother was assaulted by Levi. So, you can add that to your list of things you need to make penance for."

With that, she left, fed up with the lies and secrets, as if the entire Knox family didn't have the blood of twelve women on their hands.

CHAPTER 37

Trinity's dash read one in the morning, the shadows of the early morning eerily enveloping her as she aimlessly drove around. She couldn't sleep, and even talking through the case with her dad had her head spinning. So, she had left her parents' house hoping a quiet drive would clear her mind.

She couldn't shake the feeling she was missing something. There were so many lies and secrets. And when they'd gone to arrest Levi at the Knox compound, he'd already disappeared into the night and Theresa and Dianne were tight-lipped and visibly terrified.

It was clear they would rather go to jail than risk Levi's wrath. Which they had.

Now, they needed to find him before he completely vanished. Or started a killing spree. Which, at the moment, was a very real possibility.

Trinity didn't think he'd left town yet. She suspected he'd go after Ali as soon as the opportunity presented itself, as she was the reason the police were so hot on his trail. And if anything happened to her, Jax would throttle Trinity and the rest of the team.

Running a hand through her hair, she tried to get inside Levi's head. Serial killers almost always have a place that's special to them, somewhere they might go to reminisce or hide their trophies. She considered the family home, but that seemed too obvious. Missi's dump site could potentially hold sentimental value to him, but because he killed adulterers, she wasn't so sure about that.

Then it hit her.

The schoolgirl.

His first victim.

She yanked her car into a U-turn and drove back toward the high school. The report mentioned a clearing in the trees, which might be difficult to see now with the shroud of darkness. Pulling out the map from the case file, she slowly drove past the wooded area.

The canopy of emerald gave way to a thin opening.

She parked and pulled out her phone to call Thiago. She'd learned the hard way what could happen if people didn't know where you were. She'd almost died because of it.

But she wasn't a kid anymore. She was trained and armed and knew how to use her weapon. She'd never be taken advantage of again. But while she had a gun and badge, Trinity wasn't stupid. She was going to call for backup, even if he was making a damn booty call.

On the fifth ring, Thiago answered, voice groggy. "What is it?"

"I think I know where Levi is. Meet me at the wooded area near the high school, where the first victim was found."

"Now? Are you sure? I'm kind of busy."

Trinity rolled her eyes. What was up with the whole team? Did anyone understand being single was the best thing for the job? Well, Jax had. Now look at him; googly-eyed for a witness.

She couldn't blame him, though. Ali was kind and beautiful.

"Yes. You'll see my car parked." She felt bad for pulling Thiago away from the woman he was with, but duty calls and she wasn't trying to get trapped with no one to help her.

"Okay, give me fifteen," he said, ending the call.

Somehow, he managed to make it in ten minutes, something she was glad for. Since pulling over, she'd been anxious to get into the woods and see if her hunch was right. He maneuvered his vehicle behind hers and cut off the engine.

"Who were you with?" she asked as he climbed out of his sleek black Dodge Charger.

He smirked. "An old fling. Her name is Carmen. We dated in high school and things didn't work out. She's back visiting her parents. We happened to bump into each other at a bar, and she invited me to her hotel."

Trinity lifted a brow. "No strings attached?"

He shrugged as he pulled his gun from its holster and turned on his flashlight. "Not for me. It's not really my problem if she thinks it'll be more; she should know better."

"What an ass," Trinity said, giving him a disapproving look.

Ignoring her slight, he nodded toward the woods. "Come on, let's go find this guy."

They followed the thin dirt path into the dense trees, the darkness nearly swallowing them. It was clear there hadn't been much traffic through the area, and Trinity guessed it was because of what had occurred here twenty-five years ago.

She followed Thiago, their movements swift and wordless. Her heartbeat quickened as her senses sharpened, the thrill of the chase tangling with the angst that always shadowed her steps when she ran toward danger. The sounds of the night echoed through the thicket, putting her on edge.

Levi appeared as they came upon the clearing. He pushed a shovel into the soft ground, dumping the dirt into a pile. The hole was quite large, and Trinity was curious as to what he was up to. She hoped he wasn't digging a grave, though that wasn't his typical M.O.

Seeing their suspect, Thiago gestured to the left and to the right. Silently, the two parted ways, circling Levi to close him in.

Getting into position, she trained her gun on him as she emerged from the trees. "Don't move, Levi. Drop the shovel and slowly put your hands up."

Levi froze at the sound of her voice, then turned toward her. "If you know what's best for you, you'll leave me be, Detective."

Not wavering, she said, "It's 'Agent.' And go fuck yourself. I've seen what you've done to all those women. You're not getting away with it."

He smiled and took a step toward her, and she tightened her grip. "I see you've talked to Cam, always the snitch."

Trinity didn't respond. She wasn't going to engage with him.

The two locked eyes and she didn't break his stare. The shift in Levi's energy had her straining to hear Thiago's footsteps. But she was only met with the sounds of the night. She innately knew danger was growing. She'd hunted enough monsters to know that when they were cornered, they became completely unpredictable.

Where was Thiago?

Levi gripped the shovel. "You know, I'm surprised things played out the way they did. I would have never anticipated things getting this messy."

"Well, when you slaughter women for fun, that can only last for so long," Trinity quipped.

He nodded slowly. "There's something you're missing, Agent. And Ali will die if you don't figure it out."

He took two steps toward her, and she tightened her grip on her weapon, ready to shoot if necessary. "Don't fucking move!" she commanded.

Levi tilted his head. "Or what, you'll shoot me?" He chuckled. "Trust me, you need me alive or you'll never figure out the truth."

Leaves and underbrush snapped like faint whispers, and she shifted her gaze toward the sound where she saw Thiago coming through the clearing. Taking advantage of her distraction, Levi quickly latched onto the shovel and swung.

The metal connected with her skull and she shrieked in pain, crashing to the ground in a heap. Blood leaked down her face before she realized what had happened. Lifting her head, she watched as Thiago approached her and Levi disappeared into the woods.

"Trinity!" Thiago shouted. His brows were pulled together, worry lining his face.

She tried to pull herself to her feet, but her head swam and she fell back into the dirt. "Don't worry about me. Go get that bastard!"

"You're bleeding. I need to get you to the hospital." No longer concerned with Levi, Thiago scooped her up and ran back into the dense darkness from which they'd come earlier. Branches lashed their arms and legs as he pushed through, the sounds of the night now disappearing as she slipped toward unconsciousness.

"My mom is gonna freak," Trinity said as they emerged from their covering.

Thiago gently laid her in the back seat of his car as he climbed into the driver's seat. "She's used to your stupid choices." He dispatched the police and asked them to dispatch the hospital as he flipped on his lights and sirens and slammed his foot on the gas.

And Trinity watched through the window as the streetlight blurred, reflecting on what Levi had said.

Juliette heard the pounding before her mind registered it wasn't actually in her dream. Grumbling, she rolled over and grabbed her phone off the nightstand. Two o'clock in the morning. Sitting up quickly, she threw open the drawer on her nightstand and pulled out her gun.

Friends didn't show up pounding on your door at two in the morning.

The thudding continued and she quickened her pace.

She tiptoed to the front door, curious and cautious as to who may be standing on the other side. She peeked through the peephole, pivoting slightly to keep herself out of the line of fire should anyone be aiming at the door.

Sighing, she punched her code into the alarm system keypad next to the door. A melody of beeps drifted through the darkened home, signaling it had been disarmed. When she swung open the door, Cam stilled.

Jules smelled the stench of alcohol before he even uttered a word. She frowned. "Cam, I told you I wanted space to think. I love you so much, but I need to figure out how I'm supposed to trust you again." Her eyes drifted over him, surprised by his disheveled appearance. He'd clearly been drinking into the early morning hours, evidenced by his messy hair and wrinkled shirt.

He gave a weak, sorrowful smile, his bloodshot eyes glassy with pain. "I'm sorry, I just needed to see you. I—"

That's when Jules noticed the dark stain spreading across his shirt, seeping through as he crossed his arms over his abdomen. A wave of panic slammed through her body as she realized he was standing in a growing pool of blood. "Oh my god, what happened?"

Cam simply stood there, swaying slightly with his eyes locked on hers. Without missing a beat, she quickly set her gun on the table by the door. And as soon as the weapon had been released from her hands, Cam collapsed into her arms. She staggered back, nearly hitting the floor under his weight.

Jules took in steady breaths in an attempt to keep herself calm. Though she stayed levelheaded seeing the darkest sides of humanity at work, this was entirely different. This was the love of her life, and he was bleeding out on her doorstep.

She clutched him, slowly bringing him to the floor as her knees buckled under his weight. She tried to keep her voice steady, but she was terrified. "Cam, what happened?"

He let out a whimper, his voice was just above a whisper, "I saved you, Juliette. He was going to hurt you."

And while Jules wanted to ask him a million questions, she didn't have time for that right now. *She needed to call an ambulance.*

Grasping for her phone, she cursed.

Damn it! She'd left it in her room.

Thinking quickly, she carefully laid him down over her threshold and he winced as the movement shot pain through his body. Tears sprung into her eyes. "I'm sorry, baby. I know it hurts, but I need to get help. I'll be right back."

Then, she reached over him, slamming the panic button on her alarm system. The piercing wail echoed through the neighborhood, alerting everyone to possible danger. Jules ignored the ringing in her ears as she yanked a sweater from the hook by the door.

Kneeling near Cam's abdomen, she pressed the fabric over the wound, hoping to stop the blood that was soaking her wooden floor.

Where was the damn ambulance?

Cam's hands wrapped over hers and she felt his body shake as he whispered, "I love you, Juliette."

She had fought to stay calm, but the tears came anyway, streaming down her cheeks. She forced a smile despite the panic rising in her chest. "Hey, I love you, too. An ambulance is on the way, okay?"

He wiped at her tears, his blood smearing across her face. "If I don't make it, take care of Ali for me," he said through each labored breath.

Sirens in the distance intertwined with the alarm's rhythmic cry into the winter's night.

Juliette's lungs tightened. "You're going to be fine, baby. You can't die..." She whispered through her sobs, "Please, don't die. Please."

Cam's eyes fluttered closed. "I'm really tired. I need to take a nap."

She cradled Cam's head in her lap and stroked his hair. "No naps, okay? I need you to stay awake."

The shriek of the emergency vehicles grew louder, but sleep tugged at his eyes. She desperately needed to keep him talking. "Will you marry me?" she blurted, the words escaping before she could stop them. In that moment, all that mattered was the hope of spending forever with him.

He winced as a chuckle escaped him. "I was supposed to say that."

She laughed through her tears. "I don't want to wait anymore." She kissed him, ignoring the smear of blood she'd left on his lips while trying to lay him down.

Jules heard an officer's voice before she ever saw the man standing next to her. "Detective, what happened?"

But before she could answer, Cam grasped her hand tightly. Through labored breaths, Cam said, "Levi...he tried to kill me."

Jules' eyes rounded as she shared a glance with the officer just as the paramedics pulled her away from him. She screamed wildly at them, desperate to stay with him. She lunged forward, but the officer held her close as a desperate cry escaped her lungs.

Juliette watched in agony as Cam disappeared into the back of the ambulance. And as the flashing lights vanished into the darkness that settled around them, each second apart from him stretched like a knife through her chest.

CHAPTER 38

J ax awoke with a jerk. His dreams of vacations with Ali had morphed into a dark vision of holding her lifeless body as the world collapsed around them. He rubbed his face, trying to calm his wildly beating heart. Wanting to pull Ali close, he slid his hand to the far side of the bed, but the sheet was cold.

He quickly sat up, listening for any movement to indicate she was in the bathroom. Only being met with silence, he threw off the comforter and grabbed his firearm. He cautiously made his way through the house until he came to the kitchen.

Ali stood at the sink, the stove's dim glow haloing her in light. She grasped a coffee mug and held it close to her chest as she stared out the window into darkness. He was curious how long she'd been awake.

Letting out a sigh of relief, he said, "Ali?"

"Hmmm?" She slowly turned to him, her face downcast.

"Are you okay? Why didn't you wake me if the nightmares were bad enough to keep you from sleeping?"

She went to him, laying her head on his chest. She cupped her coffee close and he wrapped his arms around her. "I didn't want to wake you. You need to sleep, and there's not much you can do for a nightmare anyway."

He kissed the top of her head. "Well, since we're both up, why don't we do something fun to pass the time until morning?"

Ali's grin was mischievous. "Like what?"

Jax let out a soft, knowing chuckle. "That would be fun, but that's not what I meant."

Releasing her, he poured his own cup of coffee and set it on the table before walking to his hall closet. Reaching up to the top shelf, he pulled out a few games and brought them back to the kitchen table where Ali now sat.

"We can play Clue, Operation, or...." he smiled wildly. "Monopoly."

She let out a laugh. "I told you we can't ever play Monopoly. And you're a walking cheat sheet for Clue since that's what you do for work."

"Operation it is!"

Ali said, "I'm surprised you even have board games. You don't strike me as the type to be playing Clue with your friends when they come over."

He took the pieces out of the box and set up the game. "I keep them here for when my nieces visit because they think my house is boring. Plus, I usually have people stay during the hurricanes, so I keep them for when the power goes out."

She got up to refill her coffee mug. "Do you see your nieces often?"

Jax shook his head as she sat back now. "Not as much as I'd like to, but we try to get together about twice a month at minimum. But I'm usually the built-in babysitter for their date nights."

"You watch them by yourself?" she asked, raising a brow.

"Well..."

She chuckled. "I figured."

Jax grinned. "They really only see me as the fun uncle, so when it's time to brush their teeth and go to bed, they think I'm joking. That's why I usually call in the big guns. They adore Jules and they'll listen to her."

Ali slid onto his lap and held his gaze. "I'd like to meet your family one day. I'd like to get to know the people who matter most to you."

Had any other woman said that he would have bolted. But from Ali, the words struck something deep within him. And he knew his sisters and nieces would adore her.

Jax pushed her hair behind her ear as he brought his lips to hers. "When all this is over, we'll invite them over for dinner. They're going to love telling you all my embarrassing stories."

Ali's laugh warmed the moment, and Jax found himself never growing tired of the beautiful sound. She slid back into her chair, and soon they were passing time playing the game. Each victory was met with cheers and each loss met with groans, and Jax was racking up plenty of those.

Looking out the window, the colors of dawn brushed across the sky. And though the morning was breathtaking, it was also a reminder that another day had passed, and Ali wasn't yet out of harm's way.

He sighed as he studied her profile. She furrowed her brows as she carefully held the tweezers between her fingers and concentrated to remove a body part from the opening in the board. She held her breath, afraid that even the faintest whisper of air would be her undoing.

In an attempt to rattle her, Jax yelled, "Ali!"

Jumping at his voice, the buzzer sounded and her laughter tumbled out. She playfully swatted at his arm. "Jaxon Moretti, you're a cheater!"

He was relieved to hear that sound. The past few days had left him fearing she'd never do it again. He'd even wondered if her light was fading entirely. But it wasn't. Her light was still there. He just needed to work a little harder to get it to shine right now.

Hearing his phone from the bedroom, he got up to retrieve it. Quickening his pace, he clutched the device just before the last ring. "It's pretty early for a phone call, Trinity. I don't think you've ever gotten up this early."

"It's Thiago," the agent said. "Trinity's okay, but she got hurt and I brought her to the hospital."

Jax stilled. "What the hell happened?"

Thiago's voice was low, tight with worry. "The short story: we found Levi, and he swung a damn shovel at her head."

Without hesitation, Jax grabbed a t-shirt and jeans from his drawer and threw them on. "How bad is it? Did you arrest him?"

Ali stepped into the room, drawn by the urgency in his voice. He saw her eyes widen as the gravity of the situation became clear. Without hesitation, she pulled on her clothes, instinctively matching his pace, ready before he even had to say a word.

He was grateful she didn't ask questions, just trusted him fully. He didn't take that lightly.

Thiago spoke to a nurse then returned to the call. "She's fine, bossing everyone around. I had to wrestle the phone from her just to call you."

Jax snatched his keys from the counter and sprinted to the car, Ali right on his heels. She carried her boots, slipping them on quickly once they were inside.

He made his way through the lights, speeding through every one. Once at the hospital, he and Ali raced to the ER, where they were met by a receptionist who pointed them toward Trinity's room.

He carefully opened the door, not wanting to wake her if she was sleeping. But, as he did, he saw she was fully dressed, sitting on the edge of the bed. She had a patch of gauze taped on her forehead, a scowl on her face.

Relief washed over him. "You look like you got in a fight and lost," Jax quipped.

Trinity flipped him the bird. "I wouldn't have lost had he not hit me with a fucking shovel."

Ali's eyes widened. "Did Levi do that to you?"

Trinity sighed and nodded. "Yeah, I found him in the woods. I took my eyes off him for a second and he almost knocked me out." She rolled her eyes at her slip-up. "Damn rookie mistake."

Ali immediately wrapped Trinity in a hug and Trinity stiffened at the gesture. "I'm so sorry he did that to you."

When Trinity didn't respond, Ali released her and stepped back, giving Jax room to assess his friend.

Jax's gaze sharpened at Thiago. "Where were you?"

The agent put his hands up. "I was coming around on the other side and got my foot caught in a tree limb. I was trying to get free without making a bunch of noise. But when I came out from the trees, Trinity saw me, and he took that opportunity to swing at her."

"You'd better hope Trey doesn't find out what happened," Jax said, crossing his arms.

Trinity snapped at Jax. "Knock it off. No one is scared of you."

Jax rolled his eyes. "When are you getting released?"

"If they don't bring me discharge papers in..." She looked at her watch. "Five minutes, then I'm walking out."

She meant it, too. He'd lost count of the number of times she refused to wait around in a hospital. And honestly, if she could avoid it altogether, she would. No matter how serious the injury or sickness.

"While we wait, tell me what you remember," Jax said.

Trinity shook her head. "He was kind of running his mouth mostly. Saying that Cam was a rat, and he didn't think things would spiral the way they had." She furrowed her brows. "But what stuck out to me was at the end, right before he hit me, he said that we were missing something."

Jax tilted his head. "What does that mean?"

Trinity shrugged. "Hell if I know. I've been trying to figure it out this whole time."

Thiago said, "I think it would be smart to go back over every single case with a fine-tooth comb."

Jax nodded. "Okay, let's work on that later today."

Trinity jumped off the hospital bed. "Okay, time's up. I'm outta here."

If it had been anyone else, Jax would have fought with her to stay put. But not Trinity. She would have whooped his ass for intervening.

Stepping out of her way, she pulled open the door and froze. Concerned by her movement, Jax peered around her. Juliette stood frozen, blood covering her. Her eyes were red and swollen, her breaths coming in shallow gasps.

He rushed to her, gripping her upper arms. "Juliette, what happened? Are you okay?"

She remained silent, her empty gaze fixed on a spot on the floor.

Trinity shoved him to the side and pulled Jules into the room as Thiago ran water over a few paper towels. He handed them to Ali, who gently blotted Jules' forehead.

A nurse walked in, papers in hand. Her eyes rounded, "What the hell is going on?" She looked at Trinity. "Ma'am, you need to lay back down, you haven't been discharged. And you're not medical personnel. You can't treat other patients."

Trinity glared at her. "I discharged myself since you wanted to take your sweet time." Then she continued to assess Jules, ignoring the nurse's command.

The woman's face reddened. "I'm sorry, but you're not allowed to do that."

Trinity forcefully flashed her badge. "This says I fucking can."

Juliette broke down, throwing herself into Jax's arms. He exchanged a glance with Ali, whose own eyes glistened with unshed tears.

Through each labored sob, she said, "Levi attacked Cam. He was bleeding out on my doorstep."

CHAPTER 39

J ax clenched his jaw and Ali's hand flew to her mouth, a sharp gasp escaping
her. "Jules, is Cam dead?"

Calming down, Juliette wiped at her face and shook her head. "He's okay. I
didn't mean to scare you. I was just so shaken up by it." She took another ragged
breath and stepped away from Jax.

Ali closed her eyes and let out a breath, taking Jax's hand as he let out his own
sigh of relief.

"How is he doing? Can we see him?" Ali's voice trembled, laced with hope
and fear. Her gaze found Jax's, pleading silently, as if he alone could grant her
permission.

He clenched his jaw in frustration. He wanted to move heaven and earth for
her, but this wasn't a place where his authority mattered. And he felt every bit
of his powerlessness, knowing that no matter how much he wanted to give her
what she wanted, he could do nothing but wait.

Jules closed her eyes and inhaled. "He's okay. He only needed stitches, so he
should be released in a few days. He just..." her face twisted, haunted by what
she'd seen. "There was so much blood, and I didn't know what had happened."

Jax cupped her face, wanting her to focus. "Hey, it's okay. He's safe." When
he was satisfied she understood, he dropped his hands to his side. "Did they
arrest Levi?"

Jules shook her head. "No, they were focused on Cam. And by the time
anyone showed up, he'd been long gone."

Damn it. How did Levi keep disappearing?

The nurse came back in and opened her mouth to say something, but Trinity cut her off. "Get me some scrubs for my friend." She gestured toward Jules and the dark stains that soaked her clothes, a lingering reminder of the horror she'd witnessed.

The woman glared at Trinity. "Those are for staff only."

Trinity slowly turned, her voice low and threatening. "My friend is covered in her boyfriend's blood. She just watched him nearly bleed." She pointed a finger in the nurse's direction. "So, you can either be a fucking decent human being and get her something else to wear, or I will tear this hospital apart while I find them myself. And then I'll make sure you lose your job when I'm done."

The nurse's jaw tightened as she squared her shoulders, refusing to yield to Trinity's demand, but Trinity was far more tenacious and Jax anxiously watched the exchange. Rolling her eyes, the nurse reluctantly left the room in search of the scrubs.

A moment later, she returned, shoving the blue set into Trinity's arms before leaving the room in a huff. Jax saw the flame spark behind his friend's eyes, and he gently laid his hand on her shoulder, commanding her to stand down.

"Get out," she snapped at Jax and Thiago.

Doing as they were told, the two men left the room to give the women privacy to help Juliette. Jax softly shut the door behind him and let out a shaky breath, placing his hands on his knees. "Fuck, I thought that was her blood."

Thiago nodded as he leaned against the wall. "Scared the shit out of me, too."

Jax stood back up and looked up the hallway toward the receptionist's desk. "I need to get Cam's information."

"He said Levi tried to kill him?" Thiago asked.

Jax nodded. "But she's in shock, so I want to get her statement after she's had time to settle down."

The door opened and Jules stepped into the hall donning navy blue scrubs. Trinity and Ali had tried their best to wipe Cam's blood off her face, but there was still a crimson shadow near her jawline.

Jax wrapped her in a hug again and she clung to him. "I was so scared. I didn't know what was happening."

"I know. I know. Let's get you back to my house and I'll check on Cam."

Jules stiffened and pulled away. "No. I can't leave him."

He wanted to protest, to demand she go home and rest, but he wouldn't be the one to stop her. If he were in her position, he'd tear the world apart to be with Ali.

He shared a glance with Trinity, who nodded in agreement. If she thought Jules wasn't stable enough to see Cam, she wouldn't cave to Jules' request.

Trinity stood next to Thiago, then looked at Jax. "We'll touch base with your sheriff about what we know." She rolled her eyes. "I'm going to have to give him a debrief on my situation anyway."

Not waiting for Jax's response, the two left the hospital quickly, knowing time was no longer on their side. Though Jax was beginning to think it never really was to begin with.

Jules rubbed her forehead and looked from Ali to Jax. "They had rolled Cam through the restricted doors and left me standing in the hall. I tried to follow, but they wouldn't let me. So, I've just been standing out here for a few hours, and then I saw you walking into this room, so I just..." She closed her eyes and let out a breath. "I waited for you. I didn't know what else to do."

Ali gave a soft smile. "You were in shock. It's okay. Do you know where they were going to take him?"

Jules shook her head. "They wouldn't give me any information. All I know is they said he wouldn't need surgery."

"That's good news," Jax said. "Okay, let's go find out what's going on with him."

Leading the way, he found a nurse and flashed his badge as he asked for an update and a room number. This nurse happily gave him the information he needed, a stark contrast to the one who seemed to have it out for Trinity.

After nearly ten minutes, they stood outside Cam's room and Jules gently knocked, letting herself in. The steady beeps ushered them inside and Jax clenched his jaw when he saw his friend laying in the hospital bed, sound asleep. Ali grabbed his arm and then followed Jules to his side, each of them taking one of his hands.

Cam's eyes slowly opened and he smiled at them both. "It must be my lucky day if you two are taking care of me." He tried to laugh but then winced as he clutched his abdomen.

Jules climbed into bed with him, careful not to hurt him as she pulled herself close.

Tears blurred Ali's vision. "What happened?"

Cam looked away. "I was out drinking. I've been really upset about everything, and I've felt guilty for lying to everyone." He let out a long sigh. "I just wanted to numb myself. But when the bar closed, I didn't want to go home, so I called an Uber and told him to take me to Juliette's."

Jules closed her eyes, her arms gently tightening around him.

Cam continued, voice tight. "The Uber dropped me off, and I sat on her steps for a while, trying to convince myself to knock. Looking back, I don't think I realized how late it was. Then I saw movement, and before I could even focus, Levi was on me, trying to stab me." He paused, gathering himself. "I don't know how, but I managed to push him off... but he sliced my stomach. He was about to strike again when the neighbors' porch light came on. It must have scared him, because he ran. After that, everything's kind of hazy. But I remember thinking I was going to die and Juliette's face was the last thing I wanted to see." He kissed Jules' head.

Jax watched as tears slid down Juliette's cheeks while she buried her face in Cam's chest. He couldn't undo what had happened, but maybe a ton of ice cream could ease even a fraction of her pain.

Meanwhile, Ali kept her gaze on the floor, trying to hide the sorrow in her own eyes. The brother she had once believed would protect her was now hunting the people she cared about. Jax couldn't even begin to fathom what either of them was enduring.

After the silence became unbearable, Cam looked at the ceiling. "When I said I was scared to come forward, this is why. I knew he'd try to kill me." Then, his gaze locked on Jax. "He *will* come after Ali next. We all know Levi is spiraling, and when he finds out I'm not dead, it's going to get worse."

Jules sat up while Ali clutched Cam's hand, her eyes colliding with Jax's. And for the first time, he saw terror in her eyes.

And Jax knew if he didn't find Levi soon, he might lose everything.

CHAPTER 40

Juliette kicked her shoes into the corner of her doorway as Cam slowly limped inside, neatly lining his shoes along the wall. He lifted a brow at the many jackets and pairs of pants that were strewn all over the home. As she carefully led him into the living room, he stepped over a variety of shoes that had been scattered throughout her small bungalow, and he chuckled.

Heat crept up Juliette's cheeks. "I'm so sorry. My mother comes once a week to clean, but she didn't come this week with everything that's happened." She began talking faster, nervous he'd be turned off by this side of her. "If I even *think* there's a possibility I might have company, I try to clean up, but obviously I didn't know when you'd be released and-"

Cam kissed her gently, and she immediately melted into him. He smiled and said, "It's okay. A little mess won't hurt." He glanced around. "Or a lot of mess."

She laughed and swatted at his chest. "Hey! I'm a working lady." She sighed. "Knowing I don't always clean doesn't scare you away?"

"I love you, Juliette. Not even God himself can scare me away from you. You're perfect in every way, even if you doubt it sometimes."

Jules laid her head on his chest. His words healed the heartbreak she'd been carrying around for the last two years. The heartbreak her ex-boyfriend had caused her.

She and Orette had been together nearly four years when she'd walked in on him and her best friend, Katrina. The sight of them in the bed she'd shared with him had her distraught. Orette and Katrina had both tried to talk her down and had told her it was nothing. They'd even offered to let her in on their little affair, which had made her vomit in the middle of the hallway. She had left Orette's house a shell of herself, unable and unwilling to love someone else so fully again.

Until she met Cam.

He had healed something within her, something he hadn't broken. Cam had slowly chipped away at the walls she'd placed around her heart, never pushing her to give more of herself. Jules had been up front about her ex's affair and how devastating it had been for her, and Cam had catered to the broken pieces of her heart.

Jules didn't think it was possible to be whole again, but Cam had glued her back together, and she was somehow stronger than she'd been before, despite their recent struggle.

She carefully helped him sit on the couch, propping up his feet. They'd spent the last two days at the hospital, waiting for the doctor to give him a clean bill of health. Or mostly clean, she supposed. Thankfully, the lacerations he'd received weren't deep. He only needed stitches, although those had come in a great number.

Images of that night still flashed through her mind when she looked at Cam. The knocking, the blood, the tears, the sirens. She had been terrified she would lose him, and guilt had nearly swallowed her whole. He'd been drinking because she'd been dodging his calls. And the last time they had spoken, she hadn't been kind.

So, when the doctor announced he'd be just fine, Juliette refused to leave his side. Nothing else mattered. Not the lies or the fight. She could work through those. Now, all she wanted to do was be with him.

She curled up next to him, careful not to put pressure on his wound. Grabbing the remote, Cam put on The Notebook, knowing it was her favorite movie. But before he hit play, she took his hand. "I talked to Trinity. Why didn't you tell me about the girl you went to school with?"

He didn't say anything at first, rubbing her arms with his fingertips. After a moment, he looked at her. "I hate talking about my past for a reason. I'm not that kid anymore. I was broken as a teen and made plenty of mistakes, but I worked hard to build a life for myself despite my family." He shrugged. "I guess I just didn't think you'd love me if you knew about it."

Jules lifted her head and cupped his face. "Not even God himself can scare me away from you."

Cam froze for a moment, then pulled her closer. "Good. There's no one else I'd rather spend my days with."

Jules laid her head back down on his chest and listened to his heartbeat for a moment. "Do you think you're going to ever talk to your family again? Even Ali?"

Cam didn't answer immediately, and she knew he was reliving memories that no doubt haunted him. She couldn't imagine what it was like for him, being a fourteen-year-old and finding out your mother had an affair with your uncle. A revelation that had unraveled everything and set off the cascade of tragedies that followed.

Juliette found herself heartbroken for this man she loved so much.

Finally, he sighed and said, "After Missi had died, Levi and I couldn't stay out of trouble, and we couldn't stop fighting. It was bad. And the family was acting as if nothing had happened, as if Missi had never existed or Levi hadn't been the one who killed her. We couldn't get the help we needed, so it had seeped into everything we did. It was so toxic living there, and I just couldn't pretend anymore. So, I left as soon as I got the chance. I know it hurt Ali the most, but I had to cut them off or I wasn't going to make it out of that house alive."

She was surprised by the subtle admission. Jules only knew Cam as a happy man who, while slightly reserved and careful, was also quite funny and adventurous. The fact he had contemplated such dark thoughts weighed on her.

"So, the short answer is no." Cam shook his head. "I won't ever talk to them now that Ali knows the truth. But I might reach out to her more often than I do. I just don't know what that looks like at the moment."

She climbed off the couch and went to the kitchen. Walking to the fridge, she pulled open the freezer door and grabbed a carton of ice cream Jax had delivered. Then she went to the drawer on the far side of the kitchen and took out two spoons, setting her phone on the counter. Not bothering with bowls, she padded back to the living room and sat, handing him a spoon.

"Growing up, if I was ever sad or going through something hard, my mom would sneak a carton of ice cream into my room, and we would watch a movie while we ate it." She smiled. "My sisters would always find out, so eventually they'd make their way into my room too. Then, my brothers would barrel in, poking fun at whatever movie was on. I wouldn't get much ice cream, but the way my family piled around me somehow made me feel better." She sighed. "I know it's just me here, but I figured ice cream might help a little."

Cam chuckled and kissed her. "This is perfect."

He took his spoon and scooped out a bite as he hit play, and Juliette melted into his arms.

CHAPTER 41

I t had been a week since Cam had been released from the hospital. After investigating the stabbing, the police had concluded that Levi must have been following Cam, looking for an opportunity to kill him. So, when Cam was drunk and alone, Levi had seized his chance.

Thankfully, Cam hadn't been hurt too badly, though Juliette doted on him completely.

Ali was thankful for the woman in more ways than one. And she was glad the two had made amends, though she knew Cam would have to spend a lot of time making up for his lies and secrecy.

Over the course of the week, they'd also gotten an update on Theresa and Dianne. Theresa had been released fairly quickly, only having a large gash on the back of her head. But, to Ali's dismay, Theresa refused to speak to her or return her phone calls.

Dianne, however, had just come out of her coma a few hours ago and seemed to be on the mend. Jax had sent an officer over to interview her, but the woman was a vault. She wouldn't even acknowledge the officer who stood in her room. So, the deputy had left. And Jax was irritated.

Now, they all sat in the cold, shifting in their lawn chairs.

In an attempt to get Ali's mind off of everything, Jax had brought her to the Lakeland Christmas Parade. She was excited to spend some time with him doing something other than poring over family secrets or reliving her childhood trauma.

The last few weeks had been exhausting, and she wasn't sure when it would end. Levi was still missing. There was no sign of her father. She'd even attempted to leave a bouquet again, but he hadn't responded to her message.

They were at a standstill.

And Ali was terrified of the outcome. Because, no matter what happened, she would be left heartbroken.

Cam handed her his bag of popcorn, and she happily took it from him. Then, she laid her head on Jax's shoulder, pulling her blanket around her.

Thiago let out a whistle for Miss Florida as she graciously waved to the crowd. Trinity elbowed him. "Don't be a creep," she said.

Thiago let out a huff and Ali chuckled. She found his and Trinity's relationship quite interesting. Their dynamic wasn't typical, but it seemed to work for the agents.

A schoolgirl approached the group and handed Jules a piece of candy. Jules smiled wildly. "Oh, you are too sweet! Merry Christmas!"

The girl giggled. "Merry Christmas!" Then, she dashed away, eager to be with her friends.

The parade continued, showcasing a variety of organizations and businesses, each bringing the magic of Christmas to life. Ali loved to watch the high school dance teams as they glided through the street, followed by the bands that blared different renditions of Christmas songs. Then, of course, there were the many clubs and pageants that tossed out candy, and churches that sang about a babe in a manger on a silent night.

There was something magical about watching the city come together to celebrate the holiday. Despite the horror they'd endured at the hands of her brother, they wouldn't be terrorized into staying home. And though she initially thought it was best to stay home, she was glad Jax had convinced her otherwise.

She shoved her hand into the bag and pulled out a handful of popcorn and popped it into her mouth, bristling at a gust of wind. Eyeing the end of the parade, she saw the many children gather at the edge of the street, waiting for Santa's float. But before Mr. and Mrs. Claus made their appearance, Polk County's Sheriff, Gordon James, passed by and waved.

Ali smiled, happy to have had some fun with Jax and his team. She took his hand, and he lifted it to his mouth, placing a kiss on her knuckles.

The sheriff's float stopped, waiting for the front of the parade to continue through the streets. As Ali looked closer, she noticed the steady drip of crimson as it flowed from the back of the structure.

Furrowing her brow, Ali tugged on Jax's arm and pointed. "Look at the back of the float."

Jax looked at Jules. "What the hell?"

"Is that blood?" Trinity whispered.

"I don't know," Jax said, shaking his head. He looked at Ali, then at Cam. "Both of you stay here."

Ali watched as Jax and Juliette approached the back of the float, a few other officers now aware of the possible situation. Trinity and Thiago slowly scanned the crowd, looking for a threat.

Ali held her breath as Cam clutched her hand. They watched intently as Jax carefully pulled open the back latch. Jumping back, a woman's body fell onto the concrete, forget me not flowers falling to the ground with her.

Before Ali could grasp the danger, they were in, hysteria erupted. Screams tore through the crowd as people ran blindly, unsure if the threat still lingered nearby. Mothers grabbed their children and fathers shielded their families. Police officers tried to create order, but no one listened.

Ali and Cam moved to get out of harm's way, but a large man toppled over Cam and the two fell into the grass.

Ali screamed, "Cam!"

The large man pulled himself up and continued to run, ignoring the damage he'd done. As more people rushed to safety, Cam attempted to shield himself from further injury as he climbed to his feet. As he regained his footing, he clutched his stomach.

Terrified for her cousin, Ali quickly pushed through the mob and went to him, putting his arm around her shoulders. He lifted his hand and blood seeped through the fabric of his shirt. He winced. "I think I pulled a stitch."

Seeking safety to assess his wound, they backed into a corner of a building a few feet away. Cam inhaled sharply and pulled his hand away from his wound. "I need to get medical attention. Stay here and wait for Jax, okay? If you go into the crowd, you could get hurt."

Ali shook her head. "I can help you."

"No, I don't want you getting hurt. Just stay here."

Ali watched him disappear before she could stop him. Horror gripped her as the crowd's screams filled the air and police moved to contain the growing crime scene.

Suddenly, a hand clamped over her mouth and metal connected with her back. "Come with me quietly, or I'll kill you."

Her eyes rounded.

This didn't make sense. Why would he kidnap her?

Fighting panic, she frantically searched the crowd for Jax. Lost in the surge of chaos, he was nowhere to be found, and a cold wave of fear washed over her. He couldn't help her.

So, as tears flowed down her cheeks, Ali complied.

The man slowly led her around a building to an ally away from the uproar and prying eyes. The trunk of his car was open, and her heart slammed against her chest. She instinctively wanted to fight back, but she couldn't find the courage.

The voice startled her. "Get in, Alabama."

"Please," she whispered. "Just let me go."

She flinched at the sharp bite of the needle that he'd plunged into her neck. Then, not waiting for her compliance, he shoved her into the rear hatch.

Then she watched as her Uncle Rick's face faded into the darkness.

CHAPTER 42

J ax paced the conference room, trying to keep calm. Ali had been missing for twelve hours, and he knew the odds of finding her alive were dissipating with every tick of the clock. No longer able to control his rage, he smashed his fist into the wall, the impact reverberating through his arm as the cracks splintered across the plaster.

The sharp sting of broken skin barely registered against the fire in his veins as he stomped over to his desk and threw open the bottom drawer. He slammed down a glass and watched the amber liquid swirl around. He brought the drink to his lips, desperate to numb the suffocating panic gripping his chest.

"Don't you do it, or I'll kick your fucking ass, Jaxon Moretti," Trinity threatened.

He froze, debating the risk. Getting his ass beat might be a good outlet for the anguish crushing his soul. Instead, he sighed and set down the drink as he crumpled into his chair.

Trinity sat on the edge of his desk, staring down at him. "Get it together so you can save her. I know your first reaction is to numb the pain, and I get it. But that will only get her killed. So, pull yourself together."

Jax looked up at her. "I can't lose her. I-" He let his voice trail off as he fought back tears. He didn't need to say anything more. She understood.

Jules nervously approached the two of them. Shadows lingered beneath her eyes and faint remnants of yesterday's makeup blurred unevenly across her face. "Haze finally called. He thinks we need to talk to one of the prostitutes he knows."

"Why are we bothering with that right now?" Jax asked bitterly. "Ali is running out of time, and we're focused on a damn prostitute?!" He pounded his hand on the wooden surface.

Juliette jumped, but Trinity stood and crossed her arms, glaring at him. "It matters because any information we get is one step closer to finding her. And if you want any chance at finding her alive, quit being an ass to everyone and help us find her. Think like a damn *cop*, Jax."

Upon hearing the commotion, Thiago emerged from the conference room. "What's going on?"

Jax eyed the agent. Then, after a moment, he shook his head and sighed. "I'm sorry. I'm just-"

Jules touched his hand. "We know."

He clutched her hand, then stood and grabbed his jacket off the chair.

Trinity put up her hand. "What are you doing?"

He furrowed his brow. "Going to talk to this lead."

She shook her head. "No, you're not. You're not in the headspace for it." She pointed to Juliette and Thiago. "Jules is coming with me while Thiago keeps an eye on you."

Jax stepped toward her. "I have the authority to remove you from this case and my station."

She sized him up, every inch of her defiance on display as she matched his simmering glare. They had done this dance a multitude of times growing up. He'd lose his temper and try to intimidate her. She'd cross her arms and challenge him by closing the distance between them. She'd never cower, and he'd never do anything else except glare at her. Eventually, the two would end up hysterically laughing at one another.

And if the tension weren't so high right now, that's exactly what they'd be doing.

Jax knew he'd have to bully his way into going with Trinity. And he didn't care. He would move every star in the damn sky if it meant saving her.

But, to his surprise, Trinity simply sighed. "Fine, you can come. But don't fuck this up."

"Thank God," Thiago said. "I'm tired of being everyone's damn babysitter."

Trinity rolled her eyes at her partner as some of the tension subsided. As he walked by, Thiago gently patted Jax on the shoulder and then disappeared into the conference room, Juliette on his heels.

Then, Jax and Trinity walked out of the precinct and made their way to Lakeland.

After a silent twenty-five-minute drive, Jax studied the run-down motel in front of him. He didn't even want to think about the diseases and germs that no doubt clung to every crease and crevice of the filthy building. And as his gaze swept across the property, numerous patrons quickly retreated back into their rooms upon their arrival. Lucky for them, Jax didn't care enough about their criminal endeavors to walk past the parking lot to arrest them.

"This place is a shithole," Trinity said, her mouth turned down.

"You're telling me."

A tap on their window had Jax turning to see an older woman standing outside the car. He rolled down the window as winter air wrapped around him. He nearly gagged as an acrid stench filled the car.

"You with Haze?" the round woman asked, dragging on her cigarette. Dyed an unflattering shade of brown, the color left her hair looking flat, greasy, and unkempt. Though Jax thought it may just be due to her lifestyle.

He said, "Yes, ma'am. We heard you have some information for us."

She laughed, breaking into a fit of coughs. "Sugar, you can only call me ma'am if you're taking me to bed." She eyed Trinity. "You're a cutie. You two together?"

Trinity paled. "Ew. Absolutely not."

"Ahhh, swinging for the other side? Me too, if you ever get lonely." The woman grinned slyly, showing a row of rotted teeth.

Trinity nearly failed to hide her disgust, so Jax intervened. "What information did you have?"

The woman sighed, waving them out of the car. "Come on. I'm not standing out here for people to see. Don't want people thinking I'm a rat."

Jax and Trinity reluctantly got out of the car and followed her to a street-level room. Upon walking inside, the smell of booze assaulted them. Cigarette butts were strewn across the carpet. And he was surprised by the condom wrappers littered all over the floor, along with the pipe and needle that sat on the dresser.

On edge, Jax urged the woman. "Look, can you tell us what you know? A woman's life is in danger."

She poured a shot of bourbon and threw it back, taking her time. Jax clenched his fist, irritated by her lack of concern. If hauling her off to jail wouldn't potentially hinder him from finding Ali, he would do it out of sheer spite.

Finally, she said, "There's a story about a woman who was kidnapped forty years ago. Rumor has it she killed her captor and ate his heart after being held captive for years. After her escape, she disappeared and no one has heard from her since."

Jax and Trinity shared a glance. Trinity raised a brow. "She ate his heart?"

The woman chuckled. "Okay, that part is dramatized. But the tale is true. She survived nearly five years of torture and her story is a beacon of hope. Us working girls recite it when we get snatched up." She wiggled a finger at them. "Which happens more often than you think it does. These men take us as if they have a right to our bodies and rape us over and over again, sometimes passing us to friends and family. Then they dump us in the street like yesterday's trash."

"What does this have to do with our serial killer?" Trinity said. It was clear she felt the woman was yanking their chain.

"I'm getting there, Sugar." She said, taking another shot. She wiped her mouth with the back of her hand. "I met the girl who got away when I had started working the corners. I was around thirteen then, and she'd taken me under her wing. She told me what had happened to her, how he'd held her for five years before letting her go. He'd burn her, rape her...all sorts of stuff."

Jax furrowed his brows. "Elizabeth?"

The woman froze. "You talked to Lizzie?"

He nodded. "She told us what happened to her. We opened up a case to see if we could catch the guy."

"Good, then you need to hear Jezzie's story next."

Trinity held up her hand. "I'm sorry, what does this have to do with the Scarlet Letter Killer? Elizabeth's case is separate."

"That's what you think." The woman shook her head. "Anyway, after Lizzie came back, we worked in pairs a lot. I was on the corner with my girl Jezzie. And yes, that's short for Jezebel, which is the name on her damn birth certificate."

She rolled her eyes, then sighed. "We were both fourteen at the time, almost fifteen.

"And oh man, Jezzie was a looker. She had a beautiful body and these huge boobs that made her look like she was twenty-something. And she had long, thick, black hair with piercing green eyes." She paused for a moment, getting lost in the memory. "One day, a guy drives up. He might have been about my dad's age, if I had even known my dad, and he tells Jezzie to get in. I told her not to; something about him gave me the jeebies. But Jezzie wanted to get paid, was trying to get enough money to go find her mom in Miami. So, she hopped in and went with him.

"It wasn't until about two days later that he came back to that same spot and dumped her in the street. I happened to be talking to a John and ran over to her. She was pretty bruised and bloodied. You could tell he had tortured her. She had marks on her wrists and ankles. He'd burned her with cigarettes above her chest in some weird pattern that looked just like Lizzie's. I think he smacked her around a bit too, but I don't know if that was a fetish or because she was fighting back." She shook her head. "I tried to get the John to help me take her to a hospital, but he didn't want to get involved. So, I sat on the sidewalk, holding my friend and screaming for help. But no one wanted to help the whores...even though we were babies."

A tear fell down her face. "She died in my arms, right on that sidewalk. She died from swelling in the brain due to lack of oxygen. At least, that's what the cops said when they finally got involved." She shook her head. "I think the man tried to kill her and panicked when he realized he didn't do it right. A few months later, her mother came looking for her. Said she had no idea Jezzie's father had been trafficking her and was there to take her home. I had to tell her Jezzie was dead."

She blinked quickly and looked to the floor. "Man, I haven't talked about Jezzie in... well, never." The woman closed her eyes. "The sight of the lines around her neck from where he'd been choking her is engraved in my memory."

Though Jax was still irritated with the prostitute, he felt bad for her. It was clear she'd lived a difficult life. He couldn't imagine the things she'd seen in the years she'd worked the streets.

"Do you remember what the man looked like?" Trinity asked. They didn't have time to mince words or offer condolences. Ali was running out of time and they needed answers.

She said, "Blonde hair, tan. He was handsome, too. Had a nice truck and nice clothes, so I knew he had money. Was probably well respected in the community. Those are usually the ones that get away with everything, the ones who can pay off judges and cops." She furrowed her brow and tilted her head. "And it was strange, he had someone else in the car with him. Another guy. Maybe his son? He wasn't much older than me at the time. I remember because the kid tossed down some tiny blue flowers."

Trinity and Jax shared a glance as Trinity quickly pulled out her phone and showed the woman a photo of forget me not flower. "Like this?"

She snapped her finger. "That's the one. Will never forget it."

Jax thought over his conversation with Elizabeth Norman, her last words striking him. "Did Jezzie resemble Lizzie at all?"

She nodded her head slowly. "Now that you mention it, yeah, she did. Probably could have passed as sisters." Her phone buzzed and she pulled it out of her purse. "I've got a friend coming over in a minute, so y'all gotta get going."

Jax nodded to her. "Thank you for your help. And I'm sorry for everything you've been through." He meant it too. She was a lost soul and had seen far worse evil than he had.

He and Trinity walked out the door, and Trinity immediately spun to look at him. "When I found Levi in the clearing, he said I was missing something. This was it." Her eyes widened. "Jax, there's two of them."

He shook his head. "There's no way. Serial killers don't work together; you've said that before."

"No, it's just not typical. But..."

Trinity paused for a moment and Jax could see her brain working as she connected the dots. He touched her arm. "Tell me what you're thinking, and we'll work through it together."

She sighed and nodded. "I think Levi was groomed and taught. By fifteen, he showed no hesitation marks where he carved the letter 'A' into his classmate's chest. And he'd already killed Missi and thought he'd killed Jared."

"But why would he switch to branding? They don't typically change their signatures, right? And if he was groomed, why isn't his signature the same as whoever groomed him?"

Trinity shook her head as they trotted toward the car. "He didn't. He started out branding his victims. The fifteen-year-old wasn't planned. He used the pocket knife he had on him. And besides, he would develop his own signature once he got comfortable."

"So, who groomed him?" Jax asked.

"I think it was Jared. They probably bonded over killing, but the affair screwed everything up. Levi was likely enraged by it and killed Jared. Everyone else probably thought it was on behalf of Theresa, but really it was because *he* felt betrayed. He likely felt Jared shouldn't have done anything to risk their little arrangement."

He hit the gas pedal and moved the car back toward town. Following her thought, Jax nodded. "The flower isn't for the women he kills. It's a slight at Jared."

Trinity said, "And since Jared isn't dead after all, that's going to trigger Levi when he finds out, if he doesn't know already. And I have a feeling Ali will pay the price for her father's sins."

CHAPTER 43

Trinity hated hospitals. They reminded her of her own past and trauma, a shadow that had etched itself into the depths of her. She fought back a wave of nausea as the sharp scent of antiseptic slammed into her. As she walked the hall, the steady beeps grated on her nerves. But she took a deep breath and willed herself to push forward.

Now that Ali had been missing for sixteen hours, Trinity was done letting the Knox family manipulate her. For the last decade, the family had known what Levi was. Yet, they all had kept their skeletons tightly under lock and key. And now Ali was in danger because of their silence.

So, Trinity went to the one woman she knew she could break.

Trinity knocked on the door and Dianne glanced her way. Seeing Trinity, the woman's eyes widened, and she sank deeper into the bed.

Trinity attempted to put her at ease, despite her lack of people skills. She gently said, "Dianne, I'm Agent Harbor. I'm here to ask you a few questions."

"Agent?"

"Yes, I'm with the FBI."

The beeping increased as Dianne's eyes darted over her. She was scared of Trinity, and Trinity found that intriguing.

Dianne clutched her blanket. "What does the FBI want with me? I didn't do anything wrong."

"Oh, you're not in any trouble. I just need to ask you some questions about your family. Has anyone told you about Ali?"

The woman turned her head. "No. I have nothing to say."

"Dianne, I think you know a lot more than you've told the police. We want to help you." Trinity took a step toward the bed and Dianne narrowed her eyes.

"I'm sorry, I can't help. I don't know anything about Ali."

Trinity nodded. "She's been kidnapped, and if you don't help me, she's going to die. Just like Missi."

The woman's face contorted. "Please don't do this."

Trinity pushed harder. "Levi wasn't born a monster, was he? He was taught how to hide in the shadows and flourish in the light."

Dianne shook her head, the beeping erratic. "Please leave. I can't speak to you. He will kill me. He will kill Ali."

"Who will?"

Tears streamed down Dianne's cheeks. "Please, leave."

Trinity clenched her fist. She was done babying the woman. Dianne had known about Levi and Jared, and Trinity would bet Ali's life the woman was harboring if not one, but both of them.

Trinity took out the photo of Missi on the autopsy table and shoved it into the woman's face.

Dianne shrieked. "No! Not my Missi!" Sobs rocked her body as she brought a hand to her mouth.

Trinity pointed at her. "Your daughter is dead because of you. You owe it to this little girl to tell me the truth about *everything*."

"Get out!" Dianne demanded.

"Not until you tell me the truth! You were supposed to protect her. Instead, you all but gave her to the monsters who killed her."

Dianne's cries filled the small room, piercing Trinity's ears.

They didn't have time for the games the Knox family was playing. She needed answers. Sighing, she gently touched the woman's hand. "If you tell me where he is, I can stop Levi. I can stop him from killing Ali like he did Missi."

Trying to comfort herself, Dianne buried her hands in her face. As she did, her hospital gown fell around her shoulders, revealing a tattoo. Trinity studied the pattern.

No. Not a tattoo. It was a burn.

And it was in the form of an 'A.'

Realizing the gown had fallen, Dianne quickly pulled it back up. But Trinity knew what she had seen. And she finally understood what it was she'd been missing. Trinity tilted her head and furrowed her brow. "Did Rick do that to you?"

Dianne looked away. "My husband loves me. He would do anything to protect me."

"Dianne, did Rick burn you? Was he the one who taught Levi how to kill?"

Had she been wrong about the profile? It would make far more sense for Rick to have groomed Levi. Especially given that Dianne had cheated on him with Jared. The hatred from that could have sparked his need to involve Levi in his reign of terror.

Ignoring Trinity, Dianne kept reciting the same chant over and over as if to convince herself it was true. "My husband loves me. He loves me. Rick loves me..."

Trinity shook her head. "No, Dianne. If he did, he wouldn't have hurt you. He's a sick man."

"It's not true." Dianne's voice cracked.

"I will make sure he never hurts you or anyone else again, but you have to tell me the truth. It's the only way I can save Ali, something I *know* you wish you could have done for Missi." She pointed to the autopsy photo again. "It's time, Dianne."

The woman clutched the picture, bringing it to her chest for a moment. Then suddenly, fire flashed behind her eyes, startling Trinity. She said, "My name isn't Dianne. It's Cynthia Anderson. And Henry Knox kidnapped me when I was seventeen. Theresa saved my life by convincing Rick to marry me. He wanted a wife, and I wanted to live."

Trinity's eyes rounded. She hadn't expected the Knox family patriarch to be involved. She shook her head. "Did Henry brand you?"

Dianne's eyes glossed over. "No. Cameron did."

CHAPTER 44

C am opened the door for Juliette, and she followed him inside. She'd only
been to his house a handful of times, always enjoying the warmth the
cozy bungalow brought.

He took his shoes off and lined them by the door.

"How about a spring wedding?" Juliette suggested. "I know it's kind of soon,
but I think it would be beautiful."

Cam caressed her cheek. "Whatever makes you happy makes me happy. Just
send me a bill, and we'll get it covered."

Juliette's eyes gleamed as her heart soared. How had she gotten so lucky?
Though she still needed to heal the wounds that had fractured their trust, she
still recognized he was a good man.

He kissed her. "I love you so much."

"I love you, too," she said through each kiss.

After a moment, she pulled away and went into his living room and sat on
the sofa. "My sisters are going to fist fight over who will be my maid of honor."
She laughed. "I don't even think I could pick, anyway."

Cam chuckled. "I may need to borrow your family to stand on my side."

Though he tried his best to hide it, Juliette could see the pain in his eyes. She
hadn't even considered how wedding planning might affect him.

"I'm sorry. I didn't even think about how hard this might be." She pulled
herself closer to him. "We don't have to talk about it right now."

Cam laid his cheek on her head. "Juliette, I see how your eyes sparkle and how big your smile gets when you talk about our wedding. Please, don't stop." He held her close. "I'm happy because you're happy. And that's all that matters."

She pulled herself up and kissed him deeply. She was half tempted to have him take her to the courthouse right now. But her mother would have a heart attack if she did that. Plus, her siblings would riot.

Wanting more of the man she loved, she deepened her kiss. His hands splayed over her back and her fingers tangled in his hair. She quickly moved to unbutton his shirt and shoved it from his shoulders as he pulled at her pants.

The two slowly walked to his bedroom, where they found themselves intertwined in the sheets. Juliette gave herself to Cam just as she had done many times before. But this time felt far more special. This time, she surrendered herself completely, forgetting about the scars that made trusting so hard.

Afterward, with their hearts still racing, Cam pulled her close and kissed her forehead. "I need to jump in the shower before I take some flowers to my mother." He smiled slyly at her. "You want to get in with me?"

She giggled. "Maybe next time. You know, my mom always said you can tell a lot about a man by how he treats his mother." She climbed out of bed. "I'll just watch TV while you get ready."

He nodded and disappeared into the bathroom. Juliette glanced around, finding her clothes tossed haphazardly everywhere. She grabbed her panties off the nightstand and her shirt off the dresser. Her pants had been crumpled into a heap behind the door.

Where was her bra? She put her hands on her hips, studying the small space. Getting down on her hands and knees, she reached under the bed and snatched the lace cover, blushing as she recalled how it had gotten there.

Pulling on her clothes, she walked back into the living room. Not seeing the remote on the coffee table, she sighed. Again, she got on the floor to check under the sofa. Empty-handed, she moved to the table. Leveling her cheek on the carpet, she peered underneath the crevice.

Furrowing her brow, she eyed the square of missing carpet. Curious, Jules stood and pushed the table aside. A gold handle glinted in the light, and she reached out to pull it before stopping herself.

She considered minding her own business, but she's never been able to stay out of things. That's why she had become a detective. So, she pulled up the plank and peered inside.

Three rows of DVD cases lined the small space. Each with initials and a date scrawled across the spine.

What the hell?

Her stomach lurched. Was Cam a porn addict? Was he spending his evenings watching other women, wishing she was like them?

Jules held her breath and willed the nausea away as she pulled one out, a name scribbled on the front. *Anya Jones.*

Her heart beat faster.

She grasped another one. *Sierra Brown*

She nearly let out a whimper.

Then, she clutched a third one. *Serenity Raver*

These were the names of the Scarlet Letter Killer's victims.

In disbelief, she gathered three others. This time from a different row.

Susan Holtz.

Rebecca Shock.

Holly Sap.

These names were unfamiliar to her.

She pulled out the singular case with a red piece of tape running down the spine.

Carla Hodgins.

The schoolgirl who'd committed suicide after Levi had attacked her.

A sliver of hope pierced her heart.

Cam must be doing his own investigating. He must have recorded evidence or his own theories...

But as Juliette walked to the TV, disc in hand, her heart slammed against her chest. Holding her breath, she quickly muted the box and popped the plate into the device.

Then, she hit play.

A woman appeared on the screen, naked and tied to a filthy bed. She looked to be in a basement of some sort. And though the TV was muted, Juliette could still hear the screams of terror coming from her lips.

The girl's eyes darted to the side of the camera as she vehemently shook her head, tears spilling down her cheeks. A man emerged from the shadows, his back to the lens. Slowly undoing his belt, Juliette clenched her jaw, wishing away the nausea that threatened her as she watched the man raped the woman. Finally, he got off and pulled up his pants.

Juliette let out a quiet sob. And even without seeing his face, she knew exactly who he was. But she couldn't bear to acknowledge it.

Then, as the man turned around, Juliette's heart fell to her stomach. Cam locked eyes with her, his gaze void as a sinister smile stretched over his lips, proud of what he'd just done.

Then the screen went black.

Jules covered her mouth and stood, her body registering the danger. Her hand instinctively went to her hip.

Fuck!

Her gun was in the car. She needed to get her gun. And her phone. But as she turned around, she collided with the monster himself.

He shook his head. "I wish you wouldn't have seen that."

Jules ignored the rushing in her ears. "Baby, we can fix this. If you turn yourself in, you can get a plea deal."

She knew her bartering was useless. But she instinctively felt the urge to reason with him. Though she wasn't sure if it was because she loved him or because she knew if she didn't, she was going to die.

Cam let out a laugh. "Oh, Juliette." He caressed her cheek, and she wanted to recoil. "You know better than that."

"Why? Why did you kill all those women?" Juliette wanted to keep him talking until she could get the upper hand.

He tilted his head. "You were the lead detective on my case. You know exactly why I did it." He took another step toward her, smelling her fear. He smiled. "Well, go on. Tell me, Juliette."

She didn't respond, fear slowly paralyzing her.

His eyes darkened as he grabbed her by her hair, bringing her face to his. "Answer me!"

Jules shrieked. "Okay! I'm sorry!" She inhaled deeply, trying to calm her wildly beating heart. If she didn't focus, she was going to get herself killed. "You hate adulterers." She tried to steady her shaking voice. "You think they should be degraded because...because women are supposed to serve men. And cheaters distort the hierarchy."

Cam smiled, and released her and she landed on the floor. "Good girl."

She rose slowly, gauging his temper. "What about Levi? He attacked you. Is he in on it too?"

He laughed, and for a split second, Juliette thought she saw the Cam she'd grown to love. But hate quickly pulled at his face. "You dumb bitch. I stabbed myself. You and Jax were getting a little too close, especially with the FBI whore who thinks she knows everything." He clenched his jaw. "No one suspects the victim." He clucked his tongue. "It's a shame, honestly. If she hadn't run that background check, I probably would have disappeared and you'd have thought Levi killed me." He shrugged. "But now you're going to die."

Jules sucked in a breath, readying herself for the fight of her life. In one swift motion, her foot connected with his chest, and he crashed into the coffee table, glass shards flying across the floor.

He let out a grunt and Juliette took off toward the door. But Cam was quickly on top of her and she let out a shriek as his fingers grasped her ankle, and he pulled her back to him.

She tried to kick at his face but missed and his fist slammed into her side. She crumpled to the ground and he climbed on top of her. Fear nearly paralyzed her as she fought off the panic of what he'd do to her.

But she knew she wouldn't be able to escape if she panicked. So, she counted to ten as he pinned her to the carpet, her anxiety mounting.

She squirmed beneath him, darkness filling his eyes as he got close to her face. "If you don't stop moving, I'll do to you what I've done to all the other women unfortunate enough to find themselves naked and in my grasp."

A tear slid down her cheek. "Why did you do it?"

Cam smiled. "Why not?"

Suddenly, his hands wrapped around her throat and she gasped for air. His grip tightened and she clawed at his hands, her eyes wide as she fought to free herself. And as she stared into the eyes of the man she had once loved, everything went black.

CHAPTER 45

The agent's mouth gaped open, and Dianne's body shook as she realized what she'd done. For the last forty years, she had never told anyone the truth. And for the last forty years, she'd hidden Cameron away, hoping he would somehow defeat the monster raging through his veins.

But it was time for the world to know. Because if she didn't unmask him for what he truly was, Ali would die and Missi's death would be nothing but a wasted sacrifice.

Agent Harbor asked, "Why didn't you leave? Why haven't you told anyone?"

Dianne looked at the blanket laying across her lap. "Do you have children, Agent?"

She shook her head. "No, I don't."

"Until you do, you can't understand how strong a mother's love is for her child. I wanted to believe there was good in Cameron, even when every glimpse only ever revealed evil." Dianne frowned. "I've known what my son is since he was four years old, while standing over a dead squirrel he had gutted and killed." Dianne looked back at the agent. "He laughed, you know. He laughed as he tormented that poor creature. And then I knew. And the darkness was cemented the day he raped and carved up the girl in the woods. When he came home that day covered in blood, it was as if I was looking into the eyes of Henry the first time he had raped me. Cameron is every bit the devil his grandfather was. And even my love couldn't save him."

Agent Harbor shifted as she crossed her arms. "Why didn't you tell anyone? You saw dozens of women being slaughtered and you did *nothing*."

Dianne understood the agent's anger. No one could truly fathom what it meant to be the victim of a captor who let you live. And maybe that's because it was her price to pay. She let the monsters slink in the shadows, and now she'd be treated like one.

Dianne let out a sigh. "If I told anyone, he would have killed Cameron. And even though I saw darkness festering inside him, I didn't love him enough to sacrifice him. I was selfish. And I was terrified. Because part of me hoped we could make it out alive and he would no longer be under Henry's influence." She smiled sadly. "But everything fell apart when Missi died. And now, none of us will make it out alive."

Agent Harbor clenched her jaw. "The blood of dozens of women is on your hands just as much as it's on Cam's and Henry's."

Dianne nodded. "Yes. And I will pay the price for that." She twisted a loose thread on her blanket. "He's going to kill me, you know. It's his destiny. But you need to stop him before he kills Ali."

Despite her best efforts to hide it, fear pulsed at the base of Agent Harbor's neck.

Satisfied she had the woman's attention, Dianne laid back and closed her eyes. She was ready for the end. She'd played Henry's game, and though she hadn't won, no one else would have to compete in his horrific cruelty now carried out by her very own son.

Realizing Dianne had nothing left to say, Agent Harbor reached into her pocket and grabbed her phone as she walked to the door. Before leaving, she turned around. "A police detail will be assigned to you. Someone will be here to take your statement, and I will give the nursing staff strict instructions that no one is allowed inside your room aside from your current nurses and your doctor."

The dark-haired woman rushed out the door, and Dianne couldn't help but think how much the agent resembled herself when she was younger.

A lifetime ago.

A girl who had died forty years ago in a damp and dark basement.

Confident Agent Harbor wasn't returning any time soon, Dianne reached for the phone next to her bed and punched in the number she'd had engraved in her memory since the night Missi had died.

He answered on the first ring, just as she knew he would.

She said, "It's time. I told the police about Cameron."

A beat.

He had waited just as long as she had for this phone call. For her to finally declare the devil no longer had her in chains. But freedom came at the price of suffering.

She knew what that price was.

But he didn't.

And he would never forgive her when it was all said and done.

After a moment, he said, "I'll be there in ten minutes. Go to the back side of the hospital and wait for me there. Make sure you're not followed."

"I love you, Jared." She hung up and dragged herself out of the hospital bed, gritting her teeth as pain shot through her body. She made her way to the lonely chair in the corner of the room and opened up the clear bag that held her clothes.

Once she was finished changing, she walked to the door and paused as she looked down. Blood from her attack still stained the fabric. She wondered if that would become a problem.

But having no other choice, she pulled the door and peered into the hallway. The nurses were snickering at their station, occupied with the latest gossip. So, Dianne quietly tiptoed around the corner undetected. Once she made it to the stairs, she pulled on the fire alarm and ran down the stairwell as a rhythmic shrieking filled the hospital.

She needed utter chaos to ensure she wouldn't be discovered.

She needed enough time to finish what had been started forty years ago.

Pushing against the metal barrier, Dianne stepped into the frigid winter air and waited for Jared. The endgame was about to begin.

It was time for the monsters to die.

CHAPTER 46

Ali's head swam as she tried to sit up. She didn't know how long she'd been asleep, but she hoped Jax would make her some coffee. She reached out, expecting the warmth of him beside her, but her fingertips brushed over the loose dirt spread across the icy concrete floor.

Jax?

Where did he...

Her eyes snapped open and she quickly sat up, groaning as the movement sent searing pain through her head. Panicking, memories rushed over her. The parade, the blood, the body, Cam getting hurt... Her Uncle Rick standing over her.

Adjusting to the dim light, she blinked quickly and realized she wasn't alone. Her mother sat behind her, eyes sunken in as she stroked Ali's hair.

"Ma?" Ali said.

"Alabama, you had me worried sick," Theresa said, letting out a deep breath.

Ali turned toward her, but the room spun and she reached out to steady herself. Once she regained her bearings, she studied the small space. A bed sat in the far corner, covered in mysterious filth. And there was a set of stairs opposite her, but Ali wasn't sure where they led to. "Where are we?"

Theresa looked up at the ceiling. "We're under the barn."

Ali rubbed her face in an attempt to push the fog from her brain. *Under the barn?* Her eyes trailed the area again, looking for answers. Stains of blood clung to the floor, as though it's very surface still whispered of the horror it had absorbed.

Ali shook her head, her heart rate increasing. "Ma, has Uncle Rick been killing those women?"

"He-"

A sharp *creak* echoed above, followed by rhythmic footsteps beating on the stairs. Coming into view, Rick rolled his sleeves as he eyed the two of them. "Oh, good. You're awake."

"Rick, let us go," Theresa demanded.

He shook his head as he stopped in front of them. "You know I can't do that, Theresa."

"Yes, you can. Things don't have to end this way."

Ali didn't dare say a word, worried she might set him off. She'd heard the horror stories about what he'd done over the last decade. The way he tortured women and degraded his victims. She nearly vomited as she thought about the horrendous rape they had endured in their last days.

And it had all been at the hands of a man she loved deeply. Who had bandaged her scrapes and cuts and snuck her bites of ice cream before dinner. Who had climbed up a tree to get her when she had gone too high and was scared to move. Who had taught her to ride a bike and drive. The man who had been like a father figure to her.

And it was all a lie. A facade.

Or was it? Could a monster be both horrific and loving? Could the devil still harbor the remnants of an angel?

He squatted down in front of Theresa and frowned. "You and I both knew this is how our story would end. It's our *legacy*. You know what Pops always said: 'From the monster we were born, into monsters we were forged, and as monsters we will fall.'"

Ali looked at her mother. "What is he talking about?"

Rick and Theresa's eyes locked, a shared understanding as they both ignored Ali. Finally, Theresa hung her head and Rick gave a curt nod.

A chill ran down Ali's spine. "Ma?"

"Do you want to tell her or should I? It's time she knew the truth," Rick said gently.

And if Ali didn't know any better, he would have sounded like a concerned uncle, not a man who had slaughtered twelve women.

Theresa gathered Ali into a hug. "Alabama, before I tell you the truth, I need you to remember something: you're the only good thing in my life. You are the beauty where there's only been ugly. You are the perfection where there's only been devastation. You are the light in a house of monsters."

Ali threw her arms in the air as she pulled away. "What does that even mean?!"

But deep in her soul, she knew. She knew whatever they would say would break her. And she wished she could go back to the day she submitted her DNA and never go through with it. Because, in a moment's time, her life would be flipped upside down.

Theresa inhaled deeply and took Ali's hands. "Your grandfather was a murderer. He killed dozens of women over the years."

Ali ripped her hands from her mother's grasp as tears welled in her eyes. "No. Gramps would never hurt anyone. He was kind and loving..."

But her heart plummeted as she looked around the room, a testament to the horror the women had endured. And though her heart shattered in protest, her soul bore the weight of the truth. Because, somehow, she'd always known. From the screams of the ghosts in the woods to the late-night burials her grandfather claimed to be cattle.

Henry Knox was the devil, and she'd mistaken him for heaven.

This time, it was Rick who answered her. "The scariest monster is the one that appears to be a saint." He looked away. "Gin was one of his first victims."

Ali whipped her head toward him, her eyes rounding. "How is that possible? They were married. She had both of you." She scooted away from her uncle. "You're lying! You're the real monster!"

The room grew smaller and she could hardly catch her breath. She buried her face in her hands as she steadied herself, fighting off the black spots that threatened her vision.

Theresa went to Ali and wrapped her in a hug, trying to comfort her. She quietly said, "He kidnapped her and she begged for her life. She chose to stay with him so she could live."

Tears streamed down Ali's face, soaking the dirt below, her sorrow now mixed with the heartache of those who had been there before her. She wondered how many tears this floor had consumed. How many cries still clung to the walls.

Rick stood, shrugging a shoulder. "She had learned to love him, in her own way. Then she gave birth to both of us, so she couldn't ever really leave."

Ali pulled away from her mother. "Did...did he stop killing after that?" She desperately needed to believe her grandfather had changed. That he wasn't the evil her family claimed him to be.

Theresa looked away. "She helped him get his victims. And eventually we did too."

Rick looked at Theresa, then at Ali. "When two little kids appear to be lost, it makes women vulnerable."

Theresa nodded. "We did what we were told to survive. If we didn't help him, he'd kill us."

Ali was in utter disbelief. "Why didn't you run away? Or tell the police?"

Theresa shook her head. "It doesn't work like that, my sweet girl." Her mother pulled at her shirt to reveal a pattern of burns on her chest. "I traded my life for Dianne's. I could never leave or he'd kill me and her. And, eventually, he threatened to kill you and Levi."

Ali's face contorted. "Dianne was a victim, too? Does Cam know?"

Rick nodded. "She chose to marry me. It was Theresa's idea so Dianne could live."

A sharp screeching pierced her ears as someone else opened the door.

Her heart soared. *She knew Jax would find her.*

But as the figure descended the stairs, she realized it wasn't Jax.

It was Cam.

How did he know where she was? He hadn't talked to the family in years.

He shook his head as he clucked his tongue. "Why are you telling her our secrets, Dad?"

Rick didn't respond and Theresa clutched Ali's hand.

The room stilled as reality stood before her. Her grandfather had passed away years ago. Which meant he wasn't the Scarlet Letter Killer.

Cam watched her face falter as realization swept over her. He smirked as he stood over her. "Surprise. Your favorite cousin kills women for sport."

She felt a wave of nausea. "You said Levi-"

"Yeah, Ali. I lied." He shrugged. "He'll take the fall for it anyway."

"You're sick." Ali seethed.

He bent down, their noses nearly touching. "Oh, you have no idea."

She wanted to cry out in heartbreak. It had been her very own cousin whom she and her college roommates had feared as they cautiously walked from party to dorm. He'd been the darkness that had taken twelve lives from their families. He'd been the evil that had laid innocent women on display after torturing and suffocating them.

Movement from across the room caught her eye as Levi descended the stairs. "The police will be here soon, Cam. Let them all go and get out of here before you get caught."

Cam glared at Levi. "Oh, look. One big monstrous family. Now you can all die together."

Levi stood next to Rick, close to the stairs. "Cam-"

"Shut up!" Cam yelled. "You spent your whole life trying to protect her from the monsters, and you failed." He stood toe to toe with Levi and pointed back at Ali. "She's going to die because of you."

Levi jutted his chin. "Jared will kill you. If you touch a hair on her head, he will torture you like you tortured those women."

"Maybe." Cam looked at Ali. "But I'll enjoy watching him crumble as he cries over the dead body of another one of his daughters."

Theresa froze. "Jared's alive?" She looked at Levi. "How is that possible? I watched you kill him, Levi."

Cam lifted a brow. "Yes, Levi. Tell us how that's possible. His life for Ali's, re-member?" Cam laughed. "What's with our family and bargaining, as if Gramps and I quite literally couldn't have killed every single one of you."

Ignoring Cam, Theresa pointed at Levi. *"What happened!?"* she demanded.

Levi clenched his jaw. "I thought he was dead. I stabbed him, and we dumped his body. But I went back." He looked away for a moment. "He was my hero, and I just wanted to see him one last time. But when I got there, he was making noises. So I loaded him into the truck and took him to an ER outside of town."

"How could you not tell me?" Theresa cried. "He was the love of my life!"

Levi threw a hand in the air. "Ma, he was here against his will! Are you truly that delusional? He loved Dianne, and you know it."

"No!" Theresa thrust her finger at Levi, a vein throbbing from her forehead. "He stayed because he loved me, not because of the agreement!"

Ali finally climbed to her feet, unable to contain her own anger. "What the hell are you talking about?"

The two looked at Ali, almost forgetting she'd even been in the room. But it was Rick who answered her. "My father had kidnapped a woman and it turned out to be Jared's sister. I don't know how, but Jared found her. So my father made a deal with him: his life for hers. He would let her go on the condition that he couldn't leave the compound and he had to give Theresa a baby."

Heat crept through Ali's body and her breath hitched. She had been that baby. She had been conceived in the shadows of evil. She'd always believed her parents were madly in love, but it was all a lie. Her whole life was a lie.

Suddenly, Cam pulled out a gun from behind his back and trained it on her. "That's enough. We're done talking about Jared. It's time to finish what Gramps started."

Ali flinched as Theresa quickly moved to stand in front of her.

Rick took a step. "Cameron, enough. We need to get out of here before the police show up." But Cam ignored his father. Though Rick believed he was in control of his son, it was evident Cam held all the power.

Cam narrowed his eyes at Theresa. "Move, Theresa. You know I will kill you."

But Theresa didn't flinch. Arms crossed, she planted herself like a wall between Ali and the monster that threatened her.

As Ali's chest rose and fell rapidly, anger surged through her body, suffocating the fear that had gripped her moments before. She glared at Cam. "How could you do this? How could you hurt all those women?"

Cam smiled, pride glinting in his eyes. "It's in our blood, Ali. It's our legacy to be monsters."

Ali jutted her chin at him. "Levi isn't a monster. I'm not a monster. My mother, Rick, and Dianne... they've never killed anyone. That makes *you* the monster."

He laughed. "You say it like it's a bad thing."

Theresa kept her eyes ahead. "Alabama, don't. Don't push him," her mother commanded.

Cam tilted his head as he mocked her. "Auntie Terry, don't you want her knowing the truth?"

Levi took a step toward Cam. "Are you really going against Henry's orders? He said Ali wasn't to be touched."

A chill raced down Ali's spine. There was an unspoken knowledge between everyone that she wasn't privy to. And that terrified her.

"He's dead, so I don't think he'll ever know," Cam simply said. He took a step closer to Ali and her mother. "Tell her, Theresa."

Ali's mother clenched her jaw but didn't respond.

Rick shared a glance with Theresa, shaking his head at his sister as he silently warned her not to defy Cam.

Becoming impatient, Cam wiggled his gun. "Everyone else may not have tortured and killed, but they all knew about it. They heard the sweet screams of terror, the savory pleas for freedom. They turned a blind eye. So, doesn't that make them monsters too?" He paused, tilting his head as a wicked grin pulled at his lips. "And wouldn't you know, it's your legacy too."

Without warning, he shoved Theresa to the floor and forcefully grabbed Ali's cheeks. "Yours was just cut short. But I saw the look in your eyes when the blood stained your hands. I know what you are, Ali."

Ali pulled her face from his grasp and spit at him. "I'm nothing like you."

He wiped his face and then grabbed her by the hair and she screamed in pain. Levi jumped toward them, but Cam held the gun to Ali's temple and Levi froze.

Theresa tried to intervene, cradling her arm. "Cameron, let her go!"

"Not until you tell her the truth!" he yelled.

They all stilled, their chests rising and falling rapidly as silence filled the room. Theresa and Cam were in a staring match, and Ali held her breath and clutched his hand, hoping he'd release her.

Finally, Rick quietly said, "Tell her, Theresa."

Theresa looked at Levi, who nodded and hung his head in defeat.

Cam gritted his teeth. "Go ahead. Tell her how she's just as much a monster as I am."

Taking a breath, tears streamed down Theresa's face as she looked at Ali. "You killed Missi."

CHAPTER 47

J ax's phone vibrated, and he hoped it was someone calling with good news. They hadn't received a single credible lead, and he was ready to burn down the city in an attempt to find Ali. He knew his team would bring the matches and kerosene if he asked.

Trinity's name appeared on the screen and he tapped the green button. "What did you find out?"

"Cam is the Scarlet Letter Killer. You need to get to Juliette *now*!" Trinity yelled.

Jax's heart lurched and a low roar swallowed the sound of everything but his own pulse. And for a single moment, the world seemed to pause as he tried to make sense of Trinity's words.

Cam was the Scarlet Letter Killer?

"Jax?" Trinity asked. "Did you hear me?"

Her voice brought him back to reality, and adrenaline surged through his veins. "Yeah, I'm on my way to her right now." He snatched his keys off his desk and took off in a run for his cruiser, not bothering with a jacket. If Juliette was in danger, he needed to get her. He took the stairs two at a time, nearly losing his footing. "How did we fucking miss this?! He was right in front of us."

Trinity let out a short, frustrated breath. "Monsters are good at hiding, Jax."

Suddenly, the piercing wail of a fire alarm cut through the phone and he held the device away from his face as he pushed open the back door of the police station.

"Shit. Shit. Shit." Trinity's footsteps drummed rapidly as she broke into a near run.

"What happened?" Jax demanded. He didn't have time for his team to fuck up, and that included Trinity. Whatever had happened now, she'd better be able to fix it.

Her voice came in ragged gasps as she tried to pace herself. "The fire alarm just went off, but I'm pretty sure it's a diversion." There was a pause followed by a groan. "Shit. Dianne is gone!"

"Call for backup." He hung up the phone and looked at Jules' location. Jax flipped on his lights and sirens and drove like a madman to the prosecutor's house on the outskirts of town.

Anger heated his body as his thoughts turned to his partner. Jules had fallen head over heels for Cam, and it had all been a sham. And if he touched a single hair on Juliette's head, Jax would light the man on fire and light a cigarette from the damn flames.

Pulling up to the house, only Cam's vehicle took up space in the driveway.

Where was Jules? Had she simply left and forgotten her phone? Jax didn't want to think about the second, far darker option. By now the prosecutor knew they were closing in on him which made him all the more dangerous.

And that thought scared Jax to death.

Jax had spent years studying Cam's wrath, laid bare in the files of the women who had the misfortune of gracing Jax's desk. He'd seen the torture and torment they had endured at the hands of this monster Jax once called a friend. And if Cam felt cornered, no one was safe.

Including Juliette.

And including Ali.

Hurriedly, Jax got out of the car and pounded on the front door, but he was only met with the whistle of the wind as a cold breeze whipped through the trees. Uneasy, he walked to the side of the house, peering in each window. Still, no shadow caught his eye, nor did any sound echo through the home.

Cautiously, Jax walked to the other side of the house. Cupping his hands over his eyes as he glanced inside, he nearly jumped back.

Fuck.

Panic tore through him as Juliette's limp body lay just on the other side of the glass pane.

Saving Juliette and Ali meant silencing his emotions and focusing on what he needed to do next. Instinct taking over, Jax moved with purpose. Each step precise, every muscle ready for a potential threat. He took off toward the front of the house, adrenaline pumping through his veins.

Without hesitation, he squared up, planted one foot, and in one swift motion, Jax drove his heel into the door. The door groaned but didn't give way. Taking aim, he put all his strength into a second kick, letting out a guttural yell as he did. The force splintered the frame, and the door flew open.

He pulled his gun from his holster and held it out in front of him, assessing each room for danger as he carefully made his way toward Jules. Once he entered the living room, he forced his emotions aside as he struggled to focus on the scene as if he were just a cop.

His eyes swept over the room, and he blinked away tears as he came to Jules' body. Jax tamped down the surge of panic that had come barreling through his chest at the sight of the bruise around her neck.

No longer able to fight against the emotions clawing at the surface, he fell to his knees and pulled her body close to his. His voice cracked. "Come on, Jules. You can't leave me." He held his breath as he slowly brought his fingers to the base of her neck to check for a pulse. Though faint, there was a steady rhythm below his fingers, and her shallow breath fanned his face.

He let out a staggered breath as a tear slipped down his face, falling onto Juliette's cheek. "Jules, you're safe now. I've got you." Not wasting another moment, he pulled out his phone and called 911, requesting an ambulance and a BOLO for Juliette's car.

Then, he called Trinity. She answered on the first ring. "Did you find her?"

Jax clutched Jules closer, afraid he'd lose her. "He tried to kill her, Trinity." He fought back the sob threatening him. He didn't have time to be weak. He needed to catch the bastard who had destroyed so many lives. And Jax needed to kill him before he killed Ali.

A heavy crash vibrated through the phone as Trinity's rage echoed in every overturned object. "Dammit, Jax! Is she okay?"

"She's alive. I'm waiting for EMS." He paused, then said, "Why couldn't I see it? He was right in front of us the whole time!"

"None of that matters right now. We need to figure out where he's going next. Think like a perp, Jax. This is the one time it's actually helpful for you to compartmentalize. So do whatever you need to, but push the emotions to the side and think like a cop. Get into his head. You know him better than anyone else."

He quietly nodded, despite her not being able to see him. He wiped at his face as he closed his eyes, gaining his composure. The sirens in the distance grew louder, but it felt as if the world was moving in slow motion, each second dragging like a lifetime.

Pulling him from his thoughts, Trinity asked, "Where would he go? Where does he feel safest?"

Jax ran a frustrated hand through his hair. "I don't know! I honestly don't know much about him. He's never talked about owning other properties or anything like that..."

A sharp wail swept through the wind as the ambulance pulled into the driveway. Within seconds, officers and EMS poured into the house. Fighting the urge to resist the first responder who carefully pulled Jules from his grasp, Jax reluctantly released her.

Shit. He needed to call her brother, Derek. The Reid family needed to hear this from him. After all, he was to blame. He should have protected her.

He should have known she was in danger!

Her family would fucking kill him for this, and rightfully so.

Then it hit him. Cam was estranged from his family.

Nearly forgetting Trinity was still on the phone, Jax clutched the device. "He's going back to where it all started."

Ali's breath caught in her lungs as she vehemently shook her head. She looked at Cam. "You're lying!" She glanced at Levi, then back at Cam. "You told me Levi killed her."

A wicked grin tugged at Cam's lips and Ali's heartbeat quickened. Tears streamed down her face as she glanced at her mother, but Theresa looked away.

Through sobs, Ali said, "She was my best friend. I wouldn't have hurt her!"

She was not a monster. She wouldn't have ever done anything to hurt Missi. She didn't know what sick game Cam was playing, but she no longer wanted to be a part of it.

Air tightening in the room, she tried to steady herself. But it was useless. She crouched down, putting her head in her hands as sobs racked her body. She was terrified and all she wanted was for Jax to hold her and stroke her hair as he'd done with all the other nightmares she'd had.

Cam raised a brow. "Wow. You really don't remember, do you?"

"Knock it off, Cam," Levi warned.

But Cam simply laughed at their helplessness as he trained the gun on Levi. "Tell her what happened, *cousin*. Tell her how she fucked up mine and Gramps' entire operation and everyone just let her get away with it unscathed."

Levi clenched his jaw. It was clear he was juggling whether he wanted to be manipulated or if he wanted to stand firm. He had always been her protector. And even now, he was trying to figure out how to do that. But their options were limited.

Now it was her turn to protect him. And Ali needed to give Jax more time to find them. She looked at Levi and gave a soft smile. "It's okay. You can tell me the truth."

Levi and Cam held each other's gaze, a silent pissing match. After weighing his options, Levi finally looked at Ali. "When you saw the flowers on Missi's dresser, you told Mom. You thought it was cool that you both had the same flowers. Of course, Mom immediately knew there had been an affair, so she confronted Dianne. At some point, Jared got involved..."

Ali's heart raced as memories rose to the surface. Memories she had wanted to stay buried.

Ali clutched Missi's hand, afraid she'd be in trouble for finding the flowers. She hadn't meant for anyone to get in trouble. She just thought it was cool that she and Missi had the same flowers. They were basically sisters anyway. Best friends forever.

The two of them huddled on the couch watching Mommy and Aunt Dianne cry.

Why was Mommy so sad about the flowers? Didn't she love them?

Mommy pointed at Daddy. "How could you do this to me? We have a family together!"

Rage twisted his face, scaring Ali. He almost looked like a monster.

He yelled at Mommy, "You're delusional, Theresa! I came to save my sister and I did. I agreed to stay so your father would let her go. You knew from the beginning I'd never love you!"

Ali's heart hurt. He didn't love Mommy?

His voice became hushed, "You're a monster, just like the rest of them. I'm taking the kids and Dianne and getting out of here. I don't care if he kills you."

Ali clutched Missi's hand tighter. Mommy wasn't a monster. Why was Daddy being so mean? He was never mean. Ever.

Mommy sobbed. "You're not taking my kids!"

Air trapped in Ali's lungs. Why would Daddy want to take her from Mommy? Didn't he like being with them? She didn't want to leave Gin and Gramps or the farm. She loved it here.

Aunt Dianne had been so quiet Ali almost forgot she'd been standing there. She put her arm around Daddy's. Ali didn't like that. Only Mommy was supposed to touch Daddy.

Aunt Dianne said, "We're leaving, Theresa. I've waited fifteen years to escape, and every chance we've gotten, you've refused to leave. I'm not waiting anymore."

Mommy's eyes were angry, and she put her nose close to Aunt Dianne's nose. "How could you betray me?! After everything I've sacrificed for you!"

Aunt Dianne crossed her arms and yelled back at Mommy, "What you sacrificed? I gave up my freedom and my life because of the promise we made in that basement!"

"Fuck your promise! And Fuck you! You seduced my father and my brother and now my husband." Mommy's smile was evil. "My father was right; you are a whore."

Ali and Missi covered their ears. Those were bad words. They would get a spanking from Gramps if they used dirty words. Mommy was going to get in trouble if she wasn't careful.

Then, Aunt Dianne slapped Mommy, and Ali gasped. Ali shot to her feet. "Don't touch my mommy!" Ali ran to Mommy, wrapping her arms around Mommy's waist.

Mommy looked at Ali and Missi. Then she called for Cam and Levi and sent them all to the park. It was a short walk down the long path through the woods. As soon as they got there, Ali and Missi played tag through the play area, which eventually led to making flower crowns from the wildflowers in the grassy area.

They both started giggling as they smelled the skunk who lived nearby. Anytime they came to the park with Cam and Levi, there was a skunk. She and Missi had always tried to tell the boys, but they ignored the girls, happy to be hiding behind the bathroom.

Ali thought it was gross. There were much better hiding places than the stinky bathroom that never got cleaned. But the boys didn't know she knew about their hiding spot. She kept it her special secret in case they started being bullies again. She'd tell Gramps about it and they'd get in lots of trouble.

After a long time of playing, she saw Daddy's truck on the street. He and Mommy must be done fighting. He honked the horn then climbed out of the truck. "Levi, girls, we need to leave!"

Missi jumped off the swings, but Ali ignored her father. She didn't want to go home while Mommy was sad. So, she'd stay here until everything was better.

Emerging from their hiding spot, Levi went to Daddy while Cam stayed near the bathroom. Cam looked at Levi and Daddy and his eyes were mean. Which made Ali's tummy feel weird because Cam was almost always nice.

"Ali! It's time to go, now!" Daddy yelled as Missi climbed into the truck. When she didn't get off the swing, Cam walked over to her and crossed his arms. "She wants to stay, Jared. Let her have some more fun." Cam had smiled at Daddy and Ali was happy again. At least someone was on her side.

Levi whispered something to Daddy and then jogged back to Ali. "Alabama, get off."

But Ali didn't want to go. She was so close to the clouds. If she could kick just a few more times, she'd be flying!

So she ignored her brother, eager to become a fairy who would fly through the sky and use her magic fairy dust to make kids stay little forever. She and Missi had always promised to never grow up. But they needed to get to the clouds first. That was the only way they would become fairies.

Levi looked at her, then at Cam, who was now leaning against the sycamore tree. He'd started carving something in the bark with his pocket knife, but Ali couldn't read yet so she continued pumping her feet. Harder. Faster.

Almost there...

Whatever he carved made Levi mad because Levi grabbed Cam by his shirt. "If you touch her, I'll kill you."

Ali rolled her eyes. They were always fighting over girls. Eww. Didn't girls know that boys had cooties? Especially Levi and Cam.

Cam laughed and shoved Levi off of him. "You better not leave her alone then."

Levi glanced at Ali but didn't say anything for a second. Then, he yelled back to Daddy, "I'll meet you back home!"

Daddy was angry, but he nodded and went back home with Missi.

After a few more tries, Ali gave up trying to get to the clouds. Maybe she could try again tomorrow. But her legs hurt and she needed to rest.

Running down the dirt path back home, she left Cam and Levi in the dust. She'd always known she had super speed; she just tried to keep it a secret. Once out of the trees, she bolted through the front door to tell Missi about her lonely adventure.

Ali found Missi sitting on the couch, knees pulled to her chest as tears filled her eyes while the Mommies and Daddies still yelled at each other. Ali scurried over to Missi, worried she might be scared. She wiped at Missi's tears, but before she could ask what was wrong, Uncle Rick started yelling at Daddy. He grabbed Daddy by his shirt, and Aunt Dianne and Mommy started screaming. Gin and Gramps ran into the room and tried to calm everyone down, but no one was listening. Levi and Cam must have heard the loud noises from outside because they came running through the back door and pulled Daddy and Uncle Rick apart.

"What's going on?" Gramps asked.

Uncle Rick pointed at Daddy. "He's sleeping with Dianne." Then he pointed to Missi. "He's her real father."

What did that mean? Daddy was Missi's daddy, too?

Ali turned to Missi and smiled wildly as she whispered, "Missi, we're sisters! Just like we always wanted."

Missi started crying even harder. "I don't want a new daddy."

Ali furrowed her brows. "But my daddy is a good daddy."

Missi stood up and yelled at Ali, "No! He made Aunt Theresa cry! He just hurt my Daddy! He's a bad daddy!"

Daddy was not a bad daddy. He loved Ali very much. He told her every time he brought her flowers.

Angry, Ali got off the couch and shoved Missi. Missi stumbled back as she lost her footing and fell backward. A loud crack echoed through the room as she collided with the coffee table and shards of glass splintered all over the carpet.

Ali burst into tears. She hadn't meant to hurt Missi. She was just so angry. Daddy was a good daddy. And Missi was her best friend.

She waited for Missi to get up, but she didn't. She just laid on the floor and stared at the ceiling as blood stained the carpet below her. Ali crouched down and shook Missi, crying as she did. "Missi, I didn't mean to. I'm sorry..." But Missi didn't move. She didn't tell Ali she forgave her. Ali furrowed her brows and shook Missi even harder. "Missi! This isn't funny!"

Ali's heart dropped to her tummy as Aunt Dianne started screaming. Ali quickly put her hands over her ears, scared of the sound coming from her aunt.

Aunt Dianne pushed Ali away from Missi and yelled, "Get away from her! You're just like the rest of them!" Terrified, Ali ran up the stairs to her grandparents' bedroom where she climbed under the covers to hide. That's when she realized her hands were covered in blood.

CHAPTER 48

Ali's head swam as she struggled to catch her breath. She looked down at her hands, remembering the blood that had once stained her skin. Nausea threatened her.

She had killed Missi. She had killed her best friend.

She was the monster.

Cam ignored her visible distress, slowly pacing in front of her and Theresa. "I grew up hunting with Gramps, learning about the art of killing. We would take the Jezebels to the barn and spend days bringing pain and misery." He turned to Ali and snarled. "But then you ruined that. All because you went snooping over a damn flower!" He pointed the gun right at her forehead.

Ali froze, her eyes wide and pulse beating wildly.

But then Cam lowered the gun and started pacing again. It was clear he was losing control and Ali knew that was when he was the most dangerous.

He said, "See, if Missi hadn't died, both of you would have helped me and Gramps. It's tradition. Everyone in the family helped, and you two weren't exempt. But then she died and we had to hide her body. We couldn't go to the police, or they would snoop around and find what we'd been doing. So, we had to resort to killing women in the moment, damning their harlot souls to hell right in the middle of the street. We couldn't savor it or take our time." Cam glared at her, and she knew she was looking into the eyes of the devil himself. He raised the gun again. "You ruined *everything*."

Thinking quickly, she asked, "Is that why you left? Because Gramps wouldn't let you torture women here anymore?"

Jax, where are you? You're running out of time.

Cam paused, considering her for a moment. "He found me down here one day, my hands wrapped around a whore's throat after just having tortured her for the last three days." Anger clouded his dark eyes. "He reprimanded me and forbade me from ever doing it again. I begged him, but he wouldn't let me. He told me to leave until I could control my urges, so I did. But eventually, I came back." Cam snorted. "Henry thought *he* was a God, but he never realized I was something greater. That *I* held all the power. So, I gave him an ultimatum: let me torment the whores or I'd send the cops." He grinned and shrugged. "He gave me the barn as a welcome home present."

A shiver raced down Ali's spine. Cam was sick. So was her grandfather.

Then, she looked at Rick. "That's why you wouldn't let us near the barn. You were afraid we would find the women who were being held here." She clenched her jaw. "You let them torture innocent women! You could have saved them!"

Rick simply looked away, knowing he was just as guilty as Cam and Henry.

Maybe Cam was right. Maybe the entire Knox family was nothing but monsters masquerading with human faces.

Cam shook his head and turned his gun to Rick. "You're pathetic. You could have been great like us. Controlling when someone lives or dies. But you chose to live a mortal life. And now you're going to die."

Theresa screamed, "No!" She threw herself in front of her brother just as a thunderous *boom* ricocheted through the room. Theresa went down in a heap, blood pooling from the hole in her chest.

Ali vomited, no longer able to control her body's reaction.

Rick let out a guttural cry as he dropped to his knees and brought Theresa to his chest.

Pain tore through Ali's body as tears flowed down her face. She desperately wanted to go to her mother, but she didn't dare move, afraid Cam would surely kill her if she so much as breathed the wrong way.

Suddenly, another shot rang out, and Rick collapsed onto Theresa, his blood mixing with hers. And before Cam could turn back around, Levi lunged at him, the two crumpling into the dirt below their feet. Levi pinned Cam's arms above his head and slammed them into the concrete, desperate to make Cam drop the gun.

"Ali, get out of here!" Levi yelled.

Without hesitation, Ali scurried to the steps, taking one last glance at her mother's body.

Angrily, Cam lunged toward her, but Levi bared down his weight as his fists connected with Cam's face.

Ali hurried up the stairs and shoved open the door as she climbed outside, the winter air slicing her skin. And as she tore through the barn door, sirens wailed in the distance.

Jax!

But she froze, her eyes locked on the smoke billowing from the house as a blaze of yellow and orange clawed toward the setting sun. Another *pop* rang through the sky, commanding her attention as she crouched to the ground within the tree line, trying to find the source of the sound. She watched the barn door, waiting to see who would emerge.

Had Levi killed Cam? Was she safe now?

She heard his voice before she saw him. Cam cooed, "Ali, don't make this difficult. I will kill you." He slowly stepped into the winter winds, scanning the shadows as he hunted his prey, blood dripping from his face. Spotting her, he smiled as he smeared the crimson with the back of his hand.

She let out a whimper as he stalked toward her. She wanted to run, but her body wouldn't obey her mind's commands.

Then, a voice echoed through the trees. "Cameron Knox! Let her go. After all, it's me who you want."

Ali's head snapped up, drawn by the voice. Dianne was cloaked by the shadows of trees where the emerald opening led to the clearing. Cameron stilled, and for a heartbeat, the world seemed to hold its breath.

Without hesitation, Ali took off in a sprint toward the sirens that screamed in the distance, leaving the monsters behind her.

CHAPTER 49

Dianne felt as if she was looking into the eyes of the devil himself, something she'd long since grown accustomed to. When she'd found out she was pregnant with Cameron, she prayed he wouldn't turn out like his grandfather. She'd endured so much torture and torment, and he had been the bright light that had given her hope.

But that hope had quickly dissipated the moment she realized how deeply evil had infected the Knox bloodline.

Dianne had often wondered if Cameron was born evil or if he was simply a product of his environment. But such questions had been put to rest the night he had branded her for her affair.

After Levi had killed Jared, Rick and Henry had dragged her to the barn. She had thought for certain they were going to kill her. And yet, she no longer cared to live. The love of her life had been murdered, her daughter was dead, and her son danced with the monsters.

She hadn't fought them off when they had tied her to the bed used to torture the women they brought down to the pit of despair. Henry had raped her, a reminder that he was still in control of her freedom. He hadn't touched her since the day Theresa came to see her all those years ago, but it was as if all her demons were unleashed with the hiss of his zipper.

She had begged and pleaded, but they fell on deaf ears. Theresa wouldn't save her this time.

After Henry was finished, he had victoriously climbed back up the stairs. But Rick had stood silently in the corner of the room. In the depths of her soul, she had somehow come to love the man she'd been forced to marry. He had been gentle with her, patient even. He had realized it would take time for her to love him.

And eventually she had. As much as a prisoner could love her captor.

She'd begged him to let her live. Told him she'd do anything if he spared her. He had looked away from her as soft footsteps echoed through the room, Henry descending the stairs once again. And it was as if she'd been transported in time, her heart beating wildly as she fought off panic.

But it wasn't just Henry who had turned the corner. It was Cameron who had led the way. He had clung to a metal rod, the orange glow bright in the dimmed room. Henry had followed, smiling ear to ear as he studied the devil he had created.

Cameron had held out the brand to Rick. "Let the world know what she is. She's a whore and needs to be punished."

Rick had looked at Cameron, then at the rod. But, to Dianne's surprise, he had hung his head. "No. I won't hurt her."

Cameron's face had contorted as he stepped to his father. "You're weak! That's why she ran into the arms of Jared. Whores need to be punished!"

Dianne's body had shook in fear, knowing she was about to die. She only prayed it was a quick death, that the universe would show her mercy.

The back of Rick's hand had connected with Cameron's mouth, and her son had spit blood to the floor. Rick had said, "I'm not like you." He had glanced at Dianne, anger blazing in his dark eyes. Then he had looked back at Cameron. "You can do it. But you won't kill her. Do you understand?"

It wasn't a question, but a threat. And both Henry and Cameron had understood it.

Cameron had clenched his jaw while Henry had simply given a nod. And then Rick had disappeared up the stairs. She didn't remember what had happened next; her mind had drifted to a safer place while Henry had defiled her body and Cameron had branded her as a whore.

Dianne had felt betrayed by her son, but maybe she deserved it.

Eventually, Rick had come to get her and had brought her back to their bungalow where she had continued to live, chained to the monsters. And as Dianne had cleaned her burn that night, she had vowed she would destroy

Cameron. Not because of what he'd done to her, but because she knew what he would become.

And today was the day she would finally kill her son.

Cam looked back at Ali as she ran toward the sirens, torn on which prey he wanted more.

Making him choose, Dianne took off in a sprint, knowing his hatred for her far outweighed his bloodlust for Ali.

He sprang forward, chasing after her, and she slipped into the shadows of the trees, careful not to drop the gun Jared had given her that she'd carefully secured in her waistband. She could hear his footsteps beat against the winter ground as he gained on her. But she kept pushing forward as the clearing came into view. The blue hues called to her, the forget me not flowers all but withered away, an omen of the past and the future.

Once she was in the middle of the opening, she stopped and turned toward Cameron. Memories raced through her mind: Cameron as a newborn, as a toddler, as a young man. All the moments that made her believe he could be good. But then the ugly memories came quickly after, reminding her of what needed to be done.

Dianne had remained silent as her son tortured and killed dozens of women. She had become the monster she had once detested. The girl she'd once been had died in the barn the day Theresa came to get her out. But today, that girl would be resurrected. She would do what she was never brave enough to do before.

Cameron's shadow fell into the clearing, announcing his arrival before he even stepped into view. "Did you really think you could escape your destiny, Mother? Henry should have killed you in the barn, he should have made you another notch on his belt. But he let you live, and you've destroyed *everything* he built!"

She studied his face as he emerged from the trees. How had everything spiraled so far out of control? How had she allowed evil to seep into every part of him?

Maybe she was to blame for his atrocities.

But she would be damned if she went to her grave without taking him with her, purging the world of his darkness.

Yet, sadness swelled in her chest as tears fell down her face. "The day I found out I was pregnant with you my world changed for the better. I thought I wouldn't be so alone, that God was whispering hope to the depths of my soul. I watched you grow from a baby to a toddler and then to a child. And each passing day brought what my soul feared most. The darkness, the evil, the monster waiting to be released."

Dianne's heart shattered and she desperately wanted to go to him, to cup his face and hold him one last time. But she couldn't. Because it was no longer her son who stood in front of her, but the devil himself. "One night, I came into your room and watched your chest rise and fall with every breath. You were only five at the time and had been obsessed with cars. You had lined them all on the edge of your bed..." Her voice trailed off as she got lost in the memory. "You didn't know, but I'd been watching you torture animals in the woods and it disgusted me. The night I stood over you, I knew I needed to stop you before you became a monster. If I killed you then, you would be locked away in innocence, never knowing true darkness." She shook her head. "But I couldn't bring myself to do it. I wasn't strong enough to save you from what I knew you'd inevitably become. I loved myself more than I loved you. Because if I'd loved *you* more, I would have killed you that night."

Cameron stilled, surprised by Dianne's admission. Only the sounds of the forest and the sirens in the distance danced between them. Then Cam smiled. "I knew you were just like me." He laughed. "You blame the evil on Henry, that it ran through my veins because of my bloodline, but you're a monster too. You just won't admit it. You won't admit you heard women screaming in terror and you turned a blind eye. You won't admit your bloodline flows through me just as much as Henry's. And yours is just as vile. At your core, you're no different than the monsters you've tried to escape your entire life." He took a step toward her and she didn't falter. "I'm your personal devil reincarnate. The last face you'll see is the one from your worst nightmares." He lifted the gun, aiming it at her chest.

She reached for her own weapon, mimicking Cam's movement.

His laugh echoed through the canopy and birds took flight, escaping the impending danger. "You think you're going to kill me?" He scoffed. "You couldn't do it when it mattered, when it meant saving the women you knew I would eventually kill."

Dianne didn't waiver, though her heart longed for any fate but this. She desperately wished this was not how their story ended.

She desperately wished she hated him.

But she didn't. She loved her son. She loved him so much she would kill him. Because as long as he was alive, the evil would continue to swallow him whole.

Placing her finger on the trigger, Dianne saw the sergeant in the distance as he and the agent from the hospital carefully made their way toward the clearing, two other officers following close behind. But she didn't alert Cameron to their presence.

Once the sergeant was close, he trained his gun on her and Cameron. "Cam, put down the gun." He looked at her. "Ma'am, please drop your weapon."

She ignored the man, intent on carrying out her plan.

Cameron turned his head to look at the sergeant. "Or what? You'll shoot me? Juliette would never forgive you."

The sergeant shook his head. "You tortured and murdered numerous women. I think she'll get past it."

Movement in the tree line had Dianne shifting her gaze.

No. No. No.

He wasn't supposed to follow her. He was supposed to make sure Ali got out alive.

Jared Schultz slowly emerged with his hands in the air, glaring at Cam. "I told you I'd save them, Cameron."

All the color drained from Cameron's face as darkness clouded his eyes. His eyes narrowed, but he didn't move the gun away from Dianne. "So, it's true. You're back from the dead."

Jared didn't answer. Dianne desperately wanted to go to the man she loved, but she couldn't. Because if she did, it would ruin everything.

Cameron clenched his jaw and shook his head. "Always fucking up my plans. You had to go off and be a hero, bartering for your sister's life."

The sergeant took a step toward Cameron. "Cam, put down the gun and get on your knees. I know you don't want to die. But if you don't listen, we *will* shoot you."

"Not until I've done what Henry was too weak to do," Cam said. He looked back at Dianne and Jared. "He should have killed you both. But I won't make the same mistake."

"Don't do it. Don't make me kill you," the sergeant pleaded. Dianne couldn't mistake the quiet grief in the officer's gaze.

"I know you, Jax," Cam said, his gaze still unwavering from Dianne's. "I know you won't pull that trigger. Sure, you talk a big game, but at your core, you're weak. You're a scared little boy, terrified the world will never be safe. And you're right. It won't. Because monsters like me lurk in the shadows no matter how hard heroes like you try to destroy us."

The sergeant opened his mouth to reply, but Jared stepped toward Dianne, and both the sergeant and Cam moved their weapons on him, while the agent pointed hers at Dianne.

"Don't move!" The sergeant demanded. The base in his voice echoed and birds erupted from the trees in panic. Even the animals understood the danger that lurked in this clearing.

Jared slowed his pace and looked at Dianne, ignoring Cameron and the officers. "Put it down, Dianne. It's time to let go, to move on from everything that's held you captive. You're *free*. We're free. We can have a life together. We've waited for this day for decades, and it's finally here. Please, put down the gun."

Dianne looked at the man she loved. Her heart had always been his, from the moment he had walked through the doors of the Knox home, demanding his sister's release. She'd seen the good in him. He had been her knight in shining armor and they had been so close to freedom that day... But then Missi had died and everything had burst into flames.

Now, none of it mattered. It was too late for their story to have a happy ending.

But soon she'd be free. "Cameron," she said softly, tears freely falling from her eyes.

Her son turned to her and their eyes locked. He understood what she was asking him to do. She'd expected nothing less. Though he was no longer the babe she'd once carried in her womb, there had been a time when their hearts beat together. For nine months, her body had kept him alive. And while the monster's blood flowed through his veins, so did hers.

They both knew it was time.

Without wasting another moment, a wicked grin tugged at Cameron's lips. And in the same heartbeat, they both pulled the trigger. Bullets tore from his and Dianne's weapons as shots ripped through their bodies.

Pain ricocheted through Dianne's chest, and she and Cameron both went down in a heap.

Her vision blurred and darkness threatened to overtake her.

In the distance, Jared screamed for her as he rushed to her side. He scooped her up and lightly patted her face, trying to keep her present. "No! Dianne, stay with me! You can't leave me. We're finally free." His sobs shook her as he held her close and cried into her neck.

She brought her hand to his face. "I love you. You saved me. You *freed* me."

Footsteps drummed rhythmically as the officers circled around her. As they slowly crept closer, she took one last look at Jared before turning her head away from him.

Then, her eyes met Cameron's, blood spurting from his mouth as his body jerked. And after one final breath, his body stilled.

The monster was dead.

Dianne stared at the sky as Jared begged her to stay. Forty years ago, this was where her body would have been buried had Theresa not bargained for her life. It was the perfect place for her to die, because deep in her soul, she wished she had died that day.

Taking her final breath, Dianne's spirit settled into the embrace of the decaying forget me nots.

The last of the darkness was gone, and the house of monsters was no more.

She was finally free.

CHAPTER 50

A li watched the smoke darken the atmosphere as the heat lit up the sky. The firefighters continued to put out the fire, but the damage had been done. The house was disintegrating along with the evil that had filled it. She had once thought of it as a safe haven, a place meant to protect her. She angrily wiped at her tears as memories flooded her mind, many of which were built on lies.

Now, her whole life was torn apart.

And she desperately wished Jax was there to hold her close. She stifled another sob as she brought her gaze back to the treeline.

When the crack of the gunshots had first rang out, Ali had tried to run toward the sound, terrified Jax had been hit. But Thiago had nearly tackled her to the ground, wanting to keep her away from potential danger. An army of officers had swept to the back of the property, grim-faced, prepared to secure the scene and count the tally of the dead.

Nearly fifteen minutes had passed since the shots had echoed from deep within the woods. Now, she played with her bracelet, heart beating rapidly, as she sat in the back of Thiago's Charger. She kept her eyes locked on the dense forest wall, praying Jax would emerge unscathed.

"Ali," Thiago said, pointing toward the back of the property.

She scanned the seam of the trees just as Jax stepped out from the shadows, Trinity following close behind.

Ali let out a cry as she took off in a sprint, closing the distance as she threw herself into Jax's arms. He held her close, and she clung to him and let herself break completely.

She mourned the loss of the life she had once known. She grieved her family and all the memories she'd built with them. And she wept with relief because Jax was safe.

Through broken sobs, she said, "I thought you were dead. I thought he'd killed you."

Jax stroked her hair, not releasing her from his grasp. "Hey, I'm a hero, remember. Just call me Hercules."

Ali coughed out a laugh, thankful he hadn't been hurt.

Finally, she pulled away as Trinity came closer. The agent rolled her eyes. "More like Pain or Panic. Or Phaethon, if I'm feeling generous."

"Whatever, Hades," Jax shot back.

Though Ali was thankful for the brief comedic relief, reality set in once again as Trinity pressed her lips together and her expression hardened. Ali's heart dropped knowing the agent wasn't coming with good news.

Trinity sighed and looked at the ground. "Cam is dead, Ali."

Ali simply nodded and buried her face into Jax's chest. Despite her hardest to stop them, tears wet her face. Part of her mourned the cousin she thought she knew. The cousin she had played hide and seek with, who had taught her how to play cards, who had made sure she understood the dangers of the world.

The other part of her celebrated his death.

And that tore her to pieces.

How could she celebrate Cam's death? How could she feel relief knowing he'd been rid from the world? Guilt tore through her as her emotions all fought for center stage.

Finally, she choked out, "My whole family is gone. I'm alone."

From behind Jax, the deep sound settled around her. "You still have me."

Ali's head shot up as she looked to the voice she'd only ever heard in her memories.

A man slowly approached and Ali stilled, the world unmoving. She studied the face she'd nearly forgotten. The scar, the sharp green eyes, the set jaw. Though time had left its mark, it was still unmistakably him.

Suspicion darkened Jax's eyes as he studied the stranger who had stopped only a few feet from them. Jax straightened as a faint smile tugged at the man's lips.

Ali's eyes rounded as she leaned into Jax, craving his steady presence. "Dad?" Ali sucked in a breath. "Dad!" She quickly went to him, wrapping her arms around him. The two embraced for what felt like an eternity and tears fell from Jared's eyes. She clung to him tightly, terrified he would disappear again just as he had all those years ago.

Finally, she pulled away as anger settled into sharp focus. "Why did you leave me? I needed you. For so much of my life, I needed my father, and you weren't there!" Ali tried to ignore the heat in her body, but she couldn't. She felt betrayed by everyone she loved.

Jared didn't respond for a moment as he studied her. She immediately felt guilty for her outburst. It was clear he held much of his own guilt over what had occurred.

Sadness pooled in the depths of his green eyes. "If Henry and Cam, or even Rick, found out I was still alive, they would have killed you to get back at me. You were safer without me in your life. At least until Levi could get you out of that house."

Always the protector.

Another wave of heartache washed over her as she realized Levi had stayed in order to protect her. He could have disappeared after taking Jared to the hospital, but he hadn't. He walked back into hell, just for her.

She furrowed her brow as she tried to make sense of the last twenty-six years. "But you still left me flowers."

Jared's shoulders slumped. "Levi told me you were spiraling. I was terrified you'd lose yourself completely, so I gave Levi the flowers and told him to leave them for you. Then, when you moved out, *I* started leaving them for you."

"But-"

He caressed her cheek, almost as if to reassure himself she was truly there. "Not right now. I promise I will answer every question you have, but first, it's time to leave."

She clung to him once more as Jax and Trinity approached. When Ali let go of her father, Jax slipped an arm around her waist and pulled her close as he kissed her head.

Jared lifted a brow. "I expect you'll take care of her. Protect her, treat her like a queen."

Jax bowed up at the man. "Better than you did."

Ali's mouth gaped open, and Trinity swatted at his arm. "Jax, shut up!"

But Jared smiled. "That's exactly what I'm talking about."

Trinity looked at Jared. "You don't have to talk now but be prepared to tell us everything over the next few days."

He nodded, and the three of them silently made their way back to the front of the property as officers and crime scene techs swarmed past them, trying to put the pieces of the case together. So much of it didn't make sense, and they were left with so many questions. Ali hoped her father could shed some light on most of them.

Thiago stood at the command post, yelling out orders to those who were on the scene as Sheriff Gordon James held a press conference at the edge of the driveway. They approached the agent, and he immediately looked Trinity up and down. "You look like shit."

"Fuck off," she snarled.

Thiago curiously eyed the stranger next to Ali, and she pointed to her father. "This is Jared, my father."

Thiago stayed silent, assessing the potential threat Jared might carry.

Trinity shared a knowing glance with her partner. "He's safe, for now."

Thiago nodded. "It's gonna be a long next few days while we sort through everything and get our reports written." He looked at Jax. "Get Ali to a hospital and have her checked out. And we'll send one of your guys to collect her clothes and take her statement."

Ali opened her mouth to protest, but Jax shook his head. "He wasn't asking, Ali. You're going to the hospital. We need to make sure you're okay."

She nodded in surrender. Though she wasn't happy about it, she'd do as she was told.

"And you," Thiago said as he pointed to Jared, "are going to stay right here until someone has taken your statement. You're to have no contact with Ali until you've been cleared."

Jared clenched his jaw slightly. "I'm assuming that's not asking, either."

Thiago shook his head as he pulled out his badge. "I don't ask. I tell." He patted the cuffs hanging at his side from his belt. "And these tend to be a great encourager."

Jared kissed Ali's forehead. "I'll catch up with you soon."

Then Jax took her hand and led her to the ambulance that was waiting for her. The EMT shut the door as she began assessing Ali while Jax made a call to his boss. As they pulled to the end of the driveway, Ali glanced behind her at the firefighters still battling the relentless flames. It was as if the universe itself refused to let the house escape the reckoning it deserved.

She ached to preserve the home and the memories it held, but she knew the evil inside needed to die with it.

And so, she watched the flames devour the house of monsters as it slowly faded into the distance.

CHAPTER 51

It had taken a week for CSI to conduct a thorough search of the Knox property, and Jax hadn't been prepared for what he would find while investigating the family's crimes. Then the FBI had launched an intense investigation into Jared, as they weren't entirely convinced he was innocent.

Once the FBI was satisfied he posed no threat, Jax had only slightly let his guard down. In Jax's book, any man who abandoned his daughter isn't worth trusting. And he wasn't silent about his judgment either, despite Ali's irritation with him. But because he cared for her, he forced himself to ease up, even though he still felt it was his responsibility to protect her.

The team sat around the conference room table, Jared and Ali joining them. Jax held Ali's hand as Trinity and Thiago sat across from them, Jared at the head of the table. Jules was curled into a chair in the far corner of the room, her oversized hoodie nearly swallowing her. Her face was void of makeup, and her vacant gaze was fixed on a spot in the carpet.

Jax's heart ached for his partner, and his concern for her grew with each passing day. The brass had told her to take a leave of absence, but she had refused until she heard what Jared had to say. She was searching for answers, and Jax wasn't sure she'd ever truly get them.

Settling into her seat, Trinity said to Jared, "Okay, start from the beginning."

Jared nodded and everyone instinctively shifted forward, as if hearing a scary story for the first time. He took in a breath. "I know you think this story starts in 2012, but it doesn't. It started in 1983. Or at least, the parts that are pertinent to your investigation."

"That's when Dianne, er, Cynthia was kidnapped by Henry," Thiago said.

Jared nodded, his shoulders slumping. It was clear the man had truly loved the woman he could never have. A tragic love story, ironically, like the knight and lady from the forget me not story.

Jared continued, "When Dianne was kidnapped, Henry had been keeping women for about a year before killing them. He spent a great deal of time torturing them, trying to break their spirit. He felt men owned women and they were put on this earth to serve us."

Jax recalled the burns they'd seen on Elizabeth Norman. It had taken them some time, but after the FBI called in a forensic pathologist, they had found that the pattern was in the shape of the letter 'K." Henry had been marking them as his property. Trinity had even found a photo of Ginger Knox, Ali's grandmother, with an identical brand burned across her chest.

"From what I could gather over the years, Rick had wanted a wife, but Henry was nervous to let him get married for fear they might be found out." Jared shrugged. "I don't know how, but Theresa had convinced her father to let Dianne live if she agreed to marry Rick. So, Dianne had agreed, hoping it would buy her time to escape.

"They had a 'wedding' and Cynthia changed her name to Dianne, per Rick's request. Over the years, Dianne had hoped Theresa would help her escape, but Theresa never did. She was just as brainwashed as the rest of them. Henry had even branded her the day she had begged for him to spare Dianne."

Ali's voice was just above a whisper, "Was my mother a monster?"

Jax gently squeezed her hand, hoping to bring her some comfort. He knew today would be difficult and had initially protested her being present, but he hadn't been able to tell the woman 'no.' He now wondered if that was a mistake.

Jared thought for a moment, carefully considering his words. "Theresa wasn't inherently bad, no. She was lost. She had grown up under her father's reign of terror. She'd seen firsthand what he would do to the women he brought home. She knew her mother was one of his first victims, and I think Gin helped Henry brainwash Theresa and Rick in an attempt to save herself and her children. I truly believe Gin and Theresa did what they had to in order to survive."

Trinity spoke up next, throwing her black hair into a clip. "I'm assuming Ginger knew about the other women he'd bring home to torture and kill?"

Ali's face contorted slightly, and Trinity looked away from her, an unspoken apology.

"Yes." Jared nodded. "She had actually bartered for her own life. She had told Henry she'd marry him if he spared her and she'd give him kids. She would let him do whatever he wanted to the women he brought home and she'd never speak about it, as long as he left her alone. She eventually had Rick and Theresa, but refused to have any more children because she had almost died while giving birth both times.

"Now, back to 1983. Dianne had already "married" Rick, but Henry felt cheated out of his year of torture, so he went hunting again."

Jax said, "Elizabeth Norman."

Jared smiled sadly. "Yes. Except this time, he kept her for nearly five years. I think he worried about the difficulty of constantly bringing home more girls, so he found it easier to just keep her for as long as he could."

A knock at the door had everyone turning. A dark-haired woman stood awkwardly on the threshold.

Jared froze, his face draining of color. "Lizzie?"

The woman burst into tears and the two embraced. She clung tightly. "I thought you were dead. I searched for you after he let me go, but there was no trace of you."

Jared cupped her face. "I had to go into hiding, to keep Ali safe."

Elizabeth furrowed her brows. "Who's Ali?"

Jared beamed as he gestured to Ali, who uncomfortably looked at Jax. "Ali is my daughter."

Elizabeth wiped at her face as she studied Ali's features. "She has your nose. And Momma's high cheekbones."

"I see you're married." Jared gestured to the small stone glistening on her left ring finger. "Do you have any kids?"

Elizabeth shook her head. "No. Nathaniel and I didn't want kids. And we've only been together a few months now."

Trinity stood up and placed her hands on the table. "Respectfully, what the hell is going on?"

Jared looked at the group. "Elizabeth is my sister."

Jax had been surprised by the gasps that echoed through the room. The revelation had even caused Juliette to come back to life, if only for a moment.

While going over reports and files, Jax had contacted Elizabeth again, updating her on the case with the information that he could. He wanted to tell her she'd been right and the department owed her an apology. That's when she'd asked him to find her brother. After gathering a bit more information from her, Jax had made the connection as to who her brother was. He was glad at least someone would get a happy ending and had encouraged her to come to the station to see Jared.

Jax just hadn't expected it to be so soon.

Jared pulled up a chair for Elizabeth, not asking Jax if it was appropriate. Though, at this point, Jax felt that concept had been completely thrown out the window.

Trinity sat down and snapped her fingers, grabbing everyone's attention. "Okay, let's keep this going. I'm not trying to be here all day. We have reports to write and dinner to eat."

Jared nodded. "I'm sorry, I just... I haven't seen her since I saved her."

"Saved her?" Thiago said.

This time, Elizabeth spoke, her eyes wide and mouth gaping open. "Oh my god, I wasn't hallucinating. You were there the night he let me go. For the last forty years I thought I had gone crazy that night, but I hadn't."

Jared took her hand. "When you disappeared, I went to some of the other girls that were working the same street as you, got a good description of the man who took you, and waited for him to appear again. I saw him pumping gas a street away from where he'd taken you nearly five years before. I followed him home and tried to figure out if you were dead or alive.

"I parked my truck in the tree line and watched him for nearly a week." To the group, he said, "I had seen Theresa here and there, wobbling around with her pregnant belly. Of course, she'd have Levi a few months later. Rick would come and go fairly often, but Gin hardly came out of the house. And then, one night, I saw Henry coming out from the cellar door on the outer side of the house. I waited until everyone had gone to bed to see if you were down there." He turned back to Elizabeth. "I could hardly make out your shadow on the far side of the room, but I knew it was you. Before I could even make it down the stairs, though, Rick knocked me out. Next thing I know, I'm waking up to the man who had taken you.

"They had been talking about what to do with us when Theresa came into the barn, curious as to what was going on. And when she saw the predicament I was in, she suggested what she always did: marriage. I could stay and give her another baby and save you, or we could both die." He shrugged. "The choice was easy. So, Henry drugged you and let you go."

Ali's face had gone pale, and she rushed to the restroom across the hall. Jax's heart splintered and he hung his head. She had lived her life believing her grandfather was a gentle man, a good man. Only to find out her grandmother had been a victim to his horror. Her mother, uncle, and brother had been manipulated by it. And her aunt and father had suffered greatly because of it.

It seemed that Missi had been the only one to escape unscathed by the evil that plagued the Knox family.

A few moments later, Ali walked back through the door, her eyes puffy and lips red. She held her head high as she took her seat next to Jax, grasping his hand.

Not wanting to draw attention to her grief, Jax looked at Jared. "So, he let Elizabeth go. Then what?"

"Well," Jared said, crossing his arms and leaning back in the chair. "Shortly after that, Theresa had Levi and Dianne had Cameron. Henry still hunted, but he didn't keep the women long. I tried to save another girl, but he beat the shit out of Theresa when I did. So, I never intervened again.

"It didn't take long for me to realize Dianne had been a victim of the family too. We bonded over that and made plans to escape. Eventually, we fell in love, though we kept it a secret, of course. By 1992, Theresa had Ali and Dianne had Missi."

Thiago cleared his throat and crossed his arms. "So, you're telling me you kept sleeping with Theresa knowing she helped her father with his crimes, and Dianne slept with Rick even though he basically raped her?"

Ali shifted in her seat as she looked at the floor. But truthfully, Jax was wondering the same thing. It sounded absolutely asinine.

Elizabeth quietly asked the agent, "Have you ever been held hostage, Agent?"

Thiago shook his head. "No, ma'am."

"I hope you never are. Because you'll quickly find you'll do almost anything to survive."

Jax looked at Trinity, and she quickly looked to the floor. He wasn't surprised by her reaction. She never talked about her past unless she absolutely had to. Even he knew very few details of what had happened to her the summer she'd come to Florida.

Jared took in a breath. "After Ali and Missi were a little older and Henry started grooming Cameron and making Levi help him bury bodies, we began planning our escape. But our biggest fear was not being able to get the kids out. We had entirely expected Cam to stay, as he was fixated on Henry. Levi wanted to go with us since he knew the truth about his family. But," he looked at Ali, "Ali and Missi would be the most difficult. They were too young to understand what was happening.

"The day Missi had died was the day we were going through with it. But Theresa had run into the room, screaming at the two of us. She'd found out about the affair and all hell broke loose after that."

Ali spoke up, forcing herself to look at Jared. "I ruined the plan, didn't I? When I didn't get in the truck, you had to go back for me."

Jared pulled her close. "None of this is your fault. Do you hear me? *None* of it." He stopped for a moment, gathering himself. Ali gently pulled away, melting into Jax in search of comfort.

Jared sighed and looked at the table, then back at Ali. "Cam realized what was happening at the park and had threatened to kill you. So, Levi had decided to stay behind, hoping we could try to escape later that night. I went back, but at that point, Dianne had gotten scared and didn't want to leave Theresa behind. I think a part of her still felt she owed Theresa for saving her life. Plus, she felt guilty about the affair.

"By the time you got back, it had escalated even more, and Rick and I got into a fight. That's when everyone found out Missi was actually my daughter, and you and Missi argued..."

Ali let out a squeak, tears flowing down her face, though Jax wasn't sure if she had even realized it was happening. Jax helplessly held her close, not knowing how to help. How could she carry this for the rest of her life?

Juliette suddenly sat up, causing everyone to turn their attention toward her. "You bargained for her life. You told them they could kill you if they spared Ali."

Jared slowly nodded. "Yes. And Levi convinced them to lie to her. They agreed, but they wanted Levi to be the one to kill me so he would also share the guilt. It would keep him from leaving or talking to the cops."

"He stabbed you," Juliette continued. "But you survived. And somehow you and Levi kept in touch. Eventually you contacted Dianne and sent Ali flowers, but none of them ever knew about the others."

Jared nodded and the room fell silent until Trinity said, "Jezzie was Cam's first victim."

Jared shrugged. "From what Levi told me, Cam only helped Henry when Henry allowed, so I'm not entirely sure. I think there's a good chance Henry kidnapped prostitutes so Cam could learn how to kill without getting caught."

"We're assuming he practiced his torture and kills on prostitutes until 2012 when he started his own spree," Trinity said. "He may have even continued using working girls in between his serial kills to help keep his urges under control."

Jared shrugged. "I'm not sure. But it's likely."

Juliette whimpered and rushed out of the room. Jax closed his eyes, unable to process everything Jared had revealed.

Ali asked, "Why didn't you or Levi tell the police everything when you got out?"

Jax had been wondering the same thing. He understood why Dianne hadn't, and he even understood why Theresa hadn't. But it didn't make sense for Jared or Levi to never go to the police.

Jared leaned forward. "At first, we were going to, but there was no guarantee Cam or Henry would get arrested. And if they didn't, your life would be in danger. So would Dianne's and Theresa's. And then Cam found out about Levi's daughter, Catherine-"

Ali furrowed her brows. "Catherine?" Then, her eyes rounded and she suddenly stood, taking Jax by surprise. She threw her arms in the air. "Levi knew the truth about her? *You* knew?"

Great. More secrets.

Jax wanted to scream.

Jared hung his head. "Yes. I don't know how Levi found out, but he had. And eventually so had Cam. And he used it to keep Levi from going to the police. Which, he then begged me not to as well. So we bided our time. Once Henry died, we knew we would have to act soon, but we needed evidence first. Then Ali submitted her DNA before we ever had a chance to figure out how to save everyone and still get Cam arrested."

Trinity lifted her hand. "Wait. How did Cam find out about Catherine when he and Levi didn't communicate? I doubt Levi was telling Cam anything personal."

A beat.

"Oh my god." Trinity's eyes rounded. "He was the other guy. The one Lily cheated on Levi with. He left the flower for her."

Jared tilted his head. "We think Cam kept close tabs on Levi and found out about Lily." He shook his head. "Cam had spent his whole life being taught how to be charming and charismatic. It helped that he was a looker, too. It was likely very easy for Cam to convince Lily to start seeing him behind Levi's back. I think it was just his way to wreak havoc on Levi's life, but it played out in his favor in the long run, unfortunately."

Jax shook his head. "Is that all? Is that the last of the secrets?"

Jared nodded. "As far as the ones I know of, yes."

Ali promptly stood up and walked out the door and Jared stood to follow her. But Jax gripped the old man's arm, a silent threat. Jared's gaze followed her, guilt etched on his face.

Good. Jax hoped the guilt ate him alive. Ali deserved better.

Everyone else stood and Trinity pointed to Jared and Elizabeth, her eyes narrowing. "The FBI has a shit ton more questions for you two." She sighed as her face softened slightly. "But let's take a break for lunch and then we'll reconvene in an hour."

Jared and Elizabeth nodded as they followed Trinity and Thiago out the door.

Jax took one more glance around the room that had housed the Scarlet Letter Killer's legacy. There was no case board, no photos of the victims, no notes tacked to the walls. It was all gone. They had gathered the last remnants of the

Scarlet Letter Killer's reign and sealed them away for good, permanently freeing the world from his darkness.

Then, he turned off the light and closed the door.

EPILOGUE

J uliette still hadn't been sleeping well. She'd tried taking the pills her doctor prescribed her, but they didn't help. The nightmares still flooded her mind. It had been two months since she'd found out the truth about Cam, and she was plagued by anxiety, fear, and sorrow.

She jumped at the slightest sound or shadow. She felt as if she was always being watched, studied by an unknown force. She was afraid to trust herself, afraid to trust anyone. And she mourned the man she'd once loved, oftentimes wishing to forget about the monster who lurked within.

A knock at the door had her reluctantly pulling herself out of bed. Juliette looked down at her pajamas, the ones she'd been wearing for the last week. She smelled like liquor and despair.

She rubbed her face and sighed, wanting to ignore the continuous pounding.

She hadn't worked in weeks, and she no longer bothered with much of anything. Her mother and sisters had been sending her casseroles, but she would only pick at them. Her brothers tried to force her out of the house, but she simply stopped taking their calls. Come to think of it, she couldn't remember the last time she'd done laundry or even cleaned her house.

All she wanted to do was curl up in bed and cry.

After a few minutes of ignoring the rhythmic sound, Juliette groaned and made her way to the door. Looking out the peephole, Trinity stood with her arms crossed, impatiently waiting for Jules to open the door. And if it had been anyone else, Jules would have simply gone back to bed. But Trinity would have broken through the wooden barrier and come in whether Jules wanted her to or not.

Sighing, Jules unlocked the door and stood to the side, though Trinity was already barging through. She looked Jules up and down. "You look like shit." She made a face. "And you smell like straight booze."

Jules rolled her eyes, not caring what Trinity thought. Everyone was quick to judge her, expecting her to be the same Juliette she'd been before her world fell apart. But she wasn't. And she never would be. Because she could never trust herself again.

Hell, she couldn't even be trusted to serve and protect anymore. No one knew, but her letter of resignation was stuffed into her desk drawer. She was just too depressed to send it in.

Her friend quickly walked back to Jules' room and into her closet, invading Jules' personal space. She pulled open drawers until she retrieved a sports bra and shorts and tossed them at Jules.

Juliette let them fall to the floor. "What the hell, Trinity?"

"Get dressed. We're going running." Trinity stood tall, narrowing her eyes.

But without another word, Juliette walked back to her bed and pulled the covers over her body, perfectly content to sulk in her pain and heartache. She had no intention of running, or going out, or even eating ice cream straight out of the fucking carton.

All she wanted was Cam. But he was a monster. And he was dead.

Trinity crossed her arms. "Get up," she demanded.

Jules turned over, ignoring the command as she pulled her fabric over her head.

Before Juliette could take her next breath, Trinity stormed over and threw the blanket to the floor. In one swift motion, she grasped Jules' ankle and dragged her out of bed, where she fell to the ground with a loud thump.

"What is your fucking problem?!" Juliette yelled as she pulled herself to her feet, stepping toward Trinity.

Trinity didn't falter. "You're done moping around. I get you're traumatized, but we're done with this shit. It's been two damn months."

Jules glared at her. "You have no idea how I feel. Leave me alone!"

Trinity wasn't going to stand down. She lifted an arm. "You know my past and what I've been through. I know how it feels to be betrayed by someone you trusted. To have lies and secrets rip your whole life apart and nearly get you killed. So don't patronize me, Juliette."

Jules sighed, some of her anger dissipating. Out of everyone, Trinity understood Jules' grief.

She began pacing. She let memories flood her mind. The first time she'd met Cam, he'd laughed at her as she juggled her hot chocolate, late to the crime scene. Their first date had been to one of those painting places, and his had turned out awful. She glanced at the far wall where the picture still hung.

She thought of the night he'd first said he loved her and how her soul had been set on fire. Of course, she couldn't forget how terrified she'd been the night he'd nearly bled out on her front porch. And the way he repaired pieces of her he hadn't even broken.

But then she remembered the knot that had formed when she'd found out he'd been the one to rape and brand the girl he'd gone to school with. He had been so charming he'd managed to convince everyone it had been Levi. And they'd never questioned it.

Jules couldn't stop replaying the video she'd watched in his living room. She'd watched in horror as the gleam in his eye had grown brighter as he turned toward the camera after he'd raped that poor woman. And she remembered the way his hands had tightened around her throat, the oxygen slowly leaving her lungs...

"How could I have not seen it? How could I sleep next to him and never know he was a monster?" She threw her arm in the air. "I'm a fucking cop!"

Trinity shook her head. "One thing about psychopaths is that they're great chameleons. And Cam had spent years being taught how to fit in, how to look normal."

Rage filled Jules, and she thrust her thumb to her chest. "And what about me? Did he actually love me? Because I loved him! I loved a horrific monster." Finally, Jules collapsed on the floor, burying her hands in her face as tears seeped into the carpet below her. "I still love him, Trinity. What's wrong with me?"

Sighing, Trinity sat on the floor next to Jules, pulling her close.

Exhausted, Juliette laid her head in her friend's lap, and Trinity played with her hair. She softly said, "You love the side of him you knew. And it was all a lie.

I know that hurts you, but his feelings were all a lie. You're human, Jules. You love hard and fast, and he took advantage of that. This isn't on you."

Jules' face twisted in anguish as she whispered, "But he let me live."

Trinity stilled for a moment. "What are you talking about?"

"He tried to strangle me and he didn't."

Trinity sighed. "I know you still want to hold on to the best of him, but he likely got spooked or just thought you were dead and was wrong."

Juliette simply nodded. But she knew the truth. He had strangled countless women. He was too skilled to have let her live by accident. No, Cameron Knox had left her alive.

And that haunted her.

Juliette didn't fight the tears. She let them spill down her face, as if they could wash away the stain Cam had left on her skin. She had given her heart to a monster, and she'd fallen in love with a killer. And she longed to shed every trace of him, every lingering touch, every shadow he'd pressed into her.

And maybe she couldn't change that she'd loved him, but their past had died with him. And he could never touch her again.

Jules finally sat up and wiped at her face.

Trinity gave a half smile. "You know, when I was little, my mom used to fill a spray bottle with water and call it monster spray. She would spray it under my bed and in my closet." She sighed. "We grow up thinking monsters are scary-looking creatures that hide under your bed, waiting until you fall asleep to get you. But really, the monsters are hiding in plain sight, not scary looking at all, but normal. Even beautiful. And that's the worst part. You can't hide from the monsters if you don't know who the monsters are." Trinity shook her head. "He was never going to let you find out who he was."

Sighing, Juliette stood and pulled Trinity to her feet as she wrapped her in a hug. "Thank you."

Trinity stiffened, but leaned into the embrace. "Yeah, yeah. This is the only time you'll see me be nice."

Juliette laughed. "Nice? You pulled me out of bed!"

"Yes, nice. I could have dumped ice-cold water on you."

Juliette smiled and shook her head. She nodded to the workout clothes that laid on the floor. "I'll be down in a minute."

When Trinity walked out the door, Juliette's gaze swept over the disaster of her room, each scattered item a reminder of her own despair. But it was time to move forward, to leave the Scarlet Letter Killer behind for good.

She walked to the painting, letting her eyes linger on it for a moment before yanking it from the wall. Without hesitation, she carried it to the living room and placed it among the old logs still scattered in the fireplace. A flick of the lighter and the flame kissed the acrylic, curling over the image. She stepped back, heart hammering. She watched as the fire devoured the last trace of Cam, leaving only ash in its wake.

Wiping at one lonely tear, she quickly changed, throwing her hair into a clip as she made her way out the front door.

Trinity stood at the edge of the porch, stretching. "What took you so long?"

She shrugged. "Oh, I just had to put out the fire in the fireplace." Then, Juliette took off in a sprint, the winter wind blowing through her hair.

When Ali had heard they were coming back to her family's property, she had begged Jax to let her go with him and Trinity, wanting answers. But Jax had put his foot down...or rather, Trinity had made him put his foot down. It was clear he was in trouble when it came to that woman. He quite honestly couldn't tell her no.

But, she relentlessly pestered Trinity, so his friend reluctantly gave up her fight.

Now, he, Trinity, and Ali pulled up the dirt path. The closer they got to the charred remains of the Knox home, the quicker his heart raced as he recalled how close Ali had come to death.

When he'd first come onto the scene that day, he had desperately searched for Ali, knowing she was likely already dead. So when he'd seen Ali's silhouette in the distance as she sprinted toward them, he'd gone to her without hesitation. He'd never been more relieved in his life.

He'd quickly assessed her for any gunshot wounds, and when he had been satisfied she was physically fine, he put Thiago in charge of her. Then, he and Trinity had silently followed Cam and Dianne into the clearing where they had both breathed their last breath.

A shiver raced down Jax's spine. It was eerily poetic that each of the Knox family members had died where they were most tied to their sins. Rick, Theresa, and Levi perished in the barn, the same place they had repeatedly ignored as the cries of helpless women echoed within its walls. Cam met his fate in the field where his grandfather had buried his own victims, the ground where Cam's bloodlust had begun. And Dianne, in the very spot she had been destined to rest forty years before.

And as they pulled up to the rubble, Jax couldn't help but wonder if their ghosts still haunted the place or had they been damned to hell where they belonged.

Silently, the three of them got out, as tension filled the cold air. And Jax could still feel the lingering evil that had once inhabited the place.

He looked around, taking in the sight. The farmhouse that had once stood tall was merely soot and debris, the fire having destroyed most of it. The bungalow and cottage still had crime scene tape wrapped around them, cautioning anyone who might want to take their own look at the house of horrors.

Without a word, Ali walked toward the house, and Jax decided to give her some space. He turned to Trinity. "You leaving after this?"

In the aftermath of the investigation, Trinity and Thiago had come and gone from town, offering their help and expertise when needed. She'd hated the amount of paperwork attached to the case, but Jax knew she was secretly using it as an excuse to visit her parents more.

She nodded. "Thiago and I will drive back to Miami in the morning. I thought he'd stay a little longer to see his ex, but he said he doesn't do long distance." She shrugged. "We'll take the videos to the lab and see if we get hits on facial rec for more of the victims."

Thanks to Juliette, the CSI techs had found Cam's stash of hidden DVDs. It seemed both Henry and Cam had recorded most of their offenses on a camcorder, which Cam had later made into DVDs. He'd continued the tradition, filming his own assaults and murders, each one labeled accordingly. And last Jax had heard, they had found nearly one hundred discs, though unfortunately a handful of the victims in the movies they suspected were prostitutes, and they weren't optimistic about identifying those women.

Jax was glad he wasn't the one who had to watch the videos. He didn't think he could stomach it.

He nodded to Trinity. "Keep us updated. And don't be a stranger, please."

Trinity rolled her eyes. "Quit being such a girl about it."

He made a face at her and the two embraced. She pulled away and said, "Thiago is going to get me from here and we'll head out. I just wanted to get a few photos for my reports."

She looked in Ali's direction, watching Ali study the debris that had been left by the fire. "How's she holding up?"

He shrugged. "She has her days, but a lot better now that she gets to see Jared. I think having him around helps."

Trinity stared at him for a moment, and he knew she was holding back. "What?"

She sighed. "If Missi hadn't died, Ali would have become just like her family; compliant in Henry and Cam's crimes." She shook her head. "I know she doesn't see it this way, but Missi's death saved her."

"She thinks she's a monster, just like everyone else," Jax said.

Trinity tilted her head. "She was six. It was an accident."

Jax put his hands up. "I know, that's what I try to tell her." He rubbed his face and looked toward the copper-haired beauty he'd fallen head over-heels-for. He was angered by all she'd been through and hated that he couldn't take away her pain. But he was thankful she was still alive. That they had a future together, even if he didn't know what that looked like.

And even though she'd lost a little bit of her light, it hadn't completely diminished. So Jax would spend however long it took giving it back to her.

A breeze blew through the trees and Trinity shivered as she clutched her jacket. "Look, the Knox family were fucking loony-toons. And by all accounts they were all monsters for turning a blind eye to the torment, even Dianne. But they sacrificed their lives for Ali. They did what they thought was best to keep her safe. And I don't know if real monsters would do that."

"What are you saying?" Jax asked, crossing her arms.

Trinity put her arm out. "I'm saying: some things aren't black and white. Some things are so complicated you'll never make sense of them."

Jax contemplated her words, knowing she was right. But the question still lingered: Who was more of a monster? Henry and Cam for killing, or Rick, Levi, and Theresa for not saying anything? Knowing it was an impossible question to answer, he simply nodded as she turned to walk away.

Sighing, he met Ali where she was standing and took her hand. "Are you sure you want to do this?"

She nodded. "Yes. I need to find it."

Jax walked back to the car and grabbed the shovel they'd brought with them. "Then lead the way," he said.

So, she took his hand and led him up the path to the clearing.

Ali's head pounded as the field came into view. It looked much different in person than it had in her memory. Most of the dirt had been disturbed as police had dug up body after body. Last she'd heard, they'd found one hundred and thirty women, all in different stages of decomposition. Some of them they'd never be able to name or know if it was Henry or Cam who'd killed them.

She still had a difficult time making sense of her life. To the world, her grandfather was the devil and Cam was the monster found in nightmares. But to her, they were her family. And she had loved them deeply.

And she felt guilty for still loving them after knowing what they'd done to those poor women. But she found she couldn't erase her emotions. It was much more complicated than that.

Gripping Jax's hand tighter, she pushed past her panic and led him to the two trees on the far side. "Here," she said as she pointed to the ground, a large rock marking the spot she'd forgotten about.

Not waiting a moment longer, Jax began to dig. She was glad he was there to help. That he was content with her silence. Ali had needed so much support in the weeks following her family's demise. Nightmares had made it nearly impossible to sleep, and every so often a reporter would hunt her down. She'd even had someone try to destroy her home, claiming she was just as bad as her family.

All she wanted was closure and to begin a new chapter of her life. One without secrets or lies.

And this would bring closure.

They didn't have to dig far before finding the old shoebox, though it had nearly disintegrated by time and the elements. Ali carefully pulled it out of the dirt, brushing the earth from the top of the cardboard. She smiled as she set it on the ground.

She wanted to open it but was terrified of the reaction it might cause. She worried that anything may completely break her. And she wasn't sure she'd be able to put herself back together.

Still, she needed to do this.

And Jax wouldn't let her fall apart.

Before she lost her nerve, she pulled the lid off the box, revealing the trinkets she and Missi had buried all those years ago.

The stuffed animal, the bouncy ball, the beaded friendship bracelets they'd made one summer...memories of Missi flooded her mind and Ali held on to them tightly, tears streaming down her face.

It was the only piece of her past she wanted to bring into her future.

Ali placed the lid back on the container and stood. "Let's go. It's time to leave all this behind."

Jax nodded and the two walked back, leaving behind the monsters.

FROM THE AUTHOR

What a wild ride it was for me to write *House of Monsters*! I have to admit, through so much of the writing process I absolutely hated this book. I doubted the strength of the story, the flow of the plot, and, even more so, my ability to write it. I felt inadequate and had so much more trouble connecting to the characters in this story than in my debut novel *Kept in the Dark*.

Now, fifteen drafts, two years, and lots of late nights later, I have come to absolutely love *House of Monsters* and the characters found in its pages.

Jax was so fun to write, and I enjoyed getting to know him and all his faults. Now, Ali on the other hand, was far more difficult of a character for me to write. She is largely inspired by my best friend and the two of us couldn't be more opposite. She is the Ali to my Trinity- ha! It was interesting to write a character who wasn't sassy and hard-headed and instead was soft and kind, but still strong in her own right. I hope you fell in love with them the way I did! And I hope you're ready to see more of them in the future.

So, here's to this dark and twisted thriller. I hope it gave you nightmares in the best way!

DEAR READER,

I'm so glad you decided to pick up *House of Monsters*. If you loved Jax, Ali, and Juliette, you'll get to see them again in the future. *House of Monsters* is the first book in the Moretti and Reid series, and this dynamic duo will be back with plenty more cases to solve.

Until then, we get to follow Agent Thiago Silva in my next thriller, *Vengeance*. Get ready for more mayhem, murder, and mystery. Because this one is full of it.

Fourteen years ago, Carmen Lopez's best friend vanished without a trace. But when Kimmy's body is finally discovered, Carmen is forced to return home and face the truth she's long refused to see.

Agent Thiago Silva thought he knew exactly where his life was headed, but fear has a way of rewriting destinies. Now, he must confront the ghosts from his past and the woman whose heart he shattered fourteen years ago.

And while they would both rather avoid each other, Carmen is asked to dig into Kimmy's cold case and teaming up feels like the only sensible path. But waiting in the shadows are secrets capable of shattering their fragile alliance.

As they dig deeper, they discover that every friendly face hides a secret. And soon, the transgressions that have lingered in darkness are torn from the shadows, and some sins cannot go unpunished.

Lindsey loves connecting with readers! Please visit her website to find her social medial platforms, access to character profiles, and for more information regarding event booking, book club appearances, etc.

If you enjoyed this story, I would love for you to leave *House of Monsters* **a review. Reviews help immensely in pushing out my books to other readers who would enjoy this story like you did! As always, thank you so much for your support.**

www.lindseyacosta.com